I0537079

PRIMED SON

Eden Ashley

Text copyright ©2015 Eden Ashley

Primed Son is a work of fiction. Names, characters, places, and incidents either are the product of the author's imagination or are used factiously. Any resemblance to actual persons, living or dead, events, or locales is entirely coincidental.

All rights reserved. No part of this book may be used or reproduced in any manner whatsoever without written permission except in the case of brief quotations embodied in critical articles and reviews.

Cover art by Nathalia Suellen

Summary: Kali's maturity into the warrior she once was could not have come at a better time. Still haunted by his gruesome punishment in Golden Mountain, Rhane is slowly coming undone as the pressure mounts to save this world and preserve the lives of those closest to him. But given a miraculous chance to fix mistakes from the past, Rhane and Kali soon realize that the undertaking may be beyond the reach of even their combined powers.

For the readers

Prologue

Jordan was a man of science, not a bureaucrat, and certainly not one of the company's trigger-happy, lab rat mercenaries. One of those lab rats stood over his shoulder now, watching Jordan's every move to make sure he did exactly as he was told. What Commander Zed had asked—no—ordered him to do was a deception that would cost him his job if ever discovered. But what choice did Jordan have? Something more or less than human residing within the helix of Commander Zed's DNA swam far above Jordan in the genetic pool of power. If Jordan dared to disobey, Zed would easily subdue him and maybe kill him for the trouble. Jordan's hand trembled as he reached for the phone.

It took Eleazar a long time to answer. Not surprising, since it was still hours before dawn. The old man rose with the sun, bringing with him a certain predatory ambition, and lived by the motto "neither day nor death waits upon the feckless."

When Eleazar's voice rang sharply through the receiver, Jordan dared one final, questioning look to Commander Zed. Frowning deeply, the soldier tapped the trigger of the semi-automatic weapon slung across his shoulder. Point taken. Jordan hurriedly addressed the president of Global Cures. "Mr. Eleazar, I'm afraid I have bad news, sir."

"What is it?"

Jordan took a deep breath. "There was a fire. We lost him."

Eleazar was quiet for so long, Jordan wondered if the line had gone dead. Finally, the old man spoke. "Tell me you know who did this." It wasn't a question.

Jordan licked his lips nervously. At least the hardest part was over. "You're not going to believe it, sir."

"Tell me," Eleazar repeated.

"We have video footage," Jordan said, rapidly inputting a sequence of commands across the keyboard in front of him. "I'm uploading it to your hard drive now."

On the other end, Eleazar could be heard striking several keys to open the file. Jordan knew the video playing on the old man's screen all too well, having watched it dozens of times in the past few hours.

A dark blur would move across the room at an impossible rate of speed, expanding while in motion and brightening, but not readily visible as it intersected with the Gravitron—a machine capable of generating artificial gravity many times beyond Earth's natural pull. It was also the device responsible for imprisoning the captive specimen. The force field surrounding the machine did its job, reacting violently upon contact with the blur, engulfing it with an electrical current powerful enough to kill any living thing on the planet. But then the Gravitron collapsed, and the canine specimen disappeared. Seconds later, the camera feed went dead as an explosion rocked the building, ultimately killing Eleazar's youngest son.

"You told me you had something," Eleazar said, sounding very impatient.

"Here's the same footage," the scientist explained quickly. "Frame by frame."

He sent the next video. This time, the blur became a dark-haired male in his mid to late twenties. As he ran, the man transformed into an entirely different creature. Mass doubled and then tripled. White fur enveloped his body. Two legs became four as a giant white wolf, larger than any wolf this planet had ever seen, filled the screen. The creature ripped the Gravitron apart, picked up the captured canine by its scruff, and ran out of the room…all in mere seconds.

Whatever this creature was, it had caused the explosion. It had killed the old man's son.

"You bring me that thing," Eleazar said. His voice seethed with fury. "And you bring it to me alive."

Sweat beaded across Jordan's forehead. "Sir, I don't think we are prepared for such a task. Whatever this thing is, it destroyed ten tons of equipment single-handedly. Other footage shows that this creature didn't come alone. There were others with it—others who may be just as powerful."

"Is the commander with you?"

"Yes sir."

"You tell him that I don't care what it takes, how much money, or how many men. Bring that thing to me alive."

Chapter 1

His prey was smart. Upon quickly fleeing the wilderness, the Builder used the human population as cover against the supernatural threat that hunted him. But Banewolf was patient. Tracking its prey for nearly one hundred miles, the wolf wouldn't rest until the Builder was dead. No further harm would come to its pack—its family—because of this creature's meddling.

Three Builders had managed to escape the carnage following a failed attempt to separate the immortal wolf from its vessel. Wesley David, Kalista's long-time friend and confidant, gave his life to bring Rhane back from the dead. The second fell by Banewolf's claws only minutes later. Time was rapidly running out for the third and final Builder, who had ultimately found refuge in a truck driver's good graces and now rode somewhat safely inside the cab of a forty-ton semi truck that was headed for the interstate.

Powerful muscles kept easy pace with the tanker, all while remaining hidden in the forested road side. Banewolf had long awaited the proper opening to attack. Collateral damage was best kept to a minimum. The death of innocent bystanders was not ideal, but leaving behind potential eyewitnesses was unacceptable. Weighing the consequences, Rhane decided to make a move. The semi truck simply could not be allowed to make the interstate. He would have to act now.

The wolf accelerated. Pushed to maximum speed, Banewolf surged ahead of the semi truck and changed direction once it reached a position a quarter of a mile beyond its target. Then the wolf attacked. Abandoning the cover of the forest, it charged across the asphalt and straight into the path of the forty-ton tractor trailer. Wearing an expression of confused horror, the trucker panicked and nearly lost control of his payload. The wolf was already in the air as the semi swerved left and then right to try and avoid colliding with the jaw-dropping sight. But his efforts were futile. Diamond-sharp claws peeled back the cab's metal hull, exposing the prey Banewolf so ferociously sought. The Builder's form shimmered weakly as it made one desperate attempt to escape, but the wolf's claws were there. It reached into the light, seizing the Builder's still human heart and crushed it.

The trucker was in a full panic and the semi veered irrevocably off the roadway. Banewolf leapt from his topside perch, landing next to the cab and rammed its shoulders into the sidewall, steering the truck from impact with the nearby trees. The maneuver was mostly successful as the tractor-trailer still barreled off the pavement but missed smashing head-on into a cluster of aged pines whose roots surely ran deep. But the truck didn't escape entirely unscathed. Roaring past the trees, steel grinded against wood, disfiguring the cab's frame and violently ripping away the sides of the trailer.

Caught between the combined momentum of itself and the rig, Banewolf narrowly avoided getting ensnared in the tangle of twisting metal and bark. Digging in with every claw, the wolf redirected its trajectory, managing to leverage its weight against the rear of the truck. The additional drag helped slow the vehicle, but Banewolf wasn't sure it would be enough. The tractor-trailer's speed remained wildly out of control and on a rampage, leading it toward a dense line of trees. The smell of diesel overwhelmed the wolf's nose, confirming damage to at least one of the two fuel tanks. Hitting those trees would most definitely trigger a fiery blast. Thinking he had suffered through enough explosions in one twenty-four hour period, Rhane released the wolf's claws and launched onto the roof of a trailer whose condition was rapidly disintegrating. Quickly scaling across the crumbling surface, the wolf dropped once more onto the hood of the massive truck. Impaling the steel with its claws, the wolf slung its body over the driver's side and wrenched the truck sideways.

For ten grueling seconds, impact seemed imminent despite Banewolf's heroic efforts. The truck had slowed but not nearly enough. If escape from the impending inferno was possible, further action had to be taken. Banewolf looked into the driver's terrified eyes as the man shifted a panicked gaze between the approaching trees and creature clinging to his rig. Regretting the choice even as he made it, Banewolf released the rig and leapt in one final effort to save this human he didn't know but whose death would certainly be on his head.

Nearly one thousand pounds of wolf flesh maneuvered to buffer the steel missile from a devastating collision with nature. Springing forward seconds before impact, the wolf rammed its shoulder into the truck's wheel well. The axle broke apart as the truck rocked sideways, teetering wildly off balance before crashing to its side. Buckling beneath a damaged foreleg, Banewolf couldn't avoid the trailer as it shot up and sideways, slamming into the trees with the wolf pinned beneath it.

Gritting his teeth against the pain and darkness threatening the edges of his vision, Rhane shed the wolf's form to escape through a gaping hole in the ruins of the trailer. The air inside was slightly cooler against his skin and would have been much colder to a true human. No doubt the chill stemmed from a refrigeration system meant to preserve the perishable load for the many miles stretching between its origin and destination.

Rhane considered the sludgy blend of pulverized tomatoes, melons, peaches, and berries hijacking most of the traction from his boots. *Spoiled produce is the least of this guy's worries…if he's still alive.*

Just in case the universe didn't feel like giving him a break and the fuel tanks exploded anyway, Rhane quickly slipped and slid through the rest of the trailer, reaching the opposite side as swiftly as possible. Head feeling better by the time his feet touched solid ground again, he pried away the driver side door and freed a very terrified trucker from the cab.

"Did you see it?" The man clung to Rhane's tomato-stained shirt. "Did you see that thing?"

"I didn't see nothing, man," Rhane said, adopting a dopey, slacker accent as he continued to drag the trucker away from possible danger. "Just your truck plowing through those trees. Haven't you seen the billboards? Don't text and drive, man. You're lucky to be alive."

Streaked with blood, the trucker's face grew impossibly paler. "It nearly killed me." His eyes stretched even wider as he wrenched away from Rhane's grasp and turned back to the smoking wreckage. Rhane hadn't expected the move, so the driver actually made it two steps before he could recapture him.

"You can't go back there, man."

"But there was someone with me…a hitchhiker. I-I think he's d-dead. That thing killed him. R-ripped his heart out."

The man pitched forward as his legs buckled beneath him. Rhane swore and made a grab to steady the driver, jerking him upright. On realizing the man was out cold, he lowered him to the ground and dialed 911, quickly examining him for further injuries. None were apparent beside the angry-looking gash below his temple, but the man's heart rate had sunk dangerously low. He was probably slipping into shock.

Shit.

Rhane identified the highway and last intersection noted before the crash. "Just follow the skid marks," he said, and hung up.

Hanging around long enough to make sure the guy at least held on until sirens were close by, Rhane shifted back onto all fours and trotted into the woods. He had a family to get home to.

Chapter 2

Rhane pushed through the manor's front door and found Kalista standing there waiting for him, but her presence didn't surprise him. He had sensed her as early as the first step, and obviously she must have expected him too. Taking one look at him, her eyes widened with horror.

"It's not blood," he said quickly, and she relaxed, sighing as his arms slipped around her. Within himself, Rhane felt the stresses of the last twenty-four hours slipping away. He nuzzled her neck and then kissed his way to Kalista's mouth. Her body responded as it always did. Soon her breaths had quickened and her mouth became eager against his. He longed to bend her over the table and have her right there but knew Kalista would insist on more privacy. From the smell of things, everyone was still home and in crisis mode. But when wasn't there a crisis? These moments had to be stolen.

Kalista rolled her hips into him, shattering Rhane's thoughts and making the bulge in his jeans expand to painful proportions, so he reached down and flipped her up into his arms. After giving a startled cry of surprise, she rewarded him with her most inviting smile. Then leaning forward, she whispered exactly what she wanted him to do next, while her hand slid beneath his waistband to emphasize her request with a sensual caress. Groaning as all the blood from his brain migrated south, Rhane glanced at the table next to the front door and reconsidered his options.

"Do you have any idea what you do to me?" he asked.

Raising one eyebrow, her fingers gripped him a bit tighter, causing his knees to weaken. "None," she purred. "Take me upstairs and explain it to me."

"If you keep doing that—" he stopped abruptly as her hand began to tease its way up and down the hardening length of him. Rhane dragged in the next breath, expelling it as a sharp hiss. "If you keep doing that, I don't think we'll make it to the bedroom. I'll be forced to claim what is mine right here."

Kalista laughed but the maddening strokes of her hand did not cease. "I don't think I could handle York watching us."

"You're right," he agreed hoarsely. "Forget the feathers. That guy plays with the whole chicken."

Her amused laughter rang out again. "That's the same thing Rion said." Then her stroking finally stilled as she sobered. "Maybe there is more of you left in there than you think," she said, pressing the errant hand against his cheek.

"Maybe so," he murmured, moving them toward the stairs as he found use of his legs again. Kalista's grey eyes remained locked onto his face. Watching her, Rhane couldn't help dipping his head closer to steal another kiss. She rose up in his arms only to sink into him, squashing her full breasts against his chest. Both hands pressed at his cheeks now, sealing out everything else, and it was as if only the two of them existed.

These moments, Rhane thought, and then the one scent capable of shattering that peace invaded his nostrils. His body went cold, numbed by a rush of emotions he couldn't name and didn't care to. Kalista must have sensed the change in him because she pulled away. Her expression was troubled. "What's wrong?" she asked.

"Gabriel," he said, forcing the name through clenched teeth.

"Rhane—" she began but stopped as he stiffly shook his head and eased her down to her feet. Instead of turning to face Gabriel who now stood between them and the stairway, she kept her attention fixed on Rhane and bit her bottom lip uncertainly.

"Banewolf, a word," Gabriel said.

"I'm in the middle of something," Rhane answered coolly.

The fallen Prime smirked. "Yes, I see that. But this cannot wait."

"This is my house, Gabriel. You don't get to decide what can and can't wait." He moved past Kalista, positioning himself to deliberately challenge Gabriel's personal space. It was a hard fight to drag his temper back in line when all he wanted to do was wrap his hands around Gabriel's neck and squeeze until the light left his eyes. Instead he said, "You don't get to interrupt me for any reason."

Gabriel nodded. "Perhaps this disruption between you and your...mate was ill-conceived." Despite his words, Gabriel did not look away or back down.

An involuntary growl slid from Rhane's throat. He wondered if the former Prime knew the truth of the lineage between them. Through memories of the wolf, Rhane knew the hardships he had endured as a child and the shame of being an outcast among people who despised royal blood and tormented the disgraced. Through every failure and every humiliation, he had been able to cling to the honor of being a descendant of Whytetree, one of the strongest and proudest bloodlines of Warekin ancestry. But now, even that was no more. His blood was a result of the darkness of Bllacstag.

He could kill Gabriel, erase his existence and forestall the damage that nurturing close ties with the fallen one would undoubtedly bring. Rhane gritted his teeth, feeling the canines prick his gums as they elongated. His right hand ached and seemed to grow hotter than the rest of him.

Gabriel's smile evaporated. His gaze shifted down to Rhane's hand. "When I was the vessel of the great immortal, the mark only appeared as so during times of great bloodlust. I rarely resisted on those occasions. Eventually, that behavior earned us a special moniker. *Демон волк.* Demomnwyllf."

As the burning in his palm intensified, Rhane allowed himself to glance at his hand. The mark of the wolf was actually glowing. Kalista moved closer to him.

"My eyes were not as yours. Unlike you, I was not marked at birth. It seems that the immortal was destined to abandon me for my bas—"

"*Gabriel,*" Kalista's voice cut through the air like a heated blade. "If you can't play nice, then shut up, move the hell over, and let Callan drive."

Rhane's entire spine went rigid. *Did she know?* He suddenly felt ill. He wanted nothing more than to not look at Gabriel, but that would have meant facing Kalista. If he met her eyes and saw pity in them, it would destroy him.

Then York's voice materialized from the top of the stairs, saving Rhane from an impossible choice. "Gabe, I told you to wait until after they'd bumped uglies. The big guy would be in a better mood then. You know, less likely to kill you and more likely to accept the help you're willing to give and we sorely need."

Gabriel frowned. "I do not understand this."

"I assume you mean the bumping uglies part because the rest of it was pretty clear." York descended the stairs briskly, rolling up denim shirt sleeves as he did so. The look in Rhane's eyes made him nervous. For a second there, Rhane looked as if he were seriously about to rip out Gabriel's throat. York couldn't be certain, but to him it seemed that Rhane's eyes had actually flashed from black to a troubling shade of crimson. Black was normal. But red…that would be a first…and also a very bad sign. *What bad blood has Gabe stirred up this time?*

"You know—dip the wick, do the nasty, play hide the sausage, wax that ass." York smothered a grin at Gabriel's mounting confusion. "They need to have sexual intercourse, Gabe." He rubbed his jaw thoughtfully. "Wow, it sounds really weird to say it that way."

Patting Gabriel casually on the shoulder, York formed a relaxed grip to steer the former Prime away from Rhane and toward the front door. Gabriel resisted at first but eventually yielded to York's insistent pressure. "Thanks for stopping by, but we're about to call an urgent family meeting. That means you need to leave. Kali has your number. Well, she has Callan's number." York winked. "We'll be in touch."

Shrugging off York's hand, Gabriel stopped at the door.

"That means we'll call you," York finished sarcastically, unable to help himself.

Rhane kept a wary eye on Gabriel. The fallen Prime had one foot outside, but he wasn't ready to leave. Rhane knew Gabriel wasn't done goading him and felt his blood begin to boil again. Then Kalista slipped her hand into his, quelling the burn and easing the ache beneath his skin. He was hit with a swell of gratitude that helped fortify him through Gabriel's parting address.

"I know you now recognize the truth of what I am, Banewolf."

Rhane swallowed the lump of bitterness in his throat and was miraculously able to keep his voice level when he replied. "Yeah. It has come to my recent attention that maybe you weren't the total psychopathic defector that Warekin history painted you to be. You can thank my father, Jehsi, for that."

Gabriel flinched. "Yes. I must thank him someday." And with a solemn nod, he inclined his head and left.

York observed his retreat through the closest window. "Okay," he said when Gabriel had gone from sight and was out of supernatural earshot. "That was way more tense than usual." He shook his head. "I'm sorry, Rhane. I tried to make sure you guys had a little privacy when you got back, but that asshole apparently had his own agenda."

"It's alright." Rhane rolled his neck, attempting to release a knot. "Gabriel is accustomed to giving orders, not following them."

York snorted. "Well if you can put up with that crap, we're gonna need his help."

"Why?" Rhane asked.

York nudged Kalista. "Sorry about the ugly comment, kiddo. I've never had the pleasure of seeing your southern bits, but I doubt there's anything about them that's ugly."

Kalista rolled her eyes. "I know better than to take you seriously."

"Hey! I resent that."

"York," Rhane said impatiently.

"You look like hell." York replied. He was still, for some reason, trying to distract Rhane from the subject at hand.

"Thank you for stating the obvious."

"I can't believe Kali was willing to make out with you looking like that."

"Yeah, well maybe she likes it dirty," Rhane muttered and looked down, grabbing the corners of his ruined shirt. "It's not blood." He lifted his head and met the slightly stunned expressions of York and Kalista. Rhane scowled. "What?"

"Nothing," York said, shaking his head. "And I know it's not blood."

"Right," Rhane said dryly. "I'm sure I smell like hell too."

"It is actually a little more fragrant—diesel fuel and the undertones of several tons of pulverized, greenhouse-grown vegetables." York grinned. "You made the five o'clock news, buddy."

"Shit."

"Extremely deep shit. Walk this way please."

Rhane groaned. "Is this why we need Gabriel?"

"Partly."

Rhane didn't like the suspense. It gave him the impression things were about to go south very far and really fast. He settled on the couch while Kalista took a spot behind him and began kneading his neck and shoulders. The sensations her exquisite hands extracted from his body were both relaxing and arousing all at once. Rhane didn't want her to ever stop.

"Where's Bailen?" he mumbled drowsily.

17

"He and the boys are upstairs in the library."

Rhane didn't bother trying to hide his surprise as he looked at her. "We have a library now?"

A smile brought even more light to her lovely grey eyes. "Why not? This old place has plenty of room for it."

Rhane shrugged. "True."

"And Rion might have complained about needing a quieter spot for research."

He couldn't help laughing. "Gotcha." He took her hands in his, pulling her around the sofa to be next to him. "I really don't want you to stop, but I think York has something very important to tell me, and I'll get in trouble if I can't listen closely because I'm too turned on to pay attention to his hideous face."

Releasing one hand to swat away the pillow York threw at his head, he tugged Kalista into his lap with the other as his mouth automatically went to her lips.

"Oh yeah, that's better. Nice to see how I've got your full attention now."

Mid-kiss, they both laughed. "Sorry, York." Rhane waved his hand. "The floor is yours. Tell me about the extremely deep shit."

Rolling his eyes, York called to the boys without raising his voice. "Assemble," he said. Seconds later, footsteps could be heard on the stairs.

"When did you teach them that?"

"You taught them that."

Rhane winced. "Good to know."

The boys spilled into the room and fanned out in different directions. Rion and War argued with each other from opposite sides of the room, debating the "hot factor" of a couple of women named Jennifer and Angelina.

Matthias quietly looked on, clearly lost as to what the fuss was all about. But so was Rhane.

The last to enter the meeting space, Orrin chose a wall on the farthest side of the room and leaned against it. Sensing that something was off, Rhane studied the young kin and tried to understand what it was. Orrin eventually noticed Rhane's scrutiny, nodded woodenly and let his gaze fall away.

Rhane's mouth went dry. *Shit*, he said silently. *Shit*.

"Alright. Now that we're all here," York began, reeling Rhane's attention back to the other problem at hand.

"Wait," Kalista interrupted. Standing, she went to the doorway where Bailen crouched just behind the threshold. "Won't you come in?" she asked as she stooped to rub behind his ears. Bailen whined but didn't budge. "Then I'll sit with you."

"Bailen, come," Rhane commanded. Bailen rose to his feet and padded into the room, head and tail tucked low in a submissive posture. Stopping a short distance from Rhane's feet, the canine stared at the hardwood and appeared utterly dejected. Rhane softened his voice. "Do not be afraid." He patted the sofa cushion next to him. "Come."

A trembling Bailen obeyed, bounding lightly onto the couch. Rhane took the canine's great head in his and lifted Bailen's muzzle until the honey-eyed gaze met his. "Never fear me, little one."

At last, Bailen relaxed. Resting his head in Rhane's lap, he settled with a sigh. Kalista reclaimed her position next to Rhane and his world was complete once more. Gently pressing a kiss against her forehead, he choked down a swallow.

"I'm definitely jotting this in my diary."

This time it was Rhane who chucked the pillow at York's head. "Go to hell," he said.

Laughing, York switched on the television. The screen was frozen in a split frame consisting of an on-site reporter in commune with home base. In the bottom right corner, "LIVE" was written in bold, red letters. Though, clearly, that was no longer the case.

"Wait a second, you recorded this?"

Rion raised his hand. "Actually, that was me."

"So why are we watching? I know what I did. I was there. I don't need to see humans rehash it."

"Hold your horses there, cowboy," York said, waving the remote in Rhane's direction. "Only Rion and I have watched. And it's not so much about this but what comes up afterward and steals your spotlight."

"Which is?"

"I refuse to ruin the surprise."

Rhane dropped his head back onto the sofa cushions. "Gimme a break, York. Just this once. Please. These last few months have been a nightmare. I need a breather."

"Sorry." York shrugged ruefully. "Don't shoot. I'm just the messenger. Besides, what is it that you always say?"

Of course, Rhane had no idea what York was referring to and had to search the wolf's memory for a clue. York waited while he did so. The answer was sobering. "We were bred for war." Rhane sighed. "Very well then, do your worst."

Grinning, York pressed play for the recorder. Considering the scant material available to air, the so-call breaking news report was epically blown out of proportion. There was only footage of the wrecked tractor trailer and a few grainy photos taken with a cell phone. Of course, there were three different eyewitness accounts, but none of the stories corroborated with another. One motorist swore to having seen a mutated and apparently rabid polar bear. The amateur photographer claimed it was Bigfoot. "But, you know, the Yeti version." The trucker delivered the closest account, proclaiming that a giant, man-eating wolf had ripped through the steel cab as if it were opening "a bag of chips," devoured his passenger, and then tried to eat him for dessert.

Rhane looked at Kalista. "I actually saved that human."

She held up her hands. "No judgment here. Before meeting you, I fed on humans all the time."

"Ha. Ha."

York broke in, dramatically shushing them. "Come on, you guys. Here comes the good part."

And that's when the hammer fell.

The breaking news report featuring Rhane's highway encounter was interrupted by an even more sensational story. "Real monsters in New York City subways," a pretty brunette newswoman promised. The scenes that unfolded next were shocking and disturbing even to someone like Rhane who was accustomed to the many horrors encountered on a battlefield.

Men, women, and children stood waiting on a platform, transfixed by a circle of white light floating just above their heads. A train passed in the background, as did dozens of other city dwellers, used to witnessing stranger things, or preoccupied with maintaining their hectic pace in life. But those who did gaze upon the light were transformed.

Bathed in its rays, their bodies began to change. Extra appendages sprouted from beneath blazers and skirts, while existing features melted away. Splotches of fur and gnarled knots took the place of smooth skin. Mouths and ears elongated. Noses disappeared. Eyeballs shifted and migrated to opposite sides of the head. Many were rogue. Others were kindred. As the creatures fell to all fours, shredded clothing hung from their bodies, no longer fitting their grotesque shape.

"What the hell," Kalista whispered in a voice hinting both awe and disgust.

As unaffected travelers finally began to take notice and ran screaming in all directions away from the changed humans, the light vanished. The newly minted creatures started a slaughter of the remaining humans with immense savagery. The recording continued, capturing the massacre until the owner of the cell phone was killed as he fled.

There was a person in the crowd, the sight of whom stole Rhane's breath and drove the blood from his brain. Feeling lightheaded, he stood up anyway. "Go back," he said, drifting toward the television.

"Are you sure?" York sounded doubtful. "I've seen it twice now and will definitely have nightmares."

"Play it again," Rhane ordered. "Start where the light disappears."

York did as asked, but Rhane shook his head. "Slow it down."

"Are you going to tell me what you're looking for?"

"There." Rhane touched the television. He almost didn't believe it, but there he was. "Do you see him?"

In the same moment, the memory came rushing back. Rhane heard the beating of wings and remembered the goliath of red and black cobblestone flesh with yellow eyes split horizontally by black slits. He recalled the hatred that poured from its mind and felt its hunger.

The creature opened its mouth, igniting a spark, and fire materialized within its jaws, spurting forth a jet stream of magma. In the memory, Rhane was powerless to stop it. His skin succumbed and he was engulfed. His body melted. His muscles fell away, exposing bone and raw nerves to the fire. The pain was unbearable.

Above him, the creature still hovered. But then something changed. The dragon began to shift, left behind its monstrous shape to become something else. Falling like a stone, it was much smaller when it landed. A humanoid figure rose from the ground, unfolding to stand on two feet. Dark locks fell around bronze shoulders, and the head lifted, casting aside the curtain of hair that concealed its face.

Once again Rhane looked into the boy's eyes and knew him. Only this time Rhane saw that he wasn't a boy but a man.

Chapter 3

They packed quickly and quietly. Even Rion and War had ceased arguing for the time being. Everyone seemed a bit thunderstruck, struggling to wrap their heads around what had transpired downstairs. Rhane couldn't blame them, especially Kalista. It was a lot to take in.

He had sent Matthias back to his pack because New York was no place for a young kindred still adapting to even the fundamental aspects of a human lifestyle. The city was also in danger of being overrun by rogues and kindred from extraordinary origins. Rhane couldn't guarantee Matthias' safety. He had already lost one of Ian's soldiers—a second casualty of a ward entrusted to him would be unacceptable.

Rhane felt guilty leaving with the eclipse's imminent arrival. Starting with the eve of the eclipse, Ian and his pack would become mortal for forty-eight hours. Two rogue hives were seeking vengeance for the murder of Erebus last year. Since it was actually Rhane who had killed the hive Keeper and put her sister, Nyx, on the warpath, it was his duty to protect Ian's pack from the rogue threat during the event. Rhane just hoped its onset wouldn't happen until after he and the other kin returned. He owed Ian so much. In direct relation to that, Rhane's debt to Gabriel was also rising.

The fallen Prime had agreed to watch over the kindred pack in Rhane's absence. If he had not returned by the time of the eclipse, Gabriel, aided by his army of reapers, would do what was necessary to keep the lot of them safe from attack.

Gritting his teeth, Rhane nearly snapped the zipper off the duffle bag as he pulled it closed. Standing in the shadow of Gabriel's good graces wasn't something he wanted. Hearing York approach, he tried not to tense up further, but he was alone. It meant that his second would set aside the humor and seek out serious conversation.

"Judging from the veins popping out the side of your neck, this is probably a bad time to tell you this, but Kali just called for the jet and it won't be available for hours."

"Why the hell not?"

"Scheduled maintenance," York explained. Folding his arms, he leaned against the doorframe. "They're picking her apart to make sure she keeps flying."

"Secure commercial tickets then. Bailen won't be happy."

"Kali is already on it. She didn't want to wait and figured you wouldn't either."

Rhane almost smiled. "Good thinking."

"And as for Bailen, he can always become a real boy and ride up top with the rest of us."

"He has his reasons, York. You know that." Rhane unzipped the bag again. "Put your things in here. The weapons will have to travel with you."

"I told you that antique dealer's license would come in handy."

Rhane snorted. "I can only guess that you did," he muttered under his breath.

Sliding his hands into his pockets, York considered his next move. Losing memories meant Rhane was no longer tormented by the past, but something else had a hold of him, something fierce and equally powerful that was by all evidence, disinclined to let go of his warlord. He'd tried to get Rhane to open up about it, at least to Kali, but he couldn't be sure if that had happened, and right now Rhane was wound too tight to risk broaching the subject.

There was one thing, though, York could not leave without saying. "I have a suggestion—don't tell the boys before we go."

Rhane didn't even look up. "That's a great suggestion, but Orrin already knows."

York stared at him. He was unwilling to believe that Rhane could have done something so stupid right before a big mission, but asked anyway. "So...you told him?"

"Of course not."

Leaving the doorway, York moved closer. "Then why do you think he knows?"

Rhane shrugged. "I just know."

York gritted his teeth. Even after losing his head, it seemed that Rhane's instinct to protect War and his hair-brained bad judgment calls remained sorely intact. Imprisonment within their homeland had done nothing to dampen that boy's spirit. He was as impetuous as ever and no doubt held full culpability for Orrin's recent revelation.

"It was War, wasn't it?"

"Probably." Rhane sighed, raking a hand through messy hair, still wet from a recent and much-needed shower. "And I know what you're going to say, so—"

"Do you?" York broke in with a tone dripping with sarcasm.

Rhane actually grinned. "You know something...I don't. It's the damndest thing," he finished, shaking his head and still smiling. There was no point in getting upset about it. Rhane had mostly accepted that there would be a lot of things he wouldn't remember.

"And you find that funny because?"

Rhane pulled some documents from a drawer and tossed them on the bed. "No, York, I don't find it funny, but I'm not going to cry about it either. Now, are you going to get your stuff and bring it in here or what?"

"Maybe I'll just put my things with Kali's," he said, feeling petulant enough to continue the argument.

"She won't have room."

"Oh, so you can remember *that*."

"*No.*" Rhane rolled his eyes and pointed. "Her bags are in the corner. I suggest that you borrow one of her dresses if you're going to keep this up."

York barked a laugh at the unexpected joke, and realized he was going to have to get used to this new version of Rhane.

*

They landed in New York four hours later, after a brief layover in Charlotte. Rion had spent the entire flight analyzing subway footage, and now as they gathered in one of three shared suites, he briefed the others with a theory that sounded somewhat plausible. Granted, the serious nature of his presentation sorely contrasted to the image of a fearsome wolf wearing cartoonish, purple glasses printed across the front of his shirt. On the back, "NERDY WOLF" was printed in bold lettering in a shade matching the comical frames.

"You see that open, sphere-like ring at the top of the staff?" Rion pointed to an area on a print-out taken from online footage. "I believe a missing piece belongs there."

York leaned over the desk, closely eyeing the magnified image. "And what gives you that idea?"

"Remember when Wesley came to the manor and attacked us?"

"He did *what?*" Rhane said.

"How could I forget?" York answered at the same time. Then Rhane's question registered and York's expression became sheepish. "He's dead, so it didn't seem important."

Kali patted Rhane's thigh, reminding herself not to get distracted by the feel of hard muscle beneath the denim material. "We took care of them. They won't hurt us anymore."

Though still scowling, Rhane relaxed...a fraction. "Continue," he said, and Rion resumed his explanation. "That night, Wesley told us that technology of this sort existed and the Siren's Heart was the key to unlocking it. He called it the ark. I believe that when we gave rogues the statue, they went and found it. As for the missing piece...well, Wesley also said that the ark—this staff—could be used to transform humans in quantities that would expedite the awakening of the big baddie who wants to eat us all. But look at these images." Rion spread the pictures out across the desk. "Everyone who looked at the light wasn't turned. Only those who the light actually *touched* were affected. That's why the guy who took this video wasn't changed."

"He did get his throat ripped out later."

"The point is," Rion continued, glaring at War, "Changing half a dozen people at a time—though effective at creating panic and chaos—isn't going to make much headway toward the rogue goal of bringing back their god. The sort of people who bury artifacts never make it easy for treasure hunters. Why should this be any different?" Rion tapped the picture. "I think an amplifier of some sort

29

goes there, a keystone that changes the staff into a serious weapon."

Rhane nodded thoughtfully. "Maybe it's the combination of staff and keystone that becomes the ark."

Rion raised his eyebrows in surprise. "That makes sense."

"And I think I know what that keystone is. When my service was conscripted to the rogues, they took me back to the desert outpost, insisting I help them recover a stone. They seemed pretty desperate to get it."

"*Yes*." Rion celebrated, pumping his fist once. A second later, a piece of crumpled paper hit him in the face. Aiming an angry stare in the direction from where the paper had flown, Rion met War's satisfied grin and a slight bow from the auburn-haired kin. "Hater," he grumbled.

Rhane ignored the exchange. "Good work, Rion," he said.

"Impress us some more and tell us where that stone is," York chimed in. "The rogues haven't found it yet, so I'm thinking it would be nice if we went ahead and did so."

"I'll work on it."

Kali chewed her lip worriedly. Normally, the idea of hunting for a relic would have excited her, but not if it meant leaving the city...not when they were so close. "How will we know where the next attack will be?"

"Unfortunately, there's no way to predict that. At least not one I've thought of." Rion shook his head ruefully. "But I've got police scanners set up in our suite and emergency alerts are being forwarded to my phone. We can be the world's fastest first responders."

"It seems like a long shot." Kali didn't mean to be the downer, but the words felt like the bleak truth.

Rhane squeezed her shoulder. "We're all going to split up and alternately stake out the busiest terminals in the city. When something happens, one of us is bound to be close. Rion will direct the rest of us to the hot spot. Even if we're too late to stop it, we can try tracking the rogues from there. It'll work out."

Feeling somewhat reassured, Kali nodded. Rhane wasn't the type to make empty promises or have baseless confidence.

"I want everyone to stay here and get settled. Rotations throughout the city start first thing. I get the feeling that the next hit may be at rush hour. York, you're with me. Let's go scope out where the first attack happened. See if we can find any clues. Even in the highly trafficked subway system, scents of victims could be traceable. Let's find who we can and see how they're coping."

"You want me to stay behind?" Kali already knew the answer but didn't like it.

Rhane brushed his thumb across her cheek. "Rest while you can. It might be a while before you get the chance again."

"And you won't try to find him now?"

"No." His voice held a grim edge. "I want a fresh start. No mistakes. Make the first shot count before rogues realize we're here in the city. It may be our best chance."

Bailen whined.

"Stay with your mother," Rhane said. And then he and York were gone.

Chapter 4

Urine, mildew, perfume, stale food, and sweat—so many odors permeated the subway tunnels, overpowering the supernatural nose. After boldly ducking beneath a cautionary line of police tape, Rhane and York had spent the past half hour searching for clues. Unfortunately, clean up on the scene had already begun with strong chemical compounds that effectively erased the scent markers of every living thing in the area. It took some effort and a wider search radius, but they eventually found the trail of two newly transformed rogues. Rhane thought it was possible to track them outside of the subway, but he and York decided to save that agenda for later. Right now the objective was to find *him*, but so far, the goal had seen little fruition. The crime scene was too tainted.

A stab of guilt targeted his gut each time he thought about lying to Kalista. He had wanted to tell her the truth. Sure, she may have insisted on coming, but he could have just explained to her why that wasn't possible or, if necessary, ordered her to stay behind. However, telling Kalista the truth wasn't feasible until he knew the truth himself.

The vision of the boy who appeared as a dragon only to fall from the sky in flames—was he a threat? Was he the monster this memory would have Rhane believe? Was he evil? Maybe it was a dream, but while experiencing it, Rhane sensed no recognition and certainly no love from the youthful stranger. He hated to expose his family to another potentially deadly adversary, but realized he would eventually have to unless he and York found the boy first. And even if they didn't find him, at the very least he could shield Bailen and Kalista from a grievous encounter for a few hours more.

"Tell me that you found something, York."

"I can't get anything past the rat feces. Maybe if we used skins—"

"We can't risk someone seeing us."

York sighed. "You're right. There's no need to stir up a bigger shit storm than what's already brewing."

"Thank you for showing such restraint. Did that hurt?"

Feigning ignorance, York blinked at him with wide eyes. "I don't know what you're talking about."

"C'mon. You didn't just want to take another crack at me for the roadside fiasco?"

York gave in to the grin threatening to tear apart his face. "Okay yeah. It did cross my mind." He leaned against a center column decoratively tiled in a mosaic of the city landscape. The search was getting them nowhere. "What's next, boss? Should we track down these brand new rogues…make sure they're being good little boys and girls?"

"We might as well. Things here aren't going as I hoped."

"We'll find him."

"I have no doubt about that."

York squinted at Rhane, who was making good work of chewing his bottom lip raw. "You don't sound very happy about it."

"I can't be. Not when…" Rhane stopped and then decided to come clean. "I saw him before today, York. In a vision. He was this huge, fire-breathing monster who burned everything in his path, including me. I think the Builders may have meant it as a warning."

"And when did we start trusting those backstabbing intermeddlers?"

Ignoring York's sarcastic undertone, Rhane searched the wolf's memories anyway. "They never misled us regarding any danger we would encounter."

"Okay. I'll give you that." York bowed his head thoughtfully. "What does Kali think about your vision?" When Rhane didn't answer, he narrowed his eyes in suspicion. "You haven't told her, have you?"

"No."

"Rhane."

"I know."

"Do you?"

Rhane was quiet.

"I wasn't going to say anything, but since we're on the subject—you lied to her when you said we wouldn't look for him tonight. You didn't use to lie to her."

"I feel lousy about it, York. You don't have to make me feel worse."

"I'm not trying to make you feel bad about lying to her. I'm trying to help you understand who you are, Rhane...who you were. I know things in that pretty skull of yours are wired a bit differently now and that's not your fault *but*, you and Kali have always been able to trust each other. Don't screw that up."

"I know. You're right."

York grinned. "Damn right I'm right."

Rolling his eyes, Rhane fought back a smile of his own. "So, oh wise counselor, must I confess about this particular lie, or can we just scratch tonight's incident and start fresh with the honesty come morning?"

Chuckling, York started toward the platform, perching at the edge before leaping down next to the tracks. "I'm fresh out of good advice for the evening. I say don't tell her."

Rhane dropped next to him a moment later. "Well, can I be done making good decisions for the evening and agree with you?"

"Sure. But don't throw me under the bus when you get caught."

"Nah. I'll just drag you behind it."

"Gee thanks."

They followed the scent trail down nearly two miles of track before the path of the changelings veered toward a service exit. The steel door hung slightly ajar, lock broken and metal twisted, almost completely pried from the frame. Vaulting over a rusted railing, York nudged the door open and peered inside. "There's no light."

Wordlessly, Rhane tugged a flashlight from his back pocket, clicked it on, and passed it forward. As York started to step inside, Rhane restrained him by the shoulder. "Is it weird that these scents migrated deeper into the tunnels and stuck together?"

"Maybe a pack mentality is hardwired into their DNA."

Rhane grunted. "Maybe."

"That doesn't sit well with you."

"I just don't think that explains all of it."

"You got a better theory?"

"Their markers reek of fear."

"So?"

"I'll tell you the rest soon."

York smirked. "You don't have a theory."

"I'm working on it," Rhane said, and then shoved him inside.

On the other side of the door loomed the perfect setting for a low budget horror movie. Miles and miles of abandoned track had been walled off from the rest of the city and left to decay. Parts of the tunnels were half-flooded. Four inches of dust or mildew covered the rest. York danced the beam off the walls and ceiling, making adjustments to his earlier position. The place couldn't be the setting for a horror film. It was too pretty. The tiled mosaic theme from the surface must have originated from these depths, lining the crumbling walls, and encasing the entire ceiling. Lovely arches and stained glass completed the atmosphere of eerie romance, sending a chill across his skin.

He slowed down enough to turn in a full circle, appreciating the view. "This is sort of nice."

Rhane quickly moved past him. "This way," he said brusquely.

York jogged to catch up. "What set your pants on fire?"

"Turn that light off. They're close."

Startled, York sniffed the air again. *That's what I get for being a damn romantic.*

With both their noses fixed on the trail, they moved faster through the darkness, even without the light. When the smell of the rogues grew stronger, thick and acrid enough to coat the tongue, York and Rhane slowed their pace. Soundlessly, the two men crept forward, glad that the drafty tunnels took their scent away from their quarry. Then a noise reached their ears and made them freeze in place.

"You heard that?" York whispered.

"Yeah."

"The light?"

"It can't hurt."

Switching on the flashlight, York and Rhane began to move again. Nearing the mouth of the tunnel, Rhane called out softly into the next room. "Hello there."

The weeping from inside was instantly silenced.

"I'm not here to harm anyone." Rhane stepped forward, but motioned for York to remain behind while keeping the light up. "I have a friend with me. He's not here to hurt you either."

That statement was a lie until about thirty seconds ago, but they didn't need to know that. The sight before him was a pitiful one. Huddled in one corner of the room were two men and a woman. All three looked worse for wear. Their clothes were tattered ruins, shredded by the violence of the initial transformation. A mixture of blood, dirt, and tears stained each face while their bodies were held rigid by fear. Rhane still wasn't sure they wouldn't run. A frightened animal could bolt...or attack at any moment.

"I can make sure you guys go home without hurting yourselves or your families. That's why you came here, right?"

It took a long time, but eventually one of the males nodded.

"Do you want to go home?"

The woman sobbed and began rocking herself, trying in vain to soothe her cries. One of the men finally found his voice. "W-who are you?"

"My name is Rhane. I know of others like you. I can't promise a cure for what's happened, but there are ways to control it."

Except for the part where you turn into the ass end of a troll whenever touched by sunlight, Rhane amended silently.

"Who did this to us?" the same guy asked.

"I can't answer that."

"Why did they do this?" the second man questioned in a voice broken with emotion.

Rhane searched for an answer close enough to the truth that wouldn't reveal too much. "Some very bad people are trying to start a war."

The first man spoke again. "How does turning us into monsters initiate war?"

"There are forces at work here you can't understand right now. Let me help you and I promise you will find answers soon."

"Why should we trust you?"

At that point, York started to run thin on patience. They had come down here with the intent to kill every single one of these things, and as far as York was concerned, that option was still on the table. All Rhane needed to do was say the word. "This guy is offering you the only silver lining to the thundercloud you're all cowering under like little dogs scared shitless. Let us help you. The alternative ain't pretty."

The changeling responsible for most of the speaking bared some now very pointed teeth and hissed. His eyes shone in the beam of the flashlight as the rest of his features shifted, crawling across skin that pulsated as if large worms burrowed beneath the surface. "Easy," Rhane warned as York belted out a deep warning growl. "This doesn't have to get violent. You three look as if you've been through enough."

The woman, still rocking, lifted her head from her knees. "I want you to help me."

"Okay." Rhane studied the other two. "Anyone else?"

"Please help me," said the man who had broken down earlier.

Taking a few heartbeats longer, the last changeling nodded an acceptance of their help but was unable to reverse the beginnings of the transformation. His face remained a twisted mixture of man and beast. "I can't live like this," he whispered.

"Okay," Rhane said. York aimed the beam into Rhane's face. "What now?" he added.

Rhane squinted against the light. "I need to go to the surface and make a call. Will you be okay down here?"

"As long as you'll be okay not taking the flashlight," York deadpanned.

"Fair enough." Rhane started to walk away.

"Hey," York called. "You don't seem that bothered…you know, being underground."

Rhane paused, turning back to him. "Kalista mentioned something about it. No, that worry doesn't seem to trouble me as much. Besides, we're not that deep."

"And the water?"

Rhane started walking again. "That's still there," he grumbled.

*

Once on the surface, cellular service was possible again, and it turned out to be only a small hassle to get in touch with Ian. Half a dozen calls to Matthias' cell all went to voice mail. Either the young kindred had left the phone behind at the manor or had forgotten how to use it. Of course it was also possible that he was simply out on a run. While in their natural habitat, kindred prided themselves on not conforming to human behaviors regarding clothing. No clothing meant zero pockets, which meant no cell phone. Eventually, Rhane relented and called Gabriel. The fallen Prime was nearby and tracked down Ian a short while after hearing what Rhane needed. Though he didn't approve and first had to make sure Rhane understood that.

"How are things?" Rhane asked when Ian's voice finally came over the line.

"The forest persists in its serenity, but we forge ahead with preparations. The eclipse of the blue moon is close. Nyx continues her plans to march against us. I have yet to confirm but preliminary intelligence has reported her recruitment of the largest rogue hive in North America. Many thirst to avenge Erebus."

"Ian, I will return to help as soon as I can. You have my word."

"I possess not one thread of doubt. We are allies."

"How is Gabriel working out?"

"He maintains his word to you, Banewolf."

Great. Rhane rubbed the back of his neck. He felt like a complete asshole for bugging Ian when the alpha clearly had more serious things to lose sleep about. "Ian, I need a favor."

"Name it and I will assist in any way that I may. Though I fear I cannot leave here, and those I can send to your aid are few."

"Don't worry. I only need information."

"Oh?"

"What's the location of the rogue lair in the Manhattan area?"

41

"Are you in New York, Banewolf?"

"Do you know of another Manhattan?"

"In fact, there are several."

"Point taken," Rhane said. "Where can I find the rogues of Manhattan, New York? I need an audience with the priest's son."

"Will you hold while I retrieve an address for you, or shall I call you back?" Ian presented the second option with some uncertainty, making Rhane extremely hesitant to hang up at all. This was probably only the second time the alpha had handled a cell phone since the devices had been invented.

"I'll hold, Ian."

Ian was gone for quite a while. Wondering exactly how far the alpha had to travel in order to get the necessary information, Rhane stood in a deserted alleyway between a condemned apartment complex and an abandoned factory, listening to the emptiness of the still open line fill with the incessant chirping of crickets, the occasional hoot owl and coyote yowl. *Shame on me for assuming he would take the phone with him.*

Growing restless, Rhane began to pace. The cacophony of the city roared all around him—blaring cab horns, the chatter and footsteps of pedestrians, and half a dozen musical selections playing from nearby restaurants or radios. Silence did not exist here, but neither did it in the forest. Simultaneously listening to the contrasting worlds made that plainly evident.

In the next moment, several things happened at once. Ian came back on the line, and while Rhane's mind concentrated on remembering the names and numbers Ian rattled off, another sense noticed a change in the atmosphere as air currents shifted to a flow countering their earlier course. A familiar scent lifted into his nostrils—one Rhane was certain he'd never smell again—only now it was overcome by traces of putrid eggs and ash.

Ian finished the address and in the next breath gave a needless reminder of the dangers of entering a rogue lair. The warning was still on his lips when pain sledge-hammered into Rhane's back, nearly knocking him to his knees. He rolled with the blow, holding onto the phone as he scurried to take cover behind a nearby dumpster. Breathing through the hurt slicing through his back like a hot wire, he calmly thanked Ian and hung up.

Feeling the currents change again, Rhane looked around and then up to a starless sky littered with dark, feathery clouds. A shadow cut across the nightly heavens, gliding maybe thirty feet above him, between the rooftops of adjacent buildings. Then the shadow dove toward him, priming its attack with a blaze of turbulent orange flame. Fire permeated the alley as claws slammed into the dumpster, and the creature dragged the receptacle away before tossing it aside like a paper cup.

Though Rhane had taken shelter behind the dumpster, it was the wolf that leaped through the flames and sank teeth into its foe. Seeing it clearly for the first time, Rhane realized the thing appeared to be some strange hybrid of sorts, likely the end product of a Builder experiment to create the perfect monster.

It twisted away at the last second, partially shielding the base of its throat, and the thick plate of scales covering its hide prevented the wolf's bite from being lethal. But Banewolf's fangs had bitten deep, causing the hybrid to scream in equal parts fury and pain. Beating enormous black wings into a brutal frenzy, it struggled to lift itself and the wolf away from the ground while tearing at Banewolf with razor-sharp talons. Forged from bane silver, the claws were unforgiving as they ripped through the wolf's hide, seeking to detach its iron grip. Hard-pressed to keep even two paws on the ground, the wolf released the creature and lunged away from the punishment of those hateful talons.

The hybrid suspended any counter attack, leveling its wolfish snout and horn-spiked head in contemplation of its formidable opponent. Thickly muscled legs remained bunched and ready to spring. A long tail—broad and armored with dense scales but tapered into a metallic end, curved, pointed, and no doubt equally as deadly as its claws—dragged behind it, whipping slowly back and forth. Smoke trailed from both nostrils and three angular slits on either side of the creature's chest, growing and abating with each cycle of breath.

Raising its mass onto brawny hind legs, the hybrid launched into the air, and in the next instant was gone, traveling faster than even the wolf's eyes could follow in the darkness. Banewolf, however, did not sense retreat. The dull roar that next breached the air confirmed it. Fire appeared above him, engulfing the alley as it spread like a thick blanket across the atmosphere. The hybrid dove through the orange glow, a snarling devil borne along by leathery wings with murder burning from its eyes. Saliva stretched in thick streams between the fangs of the open jaws. Claws outstretched, it reached to tear the wolf apart.

Rotating its head and shoulders at an almost painful angle from his flank, Banewolf managed to avoid the worst of the hybrid's brutal talons. Still, those nails sank in just above the wolf's withers, biting deeply as the rest of the creature's weight bore down. Ignoring the pain, the wolf rolled into the attack, driving its mass into the hybrid's momentum to make the creature overshoot its landing. As the great lizard-like creature struggled to regain its footing, Banewolf was there, setting his jaws into the hybrid's foreleg and then releasing that mouthful to sink his fangs into the armored skin of its neck. The hybrid screamed in pain, thrashing wildly to break free of the wolf. Blood spewed. Chunks of flesh flew. But the hybrid tore itself away. Staggering on three legs—for one foreleg was left crippled by the wolf's bite—the creature reared up. Its chest billowed out like a preening bird and the acrid, smoky smell permeating the alley thickened. On the creature's next breath, a jet stream of fire spiraled out from its mouth.

Banewolf withstood the blast of heat and flame, unmoving, unshaken. And then he began to smell his enemy's fear. Lunging into the inferno, the wolf seized one great, leathery wing and, snapping his head back and forth like a whip, slung the hybrid against the building. Its head smashed against the mortar with sickening crack, breaking through the wall in a halo of dust and shattered debris. The great beast made a weak effort to lift its limbs, but then the hybrid's body went slack. Heaving a great sigh, it did not move again.

Banewolf waited tensely to see if the creature would rise. The minutes ticked away. The adrenaline pumping through his blood drained away, leaving him on legs that trembled from the poison of bane silver. Still, he waited.

The hybrid began to shrivel in size. Armored scales became flesh. The thick whip of a tail and the huge, black wings disappeared. Then Banewolf found himself staring at the tan skin of human hands and feet. His eyes lifted to a bloodied torso—covered in marks of the wolf's teeth and claws—a fractured collar bone, and dislocated shoulder. As his gaze went even higher, Banewolf fell to his haunches. The wolf form receded, abandoning Rhane to the mind-numbing grief that blurred his vision and choked every breath away.

Crawling forward on his hands and knees, he stopped several feet shy of the body, unable to go any further. Breathing only made his chest constrict even more. He wiped his eyes, but they only stung with more disbelief. Gathering the courage to stretch his hand forward, he touched the boy—the young man—who had emerged from the shell of a fire-breathing monster. His flesh remained warm, though his dark eyes were open and unseeing. Rhane didn't want to believe it, but the face was the same. He was the one from the television.

So many memories slammed into his mind—powerful, palpable memories that felt as if Rhane were living them once more. He remembered holding him as a baby, then as a waddling toddler, and as a boy. He remembered long rides through spring fields of purple flowers and through mountain plains dusted in snow. He remembered teaching him how to track, hold the sword, and wield the bow. Once again, he knew the pride that threatened to turn his heart inside out as the little boy learned with insatiable curiosity and grew to be more and more like his father. But most of all, Rhane remembered that fateful day when he lost him. Because of the father's sins, the son had died. He remembered carrying the tiny, limp body in his arms, and the pain ripping through his gut, hollowing him out and doubling him over as it did now.

Rhane remembered the bloodshed that followed.

More deadly than blood silver and toxic to even an immortal, bane silver was leeching from the wounds on his back and into his bloodstream. Even if there had been a chance to save him, Rhane could not. His cells were toxic. Right now, he couldn't heal himself or anyone else.

Dropping his head back with utter grief and the wicked cruelty of fate, a moan starting in his belly squeezed past a throat raw with unspoken emotion. The sound twisted and reshaped as it emerged, ripping into the air as a mournful wail, changing again to shatter the dissonance of the city as it tore through the night as an alpha's roar. Buildings trembled. The ground quaked…and Rhaven stirred.

Chapter 5

Back at the hotel, Kali snuggled beneath a soft down comforter and the warmth of Bailen's furry body tucked against hers, lost in a restful, dreamless sleep until a sound fit for her worst nightmares dragged her consciousness to the surface and dumped her wide awake on the shores of reality. Bailen's honey-colored eyes shone in the lamp light, meeting her worried stare. Outside, the rain was pouring. Before she could speak, Orrin was pounding at the door.

"Kali, open up!"

Quickly detangling herself from the sheets, Kali raced across the room, reaching the door just seconds after Bailen. She opened it to find Orrin frowning impatiently. Rion and War flanked right on his heels.

"Did you hear that?" War asked. He was the first to move past her and enter the suite. Kali didn't mind. As far as she was concerned, he and the others required no invitation.

Kali blinked stupidly. "Hear what? War, I was asleep." Looking down, she realized the only covering of her assets came from a pair of skimpy lace panties and a sheer white babydoll negligee. Kali may as well have been naked. *Maybe they won't notice in the near darkness*, she hoped while easing discreetly over to the closet to grab one of Rhane's shirts.

The kin moved through the room like a whirlwind. Orrin checked each of the room's windows while War secured the balcony. Finally satisfied with what was seen or not seen, the twin brothers strode back to the center of the room. Water dripped from War's hair onto the carpet. "So you were asleep just now, until Orrin knocked?"

They both watched as Kali slipped into an oversized shirt. Orrin's eyes raked appreciatively over her near nudity. "Nice."

Kali couldn't stop the blush from rising to her cheeks. "I was expecting Rhane, obviously."

War winked. "Obviously."

Rion chuckled, inciting a glare from Kali. "Don't encourage them," she warned. Holding both hands up, the smile melted from Rion's face, freeing Kali to turn back to the twins. "What's going on? I had a bad dream and woke up," she said to answer War's earlier question. She studied each of them, recalling the stiffness of their movements and became aware of the palpable tension that now possessed the room. Her pulse kicked up a notch. "What happened?"

"It's Rhane."

"Is he okay?" Kali pulled the shirt tighter, hugging her arms around her body.

"We don't know. We think so." War paused, looking at Orrin as if he wanted to defer to him, but his larger brother remained silent.

"But you're concerned," Kali prodded after the silence stretched on for too long.

"He used an alpha's cry."

"A what?"

"An alpha's cry," he repeated patiently. "It's different from a rally. Rhane doesn't necessarily want us to come to him, but he needed to be heard. It woke us up. We got dressed and came over. "

Kali gasped with an abrupt realization. "I did hear him. I thought the noise was just a dream. It woke me too."

All three of them suddenly seemed visibly relieved. "So what do you want us to do?"

Shit. Kali stared at War. He couldn't be serious about dropping the decision into her lap. She'd gotten them into so much trouble in the past. But even as she looked at War, all three boys stared back at her. *Crapola.* Kali bit her lip and tried to think things through. "Okay, if the howl wasn't a rally, then Rhane obviously doesn't need us charging in to his rescue." *Like he ever does.* But yet, the sound in her dream had been so awful, both angry and desperate at once. Kali felt in her gut that something was wrong. "Did you try calling his cell?"

Rion nodded. "I did. And texted. He hasn't answered."

"What about York?"

He shook his head. "Everything goes straight to voice mail."

"Is it possible to track them in weather like this? It's a friggin' monsoon out there."

War shrugged. "I'm a pretty good tracker. I'd have to use a skin though."

Kali chewed her lip harder. "That sounds risky. With all that's going in the city right now, the sight of a mutant-sized wolf in the city would set people into a panic."

Bailen whined. Kali knelt next to him, taking his great head in her hands. Of course, not fully grown, Bailen could still pass for a large dog. "You shouldn't go out there alone. You know that." Huffing, Bailen looked away. "But you can guide War," she said, and Bailen's tail began to thump against the floor. "Go make sure your father is

51

okay." Glancing up at War, she hesitated. "And don't let him see you," she added.

*

As the shudder rippled through Rhaven's limp body, his chest expanded and then collapsed, releasing a great exhalation of breath. Blinking, his eyes became lighter, exchanging the midnight pitch for a tawny grey. Favoring his left side, he started to get up. Well, he tried to. His legs wouldn't hold the weight and immediately folded beneath him. Shaking himself from the stupor holding him transfixed, Rhane moved to catch him.

"Take it easy," he said. His voice sounded strangely uneven in his own ears. "I'm so sorry. I should have known."

Rhaven flinched when Rhane's hands touched him, and he began dragging himself away. In no time, the fight left his damaged body, giving him no choice but to sag into Rhane's arms. Lowering him gently to the pavement, Rhane backed off, relinquishing the space Rhaven clearly needed. With enough distance between them, he began to calm. His eyes remained angry and untrusting as he stared wordlessly at the stranger next to him.

It was obvious that he wasn't full grown. He possessed the build of a man, but the features of his face clung to the softness of boyhood. Rhane presumed him older than the twins. "Do you know me?" he asked.

Rhaven did not answer.

"I can set your shoulder. It will lessen the pain. As for the rest of your wounds…I'm afraid I can't help those. My blood would only hurt you."

The only reply Rhane got was a cold stare.

With nothing else to go on, he had to rely on instinct. Careful to make every movement as slow as possible and to keep both hands in clear sight, Rhane edged closer to the young man. Whenever Rhaven tensed, Rhane stopped moving until the boy relaxed again. It took a long time, but eventually he was close enough to attend the injured shoulder. Very tenderly, Rhane positioned his grip, stabilizing the joint with one hand while the other took a hold of Rhaven's arm.

"This is going to hurt," he said. Then he applied a quick, twisting pressure, forcing the joint up and back until it popped into the socket.

A furious snarl ripped from Rhaven's throat as he lashed out with the uninjured arm, striking with claws in a sweeping blow that sliced partly across Rhane's neck and completely down his chest. Making a hasty retreat to avoid further injury, Rhane maneuvered to the opposite side of the alley and waited. Rhaven's labored and harsh breathing gradually subsided. He tested the arm, wiggling his fingers and flexing his wrist before looking back at the strange man who had caused hurt and then stopped the hurt.

Rhane was sure that the boy's eyes had softened. It no longer seemed as if he wanted to rip his throat out...although he had damn near done just that.

"Rhaven," he called softly.

The boy's eyes changed as he leveled a red stare at him, and Rhane heard a deep growl rumble from across the alley. Huge black wings, spanning more than twelve feet in length, unfolded from behind Rhaven and readied for flight.

"Don't," he began, but didn't expect what happened next. Partially transforming his body, Rhaven lunged straight for Rhane's face, charging as a half-man, half-dragon creature. Ducking just in time, Rhane narrowly avoided a third lashing from the bane silver claws. He twisted around quickly enough to witness Rhaven, his oldest son who was now barely recognizable in such a gruesome state, slither up the side of the building. In mere seconds he had reached the roof, launching from it to disappear into the night sky.

Dark storm clouds brewed above, rolling in from the northeast to threaten rain with flashes of lightning and booms of thunder. While Rhane's eyes strained, searching the sky for some sign of the hybrid, the heavens opened up and released a deluge. Water cascaded from rooftop gutters and down into the alley, falling almost faster than the city drains could channel it. Drenched to the skin, Rhane forced open the door of an abandoned factory, breaking through chains and dry-rotted boards, securing it from within. Once inside, he pulled out his cell and powered it back on. He had turned it off, not wanting to risk startling Rhaven with one of the many frenetic ringtones Rion had installed. Now the display revealed several missed calls and a dozen anxious text messages from Kalista, York, and the boys.

Rhane muttered a curse. Of course, he should have expected nothing less after succumbing to his emotions and releasing that tormented cry upon the city. They had a right to be worried, but the last thing he wanted was anyone to come looking for him. He definitely didn't want to risk anyone having to tangle with Rhaven. The boy was clearly dangerous.

Wincing as he shrugged out of his ruined jacket, Rhane inspected the injuries he could see. Rhaven's claws had cut deep. The wounds were clotting too slowly and still oozed a pretty a good amount of blood. *And that's why I prefer to wear black*, Rhane thought regretfully.

Looking down at his phone, he wrote a quick message and sent it as a group text. *I'm fine. Headed north.*

The others would receive it immediately, and York would get it as soon as he reached the surface. No doubt, he was already headed this way. Rhane planned on being long gone before he arrived. Explaining what had just happened back there in the alley was at the bottom of a short list of things to do before sunrise.

Ducking out into the downpour, Rhane tossed the bloodied jacket into the dumpster and left the alleyway. Jogging three blocks, he descended the stairs into the subway, swiped his metro card even as he leaped over the turnstile and dashed across the platform, managing to squeeze onboard the red line to 42nd street just before the doors slid shut.

Even at this time of night, the subway was moderately busy. Good thing this was New York. People made it their business not to notice other people, even a guy who looked like he had just gone five rounds in a cage fight with a Siberian tiger. Still, Rhane's ultimate destination remained the address Ian had given him. Going there required a change of clothes—at the very least, a new shirt. Unnecessary bloodshed could happen if any rogue mistook Rhane's injuries for weakness, so he hopped off the train one stop sooner and walked into the first clothing store whose window displays didn't advertise skinny jeans for men.

It took him less than five minutes to locate a new leather jacket and a bit longer to find a simple black t-shirt without New York scrawled across the front. He paid for the items with a credit card, not batting an eye at a total upwards of six hundred dollars, and barely taking notice of the advances from the pretty sales girl who wore too much make-up. When his eyes finally focused on her, the girl flushed beneath the intensity of his stare. Rhane attempted to soothe her with a gentlemanly smile. In full light, most people were caught off guard by his unusual eyes. "Is it okay if I wear these out?"

"S-sure," she stammered. All of her earlier charms disappeared as her movements suddenly became increasingly awkward. Sympathizing with her struggle to remove the security ink and price tags, Rhane was relieved when the second cashier, Toya, rushed over to help. He realized it was probably cruel, but since he truly was in a hurry, Rhane stripped out of the damp shirt that clung to his skin and put on the new clothing as quickly as possible. Now both of the sales girls were blushing. The first girl, Erin, gripped the counter as if her life depended on it.

"I really hate to ask this of you, but do you mind throwing this out for me?" he said, holding the ruined shirt in an outstretched hand.

Clearing her throat, Erin took the garment. "No problem." She smiled, appearing to regain some of her confidence. "Maybe you should have a doctor take a look at that."

"We've got a first aid kit in the back," Toya blurted out.

Rhane almost laughed. "Thank you," he said and inclined his head gratefully. Striding through the store and up to the main door, he couldn't help listening as the girls whispered excitedly, unaware of the supernatural range of his hearing.

"Oh my god, he was disgustingly gorgeous."

"Hot *and* rich," Toya added. "Why didn't you ask for his number? He was clearly into you."

"Are you crazy? He probably has girls falling all over him wherever he goes. Guys like him aren't into serious, stable relationships. I'm waiting for the right—" she said, and the rest was muffled behind the closed door.

Stuffing both hands into his pockets, Rhane paused at the sidewalk to get his bearings, and then headed east. Covering the next ten blocks at a brisk walk, he didn't slow his pace until the throbbing base of club music reverberated beneath his feet and pounded his eardrums. Rounding the next corner brought the club in sight. Altun Ha. Written in electric blue, the huge, neon lettering was backlit by a rising yellow sun.

Not wanting the headache threatening just behind his ears to get any worse, Rhane dulled his hearing as he stepped onto the royal blue stretch of carpet leading up to the entrance. A burly human male sat at the doorway, wearing dark sunglasses though it was nightfall. The harsh buzz cut and rigidity of his posture definitely gave off a military vibe. Despite the severity of his outward appearance, he genially greeted the scantily clad women and fashion trendy men who entered and exited club Altun Ha.

As Rhane walked up, a restraining hand was placed on his chest, barring entry. Looking down at the thick sausage fingers that dared touch him, Rhane retracted his initial assessment of buzz cut and counted to five before speaking. "I need to see Eris, the priest's son."

The bouncer shook his head. "No humans enter this palace without tonight's code."

Good. He thinks I'm human. As Rhane neared the establishment, he had overheard a single phrase repeated by several patrons just before entering. "Red rapture," he said easily. Magic words spoken, the guard let him in.

At first glance, Altun Ha seemed like any other club. There was loud music, bodies moving to heavy base, drugs and alcohol galore. But even smoke and booze couldn't mask the unmistakable scent of rogues. As Rhane pushed through the crowded room, his nose was bombarded with the odor of wet fur and potent rose water. It took a lot to get used to.

Finding a seat at the bar, Rhane ordered a drink, finished it and started another before propositioning the bartender for information. Though the girl was rogue, she didn't seem aware of Rhane's true identity. The unfocused look in her eye and the slight slur in her movements gave him the impression that the bartender was under the influence of a powerful narcotic. Thus, his secret was safe…for now.

"I need to speak with Eris, the priest's son. Can you tell me how to find him?"

"He ain't here," she said in a clipped southern drawl. Clearly, the girl was an import.

"How can I find him?" Rhane politely asked again.

Clumsily pouring a drink intended for herself, the bartender leaned in close. "That depends on why you need him."

"We have mutual friends who are in trouble and require aid I trust only Eris can offer."

The girl sniffed air. Then she tilted her head slightly to one side. "You don't seem like someone Eris would be friends with."

"So you know him?"

"Everyone knows Eris. He's the son of Moros. Not being familiar with that family tree is like signing your own death warrant."

"Understood."

Downing a huge gulp of bourbon, the girl slammed the drink against the bar and then wiped her mouth. "I don't make it my business to know what Eris is up to, but there is someone here who does." The girl smiled slyly. "And she loves a pretty face."

"Can I talk to her?"

"Sure." She pointed to a blue door about twenty feet away, behind a wall of gyrating bodies. "Go through there."

Rhane really should not have been surprised by what he found behind that door. After all, he had ventured into a rogue lair once before. But somehow the vast number of males and females engrossed in a full-scale orgy still came as a shock. Naked flesh illuminated by red lighting, couples, trysts, and foursomes demonstrating depravities in every position, known and unknown to the most sordid textbooks.

He weaved his way through the masses, careful not to touch anything or anyone. The rogues were too absorbed in their carnal pleasures to take notice of him. Passing through the red chamber brought Rhane into a second room. This one was filled with far fewer rogues, but their passion was no less licentious. Lying on the floor and arranged in a circle, females faced outward while the males faced inward of the ring, satisfying each other's needs via teeth and tongue.

Behind them was a raised platform, serving as a stage, and a great chair covered with red velvet and black leather occupied its center. On that elevated position sat the mistress of the hive. Observing the worship of her subjects with lustful admiration, she slowly lifted her eyes from the tangle of bodies. None of the rest of her moved in the slightest fraction as she watched Rhane navigate the room. Her dark red hair formed a sleek curtain about her pale face. Legs crossed, her hands rested idly atop the armrests of the chair, allowing no show of tension. In fact, her gaze almost seemed welcoming. And it was filled with recognition.

Rhane searched the fragments of memory shared between himself and the wolf. A ball of wariness fisted between his shoulder blades. This rogue's name was Lara, and they had definitely met before.

The rogue remained seated, but raised herself to her full height, squaring her shoulders as Rhane stopped before her. "Banewolf," she announced, ending the note with a purr. "What brings the mighty immortal to this hive? More importantly, how did you come to find us?"

He quickly decided to err on the side of being intentionally vague. "It's a pretty high profile thing that you rogues are doing here—turning humans into supernaturals and then leaving them to wreak havoc upon the city. I figured home base had to be nearby, and few important members of the family tree housed within it. Tell me how to get in touch with Eris."

"Oh?" She arched one perfectly manicured brow. "So you've witnessed our handiwork. The best is yet to come, Banewolf. Our god will soon arise."

Not this shit again. No matter what, Rhane vowed to keep a firm grip on his temper. But knowing the only reason rogues were ruining people's lives—and using his kid to do it—was just because of some falsely seeded, crazy alien worship made it very difficult. "Tell me how to find Eris. Please."

Uncrossing her legs, Lara leaned forward. "Tell me first why you desire this audience with my brother."

Rhane smiled in an effort to mask his surprise. Guess he hadn't made all the connections in the family tree. "That business is for Eris and I to discuss."

"I have no reason to help you, Banewolf. For murdering my sister, Erebus, the only thing I owe you is death."

"Good luck with that." Rhane frowned thoughtfully. "Tell me again, how is it that you go about killing an immortal?"

Lara's expression turned cold. "You're a bastard."

Yes, I am actually. "I saved your brother's life. He owes me a debt that I am here to collect. Won't you help uphold his honor?"

The rogue's face failed to soften. "I see the rumors of your charm are well founded. I'm waiting for the stick."

"Very well." Rhane looked around pointedly. "Helping me would leave no reason to tear down this exceptionally depraved house of yours."

"Ah." The rogue closed her eyes as a shudder passed through her body. Rhane wasn't sure if she was frightened or aroused. "Your bloodlust never fails." Suddenly reaching out, she passed one long fingernail across the back of his hand. The smile she wore was inviting, sensual, and deadly all at once. "Isn't there something I can help you with? My brother is such a dull man."

"Can you talk Nyx out of attacking the southeastern kindred?"

"Ian murdered my sister and destroyed one of our hives. For that he must be punished."

"He was helping me save a friend. And as for your sister, it was I who happily pulled the trigger."

The rogue hissed, flashing two rows of significantly sharpened teeth. "You do not help your cause, Banewolf."

"Lara," Rhane uttered her name warningly. "I'm in a bit of a hurry, and you are trampling over already thin patience."

A veil of fury swathed the rogue's face. After a long moment, her anger gradually faded, leaving an air of calm once more around the creature's throne. "Very well. I will contact my brother. Return here in one hour."

Chapter 6

"War, what happened?"

They all gathered once again in Kali's suite. She had changed clothes, ditching the lingerie for jeans, sneakers, and a long sleeved henley. Bailen couldn't be settled, restlessly pacing back and forth across the tan carpet. Every so often he would let out a whine and seek Kali's comfort by burying his sleek muzzle into her hand.

"York sent me back here."

She stroked Bailen's fur, trying to soothe him though her own fears were mounting. "Was he mad?"

"No. Just worried. What we saw and smelled…it wasn't pretty. York thinks we'll be safer here at the hotel until he finds Rhane and learns exactly what happened in that alley."

"Warren," Kali said slowly, weaving every thread of calm into her voice. "Tell me precisely what you saw."

"Rhane and York found three humans freshly turned into rogues. They were scared, angry, and out of control, but Rhane thought it might be possible to help them. He went to the surface to make a phone call on their behalf, seeking out an ally he made while working with the rogues. Later, York heard the alpha cry, same as we did and went to investigate." War's eyes darted away and then back. "There was a lot of blood, Kali. Some was Rhane's. The rest of it belonged to an entirely different species."

"Rogue or kindred?" Rion asked.

War pursed his lips into a grim line. "Neither."

At that, Rion glanced up from the multiple computer screens and papers spread before him. He had been busy researching theories for hours while simultaneously

63

monitoring police radios and a government network he'd hacked into in order to monitor cell phone chatter. "Then what was it?"

War shook his head. "We don't know. We found Rhane's jacket in the dumpster. It was ruined, a torn and bloody mess. Whatever fought against him was something seriously dangerous."

Hearing about the jacket wasn't good news. It meant Rhane had been hurt badly, and the thought of that made Kali want to hurt back whoever had harmed her mate. But one look at War and Kali knew the young kin was still holding back. "What else? What aren't you telling us?"

Releasing a pained yowl, Bailen grabbed the hem of Kali's shirt between his teeth and began gnawing. Then he twisted away from her grasp and resumed pacing.

Focusing his gaze on Bailen's antics, War finished his story. "The alleyway was burned. Even with the recent downpour of rain, the scorched bricks were still warm from the fire. And the way it smelled…the blaze came from unnatural origins." He finally dragged his eyes from the canine to look at Kali. "The signature was almost as if you'd set the fire."

*

When the hour was up, Rhane returned to club Altun Ha as agreed. Luckily, he didn't have to venture again into the backroom orgy of obeisance. Setting a telephone on the oak counter, the bartender fixed her gaze upon Rhane with a nod, and then went back to serving eager patrons.

Rhane picked up the phone and a familiar rasp greeted him. "Hello, old friend."

"Hello, Eris."

"My sibling has informed me that you desire a meeting. Has the time arrived for me to repay my debt to you, Banewolf?"

"Yeah. I need a favor. Is there any way we could talk privately? It's not that I don't trust Lara but, well, I don't trust her. This line may not be secure."

"Lara?" Eris repeated, sounding confused. "Oh yes."

Rhane caught on quickly. "Lara isn't her real name." He should have known, especially after the time he'd spent indentured to the rogues. Their names were a precious commodity, not readily given to outsiders.

"It is not. My sister has many aliases, but she is known to us as Ratri. Leave the club and head south, Banewolf. Two blocks away, you'll find St. Valentine's Church. I will meet you in the bell tower."

"What time?"

"Now," Eris said, and hung up.

Placing a twenty on the counter for the bartender's trouble, Rhane slid off the stool and grimaced as a wrong twist made him feel every mark left by Rhaven's claws. Without a backward glance, he left behind the blaring techno beats and dizzying light show of the nightclub. Following a fifteen minute train ride and a short hike, he found the church Eris had described. Only a flimsy lock on a wooden gate barred entry to the pristine gardens walled within the church's courtyard, at the middle of which stood the bell tower. Tossing a quick glance around, Rhane climbed over the gate and landed easily on the opposite side. He jogged across the lush lawn and, from a position not visible to the casual passerby, scaled thirty feet of vertical brick to reach the tower balcony. From there he didn't have to wait long. "Banewolf," Eris called to him from deep shadows. "The door was unlocked. You could have used the stairs."

Rhane smiled. "I guess I have a flair for the dramatic."

"It is safe for us to talk here."

There was no use in not getting straight to the point. "Do you know why I have come to New York?"

"I have heard the reports," Eris said carefully. "It is a perilous time for your family to be here."

"I don't have a choice. You know I have to stop this. What's in that tomb is not what you think. That creature is not a secret weapon that can be used against your enemies, and it's not a god for you to worship. Blight is a destroyer. Your people, along with the rest of this supernatural world, will be annihilated."

"The Faction tells us differently. Blight will be this world's savior."

"The Faction is *lying*."

Eris limped into the dim light originating from oil lamps mounted within the mortar of the wall. Though his shoulders remained slightly askew, the rogue stood taller than the last time he and Rhane had met. His dark blond hair remained unchanged, but the mask that should have concealed the rest of his features was gone. And so for the first time, Rhane actually saw the face of the rogue he called friend.

Eris could pass for a human male of the mid-thirties age range. Eyes so dark blue they almost appeared black were set beneath a strong brow and even stronger jaw line currently tensed with unspoken emotion. "We are friends," Eris finally said. "But you and I fight on different sides of this war."

"I didn't choose a side, Eris. Builders used the ones I care about as leverage in order to force me to fight. The champion who the Faction selected to lead your cause—what is his name?"

"He is Wrath, and he is bound to my father's command. You and I may not agree with the methods, but my people have a noble cause and my father, Moros, will see it done."

"How can I find this creature you call Wrath?"

Eris shook his head. "Banewolf, I cannot—"

"He is important to me."

The rogue seemed genuinely confused. "How so?"

Rhane was silent.

"The debt I owe you is nearly one too great to be repaid, but you cannot ask me to betray the confidence of Moros by leading you to his greatest weapon, one that has changed the tide of this war to our favor."

Rhane clenched and unclenched his teeth, forcing his temper to stay in check. Rhaven had been given even less of a choice than he had in this stupid conflict between races hell bent on controlling this world's fate. His kid was a tool, a slave, used to commit horrible, unspeakable acts at the bidding of a madman. But the blame for Rhaven's predicament could not in all fairness be attributed to Eris. Although sired by a monster, Eris was a decent man. And that was something Rhane could identify with.

Maybe there's a chance. "That weapon you refer to," Rhane began quietly. "He is my son."

Even in darkness the color draining from the rogue's countenance was visible. "H-how is that possible?"

"He was taken from us as a child, and we thought him dead. Turns out, we were very wrong."

Eris placed one hand against the wall, leaning to it for support as he averted his face from Rhane's penetrating gaze. For a long time, neither man spoke. At last, Eris looked to him again. "I will tell you the next targets we plan to attack."

"Thank you." Rhane exhaled an extended breath. "No one can know what I just told you."

"If someone learns of your secret, trust it will not have come from me."

"There's one other thing."

Eris raised an eyebrow, his expression vigilant.

"I found three humans turned by yesterday's attack. They are too pitiful to kill, so I hope you can help them. Honestly, their predicament is the reason I called."

Wordlessly, Eris stepped forward and extended his hand. Grasping the rogue's forearm, Rhane nodded as Eris did the same. "I will give you three addresses. Leave the new rogue brethren at the third. They will be taken care of and receive instruction that will, with any hope, eventually allow them to return to their families." Eris squeezed Rhane's arm a bit tighter. "You are a good man, Banewolf. If we do not meet again in this land of the living, I am honored to have known you."

Chapter 7

York whistled with a note of appreciation and sympathy. "Bane silver huh? That element is supposed to be extinct. Bellefuron was forged from the last of it."

"I guess not." Rhane lowered the shirt, covering his torn flesh, and let the jacket fall into place.

"You really think they're going to be alright back there?" York peeked over his shoulder at the abandoned fire station that grew smaller and smaller in the distance as they resumed a brisk pace in the opposite direction. About a hundred yards ahead stood yet another church and a field of tombstones behind it. This neighborhood was nothing like the boroughs of Manhattan. Though densely populated, it was far quieter. Fewer smells bombarded their senses here. Buildings were older, nearing historical. The houses weren't as pristine, and every block seemed to harbor a different church.

He and Rhane had just dropped off their new rogue friends. Sure, York was in favor of killing them in the beginning, but in the time he'd spent with them alone in the subway, the rogues sort of grew on him like cowering strays one couldn't help feeling sorry for. Rhane made a good call in choosing to save them.

"I trust Eris." Rhane stopped walking. He needed to see York's face when he delivered the rest of the story he had yet to share. "He told me how to find Rhaven."

York relinquished a deep sigh. "Rhane, buddy, after what happened in that alleyway, do you really think it's him?"

"Once upon a time, you questioned the same of Kalista."

Nodding, York dropped his head. "Good point." He looked up again, earnestly searching Rhane's stoic expression for some sign of what his warlord must be feeling. "Give me some credit though. Kali was a harmless teenager who resembled your long-lost mate but acted nothing like her. She wasn't trying to kill you on sight. We've got the exact opposite thing going on here. That guy looks like what Rhaven could have been—at least the human part of him—but outside of that, he gave no indication of being your son. Right?"

A look of pain flashed across Rhane's face. "I have to believe he's in there, if only because Bailen so strongly believes it. Everything that poor kid has done, in some way or form, has been to reunite with his brother. As their father, I was supposed to protect them." Rhane's voice became strained. "Instead I let those monsters rip my family apart. Bailen said they were experimented on…tortured." He abruptly turned away and began walking again. The ache in his chest had become too great, and the symbol in his right palm burned as if it were on fire. Thinking of what those bastards had done to his children and seeing firsthand the abomination of creatures fused together in Rhaven—it was enough to send him into a blind rage.

York caught up to him in a few steps. The cemetery gates loomed behind them. "I can't come close to feeling the pain you went through when you lost Rhaven, and I can't imagine the hurt you're feeling now, but I get it. I'm with you, brother."

As Rhane started to speak, he turned his head toward a sound in the distance. It was a faint crack, one that barely breached the range of York's supernatural perception but was enough to propel him into action. He drove one shoulder into Rhane's chest, knocking him off the sidewalk and onto the lush cemetery lawn and brought his own body into a low crouch as he did so. Another crack bit into the night and blasted apart a chunk of cement from the headstone only inches to the left of Rhane's head. Rolling onto his side, he maneuvered his body into better cover and yanked York to safety. "What the hell?"

"Someone's shooting at us," York said, breathing heavily. The grave stone was barely big enough to shield the both of them, even with York's body stacked directly on top of Rhane's.

"Yeah. I got that part." Growling, Rhane glared up at him. "But why?"

"Well…who have you pissed off in the last nine hundred years?"

Rhane stared at York with frank disbelief. "You just got shot and still can't be serious."

York pressed a hand to his side. "It's not bad."

"You're bleeding all over me."

"Barely. That shirt was ruined anyway. You would have never gotten the smell of blood out. I just did you a favor."

"The jacket was salvageable."

York hesitated. Then he nodded. "Yeah. It was. I bet you paid five hundred bucks for that grain of leather."

"I thought I'd get more use out of it." He risked a cautious peek around the stone. No one shot at him. Turning back to York, Rhane lifted an eyebrow. "You mind?"

"Oh. Sure," York said and lifted himself into a push up position. The sound of gunfire immediately erupted, this time splitting off a section from the top of the headstone.

"Keep your fucking head down," Rhane hissed. Then he rolled quickly across the ground, taking cover at the next grave. He looked back at York, now in a much more protected position. He still clutched his side, but the bleeding seemed to have slowed. Rhane knit his brow together. "How worried should I be?"

York glanced down at his wound. "Stings like hell, but the bullet was regular lead. Already healing. Whoever's shooting at us obviously doesn't know who they're dealing with."

"Great," Rhane said flatly and slid the Desert Eagle from the holster affixed to the back of his waistband. "We need to get out of here."

"We're not going to go after this asshole?"

Rhane shook his head. "It sounds like that sniper is more than a mile away from here. That leaves way too much time to execute an exit strategy. He'll be long gone by the time we cover that distance. Eris stuck his neck out for me in revealing the rogues' next two planned attacks. That remains our priority. Getting there in time could mean finding Rhaven."

York considered the weapon between Rhane's hands dubiously. "If this guy is as far away as you think, that won't begin to touch him."

Grinning like it was the best idea he'd had all night, Rhane winked. "I'm just drawing fire while you're vulnerable since you'll outgrow that headstone as soon as you begin to shift forms. Come find me when you're done."

York nodded and began to summon his war skin. Aiming the Desert Eagle into the air, Rhane was already up and running by the time black fur began to sprout from York's exposed skin. Smaller and darker than Banewolf, York's wolf would blend into the graying night. Its black fur providing a natural camouflage would hopefully garner less attention than a giant, white wolf streaking through dark neighborhoods. Still, York's war skin was massive enough to shield a grown man from sniper fire. All Rhane had to do was stay low.

The shooter found him as soon as he stood, which was great for York, but for Rhane, dodging those fifty caliber rounds proved trickier than he anticipated. The time between shots and the accuracy at which those bullets flew made the sniper seem more than human. In the past, Rhane had outmaneuvered countless bullets aimed at him with little effort thanks to supernatural speed and reflexes. Tonight was different. Either the bane silver poisoned wounds had taken a greater effect on him than he realized or the guy behind the night scope wasn't human.

The wind of one round whizzed past his ear, forcing Rhane to rapidly alter course. The next shot went wild. The third tore through the flap of his jacket that blew behind him as he ran.

Damn. This guy is good.

Diving into a roll, Rhane popped up and sprinted in the opposite direction. This bought both him and York several precious seconds as the sniper reacquired his target. The next bullet came and Rhane adjusted his trajectory to leave the projectile's path. He leapt over a headstone directly in front him. Remarkably, and while in midair, Rhane heard the sniper make a fifth shot. But this one came from a *second* shooter. Twisting to avoid getting nailed in the head, Rhane felt the searing bite of heated metal ripping across his left cheek. Trying to miss getting shot but getting shot anyway seriously affected his landing, and Rhane narrowly missed ingesting a mouthful of graveyard dirt as his face smacked against the ground.

Rhane swore as he rolled to gather to his feet. No doubt, the next bullet had the name of one of his vital organs all over it. Hearing the shot, Rhane tensed even as his muscles moved scrambled for cover, wondering what piece of him was to be anointed with an unwelcome hole. But the bullet landed harmlessly against a massive wolf hide, splintering apart as it did so. Muttering a breathless thank you, Rhane got to his feet. Then he and York ran side by side into the darkness.

Chapter 8

"The target escaped, sir, but we got a good hit. Not the subject, but it was a known associate, and a close one. He took the bullet for our guy."

"And?"

"It's just as the lab geeks suspected. Regular lead, even fifty caliber rounds, barely scratches them."

"I presume there's a positive note to this conversation or else you would not have bothered to disturb me."

"Yes, sir," Commander Zed conceded in a clipped tone. He took a moment to rein in his temper. Zephyr looked on, shaking his head with pursed lips. Able to hear every word of the conservation, even without listening, Zephyr well knew how much of a dick their older half-brother, Luke, could be.

Jealous of the special genes inherited from their mother that allowed this change in them, one which made them more than human and unlocked abilities government agencies could only have wet dreams about, Luke used his position as Vice President of their father's company to make power plays he could not have otherwise. What Luke lacked in physical prowess, he made up in sharp intellect. The order to hunt down the man responsible for raiding their facility and killing their youngest brother in the resulting destruction, had originated from their father, but it was Luke who saw past the need for revenge and recognized this man could be the final piece of the puzzle their genetic science division needed. His DNA could very well crack the code and make it possible to give anyone the supernatural abilities Zed and his squad of merchants possessed. The military application alone could prove to be extremely lucrative financially.

Finding the patience to go on, Zed continued. "We got lucky with the facial recognition scan only because the target showed up at an active crime scene. Our team was handed the winning lottery ticket. That won't happen again. However, the bullet we tagged the associate with will leave behind a chemical tracer. Estimates from our own genetic make-up places a rate of decay at ninety-six hours. Could be less though, if his metabolism is higher. Until then, we'll be able to track them anywhere."

"Well done, Zed," Luke said, actually sounding mildly pleased. "Do not come back here empty-handed. Zenith out."

Gritting his teeth, Zed glared at the phone, resisting the urge to crush it within his fist. Luke wasn't one of them. He wasn't a merchant and was definitely not a soldier. He didn't even know how to properly handle a gun. He didn't deserve a call sign, certainly not one identifying him as the leader of the pack.

*

Morning sunlight streamed in through the hotel's window, and Kali stood in its glow, basking in the warmth. A minute ago, the light had not seemed so inviting. After an entire night of anxious fretting, dawn had come with still no word from Rhane. Now, hearing his voice on the other end of the line sent a tidal wave of relief through her. The feeling was beyond compare. Sure, she had received third-hand assurances from War that everything was okay, but it didn't compare to getting the message directly from the source and in Rhane's tired but silky baritone.

"I'm so glad you called," she said, letting cheer creep into her tone.

"Sorry it didn't happen sooner. We had a busy night."

Kali frowned. If she knew any better, Rhane was hugely downplaying things. "What happened in the alleyway? Who were you fighting?" It was the question everyone wanted to know.

"I promise to tell you everything soon, but there isn't time now. I need you to collect the others and come to this address in Midtown."

Kali jabbed the speaker function active as Rhane recited several letters and numbers—the location of a rendezvous point. Though she trusted her memory, having an extra set of ears listening in couldn't hurt with information so important. Rhane's next statement made her appreciate that decision very much.

"Kalista, I have to tell you…we may find Rhaven here. Prepare yourself."

She took a long, deep breath, forcing air into her lungs. It didn't help ease the sudden ache in her chest. Fisting one hand over her heart, she nodded, though Rhane wouldn't see. "I'll be ready. We all will."

"Okay." He hesitated, and Kali could practically hear him weighing a decision in the silence. "Just one other thing. Don't get upset when you see us, okay? We feel a lot better than we look."

She bit her lip, already imaging the worst. "I'll try not to."

"Good girl." His voice softened with affection. "I'll see you soon."

"Not soon enough," she whispered. Ending the call, Kali turned to the others. "I guess we have our orders."

Rion, Orrin, and War had already assembled behind her. Bailen stood pawing at the door. Glancing at the canine, Rion held up his cell phone. "I just got a text from Rhane with instructions on entry and positions."

War snorted laughter, while his brother fought back a grin. "Yeah, you need that," War mocked. "Learn anything useful?"

Though a rosy tint crawled across both of his cheeks, Rion directed his focus to Kali and continued as if War didn't exist. "This shopping mall is huge. It won't be crowded at this time of day but still, we won't be able to cover it all. Rhane has sent what are probably the best locations strategically."

"And the fastest way to get to them?" Kali asked for Bailen's benefit. A cab wasn't going to be the obvious choice. The subway would be faster, but putting a junior wolf on a train crowded with people wasn't going to go over well with any of the locals.

Rion answered like the perfect co-conspirator. "We should take the subway."

Everyone turned and stared at Bailen. Beating his tail against the floor once, he whined.

Kali crossed the room and kneeled in front of him. "We're not in the country anymore, Bailen. This is rush hour and people are seriously freaked out by what's been on the news. I need you to become human for a little while."

He stretched his jaws in big canine yawn of disagreement.

"Bailen," she said, making her voice a tad more firm. "We're in a hurry."

For a moment his fiercely golden eyes met hers in challenge, but Kali quietly held that gaze until Bailen relented. His dark fur began to recede, revealing tan forearms and digits of a distinctly human shape. She stroked his still canine head and thanked him gently. Backing away to allow him more room as the changes took over, Kali considered the other kin. Really, Rion was the closest in size. "He's going to need some clothing."

Rion grinned. "Awesome."

Five minutes later, Bailen was a completely ordinary looking adolescent, wearing faded denim jeans and a red t-shirt that read "Jekyll Likes to Hide" in cursive white lettering. It was difficult for Kali not to stare. She could see Rhane in every expression and gesture. And herself in his eyes. Nearly identical to her own, Bailen's steel-colored orbs possessed a veiled ferocity that knotted her gut whenever she gazed into them for too long. Whatever horrors witnessed and wrongs experienced by the boy had melded him into the warped creature he was today, twisted by disfigured morals and questionable motives even in matters of family. Bailen loved her and Rhane. She was sure of it. What concerned Kali was that she had no idea what lengths he would go to in order to get what he wanted. His schemes to assure the destruction of the Builders had actually gotten his father killed. Since then, Bailen had demonstrated shame for his actions and a degree of remorse. But if faced again with a similar choice, would he make the same sacrifice?

Kali reached for Bailen's hand, and the tightness in her belly eased when he allowed her to take it. He had been torn away from her arms before ever having the chance to be loved. Maybe with enough affection some of Bailen's scars would be healed, and they could truly be a family again.

They piled into a crowded subway train, and Bailen leaned into her ever so slightly. From observing Rhane, she knew how to spot tension within the boy's shoulders—no matter how carefully concealed. Kali squeezed his hand. For someone who had spent most of his life as a canine, it must have been a lot to take in. Either that or Rhane's distaste for tight spaces was hereditary.

After riding two trains, they reached their destination, a remarkably huge shopping complex that sent Kali's inner girl twirling in circles of delight. Even in such dark times it was hard not to be wistful of the damage she could do as an authorized user of Rhane's limitless black card. As Rion called out reminders of their assignments, Kali wrangled her mind back to the task at hand.

Orrin would take Bailen to monitor the upper level perimeter while Rion and War remained on the lower level's most southern end. Kali was to meet Rhane in the food court and cover the east exits. York was to float between the first and second floors, filling in the gaps. He was more than capable of taking care of himself, but Kali couldn't help thinking he wouldn't have to be out there alone if River was still with them.

He made his bed.

Scanning the food court provided no immediate glimpse of Rhane, but that was not surprising. The area was busy for the hour and Rhane was quite disciplined in matters of stealth. Ambling through the aisles for a more exhaustive search also failed to yield results, so Kali slid into a corner, placing her back against the wall, and waited. The position should have made it practically impossible for anyone to sneak up on her. However, Rhane wasn't just anyone.

Unyielding arms slid unexpectedly around her waist and should have startled her, but Kali was all too familiar with his touch. Recognition immediately trampled any fear she might have felt. His hands pressed almost roughly against her, forcing her to sink into the hard planes of his body. Kali's eyes fluttered shut as he buried his face into her neck and inhaled deeply, capturing all of her scent. The raw power he possessed and the gentleness with which he chose to wield it felt so erotic. It made her belly tighten and her knees weak. And when Rhane placed his lips against the delicate hollow of her neck, Kali almost came undone.

Then his hold shifted, and Rhane gently pushed her away, steadying her trembling form as he did so. The entire exchange had taken less than three seconds.

Despite the uncanny influence he exerted over her body, Kali knew she claimed equal sway over him and was determined to regain her senses first. She met Rhane's darkened irises, still hooded with lust.

"So what's the situation," she asked evenly, hiding the struggle it took to mask her breathlessness. Focusing on how pale his skin appeared and the tired circles beneath his eyes helped as worry crowded out her hunger. She gently wiped at a smudge of dried blood staining his cheek. The scar beneath it was barely visible. Though Rhane had told her what to expect over the phone, she couldn't help fretting over what wounds lay hidden beneath his clothing. Rhane always downplayed the extent of his injuries.

"Right," he answered after a moment and exhaled softly. "We think…" he began but stopped. Frowning, he peered past her shoulder.

She at once became more alert. Kali narrowed her eyes. "What is it?"

Rhane took a guarded step forward. "Stay behind me."

It was then that Kali heard the screams. Forged of pure terror, the wails were nearby but came from outside the food court. Intermingled with them were hisses and barks only creatures of rogue or kindred bloodlines could make. She followed closely as Rhane jogged toward the clamor. People within the area began to take notice, and Kali watched their faces transform with mixtures of curiosity and shock. When the monsters reached the upper floor, every human expression became one of total panic.

Kali's heart beat faster. The moisture fled from her mouth. She centered her breathing and let the weight of the daggers at her waistband be a reassurance for the fight about to come. Snarling, red-eyed, and dripping saliva from their snouts, more than a dozen creatures barreled into the food court. These changelings were nothing like the ones Rhane and York had found cowering in the subway. Wild and bloodthirsty, these predators charged toward an assured buffet of easy prey with Kali and Rhane as the only two standing in their path.

"Kalista, defend yourself but use non-lethal means if you can help it. We might be able to help these creatures."

Kali balked. They certainly didn't look savable. "I'll try."

Re-sheathing her daggers, she summoned flames to both hands. Fighting and subduing opponents more than three times greater in size was easy for Rhane, but for Kali doing so would be a bit trickier. Tricky but not impossible. What she lacked in strength she would make up in smarts.

As an enormous kindred barreled toward her, Kali waited until the heat of its putrid breath stung her skin and ducked. Rolling head over feet, she maneuvered between its legs to regain her stance just as the creature turned, bringing with it a furious swipe of claws. Kali lunged sideways to avoid what would have been a crippling blow, but not before igniting a burst of flames to temporarily render it blind. Releasing an enraged howl, the kindred launched a sightless charge that Kali easily dodged, countering with three blows with all her weight behind them. Throat. Temple. Base of the spine. Its roar cut short, the kindred fell motionless at her feet.

Kali felt pretty satisfied with herself until she saw Rhane had already immobilized half a dozen newly turned creatures. Rolling her eyes, she applied a new strategy. At some point Rhane would have to recognize he didn't need to work so hard to keep her safe. Training with York and the others had turned Kali into a pretty capable fighter.

Whispering the siren's commands, she coaxed a wall of fire to surround their foe, entrapping them behind a wall of impenetrable heat. Then Kali manipulated her flames to herd the creatures forward, and one by one, released them to Rhane's waiting fists. Working together, they made quick work of dismantling the rogue and kindred horde. The fight was soon over and Rhane immediately reached for the radio as he and Kali quickly evacuated the food court.

"York, we had a situation upstairs. No sign of Rhaven, though. How are things looking on your end?"

Static crackled endlessly until a voice sounding like Orrin's finally answered. "Stand by."

Muttering curses, Rhane slowed the pace and shoved the radio into his back pocket. Kali waited next to him when he came to a standstill. "What is it," she asked, realizing his superior hearing might have picked up on something through the static.

"They ran into another pack of mutated humans."

"But you can find them."

"Yeah." Rhane tilted his head slightly, listening. Kali kept quiet while he did so, forcing her fists to unclench at her sides. She glanced over her shoulder, checking to make sure no rogue or kindred had followed them. Their lives had been spared just as Rhane had wanted, but what happened if any of them woke up and began attacking humans? One bite had turned Jackson, the fish and game warden from back home, into something quite creepy and more than human but less than rogue or kindred. Would the same thing happen to a different human bitten by one of these mutants? Kali had no idea and sorely doubted Rhane would know either. If any uncharted territory remained between them, then they were certainly in it.

Finding what he needed to pinpoint the location of the others, Rhane tugged Kali's hand. "This way," he said, and began running.

At the top of the escalator, she caught a glimpse of the scene below. Things had obviously unfolded very differently here than in the food court. For one, there was blood and lots of it. Most came from a man in his mid-thirties whose body lay strewn across the tile floor. The guy's throat had been torn out along with a good part of his entrails. Bloody footprints stamped in all directions leading away from the body, the tracks of other humans fleeing slaughter. Those unsuccessful in escaping cowered in balls of terror, weeping and clutching their injuries. Her heart went out to a young mother who clung desperately to her child. Both were covered in blood. Kali just hoped none of it was theirs.

Beyond the survivors, the final vestiges of battle raged on as the Warekin dispatched the few remaining rogue and kindred. Without any control over their transformations, they truly were hideous creatures. Twisted and gnarled limbs were covered by shaggy fur that should have been normal skin without the touch of natural light. Knotted flesh and misshapen features robbed the rogues of all human appearance. Seeing them side by side, it was easy to understand why both races hated Warekin so much. Rogue and kindred were created as monstrosities, forever cursed to shadows. Whereas the third brethren— Warekin—had been made beautiful in every sense of the word and given the ability to live in any light. Witnessing the full wretchedness of the changelings, Kali could only pity them.

Rhane hadn't been there to decree a pardon for these rogue and kindred, so there was no chance at redemption for them. Death was their only release. She watched Rhane's face for signs of anger or regret as they descended the stairs, but there was none. Her only clue to his emotions came when he slowed from a run to a walk and moved with a slightly heavier stride, perhaps weighed down by the losses of battle.

The last surviving creature was rogue in nature, and struggled against York's bear-like arms to no avail. Only a command from Rhane could save it, but the order did not come. One final, clockwise wrench of York's hands put the changeling out of its misery. As it slumped to a floor smeared with blood, the creature's eyes darkened and the spark of life dulled within them.

Reaching into his back pocket, Orrin brought the radio toward his lips but stopped short on noticing Rhane and Kali's presence. Taking a step back, he dipped his head in a solemn nod. After returning the gesture, Rhane quietly surveyed the area and grimaced. "We need to get out of here." His gaze lingered on York, plainly evaluating the burly kin's condition. To Kali, York didn't look as worn or pale as Rhane, but he did seem to be favoring his right side. "There's no time for cleanup," Rhane finished.

Rion raised his hand. "I can at least wipe all the security feed from the control room. It won't take five minutes."

Rhane nodded. "Do it."

"Where's Bailen?" Kali asked with a thudding heart. She had done her own assessment of the scene and quickly discovered the boy missing.

"He ran off," War answered hesitantly. "I think he spotted Rhaven."

Rhane growled a curse. "Where did he go?"

"That way maybe," War said, extending a finger. "Toward the parking garage. Things got pretty crazy, so I can't say I'm one hundred percent sure."

"Okay." Rhane dropped his head. "Okay," he muttered again, more to himself than anyone else. Eventually looking up, he addressed York. "Go and take the others to the second location Eris gave us. I think it's safe to assume the rogues will consider this attack a loss and move on to the next target."

"You got it. What are you going to do?"

"I need to see if I can pick up Bailen's trail. Rhaven is extremely dangerous. I don't want Bailen running into him alone."

Kali cleared her throat. "How do you know that?" Rhane flinched at the question and Kali's eyes widened with disbelief. "Rhane?"

He shook his head slowly. A flash of pain crossed his features. Then his expression smoothed again. "Not now, Kalista."

She was confused. When Rhane had left the hotel, he promised not to pursue Rhaven. And never before had he lied to her. Kali was certain there had to be some explanation for it. But the most probable scenario took her breath away. "Was it Rhaven you fought in the alleyway?"

He wouldn't look at her, but she could see the way his jaw clenched and unclenched. Meanwhile, a stare from York practically bored a hole in the side of Rhane's head. "Kalista," he said. His voice was hard and unwavering. "I will explain later."

Undeterred, Kali folded her arms. "You said that before. It is later."

"To have any chance of finding Bailen, we need to leave now. This can wait."

"Fine." She gritted the word out. "What about the mess in the food court? Should we leave them like that?"

"I'll put in a call to Eris while I'm gone. Hopefully, he can help them. I guess Ian can decide what to do with the kindred changelings." Rhane ran a hand through his thick shag of hair. "I won't tell you what to do on this, Kalista. Come with me to find Bailen or leave with them to intercept Rhaven's attack. It's your choice. There is a good chance we'll end up in the same place anyway."

Smothering out the last flames of her temper, Kali slid her hand into Rhane's. No matter the mood or distance between them, experience taught her at least one guarantee in life. "My place is with you," she said.

Pleased at her words, the thinly pressed line of Rhane's lips finally relaxed.

But what Kali said was true. If any chance existed of mending their broken family, it could only be accomplished together. She just hoped Rhane would soon realize that as well.

Chapter 9

Unease pressed insistently upon Rhane's mind as he and Kalista walked the paved loop through Central Park. Their pace was brisk and the air between them solemn. The search for Bailen had been a fruitless one. Of course, of all the skills to inherit from his mother, the boy would have acquired the ability to travel without leaving a trail. Like Kalista, Bailen could voluntarily inhibit his body's natural tendency to produce scent markers, rendering his whereabouts completely untraceable even to supernatural senses. The boy had not wanted to be followed. Therefore, tracking him was impossible.

"It happened like this before."

Kalista's voice jerked Rhane from dark thoughts. "What?"

"After the Builders took Bailen and held him in the facility owned by Global Cures, it was nearly impossible to trace him. We lost hours before Orrin found the trail."

"We don't have hours, Kalista." Rhane cringed at the edge in his voice. The comment had come out far testier than he meant it too. He had treated her with a lifetime's worth of harshness in one day.

"I know," she answered softly, but didn't look at him.

"I'm sorry." Rhane hung his head and pulled her to a stop next to him. "I must be getting lost up my own ass trying to deal with everything that's happening. No need to take it out on you though." He stroked one finger down her cheek. "Please don't be cross. Forgive me."

Grabbing his hand, she met his gaze with sympathetic eyes. "There's no need to apologize. I only wanted to tell you I get why we stopped searching. Maybe Bailen can't be found now, but we know where the next attack will be—and possibly Rhaven will be there as well. We might still be able to make a difference."

"My beloved Kalista," he whispered and drew her close. Leaning forward, he rested his forehead against hers. She was one in a billion, his true soul mate. A powerful siren placed on this earth as a prize for the strongest warrior who could lead their creators to victory, somehow she had become his. He had been so young, over half a millennium from reaching primehood, experienced but far from wise, deeply damaged and unevenly tempered. Born of the royal mountain, Rhane was only a babe when he was cursed to live in disgrace amongst the people of the plains and grow up despised by a mother whose fall from glory was carried out by no hand but her own. Roma should have known a bastard firstborn would've never been accepted within the nobility.

Once Rhane learned to fight, he had never stopped. Mercifully claimed by Jehsi, the bastard outcast became the son of a Prime from the powerful line of Whytetree. The status afforded Rhane protection from the harshest of punishments and retaliations…but not from scorn. In the military, fellow recruits promptly learned respect for the fits of rage that overcame the young warrior whenever pressed too hard or bullied too often. And when the mark of the immortal wolf branded him (inherited from his true blood line of Bllacstag) things really changed. Rhane became the unbeatable weapon. His powers were utilized to the fullest and he was well-rewarded, climbing the ranks of their army to lead elite units, become commander of his own legion, and finally gain appointment as Warlord of the entire Warekin army.

Even in all those achievements, Rhane now knew he had still not deserved her. Perhaps his younger self knew it then, deep down. He had failed to protect her. He had failed to protect their children. Because of it, his entire world was lost.

He recalled losing her—the pain was as raw and thick as the day it happened—but he didn't remember living without her. And the life they shared together, as well as his life before that, could only be seen in snatches of memory and moments. That absence changed him. Not only could he feel it, but he could sense it in the way the others regarded him. His thinking was different, his control lessened, and his reactions altered. Losing so many memories had caused an inescapable divergence in Rhane's personality.

Surrendering a deep sigh of regret, he faced what was between them. "I am the same guy you rescued from shipwreck and brought ashore years ago, but I am not the man you knew in this life. The trials at Golden Mountain changed me. Though I strive to be what I was, I'm afraid I'm just a bullheaded half-wit, mired in deeper shit than he can handle but too damn proud and scared to admit it. I am different, Kalista, but I selfishly ask you to never despise me for it."

Tears sprang to her eyes and she looked away. Slammed by sudden misgivings, Rhane waited anxiously with his heart in his throat. Maybe what he asked was too much. He stroked the tears at her cheeks. "I promise you, Kalista, I will rise again."

"No," she said, shaking her head. "How dare you ask such a thing of me?"

Crushed by her words, a great ache cleaved through Rhane's chest. The feeling was worse than any battle wound ever received.

"I could never despise you, Rhane. Just as you have loved this version of me, I will love every version of you."

Gripping her harder than he should have, Rhane forced his hands to relax as he clung to her. Relief, gratitude, and affection swarmed inside him, battling for domination. He expelled a breath he didn't realize he had been holding. Then his lips found her mouth, warm and inviting as he sank inside her, prodding gently with his tongue as the kiss intensified. She sucked him deeper, meeting each of his thrusts with long, slow strokes of her own. Soft curves melded against him, making him aware of every smoldering inch of her body. Groaning, his hips reflexively drove forward, no doubt alerting her to the measure of his arousal.

Something between a moan and purr erupted from the back of her throat, but her hands slid to his chest as she gently pushed him away. Equal parts lust and regret shadowed the lightness of her grey eyes. When she spoke, her voice was thick and low, but as welcoming as velvet. "Promise me that we will finish this later."

Rhane grinned. Were time not a factor, he would have taken her right there on the very public trail. Crisis first. Primal gratification later. "I promise," he said. He didn't need a perfect memory to know it was a vow he would keep.

*

The second address provided by Rhane's rogue friend, Eris, was a movie theater of impressive proportions, but covering it was proving less of a challenge than the shopping mall had been. Kali was feeling pretty confident about their chances. Even Rhane's moodiness had turned a corner for the better.

Not surprisingly, Rion took it upon himself to perform an easy hack on the theater's computer systems. His justification being that it was the easiest way to determine which screens had sold the most tickets, thus making them the likeliest targets. Kali wasn't sure she agreed it was the easiest. With a simple inquiry, the person behind the ticket counter would have readily given out the same information. But maybe it was the most inconspicuous approach. Six people purchasing tickets based on theater room occupancy might have raised an eyebrow. If things went as far south as they had at the mall, it would be unwise to give anyone at the theater cause to remember them.

Thirty minutes after buying their tickets, Rhane and Kali sat left of center in the top row. She couldn't help but remember the night she had first laid eyes on him—at least in this life—in a crowded movie theater much like this one. The teenage girl who sat next to him then seemed almost a stranger to Kali now. Clueless of her past and afraid of what she was, her survival had hinged solely on Rhane's protection and unwavering courage. She had grown so much since then. Strong enough to safeguard Rhane when he needed it, smart enough to lead in his absence, and brave enough to accept her new roles as mother and mate.

What strange irony in how major changes had come to both of them but in wildly opposite directions. Where Kali gained assertiveness and some recollection of her past,

Rhane had lost self-confidence and much of his memory with it.

Even with the pivotal task at hand, it was hard not to look at or touch him, in an effort to feel whatever he felt in this moment. Knowing Rhane, the hardened warrior within allowed no room for sentiment during battle. His mind was probably filled with strategy and as focused as ever. Realizing her demeanor should be the same, Kali discarded emotion and set her attention on the crowd.

The movie was halfway finished with not a word passed between them when the radio on Rhane's belt crackled to life. *"He's here. Theater seven."* Kali couldn't discern who the urgent whisper belonged to, but guessed the owner was either Rion or War because Bailen wouldn't have a radio, York always kept his cool in tense situations and Orrin was rarely insistent about anything. But there was little time to dwell on the mystery as she and Rhane had already launched into action. Reaching the aisle, they navigated the stairs as quickly but as casually as possible. Behind the wall between the audience and outside corridor, Rhane pulled the radio from his belt. "Hold your positions and do not engage. Kalista and I are on the way."

"Impossible," the voice rushed out. *"I repeat. That is a negative. It's already happening."*

Rhane gritted his teeth. Clenching the radio so hard Kali feared it might be crushed, Rhane started to run. "I'm coming," he said.

She followed closely, straining to understand the events unfolding through a steady stream of sounds from the radio. The voice of the kin became barely audible, drowned in a sea of horrified screams. *"He's changing all of them. He's coming this way. We're gonna have to fight. Rhane, hurry."*

The radio clicked off, and in its silence were echoes of pure terror. The screams, now audible from Kali and Rhane's position, gave full witness to the absolute carnage taking hold in theater seven. But when she and Rhane burst through the black double doors, the hell before them was far worse than anything she could have imagined. Dark smears of blood painted the walls. More splatter dotted the ceiling. Black liquid and fleshy tissues drained from chairs to puddle on the floors in wet slicks of gore. The aisles were littered with dead and dying, both human and changeling.

Kali didn't understand. Perhaps trapped in the room, the creatures had turned on each other, and those unfortunate enough to remain human were torn to shreds by newly emerged monsters. Whatever the reason behind the slaughter, the horror wasn't over.

At the front of the room, two bloodied wolves embattled a fearsome opponent. Everything moved as if in slow motion. Fur flew. Fangs bared. Furious snarls got buried by a roar borne from the worst nightmare, and that nightmare was her son, Rhaven. He stood on two feet like a man, but broad scales lay where flesh should have been. Black and deep red, the bony plates linked together like a suit of armor to shield him from the worst of the kin's teeth and claws. Colossal wings sprouted from Rhaven's thickly muscled torso, beating down the air and ripping through the movie screen when the great appendages lashed against it.

But as fearsome as Rhaven's charge, War and Orrin seemed to have launched a successful assault. Faster and more agile, War's red wolf drew attack while the brawny brown wolf pressed Rhaven's flank. Kali watched as Orrin's teeth found a true home, buried into one of Rhaven's enormous wings, making him roar in anger. Whipping back his head, a stream of fire breathed from his scaly lips and blanketed the theater in flame and ash. Amazingly, both wolves stood untouched in the inferno.

Bracing for a blaze that did not reach him, the red wolf realized itself unharmed and dove beneath the river of fire and latched its jaws around Rhaven's neck. Kali screamed. Rhane's boots lifted to the stairs. Rhaven roared again. The brown wolf sank its teeth deeper, further mangling the injured wing.

Whatever held back Rhaven's flames was undone then, and the fire engulfed both wolves, and Rhane, who stood on the stairs. The moment seemed frozen in time. Kali had screamed again, but this one hung in the silent beat between seconds. Calling inward, digging for everything she knew and reaching for that which she had yet to understand, she raised her arms and commanded Rhaven's fire to cease. When she opened her eyes, the theater had cleared of all flames. Rhane had finally reached the bottom of the theater and was pulling War to his human feet. Orrin checked his brother's injuries with murder in his eyes. And Rhaven…Rhaven was gone.

Chapter 10

"Where the hell were you?" Rhane asked, striving to keep the question without accusation but sounding only half successful to his own ears. Everyone was assembled in one suite. The door had barely closed, but it was time for answers.

The mission at the theater had been a disaster. Orrin and War had disobeyed an order but given their situation, that insubordination was understandable, even if not excusable. York's absence, however, remained a thing of mystery. During the entire ordeal, he had been out of contact, only checking in nearly ten minutes after the skirmish between the twins and Rhaven had ended. Now Rhane needed to know why.

York showcased some serious skill at avoiding eye contact, and it was Rion who surprised Rhane by blushing. "We were on the wrong trail," the boy blurted.

"Elaborate."

Massaging the back of his neck, York glanced sheepishly at Rhane. "There was a decoy. I still don't know why we fell for it. After the incident at the mall, rogues must have thought to send reinforcements for the guy...not that he needs any."

"When War called in for help, why didn't you recognize the mistake then?"

Rion's blush deepened. "I lost the radio."

"What?"

"Well, the guy we were chasing, it turns out that he was a really big, steroid using rogue. He smashed the radio."

Starting to get a clearer picture of what had happened, Rhane began to nod.

"The bastard was hard to pin down, but I guess that was the point," York continued. "As soon as he was eliminated, we circled back but you guys were already gone from the theater. We phoned in and met up ASAP." York decided to go with a more concise summary of events. He could understand why Rion was embarrassed. The kid had damn near gotten his brains knocked out. Hell, York was embarrassed too. His back was still bruised from the hammering he had taken, caught off guard by a particularly clever counter attack from the big rogue. It was good that Rhane wasn't the type of guy to instigate a blame game. Their egos were already damaged enough.

Rhane turned away from them, looking to the window, distracted for a brief moment. "I'm glad you guys are okay," he said as his attention settled back onto them.

Relieved to be off the hook, York offered further apology. "Sorry that we didn't back you up."

"It's alright. War and Orrin had it handled." Rhane didn't add how he thought the two had received extra help from an unseen source. He couldn't be sure of that hypothesis until he questioned Bailen, and so far, the little guy was nowhere to be found.

"Where do we go from here?" War asked from his post against the far wall. The question was addressed to no one in particular as he chose to keep a concerned stare fixed in his brother's direction. Orrin lay stretched out on one of the two king-sized beds in the suite and had been silent since the theater. Normally a quiet guy, he had been more solemn than usual. Orrin's grave mood was likely caused by the knowledge of Rhane's true role in their father's death. It was a deception that he himself had needed some time to recover from. Orrin would be okay…as long as he didn't let his anger interfere with the operation at hand.

"Eris only provided the two addresses," York said, answering when no one else did. Kali had wandered to the large window overlooking the city landscape, moving as if in a daze. York couldn't blame her. Though her human body still clung to adolescence, Kali had matured into both a warrior and leader, capable of solid decision-making and ruthless violence in defense of what was hers. But York feared the girl was not properly equipped to handle mothering or even understanding two children as warped and twisted as Bailen and his severely damaged brother.

Maybe of similar thought, Rhane went to her side and slid his arm about her slender but strong shoulders. She leaned into him, ever so slightly, and York experienced a renewed gratitude for what stood between the two of them. With Rhane and Kali united, there was little this family could not overcome. They would win this fight or die trying.

What York didn't expect was for Kali and Rhane to spin away from the window wearing expressions of unbridled fear as they charged toward the other kin.

"Get down!" Rhane shouted, shoving Rion to his knees as he dove to the carpet.

No time for questions, the rest of the kin followed suit, even as the window shattered, exploding a hail of glass into the room. The shards sliced through skin and clothing, but that pain was nothing compared to what followed. Fire erupted throughout the room, and the head of a demon followed close behind it. The heat of its rage burned against York's body, feeling as if it ate through the very layers of his skin. Hearing a scream, he couldn't be certain that it wasn't his as pure misery tore through his body.

Then the burning suddenly ceased, causing him to believe it was simply because his nerve endings had been devoured by the inferno. But when York opened his eyes, he saw the respite's true cause. Grey fire now glowed between the orange flames and his skin, its light a cool barrier to the suffering. Peering through the haze, he saw the grey light encasing all of the kin, saving them from destruction. Unfortunately, fire wasn't the only danger they faced.

A furious roar bellowed from within the orange atmosphere, and an agonized shout followed. York staggered to his feet just in time to see War being dragged backward through the window by Rhaven's claws. His eyes, wide and frightened, held York's for several heartbeats before Rhaven released the boy into the darkness to fall to his death.

York stumbled forward, questioning why his legs dare betray him as he sank to his knees. Raising his head again, he witnessed Rhane's daring jump from the window, fading out as the night swallowed his friend. Then his vision blurred, darkened…and he at last gave in to the depths of unconsciousness.

*

Descending rapidly in freefall, there was little to think about except War's survival. With the bane silver of Rhaven's venom in him, War wouldn't be able summon a skin or hope to live through a fourteen story fall. His only chance was Rhane. And that was if he could reach him in time.

Streamlining himself as much as possible, Rhane accelerated his dive toward the boy with desperate abandon as the ground rushed toward them. War's arms were outstretched toward Rhane, his hands grasping, his face frightened but hopeful. Above them, Rhaven circled the dark skies growling and roaring like some beast of the apocalypse. Wrath, the rogues called him. Builders had truly created a formidable weapon.

With not quite three stories remaining between War and the ground, Rhane seized the boy's hands in an unbreakable grip. He twisted his body around, placing himself at War's back to buffer the blow in the final seconds before impact. Then time ran out for them both. Rhane tightened his arms about War as he slammed spine first into a large sedan. Vaguely, his brain registered the explosion of the car's windows and the blaring alarm that sounded afterward. The pain only lasted a moment, followed by numbness and dark spots clouding his vision. His grip loosened, and his hands slid away from War's torso.

They both lay stunned, trying to orient beneath the spinning night sky and the sudden outburst of activity in the streets. Then War started to stir, carefully rolling away from Rhane to slide down the car's hood. Rhane tried to rise, but his legs refused to obey his urgings. A dull echo of gunfire increased his sense of urgency, so he began to drag himself, cursing the uselessness of his lower extremities. Recognizing Rhane's plight, War helped him, but the boy's face was pinched with pain. Both shoulders had been bloodied by Rhaven's claws. A harsh limp left him heavily favoring his left side.

Bullets now rained down around them from all directions. Rhaven's roars grew more enraged, but he hovered in the sky and did not attack. Pausing to catch his breath, War lowered Rhane to the pavement, letting the doubled wheels of a tractor trailer shelter them.

"So," he panted. "Any guesses at who's shooting at us?"

Resting against the tire, Rhane drew himself up higher. He thought of the recent encounter at the graveyard after returning from their meeting with Eris. "I have an idea."

War raised one eyebrow. "Oh yeah?"

"York and I took sniper fire while delivering a few refugees to an ally. Near perfect shooting. Large caliber rounds." He paused for a breath and winced. Pain was good. And he could wiggle his toes now. "These might be the same guys."

"Not that I don't think what you're saying is possible, but New York is a big city. How could they have found you again so quickly?"

"I'm still working on that one." Rhane attuned his hearing toward the sound of gunfire in order to determine a more definite conclusion, but his ears were still ringing from the fall. "Tell me what you hear, War. How far are the shooters?"

"There are two of them." He paused, listening. "One targets us from the south, ninth floor or higher. The other is just west of the first shooter's position."

Rhane didn't need to ask about the rest of the gunmen. Automatic weapons bombarded them at a street level and came from almost every direction. Even in a concussive state, that trajectory was easy to follow. He looked up to the shattered window of their hotel room, still pouring smoke and flames. There was no sign that anyone else had escaped the room. Rhane's gut twisted. Standing the closest to Kalista when Rhaven attacked, Rhane was protected from the flames. It had taken her a moment longer to gain enough control to extend her protection to the other kin. From what Rhane could tell, Orrin and Rion had only been mildly burned. But York had taken a bad hit. His luck was shit enough to have been standing directly in the path of Rhaven's firestorm. Rhane pushed the memory of York's horrible burns from his mind in order to focus on the problem at hand—saving War's life.

"I know how we're going to get out of this," he said.

Something in his face must have clued War in. "I'm not going to like this, am I?"

Rhane shook his head. "No. But that's why I taught you to follow orders."

War grinned. "You certainly have made a valiant effort."

He wanted to laugh but knew doing so would hurt too much. "How fast can you move on that leg?" It would have been great if he could have just healed him, but with traces of Rhaven's venom still coursing through his veins, Rhane could barely heal himself. Fixing any of War's injuries was out of the question.

War tested the extremity. Not much in the way of movement happened. "I think it's broken. But I can do whatever you need me to."

"On my signal, I just need you to get out of here."

"What are you going to do?"

"I'm going to use the wolf and kill every one of these guys."

War's gaze rolled over him dubiously. "You can summon a change right now?"

"Yeah," Rhane lied, hoping he could pull off the minimum necessary to be convincing.

Still not appearing to be one hundred percent convinced, War nodded. "Okay. What's the signal?"

Digging deep for every ounce of strength he could muster, Rhane forced the changes. His senses sharpened. White fur rippled across his skin. A growl rumbled in his chest, and he nurtured the guttural sound into a powerful roar, unleashing it onto the night. *"Run!"* he bellowed.

War obeyed without hesitation. Springing into action, he scurried from the shelter of the tractor trailer, taking new cover behind a smaller sedan before vaulting over it and onto the sidewalk. Even as the boy moved, Rhane stood—fully human once more—with both arms raised in surrender. Many weapons trained on him, but thankfully did not fire. Inevitably harmless, regular lead still hurt. "It's me you want."

No one moved. No one spoke. Rhane prayed that War didn't do anything stupid in the interim.

A well-built man appearing even bulkier beneath a suit of full tactical gear stepped forward and spoke brusquely into the radio holstered at his shoulder. "Confirm the target."

An answer came quickly, ringing loud and clear in the distance between them. "Target is confirmed."

Eyes glittering unnaturally in the streetlight, the soldier leveled an eager gaze in Rhane's direction. "Move in," he ordered. "Secure the prisoner."

Nearly half the unit broke off at his command and marched slowly toward Rhane's position. With rigid, halting steps and fingers resting tightly on hair triggers, the soldiers seemed just as keen as their leader. Rhane tried not to tense as they closed in, forming a tight circle around him. It was harder not to react when the butt of a semi-auto rammed into the back of his already bleeding head. He staggered forward but did not fall, gritting his teeth against the explosion of pain that radiated from the base of his skull and down into his shoulder. Rhane pulled himself straight against the protest of quivering legs and a bruised spine. The gun came down for a second and third time. Pain slammed through his skull. The sight in his right eye was lost and along with it the hearing of the same ear.

Rhane grunted, powerless to stop the pavement that rushed to meet his face. Another one of Rhaven's fearsome roars tore through the atmosphere. Swimming on the very edge of consciousness, Rhane was only dully aware of the sound. Gunfire bombarded the streets in an attempt to suppress the new threat bearing down on the soldiers. Rhane pushed blindly to his knees and hoped those bullets weren't aimed at Kalista or the others, but feeling the unmistakable heat of her flames, he feared the worst.

Rhaven's cry tore through the night yet again, punctuated by screaming soldiers who were ill-equipped to handle the monster that hungered for their souls. One by one the men fell, some with the very flesh melted from their faces. Most died by fire. Others were slain by Rhaven's razored claws.

Suddenly hammered breathless by a pounding blow across both sides of his abdomen, Rhane collapsed. Instead of hitting pavement, his body drew further and further away from the asphalt. The pain in his sides faded to a dull ache. Tracing one hand to his wounds, he felt the steady seepage of blood and the rigid plates of scaly armor. It was only then he noticed the strong wind in his hair and against his face.

Shit. We're flying, he thought. And then Rhane relented to the darkness.

Chapter 11

Kali didn't know what to do.

The plan was in shambles. York, barely conscious, was in terrible shape, and wouldn't be of any assistance in rethinking their next move. War's condition wasn't much better. Bailen was still missing, and now Rhane was gone too. That left only Orrin and Rion to help bandage their wounded and pick up the pieces.

After a mandatory evacuation for all occupants in the burned building, Kali and the others had at least relocated to another hotel, nearby in case Rhane or Bailen returned, and in a room closer to a ground floor at Orrin's request. He thought it would be a more defensible position from an enemy who could so easily take to the skies.

York and War were both resting in the same room of a double suite. Thanks to Rhane, War was much further along on the road to recovery and continued to heal quickly. Orrin refused to leave his side.

"York," Kali called softly. "York, you have to drink something." He eventually opened his eyes and nodded, grimacing as he did so. Rion gently lifted York's head while Kali pressed the warm mug to his chapped lips. Severe burns covered at least half of his body, placing him at risk for severe dehydration as fluids leeched from the damaged skin. His throat barely worked as he drank. One hand lifted, weakly pushing the beverage away to signal he'd had enough. Kali quickly inspected the cup, noting York's intake. Rion met her eyes and shook his head. "York, you need to drink more. The herbs in the tea will jumpstart your system to heal. There's also something in there for pain."

York cleared his throat. "Did you brew that poison yourself?" He seemed to muster enough strength to level an accusing glare in the younger kin's direction. "It tastes like the business end of a toilet brush."

Rion scrunched up his face. "Dude, why are you licking toilet brushes? That's gross."

Smiling, York dropped his head back to the bed. "I thought it would help me remember what I had for dinner."

"That's just foul, you guys." Kali shook her head. Even while clinging to life on a crumbling ledge with bloodied and torn fingernails, York could still be counted on to crack a bad joke.

"Sorry," York said with a grin that conveyed the opposite. He started to say more but was seized by a fit of coughing, obviously causing him a considerable amount of pain.

Rion frowned worriedly. "Look, buddy. Rhane isn't here to fix you, so bandages and shitty tea is all you got." He lifted York's head again and nodded to Kali. "Drink up."

He stalled as the cup came to his lips. "Doesn't War need some?"

She could see Rion fighting hard not to laugh. "Drink the damn tea."

With only one or two final weak protests, York eventually did as he was told and drained the mug empty. He was asleep less than a minute later. The medicine was doing its job.

"Okay." Rion scrubbed his face with both hands. "That's done. What now?"

Kali bit her lip. "I wish I knew." They were thousands of miles away from home and any allies they could call upon. It was possible that York knew how to get in touch with the old rogue Rhane had befriended during the stint spent working with those creatures at his Mothers' behest. Of course, Kali really should have thought to ask about that before the tea had rendered York completely unconscious.

Not having an answer wasn't going to be good enough. York would be out for hours, so until Rhane returned, it was up to her to give the others some sort of direction. A decision rested on her shoulders. "We already tried tracking them, Rion, but Rhaven taking to the air left nothing for us to go on." She jerked her chin toward the corner of the room where War was tucked away and resting. "There's no way these two can travel. I doubt Orrin will leave his brother's side anyway. Nor would I ask him to. That leaves the two of us."

Rion nodded. "We go looking then?"

"No." Sighing, Kali leaned back to rest her weight on her forearms. "We don't know how those soldiers on the street found us. We don't know what they want or when they may come again. I don't think we can afford to leave York and War unprotected while they're still so vulnerable. But as soon as they're able, I think we should move to a different location…something with more exits."

"More exits would mean the spot would be less defensible."

"You're right, but right now we don't need another fight. We need an escape. We need something where we can see the enemy coming and evade them."

"I can handle that from here. My computer survived the fire. Using city records—blueprints and stuff like that—I should be able find the perfect place."

"Thanks, Rion."

Patting her leg with a smile, the young kin hurried off to tackle the task at hand. Next to Kali, York made an odd sound in his sleep but quickly quieted. War shifted restlessly, still dozing, while Orrin stood as granite, a sentinel to guard the night.

*

It felt like falling within a pool of seemingly endless darkness, only to surface at the bottom and break through into the land of consciousness. He became aware all at once, but didn't move or open his eyes. Instead, Rhane lay stock-still, keeping his breathing shallow and steady while he used every other sense to decipher his current predicament.

The grass was soft beneath his fingertips, tickling his face as a cool breeze disturbed the fine stalks. A farm was nearby, perhaps within twenty miles. He could smell livestock, as well as hear faint but constant baying of playful calves. Stretched out farther beyond them were the familiar sounds of the city. Rhaven had traveled far, saving Rhane from capture, but to what end? And where was he now?

Shutting down all other senses, Rhane focused his hearing until the "picture" came into view. The resonance of every living thing, moving or breathing, appeared within a mile of his position. Following those echoes, Rhane "walked" through the crowded wood, mapping out rustling trees, scurrying rodents, grazing deer, and even a pair of stealthy foxes. Finally, perched within the bowed branches of an aged spruce, he located the heartbeat of the one he sought. Too large and strong to belong to any four-legged mammal, the solidly paced pumping could only be the heart of a warrior.

Letting go of the image, Rhane slowly rolled onto his back. A soft growl followed the movement, drifting from high up in the trees. He waited until the sound stopped. Then cautiously pushing to his knees, he rose to both feet.

The beginnings of dawn threaded dim light through the forest, effectively marking the passage of time. Gone were at least eight hours. Kalista and the others had to be worried shitless. He wondered if War had fully recovered and how badly York had been hurt. Rhane's own injuries had mostly healed. Those things, though valid concerns, were really the least of his problems. Looking him in the eye was the biggest failing of his life and Rhane wasn't sure how to face it.

But Rhaven wasn't giving him time to figure it out.

Black and red wings forged from darkness unfolded, carrying a long figure through the trees. Only half of his form was clothed in linen trousers, leaving his naked torso and the ugly scarring that stretched across it in full view. Landing a few feet away, the wings tucked away and the young man strode forward. His face was angry. His voice sounded cold and confused. "I know you," he said. Accusation lined his words.

Instinct told Rhane to retreat from that anger, but the father inside of him simply could not. "Yes. You do."

"But I don't!" Rhaven shouted as his hands came up and ripped at his own hair. "I don't," he said again as his voice became soft and bitter. Whirling away, he began pacing.

"You were taken away from your mother and me a long time ago. You were only a youngling."

Rhaven looked back at him. A storm of disbelief brewed darkly in his eyes. "I've seen your power," he said quietly. "How could anyone ever take me away from you?"

Rhane swallowed. His mouth felt as if packed with cotton. "It was a difficult time…our people were at war, and I failed to see the true enemy. I left to fight, thinking you were safe. But you weren't. You were killed, Rhaven. You died as a little boy. Somehow the Builders brought you back."

Rhaven's pacing ceased. Understanding rippled briefly across his features, but then the anger was gone and replaced by full blown rage. Eyes and throat glowing orange, he threw back his head and screamed. The sound deepened, transforming into a guttural roar as his wings spread and fire spewed from his mouth like an erupting volcano. Once the combustion receded, Rhaven turned back to Rhane. He was shaking with emotion and the surface of his skin glowed as if backlit by the embers of a dying fire.

Never entertaining the idea that Rhaven wouldn't hurt him, Rhane held his ground. No amount of pain the boy could inflict would compare to agony of watching his oldest son suffer as he did in this moment.

"They made me like this." Rhaven stretched out his hands, staring as if seeing them for the first time. "Wrath. I am what they call me. A monster."

"We're all monsters, Rhaven."

"But I'm a murderer."

Rhane nodded. "We're not so different."

112

Dropping both hands to his sides, Rhaven looked at him but said nothing.

"You've done some bad things, but so have I. Sometimes evil is necessary to protect what you love."

Tension crawled through Rhaven's torso and even stiffened his wings. "You think I'm protecting someone."

"I think you and Bailen have been taking care of each other for a very long time. I think the choices you're making now are to somehow keep him safe. And I know for a fact that he is working very hard to save you from the hell you currently reside in."

Steady beneath Rhane's scrutiny for a long time, Rhaven finally glanced away. His throat worked hard as he swallowed. "I don't want to help them anymore," he said softly.

"Then don't. Come home with me."

"I can't. I was given to Moros and must do his bidding now." Rhaven tapped one finger against his temple. "When my master calls me back, something inside hurts when I don't obey." He gazed at Rhane sadly. "He calls me now."

So angry he wanted to throw up, Rhane swallowed the clump of bile resting at the back of his throat. But the bitter taste wouldn't leave his mouth. He concentrated on controlling his voice, banishing emotion from his speech. "Then how are you here?"

"I am fighting it."

"You mean you're in pain."

Rhaven nodded. "I can't give Master what he wants. My blood doesn't work. But if I stop trying...if I don't give him something, he won't hesitate to kill me, and I fear

Bailen will be forced to take my place. He escaped this life. I won't let him be dragged back."

Hands fisting at his sides, Rhane forced them to relax. He didn't want Rhaven to mistake the source of his anger. "I am a lot stronger now than I was then. Bailen is in my care now and he is safe. Let me help you."

Still uncertain, Rhaven took a step back. "The hunters that travel with you—identify them."

While Rhane wouldn't have called them hunters, he saw no pressing need to argue the point. "They are your family, Rhaven. The woman you saw is your mother."

Suddenly, Rhaven's wings expanded, sounding a forceful snap before they folded shut again. Odd spasms seized control of his face, but then he was still. "And the young men…they are all your sons?"

"Though I did not sire them, they have become like sons to me."

"What of me then?"

"You are also my son."

"Then why did they try to harm me?"

"You know why, Rhaven. You were hurting people. Their orders were to stop you."

"Now you speak of them as soldiers."

Rhane considered that for a moment. "They are both," he finally answered.

"And you ordered them to hurt me?"

Rhane shook his head. "I did not."

The spasms returned, all but reshaping the boy's features. "I want to trust you," he uttered with some difficulty.

"Go with your instincts."

Gasping, Rhaven dropped to his knees. Growing pale beneath his bronzed complexion, his chest heaved as he struggled for the next breath. Rhane hurried to the boy's side, holding out a hand as he knelt but stopped short of touching him. "Rhaven?"

Gritting his teeth, he opened his eyes. "You must swear to me that you can protect him."

"I am stronger than I was when I lost you, Rhaven. I will protect Bailen and I will not fail you again."

Visibly shaking now, Rhaven appeared to be losing whatever war was raging inside of him. He rose to his knees. "I must go now."

"Wait." Rhane stood with him. "At least tell me how to find you again."

Lifting himself with the power of his wings, Rhaven hovered just above the ground but purposefully out of reach. His soundless flight moved him farther away even as he spoke. "My master wants the stone which powers the staff. Free it from the mountain and they will come."

Unease folded Rhane's stomach inward. He lifted his eyes to meet Rhaven's orange gaze. He had asked for his son's trust, but could Rhaven be trusted in turn? "If Moros gets the keystone, that staff you carry will become the vessel by which hell is unleashed upon this world."

"Then we must not let him have it," Rhaven called down to him. "We will destroy him first."

"When should I do this?"

"Go now. The mountain awaits your blood." Rolling mid-flight, Rhaven turned away and was gone.

Rhane stood in the forest, unable to ignore the sinking feeling taking root in his gut. When he thought of seeing Rhaven again, dread crashed over him in a ten foot wave.

He watched the sky until the black spot all but disappeared from his sight and then he called out softly. "Bailen," he whispered. "You can come out now."

It was a while before padded footsteps on the earth behind him confirmed what Rhane had suspected all along, but brought him no closer to understanding the sons who were lost to him.

Chapter 12

"Rhane, I know what we have to do, but I don't like it. There's not much about this whole damn thing that sits well with me." York, looking and feeling much better than he had the last time he and Rhane occupied the same room, couldn't let his objections go unvoiced. In such a situation, he considered it his duty to express every misgiving.

Rhane couldn't blame him one bit. He leaned against an opposite wall, his back to the room while he quietly stared out an open window. There he had remained since tendering his plan for the next forty-eight hours. Rhane fully realized what he was asking of them. An almost blind faith was needed to enlist obedience. Because of that he was willing to consider every doubt and forgive any resistance. Eventually, they all would come to terms with the mission. And after a consensus was reached, Rhane sorely needed to have a separate discussion with Kalista and Bailen.

The canine sat next to his mother's chair, pressed close to Kalista and stubbornly avoiding eye contact with Rhane at all costs. Once upon a time, he had thought himself beginning to understand the boy's cause. Sure, Bailen had made decisions that put them all in danger, but nearly getting Rhane killed had not been intentional. Bailen didn't want him to die. He simply needed to get his brother back. Perhaps more than anything else, Rhane understood sacrifices made to protect one's family.

Rion nervously cleared his throat. "Are you sure you're strong enough?" The unease in the young kin's voice painted in Rhane's mind a clear picture of the nervous expression he wore.

"I am strong enough," Rhane answered without turning. "We all are."

The bed creaked as York shifted. He sighed heavily. "If this gets out of hand, a shitload of people could get killed." A heavy silence followed and when no one else spoke, he added, "Kali, even your family might get hurt."

Rhane gritted his teeth. "Her family will be safe."

"Oh yeah?" Still not convinced, York wasn't letting him off easy. "We'll need every ally to ensure that happens."

"They'll be there."

"Even your new rogue friends—you're sure you can bring them on board?"

"They will help us, York."

"If only confidence could win wars," York muttered. "Oh what the hell? Let's get started."

"Anyone else?" Rhane asked, finally moving to face them. He focused his gaze on the twins. "You have yet to voice any concerns."

War inclined his head. "I will follow you anywhere, Warlord. I trust you."

Scowling, Orrin abruptly stormed out of the room. Looking from his brother to Rhane, War shrugged apologetically. "He'll come around."

Rhane nodded. He could always count on Orrin in battle. But never again would he stand upon the pedestal of respect and admiration the young kin once held him upon. "In a few hours, I should be able to use my blood to complete the healing for both of you." He checked his watch. "It'll be around first light, so we will leave then. Rion, can you handle transport?"

"Consider it done."

"Thank you." Rhane proceeded to the door. It was time to let them to rest. They would all need it come what was ahead. "Kalista," he said, holding out a hand. "A word please?"

She came without hesitation. "Sure."

"Bailen, you too."

The canine whined, but followed at his mother's heels. Rhane led them outside, beyond the parking lot and across the street. With a noisy highway between them and the hotel, he hoped the ensuing conversation would be past the reach of supernatural ears. Looking at Bailen, Rhane leaped straight to the point. "Harness your human form."

Tail drooping almost between his legs, Bailen lowered his head and pushed against Kalista's legs. Absorbing the weight of his quivering body, she was forced to take a step back. She glanced at Rhane with wide, uncertain eyes and gently stroked the canine's immense head.

"Bailen, I said earlier that you must not fear me. That still stands because I will never hurt you. Now, I won't ask again."

Tanned skin came into view as Rhane's command was finally heeded and a young male stood before him, all but a teenager of no more than sixteen years to the unknowing eye. The human expression he wore showed no less chagrin. Admittedly, Rhane wasn't sure it wasn't just a performance.

"Bailen, it's time to level with us, and I want nothing less than the absolute truth from you. Why go through all the trouble of tracking down your brother but then fail to show yourself when the opportunity arose? You left the mall without telling anyone where you were going or why. You've been missing for over twenty-four hours, leaving your mother and me to worry about your safety, as well as your intentions." Sucking in a breath, Rhane stopped himself. Justifying a simple question had derailed into a full blown rant.

Bailen's gaze drilled into the asphalt. "You don't have to worry about me," he said.

"We're your parents, kiddo," Kalista said, touching his shoulder. "Worrying kind of comes with the territory."

The situation was quickly becoming a good cop, bad cop showdown. *I'll play along.* Rhane folded his arms and remained silent.

Something in Kalista's kind demeanor must have appealed to him, for Bailen gradually relented. "I came to the theater. You just didn't see me."

At first, Kalista's confusion mirrored his own, and then almost simultaneously, the light bloomed for both of them. "That's why the boys didn't get hurt. You held back Rhaven's flames," she said.

The revelation left Rhane feeling a small measure of relief. Orrin and War could have been seriously injured, but Bailen had chosen to save them. He put their well-being above his own agenda. That gave Rhane hope.

But Bailen didn't look happy. "I stopped him from killing them, and then they hurt him."

"People died at that theater," Rhane said, trying to win over the boy with reason. "Orrin and War were only trying to prevent more lives from being lost. You can't be angry at them for that."

"I am not. But I couldn't allow them to keep hurting him."

"Okay," Rhane said. "I get that. It was a tough choice, but you have to see why we are concerned. If it wasn't for Kalista, either of the twins could have easily been killed at the theater. There's a definite pattern of you choosing to help Rhaven but allowing people to seriously get hurt in the aftermath."

"Their deaths were not my intention. Nor did I wish them harm. They have been very kind to me." Bailen finally lifted his head to see them, and touched Kalista's hand. "And we would never cause harm to our mother."

Kalista smiled sadly. "Oh, Bailen, but what about Rhane? He is your father and he loves you as much as I do, even if he never says it."

"I know," Bailen agreed solemnly. "But he will have to suffer."

"Bailen!" Kalista exclaimed. The boy's gaze was as steely as the color of his eyes. "He is immortal, *uskai*. He will not die."

Kalista drew back, clearly horrified. "Bailen—" she began, but Rhane stopped her. "It's okay. I'm not afraid of pain. I will do whatever it takes to prove to these boys that we can be trusted…and goddamn it, Bailen. One day you will trust me."

"I do trust you, Sire."

"Then tell us what is going on," Kalista insisted.

"I do not know Rhaven's plan to share it."

Not ready to buy that statement, Rhane pressed the boy for more. "I find what you're saying hard to believe. You and Rhaven were obviously very close. You escaped but wouldn't have left him without a plan."

"I was supposed to find you and then a way to destroy our captors by using the combined strength of Banewolf and the siren. Far more powerful than me on his own, Rhaven was to work toward the same goal on his end. Once all Builders were destroyed, we would be free to be a family again." Bailen stopped. He seemed to be deliberating, struggling with a decision.

"You mistake my fear, Father. I am not afraid of you, but I am afraid for my brother. His actions no longer coincide with our common goal. I didn't show myself in the forest this morning because I didn't want to question his motives in your presence. Helping rogues like this— the mass conversion of humans—it was not a part of the plan. Maybe they have broken him. Rhaven's mind is not whole. You can't blame him. What they did to us, especially to him…he is prone to fits of rage even I cannot dispel. You say you fear for my conscience. Rhaven has none. There were whispers that his soul did not return to life with him."

Bailen's tone softened, pleading for understanding. "But he is good. He shows affection. He remembers having a family. And I am sure that he loves me."

The boy's words traveled far toward explaining Rhaven's perilous temperament. "So be honest, Bailen. If we get this keystone for Rhaven, can he be trusted? Or do you think he is really helping the bad guys?"

Bailen's mouth pressed into a firm line as he shook his head. "No. He hates them more than he cares about anything in this world."

"Okay. I believe you. If at any point during this mission you begin to suspect things might turn sour, I need to know in the same instant. Can I count on you for that?"

"Yes sir."

"Don't call me sir." Relaxing enough to smile, Rhane leaned down and touched his forehead to Bailen's. "Hug your mother and then get furry again. I know it's what you like best."

Bailen surprised Rhane by wrapping a pair of lanky arms around his waist and squeezing tightly. "I'm so glad I found you both," he said. After embracing Kalista with equal affection, he quickly dropped to all fours again.

"Let's get some sleep," Rhane said. "We've got a long journey ahead of us."

Chapter 13

To say she was cold would've have been ridiculously understated. With every mile the temperature seemed to plummet, approaching zero at a rate Kali wasn't sure she was ready for. Rocky, snow-dusted terrain gradually gave way to an endless landscape of snowdrifts into which Kali sank past her knees.

Traversing through regions inhabited by local tribes, Rhane didn't give the order to switch from human to wolf skins. Dressed in parkas, spiked boots, and mittens, the kin were probably almost as miserable as Kali. For the last few miles, no one had said much. Except for York. He hated the biting cold and didn't hesitate to remind everyone of the fact. His complaints came like clockwork in ten minute increments, but he somehow found a way to express each one with a completely new and original vulgarity, using a cache of various languages. If not distracted by thoughts of freezing to death, Kali might have laughed at his woe.

They walked in a single file formation with Orrin on point. He was kind enough to volunteer for the task, breaking through miles and miles of packed snow for the rest of them. Always pretty quiet, especially when compared to the rest of the kin, Kali couldn't tell if he was still as upset as he had been last night. Orrin's anger was easily understood. Finally knowing the true circumstances of his sire's death was bad enough. Adding insult to injury was that the secret was kept so long…and by his sire's killer…who was also the man who raised him. Kali wasn't sure how she would have dealt with the information. That Orrin continued to follow Rhane at all right now was a testament to his character. His brother's discovery of the secret came during an exceptionally difficult time, so maybe War had been forced to come to terms with Rhane's betrayal at a faster rate. Rhane suffered so much at the hands of his people, refusing to escape when he easily could have, letting his blood be spilled only to preserve War's life. Perhaps his sacrifice expedited the young kin's forgiveness. Kali couldn't help wondering what it would take for Orrin to put the deception behind him and move forward. The twins of course had not kept the truth from Rion, but the youngest kin must have received the news with barely a shrug of anger. He plainly wasn't interested in harboring a grudge for an act committed so far back in a past he barely remembered. Kali found herself feeling even more incredibly grateful for his forgiving attitude and unflappable temperament.

Walking next to her and carrying a backpack of supplies that included a tent to provide shelter through the night and from infamous storms plaguing this particular stretch of the Himalayan range, Rhane broke the silence between them. "You okay?"

Kali smiled at him fondly. Really it was a stupid question. *No*, she wanted to scream. *I am not okay. I'm marching through one of the coldest places on this planet, about to freeze my ass off.* But she wouldn't complain. York was doing enough for the entire lot of them.

Besides, thermal underwear beneath her snowsuit was doing a good job of keeping her core temperature where it should be. It was only her extremities that weren't faring quite so well. But Kali was closing in on a solution.

"I'm fine."

"Of course you are." Rhane stopped walking and grabbed her hand, pulling her to a halt beside him. War and Bailen slowed, looking back with questioning gazes, but Rhane waved them on. Tugging off one glove, he moved the fabric that shielded the bottom half of her face from the bitter wind and pressed a hand against her cheek. His touch was so hot it almost burned. "Are you sure?" he asked, pinning her with his otherworldly eyes. "Because if you need to stop I don't think the others will mind."

The lust in his gaze revealed his true motives and nearly drew Kali in, but there was still too much ground to cover before darkness fell. There was a mission to complete.

"We should keep going," she said, and regretted the words. Rhane's subliminal proposal sounded like a hell of a lot more fun."The more ground we cover, the sooner we'll be out of territories frequented by local tribes. You all can shift to war skins and be a lot warmer for it." Kali tried to move forward, but Rhane didn't waver.

"That still leaves you out in the cold." He moved closer, completely dominating her space. Kali sucked in a deep breath. She wanted him bad. It was amazing that he still had such a crazy effect on her. "Am I a complete asshole for wanting to take you right here, right now on this frozen ground?"

Before she could answer, his mouth surrounded hers and his tongue pierced into her, making a deep and prodding exploration between her lips. She moaned against his mouth, sucking him deeper, surrendering to the tide of heat that rolled over her body. Through all the layers between them, his growing need was evident and pushed into her belly. "Rhane," she breathed his name huskily, prying herself from his arms before it was too late.

"I'm sorry." He too broke away, letting her go. His breathing sounded slightly ragged as he composed himself. "You're just driving me insane today."

"I don't mean to," Kali said, confused as to what she could possibly be doing differently. She certainly hadn't set out to seduce Rhane as they hiked through a barren wilderness seeking to kill them all with arctic temperatures.

"It's okay. It's not your fault." He took her hand. "We better catch up."

But Kali hesitated, taking a moment to plant a tender kiss against his lips. "Tonight," she promised.

His face broke into a grin. "Can't wait," he said.

They trudged through the broken snow, and thoughts of what tonight would bring distracted her so much, she almost didn't notice when the ground suddenly turned solid again. Only it wasn't earth beneath her feet, but a frozen slab of ice. The spikes in the soles of her shoes removed the challenge of walking across such a surface, but first Kali had to come to terms with the shocking beauty stretched out in front of her. On the way over, she'd accomplished a little research and knew what to expect before the twin engine plane landed on the frozen tundra. But now they had reached the base of the Himalayan mountain range and she was standing on an actual glacier. A perfect reflection of the blue sky across the ice made the horizon almost indiscernible.

"It's beautiful," she whispered.

"You see that peak?" War pointed to a snow-covered mountain mostly obscured by clouds in the near distance. "That's the monster we're after."

York didn't look at all impressed by the natural marvel. "Do you remember my promise, Rion?"

"Yeah, yeah. You'll throw me over if this is all for nothing. I remember." Rion shrugged. "I checked and rechecked the data. Of the final two remaining sets of coordinates, this is where we need to be. I'm sure of it."

"And what is here exactly?" Kali asked.

"It's called K2." An excited gleam took hold in Rion's eyes as he launched into a brief history of the mountain. "The summit isn't well known to the general population, but when comparing the number of climbers who attempted to conquer K2 versus the numbers who've died trying, this mountain is deadlier than Everest. And it's especially unkind to women."

Kali tilted her head to one side. "Are you trying to scare me, Rion?"

"Of course not." The young kin blushed.

"She'll be fine," York said. "Push come to shove, we'll pretend we're sled dogs and sleep on top of her."

Kali laughed. "The last place I want to be is at the bottom of a dog pile of war skins weighing over three hundred pounds each. I'd probably suffocate."

York winked. "How about we play big spoon and little spoon then?"

Rhane shoved York with one hand, sending the big guy skidding across the ice and scrambling to regain sure footing. The fight was lost and he fell face first onto the ground. Of course, it being York, the lesson didn't take. He lifted his head and was smiling. "Come on, Kali. This sexy fur will be all you need to stay warm at night."

Growling humorously, Rhane launched a snowball. It slammed into York's cheek and disintegrated on impact. "One more word out of you and I'll skin your hide."

"I'm sorry," York retorted, clearly undeterred. "You're talking to me or Kali?"

Scowling, Rhane started forward. Kali grabbed the tail of his jacket, pulling him backward and laughing hysterically even as York threw up his arms in surrender. "Okay. Okay. That was the last one. I swear it."

It was good to see some things would never change.

Two hours later, Rhane gave the order for skins to be used and things would have gotten a lot lonelier if not for Rhane remaining human and at her side. Falling behind the others, Bailen joined them, and Kali imagined they were normal parents on a sort of strange camping trip with their kid.

Rhane had the foresight to make sure their supply packs could be carried on the backs of the wolf forms. Together, he and Rion rigged bungee cables, several yards of rope, and a few other materials to fashion the harnesses now worn by the dire wolf-sized kin. Now the snow drifts were easily traversed thanks to over a dozen massive paws breaking a trail Kali and Rhane could easily follow. Just before darkness fell and with the menace of a storm brewing in the near distance, three tents were pieced together, cocooning pairs of them within bright yellow walls constructed of materials specifically engineered to withstand the severest temperatures.

Kali was nearly finished unpacking their bedding when Rhane returned from a visit to York and Orrin's quarters to discuss the next day's strategy. Sealing the tent's heavy nylon fly, he crossed the room in two strides and she had barely enough time to utter a greeting before he was grabbing the sleeping bags from her hands and tossing them aside. He kissed her fervently, overwhelming her body and mouth with the sudden onslaught of his passion. It wasn't until the slight chill tickled her skin that Kali realized he had already stripped her down to her underwear. He shrugged off his snow suit while still kissing her, controlling her mouth and robbing her of coherent thought as his tongue dipped into her mouth and his teeth nibbled at her lips and neck. He stopped only when the stubborn laces of the calf-high snow boots required his full attention. The break gave Kali a moment to breathe…and to think.

"Where's Bailen?"

"He's staying with War and Rion for the night."

Feigning annoyance, Kali placed her palm on one cocked hip. "You did not kick our son out of this tent just because you're horny."

Rhane looked up. No sign of regret crossed his features. A slow, wolfish smile overtook his lips and Kali noticed how his eyes had darkened, nearly black in color. "I didn't have to because he volunteered. The kid has a great sixth sense."

"Do you think he gets it from me or you?" Kali backed away, casually redirecting her attention to unrolling the discarded sleeping bags. Ever so slowly, she bent over to retrieve them and was rewarded when Rhane growled softly behind her. Once again, the bags were torn from her grasp as his large hands grabbed her hips and pulled her roughly into him.

"You know what that does to me," he whispered roughly into her ear. "You're so fucking beautiful." Kali

131

shivered at his words and the solid length of him pressing firmly against her backside. Thrusting backward, she grinded her bottom into him. A rather inhuman sound rumbled from deep in his throat as his fingers tightened, digging into her hip. She rolled against him again and this time his teeth clamped onto her neck. Rhane was aroused before, but now it felt like a steel shaft waited to burrow into her depths. His hand moved to her throat, squeezing lightly as the other slid between her thighs. Soon she was trembling, sagging as her knees weakened with every moan coaxed from her lips. She gave into the pleasure, calling his name as the intensity built and lit sensitive nerve endings afire. Bucking violently forward, she collapsed into his rock solid arms—her only support as she was lost in a storm of spasms that rocked her body in an endless seizure of toe-curling contractions. Kali didn't realize the sudden noise that filled the tent was her screaming until Rhane's hand clamped over her mouth.

He held her up until her spent legs found enough strength to support her, all the while leaving trails of kisses along her neck, shoulders, and back. As good as her release felt, she was hotly aware of the matter of Rhane's urgent need still pressing relentlessly into her flesh. The desire to feel him inside of her was almost too much for words. Digging her nails into his forearm, Kali threw her head back and kissed him, moaning ardently into his mouth. Then leaning forward, she grabbed her ankles. It was all the invitation he needed.

Kali cried out as his rigid length pierced into her. She adjusted her hips, rising on tip-toe to accommodate every inch and take him even deeper. Then he withdrew in a torturously slow motion, only to slam into her. He repeated this again and again, bringing their bodies together in the most primal fashion, ripping from her throat a symphony of moans and whimpers. He adjusted his pace, thrusting faster and harder, pounding her senseless until she broke again. Kali couldn't help shouting as every muscle group in her body tightened as if turning to stone. But the pain was dulled by the pure ecstasy experienced in the same moment. Far from finished, Rhane continued to rock against her hips, coaxing her aching body into yet another climax, making Kali see stars. She gasped his name and felt the warm gush of seed spilling inside of her. Legs no longer supporting her weight, it was only Rhane's strength that kept her upright.

Still trembling, he eased them both to the floor where Kali fell limp against his chest while she gasped for air. He pushed her curls away from her face, checking her over with troubled eyes. "Are you okay?"

Not quite able to speak, she simply nodded. Trying to sit straighter, she attempted to pull herself upward and realized too late they were still joined. Hissing, Rhane seized a fistful of Kali's hair, holding her still as his body twitched uncontrollably, hips pumping upward as another surge of fluid filled her womb.

Quietly shaking, they sat together with their hands entwined, listening to the wind grow stronger outside. Rhane eventually untangled himself from her grasp long enough to unfurl the sleeping bags. Then he pulled her inside to lie alongside him and planted a gentle kiss against her forehead.

"I am yours forever, Kalista," he said softly.

"And I am yours," she whispered.

Chapter 14

Just before dawn, everyone convened in the largest tent for a breakfast of powdered eggs and sausage. Melted and filtered snow served as drinking water and for some became the base for a mug of pretty terrible tasting instant coffee. "Ugh," Kali said after becoming the concoction's first victim. "Rion, where did you find this stuff?"

"Hey, don't look at me," he protested around a mouth full of egg. "York insisted. Said it was good stuff."

York gave a thumbs-up. "I like it."

Orrin tested the beverage and then drained the cup. His expression remained unchanged as he drank. Finished, he turned to York. "Kali's right. This is gross."

"Whatever. It'll put some extra hair on your chests."

"I don't need any extra hair on my chest." Kali barked a laugh as she considered her words. "I don't need *any* hair on my chest. What I need is decent coffee." She looked at Rhane who was drinking the coffee without complaint. Noticing her gaze, he smiled over the brim of his cup. York saw the exchange, and a glint came to his eye.

"Would that be because Rhane wouldn't let you sleep last night?"

An unstoppable blush rose to her face, betraying her embarrassment. "I slept fine thank you."

York fired back without hesitation. "Well, we didn't."

Kali's blush deepened. Mortification left her speechless.

"If you're not knocked-up and sideways after that, I think Rhane should really get his balls checked. He might be sterile."

Rhane finally broke his silence. "For Christ's sake, York," he said as Orrin offered his two cents. "At least the smell is gone." Rion cringed while War nodded in agreement.

"*The smell?*" Kali repeated, completely aghast. "What *smell?*"

"Enough." Rhane stood abruptly. "Pack the site. We leave in five." He rushed outside like the tent was on fire, all but dragging Kali with him. She dug her heels in. "Rhane, what is Orrin talking about?"

"Nothing, Kalista." Letting go of her hand, he kept walking. "Orrin is still angry and just trying to make my life difficult."

"Uh, I take it then that what he said means something."

When Rhane didn't reply or halt the long strides putting distance between them, Kali ran to catch up. She grabbed his arm. "Rhane!"

Sighing, he turned to face her. "Yeah?"

"Be straight with me."

"I am being straight with you. Orrin pretty much hates me right now."

"You know what I meant." She folded her arms, incredulous at the implications of what was happening. "I mean, you would tell me if I had skunk arms or something, right? We hiked all day, but I cleaned up. Besides, we're in freaking arctic temperatures. How can they smell anything?"

He put a hand on her shoulder. "Calm down, Kalista. You're fine."

"Well there's a tent full of supernatural noses back there that don't agree."

Rhane grinned. His uneasiness had become obvious amusement with her display of self-conscious panic. "It doesn't matter what they think. You're mine, Kalista." Holding her chin, he stooped to press his lips against hers. As bothered as she was, Kali couldn't help sinking into the kiss as she basked in the warmth of his touch. Beneath his parka, Rhane's heart beat strong and steady, unlike hers which stampeded like wild buffalo. Finding enough resolve to pull away, she narrowed her eyes suspiciously. "This discussion isn't over."

Rhane was unfazed. "It is for now. We need to break camp. York and I have already plotted the course for today's journey. There's a lot of ground between here and the summit, and probably a hundred ways you could get hurt." Frown lines creased the smoothness of his forehead. "Would you consider riding today? Orrin has agreed to carry you."

"And where will you be?"

"I need to remain as human."

"You'll ride on York's shoulders?"

Rhane looked offended. "Absolutely not. I can make my own way."

"So, I'm the only one getting the invalid treatment."

"We'll run flat out these last six miles until we reach the pass. From there, we aim to climb at least ten thousand feet before nightfall."

"Enough said." Kali threw up her hands. "Go ahead and saddle the horse."

*

Having recently sat astride Banewolf's powerful shoulders, the movements of Orrin's war skin felt familiar beneath her. The effortless, loping gallop of the wolves covered the distance to the pass in just over five minutes. Realizing she would have never been able to match such an extraordinary speed on foot, Kali felt a surge of gratitude for Rhane's insistence that she ride.

Running behind them, Rhane kept pace easily enough with the four-legged entourage. Still, Kali couldn't help feeling a spurt of sympathy for him as he was constantly showered in sprays of snow kicked up from the kin's tracks. Bailen followed in Rhane's wake, benefitting from the ease of running in a ready-forged trail and the added advantage of using his father's body as a shield against the flying snow.

At the base of the mountain, Kali slid from Orrin's great brown withers with Rhane's help. "So why didn't we just do this from the start?" she asked once her feet were back on solid ground.

"Besides not wanting to take a chance of being seen by native tribes," Rhane explained as he deliberately removed the snow from his ski mask and goggles, "their skins can't maintain that tempo for distances much longer than that."

She nodded. "So, what now? Why are we stopping?"

"First of all, I can't see a damn thing around all the snow coming off their huge asses. But more importantly, nearer to the summit the winds can reach up to one hundred miles per hour—too strong to risk riding atop anyone's shoulders. You might need to journey on your own for awhile, so I want you to get used to what climbing will feel like down here where it's easier." Digging into the pack strapped to York's back, Rhane removed some essential pieces of gear, including rope, an ice axe, and two harnesses. Rhane handed her the smaller of the two. "You remember how to put this on?"

"Yeah, but you should check after me anyway."

Rhane grinned. "It'll be my pleasure."

Kali stepped in the assembly of straps and buckles, making the necessary adjustments until the harness fit snugly around her waist and thighs. After doing the same to his own, Rhane stepped over to examine Kali's handiwork. His hands moved slowly over her legs, taking their time to test each buckle and then travel upward. Lightly cupping her ass, he pulled her closer. They locked eyes and he gave one final cinch to the belt encircling her waist.

Standing slightly ahead of them, one of the others snorted impatiently and pawed the snow. A glare from Rhane and the kin settled immediately. When he looked back at her, Kali searched his mouth with a slow kiss but didn't linger. She smiled at the dreamy satisfaction spread shamelessly across his face and wanted to keep his body against hers until satisfaction turned into a burning need that could only be filled by only her. Unfortunately, time was not on their side. If she and Rhane were going to help their children and save the world, they had to get a move on.

"Let's start climbing," she said.

An hour later, both Kali's legs and lungs were burning. On a positive note, she wasn't cold anymore. Tethered to Rhane by a six foot stretch of rope, some leeway was allowed but ultimately she was forced to match his long stride and rhythm as he pushed them near her limits. Across most stretches of the steep landscape, Kali could still walk mostly upright. Other areas were trickier and put her almost on all fours as she scrambled across the mountain's rocky, white-capped surface.

"Are you okay?" Rhane called down in a voice hinting of concern.

"I'm good," she yelled. Kali was hanging onto a precarious ledge, shoulders burning as she pulled herself along a few inches at a time. *This shit is for the birds*, she grumbled inwardly. A span of rock approximately the length of her body stood between her position and the top, aka the next stretch of somewhat flat terrain where she wouldn't have to channel her inner spider monkey so as not to fall to certain death. Digging deep, Kali ignored the pain in her muscles, cramping fingers, and protesting joints to conquer the remaining distance. She grabbed a hold of Rhane's waiting hand and was hoisted onto the plateau where she lay on her back, panting for air.

Rhane's green eyes stared down at her sympathetically. "Only twenty-six thousand more feet to go."

"That's not funny."

"It was a little."

Groaning, she rolled over and pushed to her feet. "What are you doing?" she asked as Rhane unclipped the snap hook from his belt.

"I'm confident enough in your ability here, so you should ride again. It'll be safer to tether you to Orrin now."

Kali was confused. Certainly Rhane wasn't concerned about his ability to control the wolf...at least not around herself and the kin. Banewolf would have all their scents and at least some limited memory of each of them. It would be more than enough to assuage the immortal's thirst for blood. "You're not changing?"

He nodded after only the slightest hint of hesitation. "I am. But I will be constantly scouting behind or ahead.

Someone needs to make sure we're not followed and this route remains a reasonably safe option."

"Okay," she said as Orrin slid his forelegs parallel to the snowy ground. It was the signal to mount. Kali threw one leg over the brown wolf's lowered shoulders and scooted until she straddled almost midway on its back. "Be careful," she said to Rhane.

"Don't worry," he assured her. "I'll be as cautious as only wolves can be."

Moments later, Banewolf stood before them all, blending into the white of the land like a colorless phantom. The enormous wolf moved away from the pack. After Rhane left, Kali didn't physically see him until night fell again, though she could always sense he was there.

Without Rhane, it was a quiet, almost lonesome journey. Beneath her, Orrin, along with the rest of the kin, concentrated on the precarious passage. War skins were hardily designed and virtually indestructible against Warekin enemies, but no one wanted to test what would happen if one of those skins fell ten thousand feet down a mountain. So Kali held on tight and kept to her thoughts so as not to be a distraction.

Reaching the desired altitude only an hour before dusk, the kin shed their outer skins and resumed human form to set up camp once more. Finishing a quick dinner of MRE vegetarian chili, Kali retreated alone to her tent to wait for Rhane's return from the wilderness. Even with the heater, the space seemed so much colder without him.

Midnight had passed when he slipped inside their tent. Kali was dozing, dressed in long thermal underwear that did a good job to ward off the cold, and cocooned in a double-walled sleeping bag. The layers did well to protect her body, but not her mind. Her dreams resembled nightmares. In them the skies burned in hues of orange and grey, set aglow by flames of her making and those of her son. Beneath the atmosphere, the earth was transformed into a desolate landscape, razed of all life and barren of sound except for the wailings of a desperate child. She stirred in her sleep at its voice, mumbled unintelligibly as she called out to it.

When the covers lifted and a wall of heat and hard muscle sidled up next to her, Kali rolled over, but her eyes wouldn't agree to fully open. "Hey," she said sleepily.

Rhane pressed a tender kiss against her forehead. "I'm sorry I woke you."

"It's always okay for you to wake me." Pulling her closer, he captured her mouth and nudged his tongue inside for a brief but intimate kiss.

"Did you find anything interesting out there?" Kali asked once they had parted.

A flicker of hesitation crossed his features. "We're not alone up here."

Propping up on one elbow, she was suddenly wide awake. "Tell me."

"I scouted almost to the top of the pass and encountered some pretty high winds. Complete whiteout, visibility was nearly zero. But I found a camp. At first I thought they were mountaineers trapped by the storm. Then the winds abated and the camp didn't move. It's maybe fifty rogues, and I think they are waiting for us."

Kali groaned. "Maybe Rhaven told them we would help."

"Maybe."

"You think it's an ambush?"

Rhane's expression was carefully blank. "I don't know what to think."

She fought the rising lump in her throat. They couldn't even trust their own children not to try to kill them. How messed up was that?

Probably reading the misery on her face, Rhane kissed her hair. But Kali shook her head. "We've destroyed most of the Builders, but some of them remain. The Faction is working with the rogues, so they're still out there, and these things have proven how powerful they are. If this is another trap, I don't want you getting hurt like before. I can't survive it."

Shifting beneath the covers, Rhane's mouth pressed into a thin line. The poor guy didn't have many memories, and Kali was afraid that all his new ones would be etched in pain. When Rhane finally spoke, his voice had grown noticeably quieter. "We'll just have to keep each other safe," he said.

"I can't keep you safe if you're out there roaming around the mountain all on your own."

He nodded. "Okay. I'll stay close tomorrow, and we will face whatever comes together."

Chapter 15

Taking York and Rion, Rhane soldiered ahead to conduct extra recon. They needed to find out exactly why rogues were on this mountain. A lot of scenarios made sense. It could have been an ambush, or the camp could have been a part of a larger operation further up the mountain. Perhaps the rogues hadn't given up on retrieving the artifact locked behind the blood seals. It was even likely Rhaven had told the rogues of Rhane's impending arrival and attempt to free the keystone for his son's sake.

Whatever their reason for being stationed on the mountain, Rhane thought the best course of action would be to avoid any unexpected encounters. In order to do that, it needed to be determined where the rest of the creatures' numbers were located, and their intended route. As they crossed into the coordinates of the camp's position from the night before, Rhane realized that getting information was going to be a lot harder than he initially thought.

Closing in on the target, but still nearly three hundred yards away, they shifted to human form. Rhane's white wolf had a natural camouflage for the Himalayan landscape, but hiding a brown and particularly large black wolf would have proven too great a challenge. Glancing at Rhane, York fisted both hands at his hips. "Are you sure this is the spot?"

"I'm sure." He stared out at the empty wilderness. There was no trace of any camp...or any sign that anyone or anything had ever been there. "Maybe another storm blew in and covered the site."

York nodded but looked doubtful. "I don't smell any traces."

"They were here, York."

He spread his hands. "Hey, I don't doubt that. You lost your head and pretty much all memory of everything you care about, but your ability as a tracker seems to have remained intact."

Rion shook his head, appalled by York's insensitivity. "Why are you guys friends again?"

"Apparently, he saved my life once," Rhane said, scowling.

"Twice," York corrected. "And I was only suggesting that maybe the Faction—they are Builders after all—used some supernatural trickery to conceal the camp from us."

"It didn't sound like you were going to suggest that."

"You didn't give me time to. You know what they say about assumptions. They make an ass out of you and me." York grinned.

Rhane's frown deepened.

Rion wandered off, following an eastern pass around the mountain side. Rhane had become noticeably more tolerant of many things since returning from their homeland, and York was taking full advantage. Come to think of it, so was Orrin. The insubordinate shit War's twin had pulled lately never would have flown with the old Rhane, at least not for this long.

Picking his way across the trail, a faint noise reached Rion's ear, drawing him closer to the edge. Dropping to his hands and knees, he crawled out onto the precipice and heard the sound again but couldn't see anything to pinpoint its origin. "Crap," he muttered and shimmied out further. In the end he was forced to climb down fifty feet, follow the sound to the end of a second ledge, and then hang by his ankles to find his quarry. What Rion saw sent him scrambling back to Rhane and York as fast as he could.

"Hey guys," he called in an exaggerated whisper. Standing back at the spot where he last saw them, York and Rhane were nowhere in sight. "I found something you need to see."

Almost simultaneously they appeared, each approaching from a different direction.

"What is it?" Rhane asked. Though he didn't quite whisper, he spoke in a cautious volume.

"This way," Rion said and quickly turned, leading them to the ledge.

"Holy shit on a sundae," York softly exclaimed as he peered over and saw what sent Rion running to fetch them. "Is that what I think it is?"

Rhane swore. "Fall back. Now," he ordered.

After making sure they weren't followed, the three of them hightailed down the mountainside, covering their tracks as they went. When he thought they were a safe distance away, Rhane called for a halt. York couldn't stop looking over his shoulder. He was clearly shaken. "How do you think they found us?"

"I don't know," Rhane said. "But they're definitely tracking us somehow."

"You seemed just as surprised. Isn't it the camp you spotted earlier?"

Rhane shook his head. "No. The campsite I saw was inhabited by rogues. This is different."

"First, they shot as us in the graveyard. Got lucky and hit me. Then they turned downtown New York into the

OK Corral while your kid melted our hotel room. Now we're on a freaking mountain top. I don't want to be target practice on a mountain, Rhane. There's nowhere to hide."

"Stop freaking out. That bullet barely hurt you."

"It hurt enough."

"What a sec." Rion snapped his fingers together. "What if that's how they're tracking us?"

York frowned. "What are you talking about, kid?"

"They shot you in the graveyard. What if the bullet had some kind of tracer in it? They must be using you to track us."

"You've been watching too much television."

"C'mon. My theory explains how they showed up again in downtown New York so quickly and especially how they are here now."

Rhane had to give Rion credit. A tracer bullet made sense. "Even if it is true, there's little we can do about it. The bullet is no longer inside of him, so the materials have surely absorbed into York's bloodstream."

"Yeah." Rion scratched his chin. "These mountains and the storm have gotta be affecting the signal. Otherwise those soldiers back there would already be on top of us."

"But this storm isn't going to last forever. So, what do we do about it, smarty-pants?"

Rion shrugged and looked at Rhane, who made a pained expression. "I wouldn't want to say it either."

"What?" York's gaze went back and forth between the two of them. "Say *what*?"

"We're going to have to drain your blood, York."

"No way." His eyes flew wide as he retreated a huge step backward.

"Of course," Rion said, catching on. "It's the best way to remove the tracer. With a few large but precise cuts at several major arteries…what do you think, Rhane?"

"The carotid, femoral, brachial and radials ought to take care of it."

York crossed his arms. "You two are out of your goddamn minds."

Losing it first, Rion doubled over with laughter. Rhane quickly shushed him, fearful the wrong ears might overhear, but let out a soft chuckle of his own. "I'm just messing with you." He slapped York on the back. "Relax."

"Oh if you could have seen your face," Rion said, still grinning from ear to ear.

"Very funny. So what's the real plan?"

"We need to haul ass. Get to the top the mountain and grab what we came for before those freaks find us again. Hopefully the storms up there will disrupt the signal they're using even more."

"This plan kind of sounds like a Hail Mary to me."

"Would you rather revisit the bloodletting?"

York grimaced. "Haul ass it is."

*

The pace he pushed them to was a grueling one, even for war skins. Banewolf climbed just ahead of York's immense black wolf, leading the pack, urging them to be stronger and faster. He glanced over his shoulder. Astride Orrin, Kalista practically held on for dear life. The rock face they ascended was a vertical wall with few footholds. Relying on brute strength and nearly tireless muscles, the skins navigated the cliff, using their power to punch holes into the rock as they climbed, forever reshaping K2's landscape.

Banewolf's heart lost a beat when War's red wolf lost traction and slid twenty feet before finding sure footing again. He whistled to the young kin, eyeing the tremble in his forelegs. *Are you okay?*

War's reply came quickly. *I'm fine.*

Of course you are, Rhane thought. Stubborn and resilient, the twins came from a bloodline sire to a lineage of formidable warriors who didn't quit until the job was done. During a village battle to suppress recurring attacks by a barbarian horde, their grandfather had fought for hours with the business end of a spear wedged deeply inside his chest cavity. Seeing the grave wound, the commander told Alain to stand down and tend his injuries. Alain responded by striking down ten more barbarians and saving the commander's life. At least, that was the way the story was told. Rhane paused for a moment and mulled the thought. The legend must have been an important piece to understanding the twins if the wolf's mind had held onto the memory.

Reaching the next plateau, he didn't think he'd ever felt so happy to feel snow beneath his paws. *We rest here.* At the rate they were ascending K2's peak, they all deserved the respite. He just hoped they could afford it.

Lowering his haunches to the snow, Banewolf watched as each one of them mastered the climb to flatter terrain. When Orrin's wolf reached the plateau, he was surprised to see Kalista sitting astride him with a radiant smile plastered across her face.

Shifting into human form, Rhane immediately wrapped his arms around his torso. Damn, it was cold. So why did she look so oblivious to the sub-freezing temperature? "What is it?" He had to ask.

She held up a hand as if to show him. At first Rhane didn't know what he was looking at, but then he saw colorless waves flowing outward from her palms, and her smile grew even wider. "I figured it out."

Rhane lifted one eyebrow. "Oh yeah? Did you raise your core temperature?"

Nodding, she slid down Orrin's shoulders. The brown wolf began to shrink, retreating in size until only a human form remained. An involuntary shiver moved through his body. "She did one better," he said, making an extra effort to look Rhane in the eye. It wasn't easy. But damn it, at least he was trying. "She externalized her heat, sharing it with me."

"Son of a—" War started, but Kalista's bell-like laughter and a sudden wave of heat startled him enough to leave the rest of the insult forgotten. The air around them grew at least twenty degrees warmer, halting the relentless arctic chill dead in its tracks.

Rion rubbed his hands together and smiled appreciatively. "Okay, that's pretty awesome."

"Well done, Kalista," Rhane added. Everyone's spirits seemed lifted by the cheering warmth called forth at her behest. She was a singular creature, truly unique to a planet of billions.

"Let's rest up here. We can spare an hour."

Yawning, York extended his arms and spine into nice, long stretch. "Great idea," he said and bent his knees to lower himself to a small outcropping. It was the perfect spot to relax until the time came to get moving again. As long as Kali kept doing her thing, he could pretend he was sitting next to a warm campfire. Ever the opportunist, Bailen cuddled up right next to Kali, practically crawling into her lap. York really couldn't blame him though. The poor kid was only half kin and hence slightly on the pickish side with not enough fat on his hide to keep warm in these temperatures.

Everyone else began to settle in. Everyone that is, except for Rhane. He stood next to Kali, his unusual eyes watching York expectantly. *Damn it.* York shifted to a more comfortable position. Maybe he could stall for five minutes…at least give his ass a chance to get cold against the snow. Unfortunately, Rhane's expression of increasing annoyance said otherwise. "Okay. Okay." York stood up. "Where do you need me?"

"We won't go far. I just want to affirm there's good distance between us and the enemy."

"Of course."

Squeezing Kalista's shoulder, Rhane bent his head to kiss her. "We won't be long. I made a promise to you and I intend to keep it."

Color flushed her cheeks. Her fingers gripped his wrist. "Thank you," she whispered.

Wanting to leave no more than York did, Rhane tore himself away. There was a reason the word tireless often preceded the word leader. He didn't think it was because of any active choice on the head honcho's part.

As they left the site, York turned to others, clicked his heels once and saluted. "Stay toasty, my friends."

Rhane grabbed his collar and dragged him backward. "Let's get this over with."

Chapter 16

About one thousand feet from K2's summit, they found the secret entrance to the inside of the mountain and something became crystal clear to Kali. Builders were creatures of habit. Like the doorways to all other locations, this one was also composed of stone and sealed in blood. Only those with the proper DNA would activate the now familiar symbols of an archaic language, glowing bright blue before revealing the passageway to a priceless treasure. She wondered if Builders had always known their ways would lead to this—a fissure in dogma and ultimately two sides battling for wholly opposite ambitions. Why else would they entrust their most precious artifacts with royal bloodlines of the Warekin race? It was no coincidence these doors would open solely for specific genes and that the champions chosen by either side possessed the very DNA needed to unlock them.

There was one glaring difference between this doorway and the rest. Rogues had refused to allow a blood seal to stop them from getting what they wanted.

War fingered the ruined edges of rock, ragged and charred with black burn marks. "It looks they used C4...and lots of it."

"What a crazy thing to do in a place like this." Rion shook his head in disbelief. "The chances of ending up dead from the resulting avalanche or rockslide would have been astronomical."

"Something about this time was different." War's shoulders lifted and dropped. "Maybe there wasn't a nerd on their team to inform them of the risks."

"Just be careful and keep your eyes open." Rhane moved past everyone to step inside the mountain. "This place could have a few surprises of its own."

"I have no doubt," Kali muttered. She couldn't think of one occasion when she'd entered into one of the Builders' strange realms and not received an unpleasant surprise. She was certain that nothing about the coming experience would be different.

Debris covered the bottom of the passage, most of it sourced from surrounding rock. Fragmented boulders and shard-like pebbles lay everywhere she stepped, whereas a fine powder coated the walls and ceiling like a mist of dark silt. But other bits of wreckage had origins of a far more gruesome nature. More than a dozen visible body parts were scattered about. Some were easily identified. Others were merely pieces of tattered flesh, broken bone, or mutilated clothing. Kali tried not to gag as her shoe bumped into a severed arm, bloodied but mostly burned black from the explosion. Her eyes began to water, blurring her vision and almost making her stumble into a pile of unrecognizable fleshy matter. Rhane steadied her shoulder, watching her with an unrelenting gaze until she nodded she was okay.

War, of course, didn't allow the gore to unsettle him at all. Retrieving what appeared to be a long thigh bone from a wedge between two pieces of blood-spattered rock, he lifted the remains to his nose and sniffed. "It's definitely a rogue. And now I'm sure they didn't have a nerd on their team."

"Never mind causing an avalanche. Those idiots didn't leave enough time to clear the blast."

Kali groaned. "Does that mean what I think it does?"

"Yup." War grinned. "We probably just climbed over a graveyard of rogue popsicles and didn't even realize it."

"Don't worry, Kali." Rion offered her a look of sympathy. "There was maybe ten feet of snow between your boots and the nearest corpse."

"How reassuring," she said flatly.

"No sense in concerning yourself with it now." Rhane took her hand. "Just watch your step for the next fifty yards or so."

Kali balked. "Pieces of them are strewn that far?"

"I'm afraid so."

"Ugh."

They couldn't cover ground fast enough to outrun the wave of revulsion clamoring to overtake her. Nausea sat in her gut at first. Then it moved on, bubbling into her chest and up her throat. Her foot slid against something slimy, releasing a stench of decay even her nose couldn't miss. Unable to stand it any longer, Kali gagged. Pushing away from Rhane, she doubled over and released the contents of her stomach onto the cave floor.

They were deep enough in the mountain that daylight didn't reach them. With her weaker eyesight, Kali was basically blind in the darkness. Only Rhane's guidance and following the sound of the others' footsteps had gotten her so far without incident. Stepping in dead rogue wasn't the most horrible thing that could have happened, but for some reason it was enough to send her over the edge. Thinking of the mess clinging to the bottom of her shoe, Kali coughed violently and heaved again. Rhane pulled her hair away from her face and rubbed her back, soothing her.

Feeling like the worst was over, Kali straightened. "I'm sorry."

York's voice called ahead from in the darkness. "It's not your fault, Kali. Rhane could have totally led you around that dead rogue goo. He's just a sadistic bastard."

Ignoring him, she tried taking a step but faltered as her boot slid. Closing her eyes, Kali took a moment to steel her wits. She was not going to puke again. Scrubbing the boot in the dirt until it felt reasonably dry, she started forward again, resolute in stride. "York, sometimes I wonder if your true form is the animal and you're just pretending to be a human being."

"Ouch."

Everyone laughed, including Rhane. "No," York protested. "That really hurts my feelings, Kali."

"I'd say I'm sorry, but I'm not."

"Well the guy next to you is where your adorable little insults should be hurled."

Rhane unloosed an exasperated sigh. "I really didn't see it." He squeezed her hand. "You feel better now?"

"Yeah." Still tasting bitterness on her lips, Kali wiped her mouth again. "I overreacted. It really wasn't that bad." Though he hadn't given the word yet, she risked igniting a tiny flame in the palm of her hand so as to see him. She loved the way he looked in firelight...capable of anything...sexy and dangerous. "Is this alright?"

"It's fine." Rhane angled his left ear toward the cave opening. "Actually, make it brighter," he said. "We need to hurry."

They all started to jog at once, keeping a steady, rhythmic pace that reminded Kali of Roman foot soldiers. Only these warriors were far more deadly and completely silent. No clashing of shields or roar of one hundred thousand marching feet would announce their presence to the enemy.

Dropping back to allow Orrin to run point, York positioned himself slightly ahead of Rhane's flank. He tugged pointedly at the collar of his snow suit. "It's getting warmer in here. Kali, are you doing that?"

"It's not me."

"Great," he said, putting enough bleakness into one word to set her nerves in a state of unease. And he wasn't done. York lowered his voice. "I can't shake the feeling we've got a serious fight coming to us soon."

Rhane looked about as grim as York sounded. "We've been headed toward this since the moment Kalista and I first reunited. But I understand your meaning. We'll face it together."

"I know we will, buddy." Glancing around at the others, York leveled a serious gaze at Rhane and smiled sadly. "But we may not all survive this one."

Rhane opened his mouth to respond just as the tunnel unexpectedly changed directions, but Orrin's shout startled them all. "*Stop!*" he bellowed. One word communicated all the urgency and fear of what he had encountered but the rest of them had yet to see. "*Go back,*" he yelled. "Quickly!" They obeyed his initial instruction, ceasing all forward progress, but without seeing him, Kali and the others could not possibly retreat.

Moving past all of them, Rhane crept forward, and Kali stuck close to his heels. Rhane turned at once, eyes narrowed and shoulders tensed. For a moment she thought he would tell her to stay. Then his gaze shifted past her. "Wait here," he commanded the others.

What they witnessed around the bend surpassed, in Kali's mind, every other environment fabricated by Builders. It also explained the spike in temperature.

Hollowed out except for hundreds, maybe thousands, of tiny protrusions too small to be called pedestals, the center of the mountain was all but engulfed by the fires of hell. Orange and black flames rose from depths of three hundred feet or more, far deeper than Kali's eyes could see. Encircling the vast pit was an extension of the trail, severely deteriorated and crumbling to give way beneath their feet even as Kali and Rhane approached the jutted protrusion onto which Orrin frantically clung. Each time he attempted to pull himself up, the ledge only disintegrated more, turning to ash under his fingertips and refusing to sustain his weight. Every effort to save himself only deposited him deeper into the furnace.

Looking down, Kali noticed black fissures snaking out like spider webs of cracked glass within Rhane's footprints. The cracks worsened, turning solid rock to powder as Rhane walked. Screaming for him to stop, she leapt from the trail behind him and sought sturdier footing further up the path. Shaking, Kali looked down again. The ground appeared to hold.

Rhane watched her with wide eyes, frozen in his tracks and still about twenty-five feet from reaching Orrin. Sweat beaded across his forehead and dampened his collar. It wasn't because of adrenaline. In seconds, the atmosphere had grown unmistakably hotter and yet the temperature was still rising.

And then even as she watched, the worst thing began to happen. Rhane started to sink.

"Rhane," Kali pleaded. "Go back."

He shook his head. "I can't leave him."

"You can't reach him. The ground won't hold." The dull groan of shearing rock echoed throughout the cavern as if the very mountain were in agreement. Then the earth where Rhane stood buckled, dropping another six inches. He jumped backward, seeking firmer ground, but even there the rock started to crumble beneath his feet.

Maybe it was despair or subliminal observation inspiring the theory in Kali's brain but she saw no other choice but to enact it. Orrin's life depended on it. Holding her breath, she took another step forward. When the ground didn't budge, Kali leapt to the edge of the rock face with Rhane's screams to stop pounding against her eardrums. Scrambling farther forward, she slid onto her belly and scuttled downward, hanging onto the ledge with muscles she didn't know existed. She grasped Orrin's hand just as the rocks beneath him gave way again, staying his fall but unable to hoist him upward. Strangely, there was no fear in Orrin's stoic expression. Either he possessed an extreme confidence in her ability to deliver him from tragedy or Orrin was unnervingly primed for his own death.

Squeezing tight enough to break his fingers (were that possible), Kali leveraged against the rock and called up to Rhane. Currently yelling some unintelligible threat, he quieted at the sound of her voice. "Rhane, I have Orrin! Send Bailen to me!"

Rhane sounded confused. "What? The ground is falling apart, Kalista!"

"Send him now!"

"Kalista—" Rhane began but stopped and muttered another curse. "He's here. *Hurry.*"

Though he didn't appear to need it, Kali took a moment to reassure Orrin. "It's okay. We're going to get you out of this."

Orrin smiled. "The ground does not shift beneath you."

She winked at him. "Yeah. I noticed."

"Kalista!" Rhane shouted.

She shook her head. "He's really freaking out."

Orrin grimaced. "Perhaps you should hurry."

"Bailen," Kali called. She tried to sound persuasive and embody in her tone the confidence she felt. "I need you to be human right now. This mountain will yield to the siren within you. But you gotta be human." Receiving no answer, Kali closed her eyes and silently prayed the kid's stubborn side wouldn't rear its ugly head in this moment.

"I am here, *uskai.*"

Relief poured through her at the sound of Bailen's cool tenor. "Thank you, Bailen. Can you climb down for me?"

He descended without hesitation, reaching them in no time at all. Naked except for thin linen trousers, Kali could see every muscle in his lithe torso straining as he took hold of Orrin's opposite hand and begin to pull the larger kin upward. Together, they brought him back from the brink. "Don't let go of us," Kali instructed just before stepping once more onto the compromised passageway. "And move quickly."

Relief shadowed Rhane's features on catching sight of them. Taking a proper cue from their movements, he wasted no more time retreating deeper into the mountain corridor. There the others waited restlessly with War showing significantly more distress than the others. Sympathizing, Kali took his hand and gave it a light squeeze. It had been a close one.

"We can't stay here," York said to Rhane. "Company is on its way."

"Do you refer to rogues or the fire," Bailen questioned calmly. Before anyone could ask what he meant, the boy pointed, drawing their attention to the wall of flames surging straight toward them. "The mountain does not want us here."

"Welcome to the treasure hunt kid," York said as they turned and ran. "Builders are bitchy like that."

Back the way they came, an inferno of deep reds and gold had risen up, engulfing the ceiling and walls of the tunnel entrance. Kali licked her lips. "Rhane," she said nervously.

"We'll be fine," he said with more calmness than Kali was sure he actually felt. Then Rhane called ahead to Orrin who, despite the recent brush with death, bravely insisted on continuing at point. "To the right! A new passage has opened."

"I see it," Orrin answered tightly.

Behind them fire nipped at their heels. The heat grew more intense, becoming evident now even to Kali. They entered the new tunnel but it was only prolonging the inevitable. This mountain wouldn't rest until they were all turned to ash.

The route narrowed, constricting until they were forced to run single file. Light from the pursuing inferno illuminated the rock walls and ceiling in an eerie dark orange glow. One thousand feet later, the passage suddenly expanded into an open cavern nearly the size of a football field. And Kali couldn't see a way out.

"There's an exit about twenty feet above ground," Rhane said as if reading her thoughts.

"That's going to be a tight fit," York yelled.

As they drew closer, she realized he was right. This opening was even smaller than the last tunnel. Standing upright would be impossible. The kin would have to crawl through one by one. *They'll never make it.*

Reaching the bottom of the wall, she turned to watch the fire approach. Rhane grabbed her arm. "Kalista, you need to go."

"No," she said as firmly as she could. "Fire won't hurt me."

"That fire was designed by Builders. We don't know what it can do, and we don't have time to argue about it."

Letting her gaze wander to the others, she met each of their intense stares of varying degrees of apprehension. "Please go," she whispered. Then extending her right hand into the air, she lifted her arm and called to the fires within her. Warmth built inside her core, traveling to her extremities where it burned hotter and brighter. Kali released the store of energy, commanding, "*Orrece*," to the mountain fire. The blaze faltered, slowing to a halt as it flickered through a cycle of lighter colors. She dared a look over her shoulder and saw the kin were climbing up the wall, escaping through the tiny passageway. But only two of them were through. They needed more time.

When Kali looked back, the flames had darkened. Only tiny flecks of red dotted a wall of almost completely black. The fire roared, and the sound filled the cavern, echoing with the vengeance of a beast from the underworld. Kali's resolve stood fast, though she briefly wondered if Rhane had been correct about the origins of these fires and its ability to harm her. However, there was little time for second guesses. As often as Rhane and the others had stood on the front lines to shelter her, Kali was more than ready to return the favor. Rhane and the others didn't often need protection. But this…this was something she could actually save them from.

Unleashing a second howl more terrible than the first, the inferno surged forward to destroy them. Lifting her arms higher, Kali held her ground. The burning wall would not move past her. *"Ejo juloute bevando,"* she commanded. *"Gallay niema verdus."*

The fire again slowed, but Kali felt resistance lashing against her mind. She realized the fire wasn't just some inanimate force raging unchecked throughout the bellows of the mountain. No, this was a living and thinking entity, undoubtedly another abomination created by Builders.

"Gallay neima verdus. Gallay neima verdus," she repeated, willing the command to hold. The creature lashed out and Kali pushed back, hammering down obstinacy. *"Neima verdus."*

Liquid oozed from one nostril, trailing thickly onto her lips and Kali tasted blood. Her blood. The fire screamed but its fight weakened. She checked on the kin. Only Bailen, Orrin, and Rhane had yet to escape the cavern. Three red tendrils erupted from the dark mass and lashed out, striking at Kali's dark energy. Strong enough to hold the first two, the third projection snaked through and snapped like a whip as it lashed across her face. Blackness flashed through her vision even as the pain rocked through her skull. Dropping to her knees, Kali took a deep, painful breath.

Behind her, she heard arguing. Orrin sounded angry. "We shouldn't leave her."

Bailen yelled, "Go! The longer you stay, the longer she has to fight it."

And Rhane's voice cut above them all. "If it's alive, then we can kill it."

A throaty hiss vibrated through her chest, sounded in her ears like the song of fifty vipers. Anger warmed her blood, electrified her arms, traveling into hands and fingertips where grey scales now covered her skin. Black nails elongated, gouging the rock with their length. Her tongue slid oddly against sharpened teeth when she spoke, and Kali could not even recognize the voice. "*I said leave,*" she hissed to the others.

Kali flashed to her feet in a single movement. Dropping her hands to both sides, her entire body became engulfed in flames. *"Ejo juloute ome starres!"* she screamed, igniting the surrounding aura even brighter.

She poured her fires into the creature, enveloping the black and red conflagration with her grey flames. The next howl emitted by the creature betrayed its fear, and the siren answered with its own song, an awful wailing noise that raked through the mountain like metal grinding stone to dust. When the creature tried to flee, Kali tightened the circle around it and intensified the heat, making the very ground glow orange as it liquefied and pooled into magma.

Then the howl stopped. The mountain's fire was snuffed out, and she could no longer feel the presence of the entity. The creature was gone.

Gradually, Kali relaxed. She stared down at her hands. The flesh there was still covered in scales, more reptilian than human. Long claws took shape where fingernails should have been. Touching her face, she gasped. More scales. Barely-there lips and long, thin teeth ended in rigid peaks capable of making a Great White proud.

"Oh my god," Kali whispered. She stared at her monstrous claws, begging them to change back, to become human again, but nothing happened. Kali moaned. Her hands began to shake.

Strong arms slid around her, pulling her irresistibly against a familiar solid warmth. "It's alright," Rhane's voice soothed her. "Everyone made it out. Thank you."

Spinning around, Kali hid her face in his chest but pressed closer to him. Were it possible to crawl into his skin, she would have.

"Don't hide from me, Kalista." His voice remained gentle, yet firm.

"I don't want you to see me like this." Muffled by Rhane's shirt, her voice sounded closer to normal.

"Seeing the part of you that stays hidden from the rest of the world makes me treasure you even more."

Sighing, Kali relented. She could never deny Rhane for long of anything he asked, especially when he said all the right things. "Happy now," she asked, shrugging her shoulders in defeat.

Rhane replied by kissing her. One hand gently held her face while his mouth carefully worked against hers. Afraid the three rows of razor sharp teeth currently in her mouth would cut him, Kali was afraid to kiss him back. But Rhane persisted. He tenderly explored her mouth with his tongue. Taking his time, he covered each lip with lingering kisses. She eventually relaxed beneath his passion and certainty, succumbing to the moment and feeling her love for him grow with every passing second he dared embrace such a hideous monster.

Ending the kiss, Rhane pulled away and tangled his hand in her hair. He was grinning like an idiot. "What?" Kali asked, wondering what he could possibly be so excited about. Warekin had a somewhat useful habit of brushing off near-death experiences way more quickly than what could be considered normal. She was willing to bet psychology journals would have a field day with any one of them.

"See for yourself," he said and held up her hand.

Rhane's smile immediately became contagious. Her flesh appeared human again. Kali touched her face and teeth. All were normal. Exhaling a huge sigh, she laughed. "Thank you."

"No need to thank me. You only needed to relax." He tugged at one of her curls. "And accept who you are."

Kali snorted. "Yeah, a monster."

"We're all monsters."

"Well, when you put it that way…" Thinking back, she frowned and punched him in the arm. He didn't react at all. It may as well have been a fly that hit him. "I told you to leave. You didn't listen to me. You didn't think I could handle that thing, did you?"

"I crossed to the other side to make sure the others were safe and then came back. I know you can take of yourself. In the past year, you've grown tremendously. Today marks the first time you've changed willingly and not because you lost control. Kalista, you're so much stronger than before." Unreserved praise did wonders to help banish the mild irritation she felt and Rhane took advantage. Leaning forward, he kissed her forehead and stroked her cheek. "But I will never be able to leave you behind. *Je 'liefimo, Eefmeri amala,"* he whispered.

166

She didn't understand, but the words filled her with warmth. Even if Rhane had never said "I love you," she felt his love always. "What does it mean?"

Rhane shook his head slightly. "Perhaps one day it will come to you."

And just like that, she wanted to punch him again. Kali groaned. "That's so not fair."

"You can hit me again if you like."

She considered for a moment and then laughed. "Let's get out of here." Jogging toward the tunnel exit, two sharp pangs drove through her side and nearly stopped Kali in her tracks. Hearing her sharp intake of breath, Rhane was instantly at her side. "What is it? What's wrong?"

"Nothing." Kali pulled away from him. "I'm fine," she lied. "I just need to eat, that's all."

"Okay," Rhane said but didn't seem quite convinced. "Human food or me food?"

She laughed to cover her fear. "Maybe I'll have a little taste of both."

Chapter 17

Witnessing the look of astonishment on Kalista's face as she crawled from the narrow passageway had momentarily made Rhane forget the squeezing panic of the walls and ceiling closing in from all sides. If he had to inch through that tiny space one more time, there was no guarantee he wouldn't lose his mind. At least now the overhead cloud cover helped that feeling go away almost entirely. Yep, clouds.

When he and the others initially crossed over, the freak storm was only in the beginning stages of formation. The electricity before a storm was felt in the atmosphere, tingling across his skin, lifting tiny hairs erect. A slight breeze circulated the scents of a thousand different species living in a dense forest in the valley below. Nothing escaped the fine mist covering it all. It was a chilling contrast to the hellish monster they ran from.

But when Rhane returned with Kalista, it was a different picture. A full blown thunderstorm was in effect. Buckets of rain fell from impenetrable dark clouds forming an ominous blanket across the ceiling. The valley forest was hardly visible. Flashes of lightning illuminated the eerie scene in finite intervals.

The seven of them stood beneath the shelter of a ledge overlooking the gorge. It was up to Rhane to give the go ahead, but he wasn't sure he wanted to. The power of the storm limited the kin's senses. It was impossible to hear over the storm or determine exactly what sort of life forms awaited them below. After being chased by a wall of fire that turned out to be a living entity, Rhane was sore for more surprises. Kalista had destroyed the volatile inferno, so maybe backtracking was safer. There could be another route, a safer way of reaching what they sought.

York squinted at Rhane through the next flash of lightning. "A shilling for your thoughts?"

"Well," Rhane started. "It's a nice change from the hell behind us."

"And the cold before that," Rion added.

"I sense a 'but' coming," York said.

"I don't like it." Rhane moved away from the ledge and deeper into the shadows. The rain started to blow even harder, spraying them with hard droplets. "This place was utterly different when we first came through. And now look. With the rain and wind, we're going in there blind."

Nodding thoughtfully, York scratched his chin. Rion supplied information that only increased Rhane's apprehension, but also made it impossible not to proceed. "The storm started only minutes after we arrived. It's like the mountain senses our presence."

"Yeah," War agreed. "But is it telling us to go forward or back?"

As much as he hated it, Rhane knew the answer to War's question. "Forward," he said and stared grimly into the dim forest knowing something far more terrible awaited within it. "We have to go forward."

York eyed him warily. "You don't sound happy about it."

"That's because I'm not." He surveyed the area beneath the overhang and began unzipping his snow suit. "Here is as good a place as any to stash some of our gear. Load up the essentials into two packs. We'll carry those with us in case we can't double back."

As everyone else was getting comfortable, Bailen took that as his cue to resume to a four-legged appearance. Rhane didn't blame him. The skin was a weapon and the first line of defense against whatever came next. Plus, each time Bailen stayed human for any extended period of time, it was hard not to miss that he was aging. Living in canine form 24/7 had essentially cocooned him from the aging process. Though close to Rion's age in years, Bailen had the appearance of a boy at least ten cycles younger. Still, to a human eye, the kid could yet pass for sixteen. Rhane hoped that since finding his family (though a happy reunion eluded them), Bailen had made peace with the inevitable process of maturing to his true age. Otherwise, he and Kalista would have to reinvent the suburban family with a family dog sitting alongside the family dragon.

Noticing not for the first time how Kalista was unusually quiet, Rhane slid over to stand alongside her while the others finished making preparation. "Did you feed enough?"

"The scratches on your arm should answer your question," she said without looking at him.

His fingers reflexively went to the raised marks slashed across both forearms where Kalista had fed just before they started the climb to the open tunnel. The process had been pretty rough, but the cuts were mostly healed and no longer hurt. "That wasn't exactly a yes."

"It wasn't a no either," she replied testily. Seeming to catch the hardness in her tone, she finally met his concerned gaze. "I'm sorry. I'm just tired, and I don't want you focused on me instead of what's out there. I promise I'm okay. When the next fire-breathing monster comes along, I'll kick its ass too."

From the set of her mouth and the way she stood with one hand at her hip, Rhane could tell she meant to make good on her threat. He couldn't help being turned on by that. Perhaps she had always been powerful enough, but now Kalista was even more dangerous after gaining confidence in her abilities. He couldn't thank York and the others enough for the role they'd played in her training while he was imprisoned in Golden Mountain. Her skills had grown immensely. Evidence of the fact was plain to see. She neared the level of ability in his oldest memories of her.

The others were not quite done sorting the gear, so Rhane stepped closer to Kalista and let one hand slowly roam to her ass. The hope of stealing a quick kiss evaporated at the sound of York's voice. "Oh come on," he complained loudly. "We turn away for five seconds and you two are all over each other. Rhane, you're like a horny teenager. You realize this is a serious mission, right?"

Rolling his eyes, Rhane leaned in and kissed her anyway, drowning in the smell of her skin and the feel of her body against his. Breasts and thighs squashed into him, and he wondered if he could ever get enough. York cleared his throat, no doubt to sling another insult, but Rhane headed him off, extending his middle finger for his friend's benefit even as he continued to kiss his mate.

"That's mature," York grumbled.

Finally releasing Kalista and pleased to see a lusty smile spread across her face, Rhane turned to York and grinned. "You only live once."

"Bullshit," York said and tossed Rhane his sword. "You died last year, so technically this is your second go round, pops."

"You're beginning to sound bitter." Rhane deftly strapped the weapon across his shoulder blades. "When this is all over, I want you to get out there and find someone."

"Oh, he already did," Rion said, and York's eyes began to bulge out of his head. Rion knew York didn't want him to reveal the next part, but it was too good not to tell. "He and Cixi have been banging like rabbits for a couple of months now."

War's face went from shocked to grossed out. "Eww," he said. "Sloppy seconds, man. Raise the bar."

Orrin coughed and cleared his throat. "Or thirds."

"Shut up, both of you," York growled. More embarrassed than angry, it took an extra effort to meet Rhane's gaze.

Really, it was a double-edged sword. On the one hand, having York's attention (if not his affection) directed toward the kindred beta would in theory alleviate the scorn Cixi threw in Rhane's direction anytime the two were in the same vicinity. Then again, York being involved with Cixi meant her visits to the manor could be much more plentiful. Rhane winced. Maybe things didn't balance out after all.

"We really should get moving," he said and stepped out into the rain.

The trek down into the valley wasn't easy, but it was quick. Plant species none of them recognized grew in stalks as tall as trees. Leaves the size of umbrellas clustered together to form dark red and green canopies, providing brief intervals of shelter from the drenching rain. Something about the ground felt terribly wrong; Rhane noticed the moment his boots sank into it. Each time lightning flashed, he made an attempt to examine what was beneath their feet but couldn't readily make out what was extraordinary. Slowly and quietly, he drew Bellefuron.

Already vigilant, everyone switched to red alert.

The crowded foliage made it difficult to see more than a few yards ahead. The pouring rain made it impossible. Rhane hated this place. And when their feet sank into ankle deep water, he loathed it even more.

Difficulties aside, their progress was steady and uneventful. Then the ground shifted, Orrin's sharp whistle signaled immediate danger, and everything changed in an instant.

"Skins!" Rhane yelled as the earth rose up and shook them off.

The first to complete his transformation, War dug his claws into the rising beast and held on, dangling thirty feet in the air while mud, rock, and putrid organic matter sloughed off a marbled hide. A foul smell exploded into the air. So powerful, it bled into Rhane's mouth and left the taste of decay on his tongue.

The next strike of lightning allowed a clear picture of the nightmare they faced. The creature was immense. Shaped like a giant earthworm, its girth easily measured twenty feet in diameter. The heavy tonnage of its body sank into the mud, making loud sucking noises each time it raised up. Rhane couldn't begin to guess the extent of the creature's true size. Thirty feet of rotund and slime-coated hide appeared above the surface, shuddering and shedding debris with every movement.

With the light Rhane realized what he thought to be mud was actually excretions from the creature mixed with earth, enriched by decomposed matter of unknown origins. The thick ooze actually repelled water but adhered to anything else that touched it, including Rhane's shoes and the lower half of his jeans.

As he moved to check on Kalista, the colossal worm rolled sideways and crashed its girth into the ground. Only quick reflexes kept them from being squashed. Rhane rolled away and then back, attacking the white and green hide with Bellefuron. The blade split the ribbed flesh wide open, and a slew of dark sludge spewed from the wound. Overwhelmed by the stench, he gagged and moved quickly to duck the worm's enraged retaliation as it swung what looked like a tail.

Thinking it better to ditch the rodeo, War slid from the worm's back, streaking a runway of claw marks from where more foul-smelling liquid spilled. His paws landed in the sludgy mixture of worm slime and dirt. The wolf sank but not as deeply due to the wide spread of its feet.

Rhane's voice shouted above the storm, telling them to fall back and hold. War happily obeyed. Having four feet buried in nasty compost was bad enough. He was nowhere near ready to put his mouth on that thing. He was curious, though, as to why they weren't attacking. And then he saw what Rhane must have.

Already healing from the wounds inflicted by his claws and Rhane's blade, the creature whipped the protruding part of its body back and forth almost lethargically. With one great and final shudder, it released more of god knows what into the weird mixture beneath their feet. And then the worm-like monster grew still.

"Is it dead?" Kalista asked.

"No," Rhane answered. "I hear its hearts beating below ground."

"So it wasn't trying to eat us."

"I think it was reacting rather than attacking. And I think we will meet more of these things along the way." Raising his voice over the raging storm to ensure the order was heard, he said, "From here on out, we do not fight these things. Stay close and do not engage when another rises."

Certain his command was received and understood, Rhane headed the formation on a march through the unnatural ecosystem. He listened to the hundreds of heartbeats vibrating beneath their feet and felt the flow of energy moving between the creatures in electrostatic waves that caused hairs to bristle from his skin. The worms were talking, and he had no idea what they were saying.

For the level of threat they faced, leading as Banewolf wasn't practical. It would be like using a sledgehammer to kill cockroaches. Besides, even when speaking skin to skin their language was a limited one. Communicating with someone not of Warekin bloodlines, while not impossible, was even trickier. In human form, Rhane could speak freely with both Kalista and the others, but if he were to also transform, she might miss a lifesaving warning. Within this mountain—and especially within this strange jungle—there were just too many variables to risk it. He and Kalista would have to protect each other, just as they had agreed.

York's huge black wolf whistled softly. *This place gives me the creeps.*

All of them were jumpy, but Rion's wolf seemed especially unsettled. *I feel them talking.*

"Settle down," Rhane said, trying to calm them all. "I feel them too. But right now, they are just talking."

"What?" Kali whispered, only able to hear catches of conversation. "Who's talking?"

"The worms," he answered, unable to filter the grimness from his voice.

She inhaled softly but did not comment further. Brave Kalista. Even now he smelled very little fear on her.

Walking another three hundred yards, they were forced to stop when a large body of glowing liquid, extending as far as they could see, barred further progress. Rion padded closer to the edge of the pool's surface. Naturally more curious than the others, his love for matters of science would always overrule whatever fear he felt. Using both nose and tongue, he tested the substance. The rain immediately stopped, causing everyone's eyes to roll upward.

Still studying the sky, Rion's wolf whistled his findings. *The liquid is not water. More acidic than neutral but harmless.*

Scout another way? War's russet wolf suggested, already searching the darkness.

I repeat. Harmless.

Sorry. I heard acid. The red wolf looked back at Rhane. *Scout another way?*

The unease in Rhane's gut thickened. He was apprehensive to enter the strange pool, but the idea of separating scared him more. "No. We stay together and swim across."

As soon as their feet touched the cool liquid, it began to change, transitioning from a translucent blue into a kaleidoscope of vibrant colors originating from the area around their bodies and flowing outward. "Wow," Kalista breathed. "It's beautiful."

The vise around Rhane's chest squeezed tighter. Several minutes into the swim, the pool grew much colder than when they first started and the pretty patterns accompanying their movements began to fade as the fluid darkened.

Settled in an easy freestyle just to his left, Kalista's smile didn't waver, but now the expression appeared slightly forced. "The color looks like we're swimming through molten rubies."

"Or blood," Rhane muttered.

"I was trying to think positive."

He winced. "Thanks."

Ten minutes passed and the pool was even colder and darker with a surface the color of deep burgundy. The liquid still glowed, eerily casting a red light across the kin's bodies and Kalista's face. Rhane repeatedly told himself to relax, but with no end in sight, that was difficult to do. It was if they'd begun an indefinite swim across a blood ocean.

The temperature plummeted another twenty degrees and Rhane started to shiver. Protected by their skins from such extreme temperatures, the others didn't notice the cold. The passage of time, however, did not escape them. York was the first to acknowledge it. *How long have we been swimming? Feels like hours.*

Rhane checked his watch. "Twenty-three minutes," he said and could barely stop his teeth from chattering as he spoke. "Kalista, how bright can you make it in here?"

"How bright do you need it?"

"I want to see if this will be over soon."

She nodded, giving him a look of sympathy that made him feel pathetic. He knew it wasn't her intent. The embarrassment he felt was his own fault.

Speaking in her native tongue, Kalista raised her hands while they all tread water. A grey globe the size of a small melon formed within her palms. Softly chanting a few more words, the ball of fire grew, expanding to a mass three times its original size before Kalista launched it up into the atmosphere. Thirty feet above their heads, she called to it again and the fire obeyed her command, breaking apart to disperse across the sky. Everything in the fire's path was illuminated, at last bringing lasting light to deep darkness.

Rhane's gaze followed the trail of flames expectantly. "There!" He pointed. Solid ground was less than a mile away. After that, their strokes came with renewed vigor, but the matter surrounding them thickened and chilled, resisting their efforts. It was like swimming through a giant vat of honey, and now the cold had intensified enough for even the skins to notice.

One by one, the kin emerged from the pool and stumbled onto shore. Rhane and Kalista followed, collapsing onto the dirt into shaking heaps of exhaustion. To Rhane it felt as if the cold has reached inside his skin and gripped his bones with fingers made of ice. His extremities were achingly numb. The only feeling from them was sharp stabs of pain, assuring him he was still very much alive but in a physical state of hell.

Rolling to his side, he noticed Kalista making a sluggish attempt to push to her hands and knees. *Get up*, Rhane told himself. *Get up.* He needed to go to her. Climbing to his feet with some very confused nerve endings screaming in protest, Rhane took one step and toppled forward. Good thing York was there to save his face from hitting the ground.

"Take it easy, buddy. I suggest you bring your body temp up before making any more sudden moves."

"I'm fine," Rhane managed, amazed by how slurred his speech sounded.

York frowned. "Clearly not."

He looks like a zombie. A very blue zombie, someone commented. More disoriented than he realized, Rhane couldn't immediately identify if it was Rion or War. He shook his head. "Kalista?"

"She's okay. She didn't get cold, just fatigued."

Lending proof to York's words, Kalista walked toward them, assisted by Orrin. One hand held a firm grip on his brown fur. "Sit him down," she said with enough authority to make Rhane proud.

York obediently lowered him to the ground and Kalista knelt beside him. She placed one hand on his chest and Rhane was shocked at how warm it was. The heat slowly spread throughout his body, reviving damaged organs and awakening numbed appendages. Cell by cell, the cold was driven out by her internal fires.

"Nice job, Kali," York said, sounding relieved. "He looks alive again."

Right on time, War whistled. *Heads up.*

This time Rhane got to his feet and stayed there. He was still a little groggy, as if waking from a long sleep, but other than that felt one hundred percent. Spotting the reason for War's warning, Rhane felt a renewed surge of gratitude for Kalista's healing touch.

"Re-harness your skin," he said quietly, without taking his eyes from the figure walking toward them across the pool whose surface had frozen solid.

"No argument there."

If not for his purple beard and matching irises, the approaching creature could have passed for human from the neck up. He was dressed simply. But the sheer materials did little to hide the odd glow and texture of the skin beneath. Rhane could think of no better way to describe it other than his flesh looked as if it had been embedded with thousands, or even millions, of radiant diamonds.

Hands so thin they appeared skeletal came together three times. "Well done," the creature said. It stopped within thirty yards of their position and studied them from the pool's icy surface. "You have come farther than most others before you."

Bailen's steady growl intensified. Rhane held up a hand to quiet him. The last thing he needed was for anyone to jump the gun. "Who are you?" Rhane asked. He resisted the urge to draw his sword. So far, the creature had given no reason to display aggression.

The creature lifted his chin. "I am Alister," he said simply.

"Are you a Builder?"

"I am not."

Rhane narrowed his eyes. "Then what are you?"

181

"You will know what I am when the time is right. For now, only see me as the guardian of all that is around you. This mountain is my home. These creatures are my experiments."

Sounds pretty Builder-ish to me. "You've been busy," he said aloud.

Kalista stepped up alongside Rhane. She clearly wasn't fond of this thing and wasn't going to hide it. "If you're not one of them, then why is your home one of the coordinates encoded in the map? One of the artifacts is hidden here."

Alister smiled. It wasn't a friendly one.

Kalista returned the expression with equal hostility. Rhane tried not to stare at her teeth as he wondered when she had learned to isolate transformations of different body parts.

Likely recognizing a silent impasse, the old creature acceded, though the answer he gave was opaque. "Because no place is more secure," he said. Alister spread his arms wide. "Something is hidden here, and my creations are a natural roadblock to those who would take it."

"Nothing about this place is natural," Kalista snapped.

Since pretty much everyone looked ready to rip this guy's throat out, Rhane committed himself to remaining calm and diplomatic. "If you're not a Builder, then you're not a part of the Faction either. Who do you fight for?"

"I do not fight, Rhane of Whytetree. I am simply an observer."

"But you know about the artifacts, so you must know what's happening. Rogues are ruled by madness, and the Faction's endgame will bring ruin to this planet. This world does not deserve what will happen if they succeed."

The creature seemed unmoved, except his diamond skin glowed brighter as he spoke. "Blight will rise. Your actions have made its awakening inevitable."

"Then help me kill it."

"Why would I help you destroy a beautiful creation, one meant to bring balance to all worlds…those which are and those yet to be?"

"I've seen the true history of the races. Somewhere along the way, we all became stranded here on Earth with a creature that could no longer be controlled. Trapped here, Blight cannot bring balance. It will only bring ruin." Rhane looked around the habitat pointedly, taking in the oddities Alister considered a home. "You don't want that."

"Wisely stated." Alister paced a few steps and stopped. "When a Builder dies, I feel its death. Imagine the agony I endured as you slaughtered them, as you destroyed the very ones who stood on your side and shared your cause. Why would I help such a monster?"

"It wasn't slaughter," Kalista said hotly. "It was self-defense. They were trying to kill him."

Alister narrowed his lavender eyes. "And you should have let them. Either of your sons would make a stronger vessel for the immortal which inexplicably clings to you."

Tired of the debate and wary of Kalista's temper, Rhane cut straight to the point. "There is no neutrality in this war. If you do not stand with us," he drew Bellefuron from its scabbard and the metal blade rang out eagerly, echoing strangely across the frozen lake, "then you are against us," Rhane finished. "Prove yourself friend or foe. If Blight cannot be stopped, then tell me how to kill it."

Alister stared at the shining blade with a mixture of dread and greed. At last, he answered. "Even Builders, with all of their power, could not destroy the evil that is Blight." The frightening expression Alister would have probably called a smile spread across the creature's face again. "Though, they broke several rules by trying."

"You're not telling me anything new, Alister. Builders are not allowed to destroy. Only create."

"You misunderstand, Banewolf. After the first culling—on a different world, one far away from this Earth—Builders realized their mistake. Most were willing to go against the sanctions placed upon them and sacrificed many, many years of life in an ill-fated attempt to annihilate the abomination spawned by their own ungodly ambition. And yet Blight lived. Absorbing the very energy used in trying to destroy it, Blight grew stronger. Its next culling was worse than the one before it. In all their strength, Builders could not defeat it then. How can you in all your weakness defeat it now?"

"You call us weak, but we were strong enough to kill the Builders. You felt their deaths, Alister. Do even ten of them remain?"

The glow beneath the robes darkened though the creature's face remained serene. "No," he said thickly.

"Then I need an answer from you."

"Blight has few weaknesses. One of them is fire." Alister rested a piercing gaze upon Kalista. "I see why they thought you could be the answer. But he will absorb you, child, and steal every ounce of your life force before you ever have any chance of killing it."

"Thanks," Rhane said and started to back away. "We'll work with that."

Alister called out as the other kin and Kalista followed. "Where do you venture now?"

"I think you know what we really came for."

"You mean this?" A glimmering blue stone appeared within the creature's palm. Without warning, Alister tossed the artifact high into the air. Arcing, it fell right into Rhane's hand. He looked down at the keystone and then up at Alister with open disbelief.

"I don't understand," Rhane said.

"I am choosing a side." The pool's surface began to change, liquefying to resemble the matter they'd initially encountered. Alister sank into it, slowly disappearing from sight. "Save them from what comes next, and perhaps there is hope for all."

Chapter 18

Finally comprehending the reasons behind Rhane's hesitation to enter the valley, Kali suspected everyone else now understood his apprehension too. It had only taken ten seconds for chaos to erupt.

The downpour fell harder than before, dragging visibility down to zero. Nonstop thunder rumbled like clashing titans. Vibrations rocked through Kali's bones and rattled her teeth. Lightning left the sky to snake beneath their feet, hissing and snapping as it crackled through the ground, seeming to shift the entire habitat. Kali struggled to stay upright as the strange being disappeared from sight, sinking into the lake from which he had arisen. But there was little time to focus on him or his warning because a new peril had materialized in the horizon. A hide of grayish white rose from the red liquid, expanding and growing at an alarming rate. Even more frightening were the fingers of electricity spreading across the creature's skin like a web of energy. When the gigantic form finally unfolded, it reached clear into the clouds. The head wasn't visible, but what they could see was fifty feet of the monster's body and neck. Any legs, if they existed, remained beneath the water. Currents moved all across its skin, evaporating liquid wherever the electricity met the water. The effect was a cloud of vapors that hovered around the monstrosity, billowing up as far as its chest.

Rhane shouted above the cacophony of successive lightning strikes, ordering the kin to retreat, but more bolts exploded from the sky, striking all around to form a circle of blinding light. Surrounded, escape was impossible. This monster would have to die first.

Kali looked at Rhane. He stood braced against the storm, sword held in mid-guard. Defiant and pissed, he looked more than ready to face this new demon. It was funny how the things that should have scared him shitless had the opposite effect.

She knew he remained human in part to protect her, but right now what they all needed was Banewolf. And Kali intended to tell him just so. She turned, opening her mouth to shout his name, and saw what only could be described as a face from the darkest, cruelest nightmares lunge from mist. Humanoid in shape, but covered by macerated cords of muscle and thin, sagging skin that seemed to melt from its bones, the skull was fixed atop a long neck of sinewy muscle that whipped toward Rhane in a blur of movement. Kali saw Bellefuron flash and heard the thud of metal hitting a solid object. At the same time, lightning struck near them, creating a reaction so bright Kali was forced to look away.

Knocked from his feet, Rhane flew backward and landed over ten yards away. Streams of smoke spiraled from his clothing. Kali screamed but he had already jumped to his feet with white fur appearing at his temples. The kin snarled, looking in all directions for the next attack but were hard-pressed to avoid the electrical charges beneath their paws.

Before Banewolf fully transitioned, the hideous head descended once more, mouth fixed in a silent scream and hurtling straight toward Kali. The sight would haunt her days and nights for years to come, but she faced the horror with only a heartbeat to ready herself. Speaking a command she'd never used or known before that moment, Kali slammed her hands together, creating a wind that dispersed the rain and a combustion which burned hotter than anything she had ever created. The fire hit the creature head on, pouring into its mouth, melting flesh, bone, and anything else it touched. Still, the monster came and she stood fast, intensifying the burn. Inches from being knocked on her ass or worse, War's russet wolf shoved Kali to the ground. Remnants of the skull and neck, engulfed in fire and partially turned to ash, sailed over their heads to crash at Banewolf's feet.

Hearing a dull roar, Kali looked to the lake with wide eyes. Separated from its head, the creature's body fell hard and fast into the red liquid. She only had a moment to glimpse it sinking out of sight because the huge white wolf called to her urgently.

Go to Orrin, Banewolf said. *Run.*

The lightning stopped with the giant's death, but Kali knew the worst wasn't over. Tremors now shook the ground and trees. Mounds of earth heaved upward and then collapsed into sinkholes where clawed hands appeared, scratching at the edges. Dark shapes began to crawl from the hollows, and then the kin were running, leaving the rest behind in a blur.

They hadn't gotten far when the screaming began. Frightening, desolate, mind-numbing howls tore through the atmosphere and bore down on them from all directions. Kali wanted to press her fists into both ears to shut out the terrible sound, but Orrin sprinted so quickly beneath her, she dared not relax her hold of his fur until the worms surfaced, leaving her no choice but to let go and fight back.

Only thickly muscled protrusions to them before, the "worms" prowled into view. Their strange tails had only been the beginning. Each was nearly five feet tall and stood on four legs. Hoofed hindquarters melded strangely with forelegs of a jungle cat. The bodies were solid, powerful, and all black. Large manes covered their necks. Fearsome teeth curved over bottom lips. The faces were eyeless. No open orbits or missing sockets, just a smooth roundness, as if the eyes had been intentionally erased. And the worst part was the maggot-like bugs constantly shedding from the creatures' skin.

This night keeps getting better, one of the kin remarked.

Gagging, Kali raised a fire to engulf the strange hybrids. Dozens of the creatures burned but joined their un-scorched companions and gave chase. There were more than one hundred pursuers. Those that did not collapse into smoldering corpses only helped spread Kali's flames to the rest of the herd. Refusing to die, the strongest of the hybrids leaped at the kin with snapping teeth and eager claws. Everyone did a good job of deflecting the attacks until one of the creatures latched its jaws around the pack harnessed to Rion and both he and it went down in a tangle.

"Rhane!" Kali screamed to alert him, even as York's wolf wheeled around to Rion's aid.

The black wolf wrestled the cat off Rion's back and tossed it aside with a flip of its powerful neck. But then others swarmed in, moving to overtake them. Banewolf jumped into the fray, quickly followed by War, Bailen, and Orrin. Together they battled back the horde while desperately searching for a way out. The kin easily overpowered the hybrids, but what the enemy lacked in strength was made up in numbers.

Then Kali had an idea. It wasn't the best plan, but maybe, just maybe giving the hybrids something else to think about would buy them enough to time to escape.

Summoning the reserves of her strength, she launched a barraged of fireballs into the air. The flaming masses pierced the clouds with enough momentum to reach the ceiling beyond and cause damage upon impact. The destruction rapidly snowballed and soon a cave-in started. Boulders plummeted from the collapsing ceiling, shattering bones and splattering the unlucky. Counting on Banewolf to shield them, the great wolf did not disappoint.

The kin at last pulled away from the hybrids and fled unhindered. Kali rained more hell behind them to ensure they were not followed. They climbed out of the valley on the opposite side from where they'd entered and far from where their gear was stashed. Silently thanking Rhane for having the foresight to keep some supplies with them, Kali prayed her snow suit was one of the necessary items being carried by the kin because without it she wouldn't survive outside. So much energy was used in getting them this far. There was no way she could generate enough internal heat to keep the arctic temperatures at bay.

Safely reaching the next chamber, they found emptiness. Kali both welcomed and dreaded the quiet. It was nice to be rid of the horrible wails and the hybrids, but her gut deeply mistrusted the silence.

Faster, Banewolf urged, and the kin doubled the pace.

For a long time the nothingness persisted. Light by Kali's hands was the only illumination, and the kin's laboring breaths the only sounds. She felt a noticeable change in the atmosphere and thought she smelled the outside air again. Her spirits lifted but Kali promptly shoved them back down. It was far too soon to hope.

Bailen whined and the kin changed positions, tightening their lines into a ring with Orrin and Kali at its center.

"Bailen, what's happening?"

Something bad.

Banewolf dropped to the rear of their formation, and Kali turned in her seat to see. The way Orrin tensed beneath her thighs was cause for extreme worry. Glimpsing what was already sensed by the others confirmed all her fears.

Whatever it was ran upright like a man, but nothing about this thing was human. Towering over even the immortal wolf, this creature blended with the darkness as if it had been formed from it. Except for flashes of gleaming teeth and steaming breaths, the only thing Kali could make out was a dim blue light glowing within its chest. But that was over ten feet above ground.

Even at top speed, the kin were not outrunning this thing. Foot by foot it gained on them. Suddenly, Banewolf spun on heel and faced the creature head on. Rhane's order to keep going sliced into Kali's mind like a hot blade. Closely following it was a boom that shook the entire mountain.

Her next breath was one of fresh air. Squeezing through an opening barely large enough to accommodate the mass of giant wolves, the darkness suddenly lifted and they were outside again.

She could have fallen to her knees with relief, but the full tide of emotion would have to wait until Rhane stood next to her unharmed. Backing a safe distance away from the cave mouth to prepare for whom or what came out first, they waited. Seconds ticked by and stretched into agonizing minutes.

And then white paws stepped out into the sunlight.

Sliding from Orrin's shoulders, Kali ran to him. The wolf was far too large to wrap her arms around, so she leaned into Banewolf's shoulder and pressed her face into his fur. She didn't care about the blood or stench clinging to the wolf's beautiful white coat. It only mattered that Rhane was okay.

Returning to human form, he signaled for the others to do the same. "Kalista, you're shivering."

The husky sound of his voice was enough to warm her. Kali hugged him tighter. "We made it."

"Yeah," Rhane said. Wrapping her securely in his arms, he called for the packs and kept Kali folded into his warmth until her snow suit was found and readied. Steadying her as she stepped inside on wobbly limbs numbed from cold, Rhane quickly tugged the zipper shut and bundled the double insulated hood around her head. "There," he said softly and touched her cheek. "You really saved our asses back there."

"I just wanted to keep everyone safe." She grabbed his hand and squeezed it. "Rhane…"

He nodded. "I know. Take whatever you need."

Studying his face, Kali noticed the way his eyes pinched at the corners and remembered it was often the only clue when Rhane was in significant pain but otherwise wished to hide the fact. "You're hurt," she blurted out.

"Just a little."

Shaking her head, Kali started to pull away but he stopped her. "You're barely standing. You need to feed."

"No. It will only make you weaker."

"Kalista, please." He searched her eyes as if begging her to understand. Finally, he said it. "Don't make them carry us both."

Worry grabbed her by the throat. "Is it that bad?"

"It's hard to know…maybe in a few hours. I'll see how I heal. In the meantime, we can at least fix you up."

Gradually, Kali conceded. But in calling to his spark, she barely drained the edges of light fueling the fires within him. Strength quickly poured through her cells and charged her blood for the trek ahead. "That's enough," she said, and broke the connection.

Exhaling, Rhane leaned into her but didn't object. "As you wish."

Trekking slowly through drifts of snow gathered at the mountainside, they joined the others. York's scrutiny was plainly evident as they approached. "At least one of you looks ready for the next fight."

Kali frowned. "It feels like we barely survived the last three. Are we expecting more trouble?"

"Hopefully not," Rhane said. "But there's a good chance rogues and especially the enhanced soldiers following us have made it this far. The last thing we want is to stroll into another ambush, so I told York to send War ahead in order to scout the pass leading out of here."

"And how long before he comes back?"

York checked his watch. "He should be returning any minute now."

Before he could finish the sentence, War crested the hill shouting. Kali couldn't make out the words, but she didn't have to. Circling high above the young kin was the reason for his distress. A huge, dark, lizard-shaped beast streaked across the sky with enormous wings stretching across the sun, casting a shadow on the snowy ground. The shadow expanded as the beast flew closer to War's position. Even at top speed, he could not outrun it. The creature dove, ramming its scaly head into War and driving him into the ground. But War recovered even as he fell and was on his feet again.

With a heart trying to beat a way out of her chest, Kali ran with the others. The black and red pattern of the scales identified this thing as Rhaven. But the first and last time she had seen him, he had least appeared somewhat human. In the beast attacking War, Kali couldn't see any of herself or Rhane. And if Rhaven truly intended to hurt War, she wasn't sure they would reach him in time to stop it.

Using its tail, the beast grabbed War and dragged him to the ground. Throwing back its head, the creature roared at the sky. An orange glow started in the chest, moved upward, and finally reached its jaws. Opening its mouth, flames spewed out across the mountainside, melting snow and setting fire to several tiny saplings.

Kali threw up her arms to protect herself from the heat and was surprised to find the blaze actually burned her. Breathing another stream of fire that stopped them all in their tracks, the dragon began to change. Fearsome claws became fingers and toes. The huge tail disappeared. Arms and legs took its place. The head and face became human in shape, taking on features of male no more than twenty years of age. Orange, reptilian eyes, enormous wings, and armored scales all remained, disrupting what would have otherwise been a full transition to a human appearance. Crouching low to the ground, Rhaven held War in place with one arm. A low, warning growl rumbled continuously, a sure signal for them to proceed no further.

Rhane stretched out his hand. "Rhaven, this isn't necessary. Let him go."

Rhaven didn't answer, didn't move. Glaring furiously, his eyes studied each of them. War was captive beneath his grasp, but at least did not appear to be harmed or in pain.

"This wasn't the plan," Rhane said, and Rhaven answered with a hissing scream probably heard for miles away.

The kin shifted nervously. Rhane clenched his jaw so hard, Kali was afraid it might crack. She finally saw what everyone else had sensed as the hooded figures drifted slowly into view. As usual, tarnished metal masks shielded their skin from the sun and hid their identities. Rogues had traded the traditional robe coverings for thermal suits to protect them from subzero temperatures. Numbering well over fifty, apparently the rogues were there with her son.

One of them stepped apart from the others. "The creature before you is Wrath," it said in a loud, sneering voice. "And he is doing just as his master has commanded."

Chapter 19

The situation was not a good one. They were severely outnumbered, nine to one, and that was only counting visible combatants. Considering their style of attack, it was highly likely more rogues lay in wait for ambush within the trees. Under normal circumstances, York would have still bet his money on their side coming out on top. Kali had shown some serious skill back in the caverns and was probably capable of taking on half the rogue army on her own. And even one thousand rogues couldn't defeat Banewolf.

However, Rhaven was crazy dangerous. War was in enemy hands, Kali wasn't feeling one hundred percent, and despite Rhane's best efforts to hide it, York knew the guy was barely standing. He'd taken a hard hit from the oversized, freak-storm-causing sea monster just before changing into Banewolf, and damage was still being done. Strange electrical pulses could be heard moving through the wound on Rhane's side and humming through his blood. Worse yet, the burnt smell permeating his skin had gotten worse.

Regardless of his injuries, York was pretty certain Rhane would have already transformed into Banewolf and kicked some serious rogue ass if not for War's dicey predicament. The fact that it was his resurrected son holding the young kin hostage also presented a problem. Still, York trusted Rhane's judgment and was confident in his warlord's ability to not get them all killed...even though Rhane's temperament had undergone a minor setback of about four hundred years.

Remaining human until Rhane gave the order for skins, York doggedly waited for a call to action. His resolve cracked when War cried out and his blood poured into the snow.

Rhane roared. "Don't!" he shouted, breathing deep to collect himself. "Rhaven, don't do this."

"Turn over the stone."

He quickly pulled the glowing blue crystal from a zippered pocket. "Let him go, and it's yours."

With a shake of his head, Rhaven dug those dreadful talons in deeper. Another scream tore from War's throat but was muffled into an agonized groan as he bit back the rest of the sound. "The stone," Rhaven repeated.

"Okay," Rhane said. "Okay." He tossed the keystone to rogue leader. "Now let him go."

Taking more time than necessary to examine the jewel, the rogue spoke with a smile. "I think the mighty Banewolf should say please."

Rhane didn't hesitate. "Please."

The rogue leader was silent for almost too long. Then he waved a dismissive hand. "Very well, then. Wrath, wait for the signal that we have cleared the area. Then you may give the immortal back his mongrel."

"Understood," Rhaven said without inflection. He lingered in a crouched position over War's body but had at least stopped hurting him. Blood still seeped from both of the boy's shoulders.

Shaking from head to toe, Bailen let out a low whine that rose to a high-pitched bark.

Rhaven hissed, giving them all a nice, long look at the forked tongue snaking from between two wicked rows of teeth. *"Don't,"* he said.

Bailen fell silent.

Rhane glanced at Kalista. Her expression oscillated between devastated and pissed off. He knew how much she hated it whenever someone dared to hurt one of "her boys." This was no exception. Except that it was. Rhaven was one of hers too. Rhane understood completely. He had been hesitant to trust Rhaven, but the betrayal still managed to slice pretty deep.

No one relaxed when the rogues disappeared. The next move was Rhaven's.

Kalista whispered something in her native tongue that Rhane couldn't quite make out. But Rhaven heard and his attention snapped toward her direction. For a moment, his eyes cleared of their serpent-like appearance and the scales covering his skin faded, lending him more of human exterior.

Rhaven grimaced as if in great pain and the mask and scales came down again. Rising to his feet, he stretched out his wings and stared directly at Rhane. "You must keep your word," he said. "Protect him." Then he lifted into the air and was gone.

Everyone rushed toward War as the young kin scrambled to his feet. Orrin held his bewildered twin in place as he checked him over to satisfaction. "Are you hurt?"

"No," War spoke with wild eyes. "It's not my blood."

"What?" They all asked at once.

"It wasn't my blood. Rhaven…he was cutting himself. He screamed in my thoughts, telling me to make it convincing. And if I didn't he would kill me for real." War stared down at the snow, now stained in blood. "That's all his."

"I'll be damned," York whispered, and looked up into the sky.

*

"Okay so he didn't hurt War, but technically Rhaven still betrayed us and because of it the rogues now have the keystone. We all know what happens next." The six of them were crammed inside the only remaining tent, and York stood with his arms folded, playing devil's advocate too well. Kali wanted to smack him.

Rhane, however, was being extremely long-suffering. "I don't think he betrayed us, York. I just think Rhaven is following a different plan."

After fourteen hours of descending the summit as fast as possible, they had been forced by a nasty storm to pitch camp. With most of their gear left behind within Alister's weird-ass lair, supplies would be extremely limited until they recovered the vehicles that brought them to the mountain's valley. So, their bellies were only partially filled after rationing out a handful of MRE dinners. Following the meal, the next forty-five minutes or so were spent debating earlier events. Rhane and Kali of course stood firm in the belief that Rhaven fought on the same side they did. Kali was pretty sure York believed it too, but for the sake of arguing the point from all sides, he was being an argumentative pain in the ass. Rhane didn't seem to mind though.

Orrin hadn't said much but wasn't entirely convinced of Rhaven's good nature. The idea of a secret agenda that could ultimately turn out to be entirely self-serving didn't sit well with him. Comfortably straddling the fence was War. Obviously, Rhaven had procured a few points in War's book by not ripping his throat out...this time. But neither twin had forgotten the battle in the movie theater where Rhaven had tried very hard to incinerate the both of them…or when Rhaven had thrown War from a hotel window more than ten stories above ground.

Different from the rest but in complete accord with his tolerant nature, Rion showed no interest in arguing sides. He would go along with whatever Rhane and Kali decided. After making his position known, he diverted his concentration to a tiny bag of trail mix found in one of the backpack's hidden side pockets.

"Well, he betrayed *our* plan," York said, continuing the argument.

There was one other person who gave no notice to the ongoing discussion. Tucked away in a far corner of the tent, Bailen sat alone in sullen canine silence. Even refusing to eat at mealtime, he wanted neither comfort nor companionship. Hard though it was, Kali respected his wishes and stayed away.

"If the end goal is the same, then it's not betrayal."

"You two are beginning to sound like parrots," Rion grumbled around a mouthful of trail mix. Totally chill in a shirt with the phrase "Look Human" printed across the front, the young kin seemed more sleepy than annoyed.

"Agreed." Kali sighed. "York, I understand your misgivings. Back in the city, Rhaven nearly killed you, but he didn't know us then. And he could have ended War back there but didn't. He even hurt himself rather than hurt him. That has to count for something. Give him the benefit of the doubt."

"And I would, except he tricked us into getting the keystone and then led an army of rogues right to our position, ambushing us for control of it. We were supposed to use the stone to draw Moros out and kill him. Now that plan is shit."

"Okay. Yes, York." Kali had run out of patience. "The original plan is moot and arguing won't change that. So how about we just figure out the next move and then get some sleep?"

York's mouth twitched. "Fine by me."

"First things first," Rhane began, hiding a smile. "We need to get off this mountain."

"Now we're all in agreement," War said. Folding both arms behind his head, he leaned against a rolled up sleeping bag. "Has anyone else realized today was Rhaven's second time grabbing me? What is that guy's problem?"

"Maybe he thinks you're cute," Rion offered.

War glared at him. "Shut up."

Waiting until they had settled, Kali looked around the tent and made serious eye contact with each of them. "We need to kill Moros."

"Whoa." Tensing, War regarded her with a bewildered expression. "That escalated fast."

"Yeah and back to where we damn started," York said. "You're gonna have to forgive me for being the voice of dissent again." He looked back and forth between Rhane and Kali. "But wouldn't it make more sense to go to the nearest and largest city—the likely destination of junior and his merry band of trolls. Maybe we can stop this upgraded staff from being used."

"It's called the ark now." Exhaling, Rhane dragged a hand through his hair. It had gotten long enough to warrant another haircut. "Where would we even start? Gilgit and Skardu both have populations of over two hundred thousand. Hotan and Kashgar boast over one million people each. How can we be certain rogues won't aim for maximum damage and send Rhaven straight to Delhi, Shanghai, Beijing, or Karachi? More than twenty million people live in each of those cities."

Kali cringed inwardly. She could find only three of those places on a map. Probably.

"Besides, we barely contained the smaller outbreaks in New York. If the keystone has amplified the ark's power as much as Rion projected, we wouldn't survive what would happen on a larger scale. And I won't put you all at such risk."

Orrin chose then to interject. "We have risked our lives for you many times over."

And cue the awkward. Kali rose to Rhane's defense. "This time is different. Can't you feel it? And if you can't, then just think about every Builder creation we have encountered up until this point. The monsters—these *freaks* are only getting worse. We're so close to the end of this thing. And the worst is yet to come. What the rogues are trying to raise is something even the Builders fear. I haven't faced anything like this before. I know you're a skilled fighter, Orrin, but neither have you.

"Let's face it. Rhaven would be impossible for us to track even without this storm. We won't know where he is with the ark until he uses it. By then it will already be too late. The best chance we've got at stopping Rhaven is to stick to the original plan. Whether Rhaven is on our side or not, we have to kill Moros, the guy pulling Rhaven's strings."

"Moros is also the head honcho of the entire rogue outfit," Rion added. "Ending him could make other problems go away."

While Kali didn't catch on immediately, Rhane nodded. "The imminent attack on the Kindred," he said, clarifying an unspoken question. "Good thinking, Rion."

York threw his hands up. "Okay. I'm on board. So how do we find Moros?"

Kali pasted a stiff smile onto her face, but felt like she was baring her teeth and erased it. "I think your girlfriend could help us with that."

*

Daylight. It wasn't a bad thing, just a frustrating marker of how much time had passed. On the positive side, after traveling over one hundred miles to a small province south of the mountain, Kali and the kin had crossed into a much friendlier climate. No snow suits or arctic gear were required in these warmer temperatures.

She stood waiting with the others near a private landing strip. The small twin engine aircraft carrying Cixi to their location was overdue by thirty minutes. Seeing York check his watch for the bazillionth time, Kali wondered if he was worried about the safe arrival of the plane or nervous about having the red beauty around now that his secret was out.

It would have been nice to have a little fun and tease him about it, but no one else had jumped on the opportunity, so Kali kept her mouth shut. There had to be a reason why the others, especially War, were showing such restraint. When Rhane moved up next to York and engaged him in low conversation, Kali dropped back to stand beside Orrin. She touched his arm. "Is it getting any easier?" she asked quietly.

Orrin looked down at her sadly. "Rion trusts easily and forgives easily. My brother is often obstinate and brash. He took months to forgive Rhane, but I will not have such luxury. We are at war."

"For what it's worth, I'm sorry for what happened to your parents."

"I moved past their deaths long ago, Kalista. My hardship is the cruelty of a lie upheld for so long."

Understanding completely, Kali nodded. "He has trouble with that sometimes. Rhane thinks he's protecting you by keeping secrets or telling half-truths. Sometimes he's right. A year ago, when Rhane first came back into my life, I would have never been able to handle knowing he was actually my mate, or the shock of learning we had a child together—one who had died. Back then I got really angry at him for keeping things from me, but once I knew the truth…I understood why he'd kept the secrets in the first place." Hearing a distant hum overhead, Kali lifted her gaze to the afternoon sky. "The hurt you're feeling, Orrin, how much sooner would you have liked to have felt it? And how long do you think Rhane spent agonizing over how much pain what he'd done would cause you?" Finally spotting the plane's approach, Kali looked at Orrin again. His expression was thoughtful, contrite even. "Rhane didn't hide what he did to spare himself. He lives by a code of self-flagellation."

To her surprise, Orrin relinquished half of a smile. "Well, version 2.0 actually doesn't seem so angst-ridden."

"Is that a bad thing?" she asked, raising her eyebrows.

Resting a hand on her shoulder, he squeezed it lightly. "Or course not, *Uskai*."

She was instantly taken aback by the formal address. "Why did you just call me that? Bailen has said it twice, and now you. What does it mean?"

Orrin glanced at the canine. Sitting at Kali's feet, Bailen seemed to have recovered from his brooding mood of the night before. "When he says it, he uses *uskai* as "mother" in our native tongue. Since I am not your blood relative, I say it to acknowledge my love and respect for you, and also to recognize my willingness to submit to your authority and wisdom."

The explanation left her speechless. Kali shrank away from the intensity of Orrin's brown eyes. But the way Bailen stared at her wasn't much better. "You honor me," she managed. Kali swallowed. "But I am not wise, Orrin."

This time Kali was rewarded with a full smile. "More than you know."

A sharp whistle from York snapped everyone to attention. "The plane is here."

War's expression took a mischievous turn as they jogged toward the runway to meet the landing plane. "Hey Rion," he said loud enough for anyone to hear. "Care to make a wager?"

"It depends. What'd you have in mind?"

"Before this is over, either Cixi or York is getting punched in the face."

Rion chuckled. "I think I'll take you up on that."

"So, who are you going with?" War asked.

Rion thought for a moment. "Does it matter who does the punching?"

War grinned. "How about double rewards if you get both the puncher and the punched correct."

Rion laughed. York huffed. "I don't like this bet."

"My money is on Kali knocking the shit out of Cixi."

"Hey!" Kali exclaimed. "How did I get put into this?"

War winked. "Just go with it." He took another second to deliberate his own choice. "Cixi will definitely hit York."

"I would like to bet too," Orrin said, surprising everyone. "I will also go with Cixi hitting York."

Kali feigned offense. "And why not put your money on me?"

"It is because Cixi allows anger to lead her too far."

"I'll accept that."

York did not look amused. "Would anyone like to win their money now and gamble on me knocking the hell out of the instigator of this little wager?"

"Come on," Rhane said, finally weighing in as the airplane's door opened. "Be a sport." He wagged an eyebrow. "I'll bet on York as well."

Though grateful for the lighter mood, Kali couldn't help feeling a spurt of animosity at the sight of the long-legged kindred beta who possessed amazing hair, awesome boobs, and a carnal history with Rhane. But in spite of all those things, the worst thing about Cixi was her domineering attitude. The beta's ongoing desire for Rhane didn't help matters either. Breathing deep to quell the rising heat in her chest, Kali abruptly worried Rion was the one who had gambled correctly.

When not running through the neighboring woods au naturel, Cixi typically dressed in a manner suited to the latest high fashion trends. Today was no different.

Admittedly, Kali hadn't given much thought to her dress these days. Other matters just seemed way more important. Now, she looked down at her simple jeans, hiking boots, and fitted v-neck, wishing she put a little more thought into the packing done for the trip.

Cixi wore all black, making the reflection of sunlight against her red locks even more stunning. Fine linen trousers further streamlined her slender hips and thighs. A sheer silk blouse hung loosely at her shoulders, tapered through the waist, and then billowed out again, perfectly completing the look.

Ugh, Kali thought. And then mentally scolded herself for being shallow.

Rhane stepped forward to greet Ian's beta. "Thank you for coming, Cixi."

She, of course, was as pleasant as ever. "You can thank Ian when you see him, Banewolf. My presence is solely at his behest. Somehow you have deceived my alpha into believing the foolish notion that you are truly a friend of the kindred."

Wow, War mouthed, turning his head so only Kali would see.

Rion wasn't as subtle. Faking a pretty convincing sneeze, he muttered "bitch" during the forced expulsion.

Rhane 2.0 was totally unaffected. If anything, his affable smile only widened. "Make no mistake, Cixi. Never have I claimed to be an ally to your species. I am Ian's friend. As a member of his pack, my tolerance and goodwill extends to you."

"Boom," Rion whispered, and Kali struggled not to laugh.

The kindred beta narrowed her golden eyes. "It's always good to know exactly where I stand with you, Banewolf."

"Cixi, what can you tell us about Moros? Finding him as quickly as possible is critical."

"What makes you think he is near this region?"

"The range needed to control the rogue champion must have limits. Rhaven was last seen here, so Moros must be close."

Cixi raised one perfectly arched eyebrow. "Rhaven?"

An infinitesimal twitch rippled through the left side of Rhane's jaw. "He would be known to you as Wrath."

Recognition chilled her smooth features. "He is the bringer of havoc throughout American cities."

Rhane nodded.

"Actually," Rion suddenly interrupted, looking down at the tablet computer he'd insisted on carrying with him to the meet. "Wrath is making mayhem a little closer to home base."

Rhane stared at him. "Clarify."

"The web is going nuts about monsters rampaging through Islamabad." He turned the tablet around so all could see the chaotic footage. "It's just like New York."

"Alright, Cixi." Rhane's tone fell grimly onto Kali's ears. "Looks like you'll be starting in Pakistan. We need to find Moros."

Chapter 20

Two sport utility vehicles raced across the mountainous region, carrying them toward an unknown destiny. Kali, Rhane, Rion, and Orrin traveled in the second car. The first SUV held Cixi, Bailen, War and York. Of course, York had strongly insisted on manning the wheel despite War's objections. Stubbornness won out and War settled for shotgun with a minimal display of resentment. The travel arrangements weren't ideal but they were certainly necessary. Rhane probably would have liked to have kept a closer eye on Cixi, but asking Kali to occupy the same space as the kindred beta for a three hour trek was a test Kali wasn't sure she was ready for. Perhaps it could have been good for her character, but more pressing was mending the rift between Orrin and Rhane. The two were at least conversing freely, though some tension was still evident. Things were getting better though and Kali was grateful.

As to whether Rion noticed any difference, Kali could only guess. His attention had been pretty much glued to his tablet since leaving the airstrip. Glancing at Rion and Kali via the rearview mirror, Rhane asked a question Kali herself had been wondering. "Rion," he said in a voice carrying a heavy note of suspicion. "How are you getting internet access out here?"

The young kin answered without looking up. "I re-tasked a government satellite."

"You *what?*"

"It was only a few degrees." He smiled sheepishly. "I doubt they'll even notice."

"And if they do?"

"I have safeguards in place. This computer is virtually untraceable."

Rhane's mouth turned down in disapproval. "I'd feel better if you said it was absolutely untraceable."

"Well, there are always variables," Rion admitted innocently. Suddenly bolting upright in his seat, he excitedly waved one hand. "Hey, the Pakistani government just shut down Islamabad's airport. All air traffic has been diverted. No one is being allowed in or out."

"Did they give a reason?" Kali asked.

Rion shook his head. "But I think we can guess why."

"Things must be really bad." She tried to envision the outbreak at the mall happening on a citywide level, but her mind shied away from the task. Carnage on that scale was too much to imagine. And the knowledge of her son being the cause of it all made Kali sick to her stomach. "How much further?" she asked.

"A little more than an hour," Orrin answered softly.

Hurriedly tapping the screen several times, Rion passed the tablet to the front of the SUV. "They've attacked a mosque."

Kali peered over Rhane's shoulder to see the video and immediately wished she hadn't. Filmed with a cell phone camera, the uncensored footage showed hundreds of changelings pouring out of a huge, triangle-faced building and into a paved courtyard, savagely killing everything thing that crossed their paths. No human was spared—old, young, man, woman, or child. Blood filled the stone grooves of the pavement until a river of red spilled out onto the grassy lawn. Kali looked away before the playback was done. She couldn't watch anymore.

"They hit the University too," Rion said.

Wordlessly surrendering the computer, Rhane snatched up the two-way radio resting atop the dashboard. "War, come in, over." Though his fingers held the transmitter in a white-knuckled grip, Rhane's voice conveyed absolute calm.

"I'm here."

"We can't take the main road into the city. The situation has escalated, and we'll need to use the back door."

"Understood."

"Check your ammo and ready the weapons. A rouge unit may still travel with Rhaven. Steer clear of using skins for now. We don't want to advertise our presence."

"Roger that. I'll relay your instructions."

Ending the transmission, Rhane settled back into the seat. "Rion, I want you to keep me updated on any new developments in the city. But once we get there, your full attention goes to what's happening around you. Got it?"

"Yes sir."

Outside Kali's window, the scene changed from dusty, wilderness roads to curvy asphalt snaking down the mountain and toward the densely populated city. From their vantage point, she could already see how right Rhane was to avoid the main highway. Cars littered the roadway, packed together bumper to bumper. As they drew closer, it became obvious many of them were unmanned. Blood dripped from open doors. Dusty windshields were smeared in crimson. The people still inside were dead or dying. Others were simply missing. Those still living desperately struggled to weave through the stagnant cars. A few were successful. Most only made the traffic jam worse.

An explosion boomed from the city center, sending a cloud of thick, black smoke into the atmosphere of the tallest buildings. Nearby, two helicopters circled in the sky, no doubt reporting on the chaos. A second explosion caught the tail of the second bird and pitched the chopper into a tailspin, sending it crashing into a row of towers.

Rhane swore. Grabbing the radio, he hailed War for a second time. "Tell York to get us off this road. Find out where Cixi needs to be and take us there."

"We're already on it, boss. The Shah Faisal is about fifteen clicks from our current position. ETA in under twenty."

Rion's eyes stretched wide. "Uh. Not good. Rhane, tell him that's not good."

"Rion, focus." The order was firm but gentle. Rhane turned his attention back to communication with the first SUV. "Please advise Cixi that Shah Faisal is currently overrun with changelings."

"Roger that," War said, and the radio went silent. Rhane squelched the noise while they waited. A short while later, War's voice crackled over the speaker. "The beta says if we want any chance of finding Moros, we have to go there. Hopefully, her contact is still alive."

"Perfect," Rhane muttered with his finger off the talk button. "So be it," he said, speaking into the microphone again. "Everyone stay sharp."

Traveling side streets and back alleyways, they moved deeper into the city with painstaking slowness. For the most part, their SUVs went unnoticed by the rampaging creatures. A middle-aged man ran up to the car and slammed his bloodied hands against Kali's window, shouting for her to let him inside. "I'm sorry," she said, sickened by his terror and her helplessness to end it. She looked to Rhane for help.

"Drop your window," he said. His voice was too hard, too calm. Kali hesitated. "Kalista," Rhane repeated in a tone with room for nothing except obedience. "Open your window."

As soon as she did, Rhane raised his weapon and fired a single shot past Kali's head and through the two inch gap. She screamed reflexively, expecting to see the man's head blown apart right in front of her eyes. Instead, a snarling kindred dropped dead in its tracks as a blood silver bullet pierced its heart. The terrified human stopped chasing them, probably just as stunned as Kali.

Rhane spoke, jarring Kali from her trance. "Secure your window please."

She raised the window with a trembling finger and took a deep breath to calm her nerves. "The next time you're going to fire a gun so close to my face," she snapped. "Give me the courtesy of a warning."

He at least had the decency to appear rueful even if Kali's soured mood served as the only motivator. "You're right. I'm sorry."

It wasn't much later when they arrived at the courtyard of Shah Faisal. Everyone climbed out of the SUVs, armed to the teeth with an assortment of knives and guns. Though capable with weapons of her own, Kali found assurance at the sight of Rhane's sword strapped to his back. Bellefuron had saved her from many tight situations over the course of the two lifetimes she remembered.

Death had certainly left its mark on the mosque. Half-eaten body parts lay strewn across the square. Gutted corpses soiled the fountain, turning what should have been healing waters into a literal bath of blood.

Kali's brain found one positive element in the entire scene and held on to it. Except for the dead, the mosque was deserted. The creatures responsible for the wicked savagery had moved on. Still, progress to the front entrance was deliberate and cautious. Once there, Cixi held up a perfectly manicured hand. "The lot of you cannot go in here. If I am to get your answers, Banewolf, and find the rogue king you seek, I must not be seen consorting with their greatest enemy."

Rhane nodded. "Fair enough. How and when will you make contact? I have a hunch the phone service around here may be unreliable right now."

"Leave a radio for me inside the Alley Café on Street Thirteen. It's only a block from here. The location should be far enough away not to arouse suspicion when I retrieve it, but not too big a distance to risk traveling alone."

"Consider it done."

"Hang on a second." Stepping into her path, York blocked the doorway. "We should escort you inside and make sure it's safe in there."

Cixi actually smiled. "I'll be fine, Yorkshire."

"Are you sure about that? Only a few months ago, you were begging us for safe passage off this very continent. What's changed since then?"

Not a tolerant woman to begin with, the beta's patience abruptly thinned. "I did not say coming here was without risk. I said I will be fine."

"Great," York said. Moving around Cixi, he snatched open the heavy glass door. "Go be fine."

Seemingly amused by his anger, Cixi sauntered forward but stopped at the threshold and sniffed the air. She turned to York, looking up at him through lowered lashes. Her voice was a purr as she spoke. "I will need a weapon."

To Kali, it was one of the oddest, most uncomfortable sexual exchanges she had ever witnessed between two people. Odd because York was pissed and Cixi was explicitly aroused by it. In turn, York's hostility flipped to a barely restrained erotic aggression as Cixi wiggled her hips like a dog in heat. Adding to it was the one thing Kali couldn't extract from her brain no matter how many times or how hard she tried—Cixi and Rhane were ex-lovers. Hating herself for continuing to think about it every time the beta was in her presence, Kali swore she would never mention it to Rhane or act on those feelings of jealously. Still, that oath didn't stop her from wanting to scream "get a room" to York and Cixi.

York didn't budge. So with permission from Rhane, War eased forward and slipped a gun into Cixi's waiting hand. Satisfied, the beta stepped inside the mosque and sashayed away without ever looking back. York stared woodenly after her until she was gone from sight. "What now?" he asked, finally turning to Rhane.

"We'll plant the radio at the café and then find a safe place to lay low and wait."

Kali surveyed the scene around them. "Is there anywhere safe left in this city?"

"There is and we'll find it," Rhane said confidently.

"And if not," War added as he twirled a semi-automatic pistol a full 360 degrees before deftly securing the weapon inside its shoulder holster. "We'll make one."

Rion shook his head. "Dude, that was so lame."

"You're lame," War shot back.

"So is your penis."

"Why do you always have to make things sexual?"

"I'm just trying to be more like you."

"Well stop it. You're embarrassing yourself."

"Oh yeah?" Rion crossed his arms. "From what I've seen, I think you're the one who should be embarrassed."

War's cheeks flushed crimson. "Not cool, bro."

Smiling victoriously, Rion opened his mouth to speak again, but Rhane's voice trampled whatever inappropriate remark was about to bubble out. "Boys," he said. "Knock it off."

The two instantly sobered at Rhane's sharp reprimand, at least until his back was turned. Then a full blown, amazingly silent shoving match ensued. Laughing quietly, York dropped his head.

Rhane rolled his eyes in exasperation. Kali guessed he'd been with the boys so long he didn't have to see them to know what was going on. Either that, or Rhane had the same eyes in the back of his head all parents seemed to possess. "Enjoy the show, York. Those two will ride with you."

Chapter 21

"Waiting sucks," War said, and Kali had to agree.

Rion yawned. "You're just saying that because you're losing."

After leaving the radio in the café, Rhane insisted on hunkering down where Cixi would easily be seen as she came to fulfill her end of the arrangement. York readily agreed, and they all ended up in an old hotel directly across the street from the restaurant.

Securing the hotel had been a tricky endeavor. The supernatural infection raging throughout the city had spread like the Black Death through Europe. Humans directly turned by the ark attacked others. Bitten survivors who didn't die from their wounds or weren't eaten outright became violent monsters and continued the cycle.

From the moment Orrin opened the hotel's front door, blood stains on the carpet and walls clued them in as to what to expect. Sure enough, a rogue, kindred, or dead body waited for them around every corner. Freshly mutated and still raging, these changelings could not be reasoned with and had to be put down as quickly as possible. Room by room, hall by hall, floor by floor, the disease was cut out until only Kali and the kin remained. Then there was nothing to do except wait.

And wait they did.

Hours passed but no one appeared on the street in front of the café except a few terrified humans and the creatures chasing them. Orrin jumped at the assignment to patrol the roof, taking Bailen with him to make sure nothing breached the established perimeter. Procuring playing cards from a mysterious source, York brandished a half-bloodied deck and issued a challenge for a game of Scat. Rion and War readily accepted. Kali passed. She didn't think she could muster the focus to play or enjoy a game of cards at the moment.

Moving to the bedroom, she sat at the edge of the mattress next to Rhane and nudged him. Until then, his attention to the east-facing window was unwavering. "I'm surprised you're not lecturing them on the necessity of staying alert," she said.

He shrugged. "We're reasonably safe here, and with Orrin on post, nothing will sneak up on us. They could use the distraction…especially York it seems."

"Yeah," Kali said, dragging the word into three syllables. "I thought it was only sex between them, but York may have actually caught some real feelings. Poor guy."

Taking a break from the window, Rhane's scrutiny shifted to Kali. "We've never really talked about it. How are you doing with all of this?"

Kali exhaled softly. There it was…the moment of truth. "You've never made me apologize for my past, and I'm not going to ask you to apologize for yours. Cixi is here to help, and despite the silly bet between the boys, I have no intentions of hitting her."

Rhane smiled, but the expression faded as he looked back to the window. He was quiet for a long time. "I'm sorry, Kalista," he eventually said.

"Don't be."

"But I really am." Taking her hand, Rhane stroked his thumb across her skin. "The worst part is I can't even give you the explanation you deserve. The memories of what happened between Cixi and I are gone. I know I hurt her, but I don't know why. York was worried about how I would react to learning about their relationship, and he should have been."

Kali flinched.

"But for the wrong reasons," Rhane added quickly. He looked guilty as hell and Kali was dying to know what had him reacting in such a manner. Besides guilt, there was fear in his eyes. And that made her afraid.

She finally harnessed enough nerve to ask. "What do you mean?"

"She's nothing to me. Only a tool serving a purpose…whether for sex or information, but completely expendable. York's interest in her changed nothing." Rhane swallowed. "I could kill her without regret."

"Wow." Kali sagged with relief but also couldn't help feeling sympathy for Rhane's ex-lover. The woman had obviously carried quite the torch for Rhane. And from Cixi's behavior, it was reasonable to conclude the flame still burned on some level. "Rhane…that's pretty cold."

"I know. What kind of person am I?"

Kali answered without hesitation. "You're the kind who will stop at nothing to protect his friends and family but still risk everything to save a world that doesn't know him."

Rubbing his neck, Rhane leaned forward and rested both elbows on his knees. "I was probably better suited to the task before having my head severed."

"You're still the same guy." Kali moved so she could see his face again. "Everything you need is still in there," she said, tapping his forehead. "Each time you ever became Banewolf, you drew on your own wisdom and experience to guide the wolf through battle. It wasn't just

221

brute strength getting you all those wins. I know it's hard but you've got to trust yourself. Stop doubting what you're capable of."

Cupping her face, Rhane pulled Kali closer. He kissed her briefly but passionately, teasing her into wanting more in just five seconds of contact. His mouth withdrew from hers but he didn't pull away. "At any point of our lives have I used a similar speech on you? Because you sounded incredibly smart just then, and I would really like to stake some claim in that."

Kali laughed. "You've given me plenty of pep talks."

"But what about that one," he insisted with a playful sparkle in his eye. "Have I given you that one?"

Still giggling, she was transfixed by his beautiful green orbs. *I love you so much,* she thought. "Maybe there was a similar one."

"Ugh," he said, faking disgust. "You mock me, woman." Then his smile faded as he brought his lips against hers in a slow, burning exploration of her mouth. The kisses moved to her neck, forging a trail of heat felt all the way down to her belly. Trembling, Kali melted into him. Rhane effortlessly lifted her and set her legs astride his lap, letting her feel how much he wanted her. Kali rocked against him, and he groaned, nipping her skin with his teeth. His mouth moved to cover her nipple, making her gasp and arch into him. Her body ached for more.

Shaking with need, she pushed him back onto the bed and lifted his shirt. Her fingers gingerly outlined the mostly healed marks of the wounds across his abdomen. Then Kali leaned forward and kissed his rock hard abs, using teeth and tongue as she traced a way down his belly. Stopping below his navel, she dipped her tongue beneath the waist of his jeans and drew a line from one hip bone to the other. A hiss eased from Rhane's lips, and Kali was further rewarded by the increasing bulge at his zipper.

Working her mouth against cold metal, she undid the button and slowly tugged down the zipper, watching his lust-shadowed face through every second of it. Blackness swirled into his eyes as she kissed the length of him through the material of his boxers and teased the tip of his arousal with her tongue. A gruff curse strangled from his throat. Loving the control, Kali moved to take more of Rhane's hot, throbbing flesh into her mouth.

Unfortunately, just then the radio came alive with Orrin's voice. "I've got eyes on Cixi. Stand by for her transmission."

"Shit," Kali said and moved aside while Rhane sat up, exclaiming a stronger oath. He finished zipping his pants right as York and the others barged into the bedroom.

Taking in the scene, York rolled his eyes. "I can't believe you guys would rather play hide the sausage than engage in a friendly game of cards with us."

Releasing a resigned sigh, Rhane slid off the bed and went to the window. "Kalista is way prettier than you are."

York pursed his lips. "You weren't in here looking at her face."

"Your powers of observation are stunning." Rhane adjusted the volume of the radio using the fat knob situated at the top. Cixi's call came through the channel only seconds later.

"Rhane, are you there?"

"I'm here."

"The infection rate in this city has reached over seventy percent. The rogues have moved on. Moros isn't here, and neither is your son. We should return to the airstrip as soon as possible."

"And where are we going, Cixi? I'm not leaving this continent until the job is done."

"Moros has sent the ark to New Delhi. Twenty-five million people will be infected by week's end, and a legion of changelings will be unleashed upon the world unchecked."

And so will Blight, Kali added silently. She cringed inwardly at the thought.

"Are you safe to meet?" Rhane asked.

"Not here," Cixi answered. "Head northeast and pick me up outside of the city."

Expressing agreement with her instructions, Rhane ended the transmission. York didn't look happy. "She shouldn't be wandering around this city on her own."

"I agree with you, but it's Cixi's decision. And she wouldn't be Ian's beta if she weren't very capable. Stop worrying."

York winced. "I sounded like a wet nurse just then, didn't I?"

"Well, yeah. But I wasn't going to say it." Rhane tossed the radio to York. "Contact Orrin and tell him the plan. We'll meet him next to the first floor stairwell." He looked to the others. "Pack up and move out."

*

Exiting from the city was mostly seamless. Things only got testy as they maneuvered the SUVs through a jam of abandoned cars blocking the road into mountains. A steep drop off to one side left no room to bypass the blockage, so several vehicles had to be physically removed from the roadway. Kali and War stood guard while Orrin, York, and

Rhane handled clearing the cars. Bailen lounged on the backseat, panting to keep cool. Rion sat next to him, busy on his computer. He'd barely spoken two words since they'd crossed city limits. She presumed it was because something geeky held his attention hostage.

Cixi, of course, showed no interest in standing guard or getting her hands dirty moving cars. Taking a quick stroll to stretch her long legs, she returned to the vehicles and waited. Kali tried very hard not to send any ill will toward the beta, and was mostly successful.

Finally looking up from the tablet for the first time in over an hour, Rion scrambled from the car, calling Rhane's name excitedly. "I don't think we should go to India," he said, and shoved the computer into Rhane's hands. "Check out the data. It doesn't make sense." Folding his arms, he watched Rhane's face and waited patiently.

"Rion, tell me what exactly it is I'm looking at. I see a map, a bunch of red arrows, and the countdown is impossible to miss."

Coming to Rhane's side, War glanced at the screen. "I think Rion has plotted the zombie apocalypse," he mumbled, and went back to watching for trouble.

Rion rolled his eyes. "I extrapolated date from satellite feed and footage from the web of what's happened in the city below us. Taking into consideration time stamps from the very first videos and news reports of Rhaven's attacks, I created a formula calculating the approximate time needed for the population to be fully decimated."

"Zombie apocalypse," War whispered loud enough for Kali to hear. Ignoring him, she tried to stay vigilant and still follow Rion's complicated explanations.

"From there," he continued, "I expanded the program to make the same calculations using neighboring populations, projecting how fast these creatures will migrate and infect other humans. In three to five days, the entire eastern hemisphere will be lost. India as Moros' next move doesn't make sense. Dude, this is already checkmate."

"Don't call me dude." Squinting, Rhane rotated the screen. "Are you saying we've lost? That in less than a week the monster everyone has been talking about will awaken, and rogues will finally have their god?"

Fidgeting beneath the intensity of Rhane's glare, Rion swallowed nervously. "I'm saying Moros isn't in India."

"Hang on a second." Rhane handed the computer back to Rion and strode to the SUV with Cixi inside. Snatching open the door, he practically dragged her from the car. Cixi tried to pull away twice, but Rhane didn't let go until he was ready. His unexpected release knocked her off balance. Amber eyes storming, she yanked her clothing straight. "What the hell?" Cixi exclaimed furiously.

Rhane stuck his nose about two inches from her face. "Are you playing us? Tell me now. Is Moros truly in India?"

"This is the thanks I am to receive after risking my ass for you?"

"I haven't killed you yet."

Stepping away from Rhane, Cixi turned her steely gaze to York. He stood with arms folded tightly across his chest, seemingly disinterested in making any move to defend her. "Answer the question, Cixi."

Murder burned in the beta's eyes, but so did tears. Kali knew Cixi would never let them fall. Instead of answering Rhane's question, she launched a glob of spit into his face and lashed out to strike him. Rhane caught her fist easily in one hand while the other wrapped around her throat. Lifting her into the air, he slammed her against the SUV with enough force to dent the car door inward. Cixi cried out, and York rushed forward. But Rhane spun on him, exhibiting features more animal than human. *"Stand down,"* he growled, and all of the kin took a step back.

Kali readied herself to intervene, though she didn't know on whose behalf it would be.

In a completely normal voice, Rhane spoke to Cixi, "I won't ask again."

Flesh turning red and then blue, the beta opened her mouth in a soundless gasp. Rhane relaxed his hold enough to allow her to speak. The words were a struggle on her lips. "I told you all I know."

Enough time passed for Rhane to either ask another question or let her go, but still he held on, slowly strangling the life from her body. Kali had no choice but to call out to him. "Rhane," she said. "Maybe Cixi isn't lying. We used her months ago to deliver the Siren's Heart to the rogues. She helped us set up a meeting with Moros and could have compromised his trust because of it. Consider it."

Taking a deep breath, Rhane closed his eyes. He released Cixi and she fell to the ground, collapsing onto her side in a violent fit of coughing as her lungs were reintroduced to life-saving air. Looking mad as hell, York held his post. His fists clenched white with the effort. "Go to her," Kali said softly. She turned back to Rhane. It was impossible to be angry. He had warned her of this very moment only hours before, and she had basically absolved him because of his good heart and noble intentions. But to watch him come so close to killing an innocent person was shocking.

"For York's sake," she whispered. "Please don't touch her again unless you intend to kill her."

Rhane nodded, and Kali accepted that. Approaching Cixi, she kneeled next to the kindred woman. "We need to speak to your rogue contacts. Can we still find them in the mosque?"

Cixi rubbed her throat. A bruise in the shape of a handprint was already forming. "If I lead you to them, my relationship with this hive will be burned."

"Cixi," Kali said gently. "You're alive now because we're assuming your alliance with them has crumbled and that is why you were given false information." Glancing at Rhane, Kali prayed that he had at least choked the stubborn streak out of the bitch. Otherwise, they were dead in the water and without a plan.

"The hive lies beneath the mosque. If you go there, they will try to kill you."

"How many rogues can we expect?"

"At least eighty are currently nesting, but no more than two hundred."

"Thank you."

Cixi's mouth formed a bitter line. Dropping her eyes, she looked away. Kali suppressed a sigh and got to her feet. She walked to where Rhane stood, now apart from the others. He was angry, but Kali didn't realize to what extent until he shoved a broken down car off the roadway and over the side of the cliff…using only his foot.

"We're going back in," she said. "We tried the nice way. Now we'll let them meet the wolf."

Chapter 22

Rhane gripped the steering wheel with one hand. "I really fucked up."

After completing the task of clearing the mountain roadway, he and Kali had taken one of the SUVs and headed back into the city. Rhane had needed some convincing to allow her to tag along. Finally, Kali had lost her temper and practically yelled at him that she wasn't asking.

"You shouldn't have done that," Kali said. "You put York in a really tough spot."

He looked at her with wide eyes. "If he gets much more serious with Cixi, he'll have to leave the manor anyway. But that's not what I was talking about."

"Wait a second," Kali said, shaking her head. "Why will York have to leave?"

"Cixi is a beta with a very dominant personality. She's used to being the top bitch and will never submit to your authority…or even to mine, for that matter."

"Well maybe if you choke the shit out of her one more time it will fix her attitude problem."

"You just said I shouldn't have hurt her."

"I thought it was what you felt bad about. But if it keeps York in the house, hell, go for it. By the way, if not the act of brutality against your ex-lover, then what are you regretting?"

Rhane stopped the car. "Get out."

Kali looked around. They had driven only to the very edges of the city and were at least ten minutes from the mosque. "Excuse me?"

Rhane opened his door and put one boot onto the ground. "We walk from here." Rounding to the passenger side of the SUV before she could articulate a valid protest, he offered her his hand. "You wanted this, remember?"

Kali bit her tongue.

They walked down a very quiet, very deserted street in complete silence, except for the occasional direction given from Rhane. Those didn't come often, though. It seemed he was making a beeline for the mosque, and Kali understood why he wanted to ditch the rental. With all the abandoned vehicles and debris, it was far easier to cut a direct path to the mosque on foot. The biggest wave of chaos had passed over as every remaining human had either died or fled. The few straggling survivors were likely being hunted down by changelings yet to move on in spread of their disease.

Realizing Rhane had yet to answer her question, Kali revisited the subject. "So what do you regret?"

"Look around you, Kalista. We've lost. And pretty much every decision I've made has led up to this."

"This isn't your fault."

"Isn't it? Once I found you again, all I could think about was keeping you safe. I should have met this thing head on, found those artifacts and destroyed them, or opened the tomb myself and killed this thing before Moros had a chance to do so much damage."

Stunned, Kali stopped walking. "You remember it all now?"

"I've been piecing some things together."

"And of course you would remember more stuff to torment yourself with."

"I guess I'm just an angst-ridden guy."

230

"Leaning toward masochism." Kali put her hands on her hips. "We have no way of knowing how differently things would have turned out if we'd done everything exactly as you say. We couldn't trust Wesley. And even back then, with the Faction helping them, rogues were nearly always one step ahead of us. Get that pretty head of yours out of the past," she said, and tugged on his hand. "The only way is forward."

Rhane smiled. "Yes ma'am."

*

Long before reaching the lower levels containing the rogue hive, Kali decided the inside of the mosque was far creepier than anything she could have imagined— dismembered body parts scattered about, as well as the copious amounts of blood that stained the walls, floors, and ceiling had a lot to do with her assessment. Additionally, the lights overhead dimmed and flickered, threatening to go completely dark at any moment.

Rhane led them from room to room and deeper into the complex, passing the point of return three times over. He walked with confidence, made turns without hesitation. If Kali hadn't known better, she would have thought Rhane had been there before.

"How do you know where to go?" she whispered.

"I don't." Rhane glanced over his shoulder to see her. "Cixi was just here, so the markers she left behind are still strong. Let's hope they lead to the heart of this lair."

Duh, Kali thought. Of course he'd be following a scent trail.

Stopping in front of what looked like a basement entrance, Rhane pressed one ear against the heavy wooden door. "I know it's a little late to ask," he whispered. "But are you sure you're up to this?"

"Are you?" Kali shot back.

He winked. "I'm always ready," he said, sounding so much like York that Kali couldn't help rolling her eyes. "Get ready, Kalista. Remember, their blood is toxic. Don't let it touch you, and don't hold back."

She nodded, and Rhane opened the door to the rogue hive. A long corridor stretched out before them. Down it, Kali hoped they could somehow find an answer to the question of Moros' true plan. She expected the darkness. The sudden chill, however, was surprising. Nothing about the place really screamed she'd just stepped into the hideaway of supernatural trolls forced to nest away from sunlight.

The door closed behind them with a soft bang, sealing off the light and reducing visibility to absolute zero. "Light please," Rhane whispered.

Bellefuron sang as the weapon slid from its sheath, underlining his request. Kali lit a small torch within her palm.

The corridor made a sharp left turn and began a descent steep enough for her legs to take notice. When the terrain leveled off, a figure appeared at the edges of her fire's soft grey light. Rushing toward her, the creature released a murderous hiss but the sound was cut short as Rhane's blade sliced through the rogue's throat, relieving it of its head.

Exhaling, Kali relaxed her grip on the hilt of her dagger. "Thanks."

"That was a sentinel. Expect more of them."

Tension set across Rhane's shoulders alerted Kali to just how serious of a situation they were in. She remembered how he and Ian had bravely stormed a rogue hive back home in search of War after he was taken and the manor attacked. She wasn't sure if Rhane had yet to retrieve the memory in full detail, but some part of his subconscious was very aware of what awaited them in this underground region.

Crossing paths with two more sentinels, Rhane and Kali were able to dispatch the creatures before an alarm was raised and their presence alerted to the rest of the rogues. Deeper into the hive, light from a different source washed over Kali's eyes and she quickly extinguished the flame within her palm. Escaping from an open doorway, the orange glow sourced from hundreds of candles arranged in parallel rows from one corner of the room to the next. Within the square's center were at least a dozen rogues engaging in frenetic acts of copulation using positions Kali didn't know existed. Male on female. Female and female. Male and male. The scene was an orgy free-for-all and would have been shocking to even the most dedicated of porn enthusiasts.

Rhane swept the room in one glance and moved on without so much as halting his stride. Kali, however, possessed a brain that took much longer to process what her eyes were seeing. She didn't realize she had stopped walking until Rhane grabbed her arm and pulled her past the doorway.

Chamber after chamber, it was more of the same. Masses of writhing flesh and undulating bodies fulfilling the most wanton desires. Faces locked in masks of unadulterated pleasure. Soft moans and heavy breathing, punctuated by the occasional hiss.

Kali couldn't wrap her head around it. "This is what they do? *All day?*" Though she'd dropped her voice to the lowest whisper, Rhane motioned for silence. *Wow. Just wow.* Shaking her head, she made up her mind not to look into any more rooms. Of course, then Rhane decided to enter the next one.

Here, there were only two rogues. Both male. One was pretty burly with broad shoulders and well-defined muscles rippling across his back. His long, dark hair was tied into a low ponytail and nearly reached the floor. Kali wasn't sure of the rogue's height because he was currently kneeling in front of the other. This one had a much leaner build and darker skin. The attractive but almost feminine appeal of his face was worthy of any runway. Eyes closed, the rogue's head dropped back and his lips parted, making sounds of encouragement to his partner. Were he not so lost in throes of pleasure, the rogue may have sensed the danger standing less than ten feet away.

"How about a little more privacy, Kalista," Rhane said and the creature's eyes opened, nearly popping out of his head. "Seal the door."

At his word, she raised a wall of fire before the entrance, one reaching all the way to the ceiling, and made the flames hot enough to melt the flesh of anyone brave enough to attempt charging through it. The kneeling rogue tried to rise, but the other had regained composure and held him down. "Keep going," he ordered.

Rhane rotated his sword, leveling it off in a high guard. "If your buddy doesn't stand up right now, I'm going to cut his head off."

Without waiting for permission, the burly rogue hurried to his feet. Kali was instantly grateful for the dim lighting. The rogue was far taller than she had imagined and burly enough in other places to make her cheeks hot. Quickly lifting her gaze, she hoped Rhane hadn't noticed her schoolgirl reaction. Version 2.0 would certainly tease her for it later.

The attractive rogue narrowed a pair of almond-shaped eyes. "We assumed that dog, Cixi, had turned traitor. Your being here confirms it."

"Are you the Keeper of this hive?"

"This hive has no Keeper."

"Then you will answer my questions," Rhane said. His voice was low but brimmed with unmistakable menace. "Where's Moros?"

"All hives know the fate of Erebus. Why should I answer your questions, when you will kill me anyway?"

Rhane shrugged one shoulder. "Erebus caught me on a bad day. I recently visited Ratri in New York. She was very accommodating and I touched not one hair on her head."

"Give me first your word—you will not harm any in our hive."

"Answer my questions. And if no one attacks when we leave, no one will be harmed."

Silent until now, the burly rogue's gaze slid nervously in Kali's direction. "What about her?"

"She speaks for herself."

Surprised by the unexpected nod to her independence, Kali smiled. "Follow his conditions and I won't hurt anyone."

"Swear it," the first rogue insisted.

Frowning, Rhane relented. "I swear it."

"Very well then." The attractive rogue drew himself taller and smirked as if he'd won. What the contest was, Kali had no idea. Then the rogue uttered the words that made her heart sink to her knees.

"Return to your people. Moros should have found them by now."

Chapter 23

The carnage along the mountain road was similar to the bloodbath in the city. Only instead of a massacre, this scene was a combat zone. Someone had been strong enough to put up a fight. But it was still bad.

The dust in the air had yet to settle as Rhane and Kali drove up the mountain roadway at speeds too high to be considered safe. They passed bodies…many bodies. Most were dead rogues or kindred, fully troll appearances beneath the late afternoon light. Claw and teeth marks scarred already twisted, grotesque limbs. Dozens of bullet holes riddled many of the bodies. Empty shells were scattered at random. Near those casings were the fallen soldiers who fired them…or at least their comrades.

Bailing from the car, she and Rhane ran across the battlefield, stepping over corpse after corpse. It appeared the men had been overrun. In some instances, Kevlar vests still protected torsos missing arms and legs. Yet for every dead soldier, there were ten dead changelings. Kali wanted to take comfort in that, but couldn't. Even from this distance she could see the strain on York's face as he paced, shaking his head when one of the uniformed men left the loose formation of a small unit of soldiers and approached. The other kin stood within the circle…but not all of them. She saw Orrin, looking absolutely dazed as he stared off at some unknown point. Bailen sat at his feet. War and Rion were nowhere to be seen.

Kali sobbed. She knew. She already knew but forced her legs to keep moving.

Her eyes finally found War. He was kneeling in the dirt, his auburn hair covered in enough dust and blood to turn its color black. Tears stained his face. Blood soaked both his clothing and the broken form cradled in his arms.

No.

Pushing through the circle of men, she fell next to them and met War's eyes through a blur of tears. Then she looked down at Rion, immediately noticing the odd concavity of his chest. Her hands shook as she reached out to touch him. His battered skin was still warm. *No.*

She could barely form a sentence. "What happened?"

Shaking his head, War tried to speak but choked on the words. He started rocking, eventually calming enough to try again. "Moros came with his army and attacked. This little shit saved me." A grief-stricken smile flashed through pain. "It should be me lying here," he said, and hung his head.

From somewhere above her, Kali heard an enraged roar, followed by sounds of a scuffle, and then York's urgent shouting. "This wasn't them. Let him go, Rhane. Let him go."

Looking up, she saw a familiar face in the crowd but couldn't place where she knew it. She couldn't think past her pain. With a heavy heart slowly breaking into pieces, she lowered her forehead to Rion's and rested her hand gently atop his shattered ribcage, above his bloody shirt. The last one he would ever wear. "Monsters Don't Sparkle."

"Oh but you did, Rion," she whispered. "You did."

At some point, she registered Rhane standing over the three of them. Swaying, he bent over, resting his hands on his knees. He finally gave in and fell to the dirt. His entire body shook. The mark of the immortal burned bright within the palm of his hand, glowing as intensely as a halogen light. His eyes changed from green to black to red.

Leaning forward, his nostrils flared as he inhaled the air next to Rion's skin. Glistening canines stretched over his bottom lip even as white fur rippled across his face and arms.

"Rhane, wait." York's voice, cracking with hurt but still somehow calm. "Moros is different from any rogue we've ever seen. He's powerful. He's old…like Dmiri. Time has altered him. Made him stronger."

"Don't follow me," Rhane said as his body continued to grow, steadily changing to become the creature so feared by the supernatural world.

Wordlessly, the soldiers moved back, surrendering space without question or hesitation. None of the men raised their guns but touched the weapons as if seeking reassurance of some defense against the awesome but frightening thing rising before them. Kali tried to imagine seeing Banewolf with virgin eyes…or at least recall the memory of the immortal's recurrence in Rhane's first fight against Gabriel. Then she realized she didn't care what the soldiers were experiencing. Rion was dead. That was all that mattered.

She looked up at the white wolf. "Don't come back until it's done."

*

The wolf ran until nightfall. Hundreds of miles. Through rural valleys. Into a different city. Maybe into a different country altogether. Things weren't clear. Hard to see anything past the scent. Past the rage. The wolf had a single focus. One directive. One mission. Nothing stood in its way. Anything that tried was killed in seconds.

Moros had many minions who attempted to stand between Banewolf and his prey. They stretched out behind the wolf in a trail of corpses.

The chase ended outside a remote village in an arid landscape. It was near dawn when the wolf heard the mechanical whir of a starting engine and then the rhythmic beating of chopper blades. Roaring, Banewolf accelerated. His prey would not live past the night.

Mid-liftoff, the wolf latched onto the landing skids and the bird tilted violently beneath the additional weight, plummeting nose-first into the sand. Banewolf rolled away from the burning wreckage and climbed to his feet, honing in on the only movement from the helicopter. An enormous rogue staggered outside. He was nearly seven feet tall, built of corded muscle and sharp edges that belied the creature's old age. Unlike the pewter masks others of his kind ritualistically donned, the mask this rogue wore was golden. Obviously suffering damage in the crash, it hung askew from the creature's face. Moros ripped the mask off, revealing deeply set eyes and half a dozen scars across his cheeks, upper lip, and forehead.

Teetering unsteadily, the rogue shook his head as if to clear it. His gaze narrowed on seeing Banewolf. "The immortal," he said and spread his arms wide. "We meet at last."

Banewolf made no reply, only stood watching the creature known as Moros. The rogue king was rumored to be insane. Even from where the wolf stood, he could smell madness. He could also smell Rion's blood. And that enraged the wolf.

"The Faction feared you and your siren could stop me. They were wrong. Nothing you do here will change the outcome of what is to happen. I have won, Banewolf. Our god will rise."

The rogue's skin began to crack. The fissures widened, spreading apart and slipping downward until chunks of skin began shed, falling to the ground in great lumps of steaming flesh. The thing revealed beneath the discarded skin was probably the ugliest troll Banewolf had ever encountered. Large, yellow eyes blinked out from a hide dark green in color. The twisted digits of clawed hands and feet dripped with black venom that sizzled upon touching the earth, melting the surface, changing sand into glass. As it breathed, its ribs expanded one at a time. And when it laughed, the entire ribcage splayed outward, expanding the torso to almost twice its normal size. Teeth as long and thin as needles clicked together excitedly.

"You took a daughter from me. I took your son. And the little one I killed back there…did he mean something to you?"

Banewolf answered by lunging for the bastard's throat.

*

The rest of the afternoon passed, as did the night, the next morning, and another afternoon before Rhane returned to them, covered in blood and filth. After insisting they move off the road and higher into the mountain, the soldiers had set up several tents and made camp. They wanted to help fight whatever plague was spreading through the East, but there was no fight without Rhane. So they all waited.

The soldiers buried most of their fallen. But neither Kali nor the kin could stand the thought of leaving Rion behind in this forsaken territory. They had to take him home.

Everyone was having a pretty awful time coping with the loss. The unit commander wanted to talk strategy, but after five minutes of dealing with York and Kali, the guy had given up and taken a step back to allow them time to grieve.

Poor York had taken a double hit. A day ago, Kali hadn't seen much of anything past the shock of seeing Rion's lifeless body cradled in War's arms. She didn't realize then that Cixi's broken form lay less than fifty feet away. Now the kindred beta was rolled in a tarp beneath the same tent with Rion's remains. There she would stay until they could return her to Ian for a proper burial.

In the end, Kali wasn't sure if Cixi had betrayed them or not. It was true the rogues had realized she was a traitor and consequently gave the beta information to mislead them. But what if Cixi knew about the ambush and led them straight into it? What if Moros had in turn returned her betrayal by killing the beta? Kali could empathize with the hurt York must be feeling but ultimately couldn't bring herself to mourn Cixi's demise.

They all took turns sitting with Rion so he would never be alone. After each of her shifts, Kali broke down into a fresh well of tears. Bailen stayed closed. Though he remained canine, he comforted her as best he could.

The two of them were sitting just outside the site's perimeter when Bailen whimpered and nuzzled Kali's arm. Lifting her head, she took in a sight that made her pulse skip with both gladness and dread. It was Rhane. He more or less stumbled toward the camp, eyes unfocused, clothing and skin covered in dried blood.

Standing up, Kali ran to him. Placing one hand on his cheek, she held his face until he saw her...really saw her. "Is it done?" she asked.

Rhane swallowed thickly. "Moros is dead." Tears sprang to his eyes and quickly flooded over, stripping through layers of blood and dirt on his face. "Kalista," he whispered, and she could hear the intense ache in his voice.

Kali pulled him close. "I know," she said. "I know." His legs gave way, and she did her best to help ease him to the ground. Taking a seat next to him, she checked for injuries, but it was difficult to tell if any of the blood sourced from Rhane. She called his name gently. "Are you hurt?"

He stared off into the camp with a dazed expression, and Kali wondered if she would get a response. Eventually, he shook his head.

"Then where did all this blood come from? You must have fought Moros as Banewolf."

Rhane nodded. "I ripped him apart, one piece at a time." He spoke so softly, Kali was forced to lean in close to understand him. "But the maniac still didn't die...so I fucking ate him."

"Oh." Kali covered her mouth. Bailen's ears dropped flat against his head.

"York was right. Moros was...changed somehow."

"So..." Kali looked down at his hands. She was still doubtful. There was just so much blood. "This all belongs to Moros?"

"No."

She was trying not to get freaked out, but it was becoming harder by the second. Rhane clearly wasn't himself. Yesterday, after seeing Rion, he'd left in a rage. Kali wasn't sure she had ever seen him so angry. What he was capable of in such a state...she already knew. After Rhaven was killed as a little boy, Rhane had completely lost it and massacred an entire legion of Warekin soldiers.

Kali grabbed his hand, willing to try anything to ground him. "Rhane, what did you do?"

He stroked the back of her hand and finally looked at her. "I went into the city...to the rogue hive. And I killed them all."

Stunned by his words, Kali reeled backward. She didn't know what to say. Biting her tongue, she remained silent.

"I gave my word I wouldn't harm them. But how could I allow the hive to continue in existence when Rion..." he stopped abruptly. Noticing a tremor in her arm, Kali looked down. Rhane's hands were shaking. "I couldn't let them live," he finished quietly.

Okay. She took a deep breath. *Okay, it could have been worse. It could have been innocent people slaughtered.* Besides, Rhane was hurting so much, a lecture on morality would have done little good in the moment.

Digging deep, Kali managed something she hoped resembled a smile. "Let's get you cleaned up," she said. "There's a shower set up in camp. It's kinda makeshift, but it will do the job. The soldiers shouldn't see you like this. They're still pretty jumpy."

With little coaxing, Rhane followed her and Bailen into camp. Posted on perimeter, Orrin saw their approach, and his eyes widened dramatically upon seeing Rhane. He started to come over, but Kali quickly waved him away. She ushered Rhane into the tent and behind the partitioned divider splitting the room into two compartments without further incident, grateful for the task of putting him back together. It meant she could stop thinking about her own grief, if only momentarily.

The shower consisted of a durable plastic bag holding about five gallons of water and hung overhead, suspended by a triangular metal framework. Operated by gravity and a simple valve, Kali knew from overhearing conversations in camp that she had about seven minutes of pressure to scrub Rhane as clean as possible. Frowning, she looked around for a means to refill the reserve of water. Seven minutes wasn't going to be enough.

After getting him stripped and soaked, Kali helped Rhane lather from head to toe, scrubbing the grime from his back and hair while he took care of the rest. They did this without speaking. A couple of times, an intimate gaze passed between them, but things went no further. Thinking about sex just didn't seem right when Rion's body was less than twenty yards away.

"Rhane," she said in one of the moments when their eyes met. "If Moros is dead, then why hasn't Rhaven returned to us?"

"I don't know, Kalista." His expression renewed with pain. "Maybe he just needs more time."

Kali accepted that answer, for no other reason than Rhane's sake.

Realizing his clothing was unsalvageable, she called to Orrin and dispatched him to find suitable replacements. He returned a short while later with tan cargos and a t-shirt of the exact same color. Smelling them, Kali wrinkled her nose. "Are these Rhane's?"

Orrin shrugged. "They came from our gear."

"Okay. Thanks." Kali met his eyes and the sadness in them rolled her stomach inside out. Fighting back a fresh wave of tears, she said, "Tell York he's almost ready." Then she hurried back inside. Rhane stood waiting at the center of the tent, in all his naked glory.

Kali wiped her face dry and handed him the change of clothes. "The commander of these soldiers would like to meet with you. He wants to help fight these things."

Rhane was slow to answer as he stepped into the thick cargos. "These are the same guys who shot at us in New York."

"Well yeah, but apparently everything that's happened in the news helped facilitate a change of heart on their side of things."

Pulling the shirt overhead, Rhane muttered something Kali didn't quite hear. He plopped down on a nearby supply box. "I don't know if we can fight this, Kalista. Rhaven could be out there right now, still using the ark to change humans into rogues and kindred on an even larger scale. We couldn't stop what happened in this city. We lost…" Rhane stopped. His face twisted with pain. "Moros didn't attack with a full army and look how much we lost."

"No," Kali said with more heat than she meant to. "Don't use Rion as an excuse not to finish this. Moros died easily by your hand. If you had been here during the attack, things would have turned out differently." She regretted her choice of words as soon as they left her mouth. From the stricken expression on Rhane's face, she may as well have punched him in the gut. "That came out totally wrong."

Rhane nodded. "Right," he said hoarsely. A look of utter defeat crumpled his features.

Kali wanted to kill herself. "Oh god, Rhane, that's not what I meant." Flinging herself at his feet, she took his face in her hands. "This isn't your fault. I wasn't there either, and I could have made just as much of a difference. I only meant that with the strength of the immortal, we have a chance."

Gently prying her hands away, he kissed each of her palms. Then he stood and strode to the tent opening. "Where are you going?" Kali asked.

"To meet the leader of this outfit."

Chapter 24

Though Kalista had done her best to help Rhane realign, he still dwelled in a dark place. His head wasn't in the game, and his heart wasn't ready for reality. Looking at the others for any stretch of time was difficult. Kalista's face was puffy and her eyes were swollen from all the crying she'd done in his absence. War was hurting pretty bad. York was an absolute mess. And to be honest, Rhane wasn't faring much better. Even after destroying the rogue hive beneath the mosque, methodically killing each of its members and using the most brutal methods to appease his appetite for vengeance, the storm of anger had barely abated. The only reason he bothered seeking out the commander was because he simply needed to keep moving. Standing still meant he had to think. Sleeping was out of the question. Rhane dreaded when the moment came that his body refused to operate any further without it. Hopefully, by then he would be dead tired and could just collapse into a dreamless sleep.

He passed the first huddle of soldiers he came across. They seemed capable enough but nothing about the men pointed toward them calling the shots. Anyone guarding equipment was also ignored. Taking in the full extent of the camp, Rhane realized this unit was considerably larger than the task force encountered in New York. He applauded them for learning from past mistakes, but Rhane knew these men wouldn't be enough to handle what was coming.

Near a tent situated toward the center of the camp, his gaze located three soldiers in deep discussion. Rhane was still far off but not too far for supernatural hearing to listen in. Strangely enough, the soldiers killed their conversation before he came within the "normal" range of human ears, and all three turned to greet his approach. Rhane read the name tape on each of their uniforms: Zed, Zephyr, and Zarek.

Gotta be code names.

Zarek, the only one of the trio who smelled completely human, jerked his chin upward. "I hope you're the guy we've been waiting all day and night for."

Appraising Rhane from head to toe, Zephyr confirmed his team member's suspicion. "It's him," he said.

Spreading his feet into a wider stance, Zarek tapped his finger against the assault weapon strapped across his chest and tilted his head sideways. He tossed a cocky glance at Zephyr. "He's smaller than the two big ones. Thought he'd be taller."

Zephyr replied with noticeable tension in his voice. "He's big enough."

"Cut the chit chat," Zed barked in a strong Midwestern accent. "We've wasted enough daylight." The commander turned stiffly to Rhane. "Confirm your identity for me, son."

Rhane could have laughed. He was more than aware of the fact that his appearance was exceedingly younger than the near millennium of living he had under his belt, but Zed wasn't a day over thirty-two and blond-haired, blue-eyed Zephyr—clearly a sibling—was even younger.

"I'm the guy you took a shot at in New York."

"Well I can't say I regret it. We had our orders."

"Which are what exactly?"

Zed showed the first hint of uncertainty since their meeting. "Last month you destroyed a lab, costing its parent company millions of dollars in damages. Several projects were rendered irretrievable secondary to the catastrophic loss of data. We couldn't let your crime go unanswered."

"You work for Global Cures." Keeping a neutral expression was difficult. The lab in question had held Bailen prisoner and belonged to a company whose CEO orchestrated the plot to lure Kali into the desert and have her sold to Gabriel and his reapers.

While Zed didn't answer, he didn't deny Rhane's assertion either. He pressed the soldier for more. "Where you supposed to kill me?"

"You wouldn't be standing here if we wanted you dead."

These guys aren't short on confidence. Patience running thin, Rhane strove to keep the flow of information sharing one way. "So what changed? You went from wanting to apprehend me to traveling thousands of miles to fight on the same side."

"Take a look around you, son."

"My name is Rhane," he snapped. If Zed called him "son" one more time, Rhane wasn't sure he'd be able to hold it together.

"Alright then, *Rhane.* That city below was devastated by an attack from an enemy unknown to us, using a weapon unknown to us. Right now it doesn't matter whose side we're on. What happened here can't be allowed to happen at home. Our unit is here to face the enemy in a direct assault and stop this disaster from spreading."

Rhane shook his head. "Well good luck with that plan, Commander, because you're out of your league here."

"Funny you should say so." Zarek folded his arms. "Don't seem to be doing too bad," he said. "We saved all of your asses...well except the little one. That crazy monster crushed him like an empty beer can."

Something inside of Rhane buckled, and for a moment everything went dark. He didn't hear, see, or feel anything until Kalista and York's voices reached out to him, begging him to stop. Then his vision slowly cleared, and Rhane was met with Zarek's horrified and bloodied stare. The soldier was pinned downed with Rhane's knee in his stomach and hand around his throat. Rhane had no memory of splitting the guy's lip or smashing his nose, but Zarek's face looked a lot like a pancake now.

"Rhane, get off of him," Kalista said with an eerie calmness. Dragging his attention away from Zarek, Rhane found her with his eyes. She was frightened. York stood next to her. Even he looked nervous as hell. "Let go, buddy," he gently urged, using a tone suitable for coaxing a terrified kitten from beneath the bed.

Shit. It took two tries, but Rhane managed to relax his hand and release the grip that had come dangerously close to pulverizing Zarek's windpipe. A ring of purple bruising was beginning to show on his skin. Maybe in three days, the guy would be able to speak normally again...if he was lucky.

Rhane backed away while two of Zarek's comrades helped him to his feet. A crowd of soldiers had gathered. All of them were tense. Fingers rested on triggers of lowered weapons, ready to be raised and fired on command. Zed didn't look happy but was smart enough not to escalate the situation. "Keep those weapons down," he ordered loudly so all would hear. "I'm sorry about that," he said more softly. "Zarek has a big mouth. But it seems like you've shut it for a while."

Heart racing way too fast and hands shaking, Rhane didn't answer. He pulled away when Kalista touched him. He couldn't bear it. He couldn't breathe. His chest ached for air. The ground shifted beneath him and the sky tilted sideways.

Get it together.

"This guy is nuts," a soldier he hadn't met whispered.

"He is not," a familiar drawl answered, making Rhane's attention whip in its direction. The voice belonged to a young soldier with sharp, almost bird-like features that gave him a much older appearance. The patch across his shoulder identified him as Zander.

Not helpful. But York had recognized him too.

"Well, that explains a lot," he said. "Hello, Jackson. I see you've found your friends."

"A lot of thanks to you."

The situation needed some humor injected into it and fast. Rhane's appearance reminded York a lot of what he'd looked like four centuries ago when Kalista was lost and Rhaven was killed. Since losing his head, Rhane's fuse had obviously gotten a lot shorter. It was almost like old times, when they were young recruits in the Warekin army and Rhane was about as level-headed as a warped two-by-four. He had already hammered in one guy's face and looked ready to take on the rest of the army. The muscles in his back were wrung tighter than guitar strings. At least he seemed to be trying to pull it together. He just needed more time. Hell, they all did.

Joking was the very last thing York wanted to do, but somehow he wrenched free from the fog of grief long enough to get his mind in the game. "I'm detecting some sarcasm there, Jackson. Totally unnecessary. I think I gave you a rather big, fat clue."

Jackson aka "Zander" rolled his eyes. It was a remarkable feat, considering how tiny they were.

"Now you, on the other hand, did not keep your promise. You were supposed to leave us alone, Jack. But here you are, running around with Captain Zigzag and his merry not-so-men."

"I've been trying to convince my team that y'all ain't the bad guys."

York winked. "And how is it working out?"

Jackson's mouth twitched. "Stand by," he said.

It was impossible not to recognize the valiant effort York had just made. The big guy was definitely hurting just as much Rhane. Doubling the effort to pull his head out of his ass, Rhane squared his shoulders and steeled his mind, shutting off all emotion. It was time to end this.

"Commander, your mission is one for fools. What's happening here can't be stopped. Withdraw your unit."

"I don't take orders from you."

"I meant no offense. It wasn't an order. I'm just trying to preserve the lives of your soldiers."

"While we turn tail and run, what will you do?"

Blinking slowly, Rhane blew out a long breath and ignored the stabbing ache in his gut. "I'm taking him home," he said.

"So you don't want us to fight, but you're not going to fight either. Unacceptable," the commander said brusquely. "If we do nothing, this entire continent will be lost."

Rhane turned away from the commander. As far as he was concerned, it was already lost.

York, however, did not share Rhane's confidence. He grabbed his arm, stopping him. "Hey, are you sure about this? We're just going to leave?"

Rhane looked his friend in the eye, the pain there mirroring his own. "See as Rion did, York. The fight can't be won here. It just can't."

A moment passed before York nodded and let go. Then he and Kalista fell into step as Rhane retreated from the commander's audience.

"Don't walk away from me." An angry edge crept into Zed's voice. "I gave the order to save your people. You owe us."

"No, Commander. Zarek was right," Rhane said. "You didn't save all of them."

Chapter 25

Rhane's legs felt as if they weighed a thousand pounds each as he walked toward the tent cover of the dead. Every step was heavier than the last, and he nearly lost the resolve to enter the makeshift morgue. Somehow, he managed to lift the flap and go inside. The sight of seven body bags arranged side by side on the dirt floor was a sledgehammer blow to his stomach. Gritting his teeth, he resisted the urge to double over with the pain but almost gave in when War turned to see him. He looked completely lost. His eyes were dull. His posture was limp. It was as if a little boy had lost his best friend in the entire world. And really, War had lost his best friend. He and Rion argued endlessly, fighting like brothers who shared an unbreakable bond. Only now it was broken.

Rhane rested a hand on War's shoulder. "We're going to take him home soon."

War cleared his throat. "That's good," he said. His voice barely rose above a whisper.

"Would you mind if I sit with him before we leave?"

Movements heavy with sadness, War got to his feet without a word. Sitting next to Rion's body for hours on end hadn't made it any easier to accept his death. Rion's final moments kept playing over and over in War's head, reminding him of how useless he had been in stopping Moros from crushing the life forever from Rion's eyes. Again and again, he saw blood forced through every orifice as Rion's body crumpled and his soul was extinguished.

"Warren."

Hearing his name, War turned back to Rhane. His expression was haunted. "If I could take this away, I would."

"I know."

"You're wrong to think this should be you lying here instead. Rion chose to save you. There will come a point when you'll become angry about all of this. Try not to resent his choice. Saving your life was the last good thing he did and the ultimate gift anyone could ever give you."

Tears streaming down his cheeks, War inclined his head and exited the tent, leaving Rhane alone at last. He squatted next to Rion, wondering how he was going to get through this day and the next. Emotionally and physically, Rhane felt he'd reached the end of an extremely frayed rope and beneath him was a pit of inconsolable darkness. If he fell into the abyss, it would never release him. Even so, Rhane stood on the ledge and wondered if he could just throw himself in.

"I thought I might find you here."

Startled, Kalista's voice wrestled him back from the void. She smiled, but it did not reach her eyes as she sat beside him and leaned her head against his shoulder. "There's something you should know."

"What's that?" he asked, making an effort to hide the true depth of his grief.

Hesitating, she studied his face closely. Rhane feared she would spot his secret. Finally, Kalista raised a finger and pointed to the plastic-wrapped body immediately next to Rion. "Cixi. Moros got her too."

Closing his eyes, Rhane groaned deeply. He hadn't even noticed her absence. *I'm such an asshole.* "What York must be feeling…" Having no idea how to finish it, he let the sentence hang. "It's time to leave this place, Kalista."

"I know."

"I borrowed a satellite phone and arranged for a jet to take us out of here. We just have to return to the airfield."

"Okay," she said. "We'll leave whenever you're ready."

Rhane had wanted to win this thing and keep everyone safe while doing so. He'd failed. Getting Rion home and giving him a proper burial was the only thing he knew for certain was right. After that, he had no idea what the next move would be, but the answer wasn't on this side of the world. Rion should have been chattering away in his ear, extrapolating data and presenting the possibilities.

"I can't believe he's gone."

Kalista took his hand and grasped it firmly. Rhane only knew she did so because he watched her. He couldn't feel a thing. He was numb.

*

The return to the States was a quiet trip. Everyone wore the same ragged expression, worn down and broken by defeat. With Rhane leading them, Kali knew they could find the strength to move forward, but first they needed to bury their dead.

Ian showed no emotion when Rhane delivered the news of Cixi's death, but Kali could tell the alpha did not take it well. Rhane didn't ask for absolution. Neither did Ian give it. He simply received her body in his arms and bowed his head as he backed away. Returning to the forest, he paused at the edge of the clearing. "The eclipse of the blue moon will be here in three night's time, Banewolf. See that you are ready and prove to me this alliance has not been in vain."

259

The alpha stood with his back to them, waiting. When Rhane didn't respond, Kali stepped forward. "We'll be ready, Ian."

Turning his head, Ian considered her with glittering red eyes. The alpha shifted his gaze to Rhane, but Rhane refused to look at him. "Very well, siren," Ian finally said. "I accept your word."

When he had gone, Kali stared at Rhane curiously. Meeting her eyes, he answered the unspoken question. "It doesn't feel right to give assurances I'm no longer sure I can keep."

"I understand," she said. Constructed the same morning, Rion's funeral pyre was erected less than twenty feet behind them, automatically placing Kali in a losing situation to challenge any of Rhane's self-proclaimed inadequacies. The discussion would keep until another time. She extended her hand to take his. "Let's go join the others."

She and Rhane took positions to complete the half circle formed around the pyre. Bailen stood with them, fully human, and dressed identically to the kin. Their torsos and feet were bare. Everyone exhibited heads of freshly cropped hair. No words were spoken. No songs were sung. They waited in absolute silence. And when the sun descended in the western sky, Kali set fire to the wooden platform and the combustibles piled beneath it. One by one, the kin tossed back their heads and began to howl a soft and hollow chorus of mourning. Their voices united to become a single voice of bottomless sadness that reached into Kali's bones and dragged her into the same pit of despair. The tears came and she was powerless to stop them. But at least she wasn't alone.

When the howls suddenly stopped, the approaching night was filled with unmatched silence. It was as if the rest of the forest knew their sadness and grieved with them. They stood motionless for hours, watching as the pyre and all it contained was reduced to ash. Then the fires died, giving them up to the darkness and leaving only sorrow behind.

After the light went out, Kali wasn't sure what to expect. Rhane had explained how Rion would have a warrior's burial and be honored in the language of the skins. Going into further detail seemed too painful and so Kali had not pressed for more. She intended to watch and listen carefully, taking any necessary cues in the ritual from the others. So, when the fires died and yet no one moved, she resolved to stand all night with them if necessary. What happened next could not have been predicted by Kali or anyone else.

By light of the waxing moon, she saw Orrin break formation. He turned in a circle, looking first at the woods and then into the sky. Lifting his head, Rhane tensed as he sniffed the air.

"What's happening?" Kali asked.

He frowned. "Something odd," he said and called out to Orrin. "Stand down until we spread the ashes."

Orrin jogged back to the group and rejoined them in facing the remains of the pyre. Reaching into the ashes, Rhane grabbed a handful and nodded for Kali to do the same. She did and the others followed, each taking heaping mounds into their hands. Facing outward, they slowly strode away from the center and each other, letting Rion's remains fall to the earth in the trails behind them.

And when they reached the edge of the field, the procession halted.

Rhane was now fifteen feet to her left, and War stood the same distance on her right. Kali glanced at each of them, waiting for the next step. She was surprised when it turned out to be spreading remnants of ash through their hair. Hesitating for a brief moment, Kali lifted her hands and raked them through her curls, repeating the process until the residue was completely transferred. When she was done, War embraced her. Grasping her shoulders, he touched his forehead to hers. Then he pulled away, offering Kali a solemn smile before moving on. It took another heartbeat for her to realize it was over. Rion was truly gone and she would never see him again. There would be no more ridiculous arguments between him and War. No more excited rants as he attempted to explain some nerdy topic she couldn't fully understand. The soft fur of his timid but fearsome wolf would never again brush against her skin. This was it. Rion wasn't coming back.

As she started to sink to her knees, solid arms encircled her waist and lent her their strength, keeping her upright. Rhane's cheek pressed against her face and his tears mixed in with hers. "We must be strong," he whispered.

Nodding, Kali released a sob and leaned into him for a few moments more. Then she fought back through the grief, finding a way to stand on her own.

York called to Rhane. His voice was still hoarse with emotion. "Do you feel it?"

"I do."

"So do I," Kali said and raised her arm. All of the hairs were standing upright. She felt rather than heard a faint hum spread through the air. The sensation amplified and then a boom of bright light illuminated the forest with blinding radiance.

Kali had already reached for her knives before she realized they weren't there. No weapons were allowed during a burial ceremony. But the kin were never defenseless, and neither was she.

"Skins!" Rhane ordered even as white fur appeared at his temples. Orrin, York, Bailen, and War immediately dropped to all fours, seamlessly shifting into the wolf forms as they assembled into battle arrangement. Ahead of them, the light disappeared and a mass of shadows moved in its place. A chorus of eager growls came from the kin in open challenge to the unknown threat. Kali worried it might be another attack from Builders. They were, after all, great with light shows.

Just as quickly as they appeared, the changes in Rhane's features reversed and he stared into the forest with a shocked expression. "Stand down," he yelled, putting himself in front of the snarling wolves.

It didn't take long to understand why he did so.

Emerging from the shadows, dozens of human figures entered into the moonlit clearing. Male and female, their garb was a mixture of dark leathers and silky linens made translucent by the moon's shining light. Many of them possessed tresses of stark white, gleaming even in the near darkness. Kali couldn't see the color of their irises, but she was willing to bet on them being clear blue.

Her eyes darted through the crowd, searching the faces of all the strangers. She didn't realize who she was seeking until her heart lurched and blood pooled to her extremities.

River.

Before Kali could react, Rhane was moving, pushing through the crowd to reach his brother. River attempted to defend himself against the onslaught, but his efforts were futile. In five seconds, Rhane had River's arms and head locked in an unbreakable hold. The look on Rhane's face was murderous. But when he spoke, his voice remained frighteningly calm. "What did I say would happen if she ever laid eyes on you again?"

Gasping for a breath Rhane wouldn't allow, River struggled to escape. Rhane kicked his brother's feet from beneath him and adjusted his grip. It looked a lot like he was about to break River's neck.

"Rhane!" Kali shouted. "Don't do this."

"I've already spared him once for you, Kalista."

"He is your brother."

"Only because our sires shared a whore," he said, and a burst of murmurs reverberated through the crowd.

York's wide-eyed stare whipped around to Kali. Shaking her head, she licked her lips and grew desperate. Rhane was hurting so much already. Right now he was furious and a little lost. Murdering River would only add to his pain. He just didn't realize it yet. "You loved him once, Rhane. You love him now. River made a terrible mistake, but you need to forgive him." Kali swallowed, wondering if she had the strength to utter her next words. "I forgive him."

Though Rhane didn't let River go, he hesitated. Then his eyes darkened and Kali turned away, knowing she could never forget if she witnessed what was coming next.

A powerful voice cut through the air, male and strangely familiar as it stirred distant memories Kali no longer possessed. "Rhane, you will not kill him." The command was delivered gently and yet demanded obedience.

The crowd parted, making way for the owner of the voice and Kali laid eyes on a man who could have been River's twin. It was more than the same white hair and blue irises. The two had matching physiques, built equally for speed and strength. Angular but solid jaw lines framed the same thin mouths. The only difference was this newcomer radiated an aura of kindness River could never hope to achieve.

In this stranger, Kali also saw Rhane. Not so much physically, but the mannerisms were there. The set of his shoulders and jaw, the same powerful stride as he walked. Just from the way he stood, the awesome depth of the stranger's might was evident. It was also clear his authority was revered …even by Rhane.

Clad in all black, the man stepped into the space where no other was brave enough to enter. No one else dared moved within ten feet of the killing floor. "Release him, Rhanelin."

The struggle rippled visibly through Rhane's body. He wanted—needed—to obey this soft-spoken stranger, but the thirst for violence was nearly irresistible. Gritting his teeth, Rhane finally let go. As River dragged in the first taste of air he'd had for several minutes, Rhane shoved him to the ground and pulled the dagger from his brother's waist. Fisting River's long hair into one hand, he sawed the blade through and through, severing the bulk of River's proud locks. He leaned in close to River's ear. "It is by Jehsi's will you now live. When that ends, you die. When he dies, you die. By my immortal breath, I will see my oath to you fulfilled."

Jehsi had managed to reel Rhane in. But it was a tight leash, one liable to snap apart with the whisper of the wrong word. Gaining composure, River kneeled before Rhane and bowed his head. "For your mercy, brother, I thank you."

Rhane threw both the dagger and River's shorn hair to the earth. "Why have you come here?" He looked at Jehsi. "Why did you bring him here?"

"We had nowhere else to go."

Kali assumed that with the matter of killing his brother set aside for the time being, Rhane was free to really consider the crowd of haggard people. "What happened?"

"I'm afraid our worst fears have been realized—the creature has awakened."

Chapter 26

It was a lot of people to fit inside the manor, but their home was huge and well-suited, as it turned out, to the task of receiving nearly one hundred refugees. It was nearly too much for a girl to take in, but Kali thought she was getting close to fitting together all the pieces. The man who had prevented Rhane from executing his brother, thereby saving River's life, was Jehsi, and he was their father. Maybe he wasn't Rhane's biological parent, but he was Rhane's father in every sense that embodied the spirit of the word. Kali wanted to know this man. To overcome the shame and scandal surrounding an unwanted child's origins was an incredible act of love. Then to go on and raise the child to become the fine and loving warrior she could no longer live without—Kali hoped for the chance to express her gratitude.

Unfortunately, she had yet to properly speak with Jehsi. The manor had bustled with nonstop activity since the arrival of Rhane's people. There was ample sleeping space, but finding and distributing enough bedding to meet everyone's needs was an entirely different challenge. Families shared. Many proudly did without. Apparently Egyptian cotton sheets didn't compare to home-cured fur bedcovers. Kali kept reminding herself that most of the survivors were royalty and completely unassimilated to any culture outside of their own. Though she didn't want to, she thought of River. These newcomers were much like him with the aloof air around them and the formal politeness with which they spoke. Orrin seemed rattled by all of it. York was less than thrilled to associate with any of them, and Bailen wouldn't come out of hiding. Having spent months imprisoned within Golden Mountain, War remained unfazed. Kali wondered how Rion would have handled their present circumstances. Always sporting a gun half-loaded outlook, he probably would have been thrilled at his first real taste of the Warekin homeland, meeting royalty and possibly even relatives from his bloodline.

When most of the refugees were settled and on the path to getting some severely needed rest, Rhane took Kali's hand and sent for York. Sagging against the nearest wall, he closed his eyes. Her gaze wandered to the purple blotches shadowing the skin just above his cheeks and the tension seemingly etched permanently into his face. Kali bit her lip. "When did you last sleep?" she asked softly.

Rhane shook his head. "Can't remember."

York popped into the room. "You rang?"

Rubbing his eyes, Rhane straightened from the wall. "I need to meet with the extant leaders. Seppina is the only Mother who lives. Two of our Primes survived as well."

"Have they told you exactly what happened?"

"No. We still need to find out."

"So, Jethra…she's…"

Rhane grimaced. "She's gone, York."

"I'm so sorry."

"Yeah," Rhane said softly and ducked his head. "It actually happened before this. She delivered War to me in the Gobi Desert outpost but then died while helping destroy two Builders. I couldn't save her. There wasn't a chance to tell you sooner."

"There were plenty of chances, buddy." Though York's tone was persistently gentle, he wasn't letting Rhane off the hook. "You just didn't want to talk about it."

"You're right," Rhane said. He sounded too exhausted to argue. "Are you going to give me hell about it?"

"Absolutely. But later."

So, Jethra was dead. All those centuries ago, Rhane's grandmother had been the only one brave enough to condemn the nefarious scheme of the Primes. She had taken action, risking herself to deliver a young Rhaven to safety and thereby freeing Kali to act. Rhane had little affection for those who called Golden Mountain home, but from the way he spoke of Jethra, Kali knew she was one of the exceptions. Rhane had loved her very much.

It stung a little to know he'd withheld the news of her death and hidden his pain about it for so long. They were supposed to be moving past keeping secrets from one another. Had Kali known he was already hurting so much from that recent blow, maybe she could have kept a closer eye on him after Rion.

"Rhane, we promised," she said looking at him seriously. "No more secrets."

York, of course, couldn't resist adding his two cents. "High five, Brutus."

Ignoring him, she took Rhane's face gently in her hands. "You don't need to go through anything alone. Not anymore. Don't shut me out."

"I know. I'm sorry." He took her hands in his. "It was a momentary lapse. I'm not hiding anything else."

"Yeah about that," York said while scratching the back of his head. "Outside when you called your mom a whore...I mean she is a total bitch, so I'm not questioning that part..."

Watching Rhane's face grow paler and paler with York's every word, Kali's heart ached for him. That he had made such a shameful admission about his heritage while in a fit of rage was a testament to the volatile state of his mind. Kali widened her eyes and shook her head subtly, trying to get York to shut up, but he ignored every hint.

"Did you really mean the bit about you and River having different fathers? I mean, you did use sire in the plural form. It would explain a lot, I mean…" York rambled on. The misery consuming Rhane's face must have finally clued him in to the field of shit he'd just stepped into. "You are more like Jehsi than River will ever be. He's an ass most of the time and you're not…most of the time. So, I can see how you two could have sprang from different seeds…that is, if you meant what you said out there. But if you didn't, that's okay too. People get mad and say stuff they don't mean all the time."

Pursing his lips together, York managed to stop himself. He looked at Kali as if begging for help. She just stared at him in disbelief. The confession had probably shocked her a little less than most everyone else because Wesley had already revealed to her the reality of Rhane's origins, Gabriel being his true sire. But even without being privy to the truth, York had to know this was probably the worst moment to go diving for more details.

"Maybe now isn't the right time, York."

"No. It's okay," Rhane said hoarsely. "You two should know. I'm obviously not handling everything so well on my own." Taking a deep breath, Rhane blurted out a detailed explanation. "One of the reasons Builders were so hell-bent on capturing Bailen was because of the immortal. They needed my kid to be the wolf's new vessel in order for him to become a worthy opponent to Rhaven and hopefully defeat Blight if the situation came to it."

"Okay?" York looked at expectantly at Rhane, clearly waiting for more. The other shoe had yet to drop. "I know they were after the little guy, but what does it have to do with your father?"

"The immortal is blood chained, York. It can only be passed from father to son."

York frowned. "What you're saying doesn't make any sense. Gabriel had the immortal before you."

Rhane's face hardened as his green eyes grew defiant. "Exactly," he said plainly.

All at once, the air seemed to leave York's body with one lengthy exhale. Horror overtook his expression. "You've got to be kidding me."

"I'm not."

Dismay became full blown confusion. "All this time? Did Jehsi know?"

"He knew."

Straightening, York shifted his attention to Kali. "You aren't shocked by this."

Biting her lip, she considered lying, but what was the point? "Wesley told me just before he died."

Now it was Rhane's turn to be stunned. "And you didn't tell me?" he said, staring at Kali with open disbelief.

"You didn't tell me," she replied indignantly. "This is why we shouldn't keep secrets from one another. Had I known you knew about Gabriel, then, yeah, I would have talked to you about it. But there was no way I was going to be the one who dropped a bombshell like that unless I was one hundred percent sure it was true. And considering the source, certainty was impossible."

"No shit," York said, still looking somewhat dazed. "Rhane, no wonder you're spinning like a raving hatter. This is too much. It would be too much for anyone."

"It's no excuse. We all lost Rion...and you lost Cixi. I think she was special to you."

Rounding his shoulders, York jammed both thumbs into his pockets. He shrugged sadly. "We weren't so close."

Rhane scoffed. "Baloney. The stars in your eyes could be seen from a mile away. She had you completely spanked."

"She cared about you too, York," Kali added.

"Alright, yeah." York threw his hands up. "I did like her a lot, but not enough to leave the pack or anything. It wasn't that serious."

"Okay," Rhane said quickly. "Take it easy."

Talking about Cixi clearly had York rattled. Everything about his body language said he no longer wanted to be in there. He crossed his arms over his chest. Toes pointed to the door, one foot tapped anxiously against the hardwood floor.

"I guess share time is over. Let's go downstairs and meet with our visitors," Rhane suggested.

"Good idea," York said, and was the first to step out into the hall. Kali and Rhane followed behind, trying to give him some space, but she had to stop abruptly when York suddenly spun around. "I'm fine. And good job of shifting the spotlight off your ass, by the way."

Rhane opted for the route of ignorance. "I don't know what you mean."

Rolling her eyes, Kali pushed past both of them. "You two are more alike than you realize."

"Well none of us seem to be so hot at these coping mechanisms, sister," York tossed at her back.

She kept walking. "What are you, five?"

"Three and a half."

Kali smiled. If York was joking again, it was a good sign he would be okay.

*

Being in the same room with the four of them was unnerving. With their pale skin, clear blue eyes, and long, white hair, Kali was eerily reminded of how vampires were often depicted. Other than those oddities, the royal kin appeared human physically. But they didn't fidget like humans. They definitely did not blink as often. And the disdain oozing from their pores was almost tangible. It was just hours ago when these people had been driven from their home. They were refugees, and they were guests. But Kali figured there was a slim chance of getting their pride to see it in such a way.

She, Rhane, and York sat spread out between the couch and armchair, facing off against the pale visitors. Drawing on old memories, Kali graciously offered to brew a batch of healing tea for Seppina and was surprised when the regal woman actually accepted. The matriarch now sat holding the mug, taking small sips in long intervals. Only the slightest wrinkle creased her stoic expression after each drink. And that was really impressive. Kali had added a lot of skullcap to the mixture. Even the extra honey wouldn't quell so much bitterness. But Seppina's tired eyes and sunken cheeks had screamed a dire need for the heavy dose.

Three royals stood at her side, surrounding Seppina's chair as if it were a throne. Kali remembered Rhane had

273

said only two Primes escaped the mountain and wondered who the third guy was. Jehsi, of course, she knew. The second Prime was easily identified. His appearance was older than Rhane's father and a lot older than the third male. But his clothing was the same as Jehsi's. Thick trousers and long-sleeved shirts cut from softer leather. Boots laced up to their knees completed the look. Really, their outfits could have been at home on any high fashion runway.

Rhane was the first to break the tense silence. "Now that everyone is settled and comfortable, perhaps you can explain what happened at Golden Mountain."

The unnamed Prime flinched. While his face darkened, the ruler did not speak. Kali began to wonder if any of them ever would. Despite Rhane's request, all three men stood with their hands folded behind their backs, uttering not a single word. Seppina's gaze was cool and unmoved as she stared straight ahead, through them instead of at them. Even Jehsi was quiet, but blotches of color spotted his pale cheeks.

It was finally the matriarch who replied. "The creature, Blight, awakened from its tomb. After draining most of Asia, it came to us. We did not know it would be drawn to our power." Something flickered behind Seppina's frosty eyes. Regret? Regret made sense after dreaming up a plot to erase the human world, having the plan backfire, and getting your own people killed.

When the Mother said nothing further, Rhane leaned forward. "And then what? No outside force has breached Golden Mountain since it was forged into our home."

"Coren and I stood against the creature, but without the power of our third sister, we could not defeat it. Nor could

274

we drive it back. Golden Mountain was lost. Blight fed, draining them all until they were but withered corpses." The cup rattled against the saucer as Seppina's hand began to shake. Carefully setting it aside, she smoothed her robes.

"Are you okay?" Kali asked.

Seppina stared at her coldly. Inclining his head, Jehsi offered Kali a kind smile. "Old Mother was greatly weakened bringing us here."

"Which was how exactly?" York asked.

The unnamed Prime turned an even darker shade of red.

Again, Jehsi responded. "You, Yorkshire, should be familiar with the unusual abilities possessed by those who rule as Mothers. At great cost to herself, Seppina transported us here through a portal of light just as the mountain was destroyed and with it, the last of her strength."

"Well that's a neat trick."

Not sharing York's blasé attitude, Kali's eyes nearly boggled out of her head. If Seppina had really teleported nearly one hundred people halfway around the world in mere seconds, her powers were incredible.

"And how did you know where to find us?" she couldn't help asking, but at least managed to hide the amazement from her voice.

"River showed us the way."

Right. Kali considered leaving the rest of the questioning to Rhane and York. They were doing a better job. Noticing how Jehsi still watched her, Kali felt a blush creeping into her face.

"It pleases me to see you again, Kalista Darkesong."

"It's good to see you too, Jehsi...uh, Prime of Whytetree," Kali finished after racking her brain.

Jehsi's warm eyes flashed with amusement. "No need to be so formal, daughter."

And that's when the second Prime finally lost it. "Enough of this!" he shouted. "These dogs should kneel before us, not address us as if we were equals."

"Silas," Jehsi hissed. "We are not in our homeland. We are guests. Conduct yourself in a manner thus befitting."

"What is not befitting is this summit with a band of mongrels. I am Silas, Prime of Greinwysh, First Son of the Old Mother, and Pinnacle of the triumvirate, and I say we should have never come to this wasteland. We should have stayed and buried our dead."

Jehsi grabbed the older Prime and pulled him close, urging him toward reason. "Had we not come here, then your breathless body would lie next to that of your wife and son. Calm yourself, Silas."

Silas responded by shoving Jehsi away with enough force to knock him to the floor. Passive onlookers to the heated exchange until that point, Rhane and York stood from their seats. But Jehsi held up one hand to stay them as he climbed to his feet. Kali kept her focus on Rhane. The dead look in his eyes made her nervous.

"Silas, you must display more control," Seppina said in a tone containing more boredom than reproach. "In time, we will regain what was lost."

The older Prime balled both hands into fists. "We shall rebuild on the bones of the human world and our legacy shall stretch from hemisphere to hemisphere. No longer can our blood be tainted or diluted by inferior filth. We had a vision, Old Mother. On my last breath I shall see it fulfilled. Blight's awakening is only the beginning. Let it purge the refuse and pave way for our glory."

Getting the impression Silas was certifiably nuts, Kali still couldn't believe what she was hearing. Even after losing his home and family, the Prime persisted in the same narrow-minded ideals that had helped get them into this mess in the first place. Jehsi turned out to be a man of infinite patience. He yet again attempted to reach the co-ruler with reason.

"Silas, you must abandon this unholy crusade. Look at where it has brought our people. You have a chance now to set right the grave wrongs of the past. Seize it."

"You are a righteous fool, Jehsi. Your Mother is dead. Your line is dead. Instead of rising to the greatness of your ancestors, you abandoned your post and claimed a bastard who can never sit as Prime. You are heirless, Jehsi, and your high-mindedness is not only unjust; it is useless. With Seppina and Corbin at my side I shall create a new order. A royal brotherhood founded in purity and might. And in this brotherhood, I'm afraid there is no room for you, old friend."

Uh oh.

Silas softened his voice to the point where it almost became sad. "It is time I did what we failed to do so many years ago."

"Silas, don't," Jehsi warned.

Shaking his head, Silas took hold of the dagger secured at his hip. "It must be this way," he said and started toward Jehsi. He had not completed the step when Rhane pulled Bellefuron from behind the sofa cushions and moved in front of his father in one fluid motion. Before Silas or anyone else could react, he drove the sword through and through the Prime's chest, piercing dead center of his heart.

Kali's stomach took a sickened twist at the sound of tissue and bone yielding wetly to the ancient blade. Groaning, Silas looked down at the wound and then back at Rhane. He opened his mouth but only gurgled as blood spurted from his lips. Falling from limp fingers, the dagger clattered against the hardwood. Rhane withdrew Bellefuron, and Silas slumped to the floor.

It was like someone had hit pause and then play on a remote control. For what seemed like a long time, no one move or breathed. And then things slammed into action. Corbin rushed to the fallen Prime's side. Possibly still feeling the drain of power, the Old Mother moved more slowly but also dropped onto her knees next to Silas. He was still alive, but barely. Bellefuron's blade was famously forged from bane silver. The metal's composition was toxic to even Warekin and with location of the wound, the poison was pumping directly into Silas's bloodstream.

"My son," Seppina called desperately. She cast an accusing glare up at Rhane. "How dare you! You must heal him."

"I will not." Rhane's voice was void of all emotion. So much blood flowed. Pooling beneath Rhane's boots, the deep red liquid spread to where Kali sat, nearly touching her shoes. She withdrew her feet and looked at Jehsi. Eyes closed, his face contracted as if in pain. Standing just to her side, York reached back and hauled Kali from the couch. For a moment, her movements were all of his volition as he ushered her farther away from the scene. She eventually worked out how to move her legs again. It was funny how shock had a way of making the body numb, but hearing Rhane's quiet, even speech helped her brain accept the reality of what was happening.

"I, Rhane of Whytetree, Vessel of Banewolf, Bastard Son of Jehsi, sentence you, Silas, Prime of Greinwysh, murderer of my son, would-be murderer of my mate, would-be murderer of my father, and slayer of the Warekin people. I sentence you to death."

Silas began to seize. His arms and legs flailed erratically. His breaths shortened, became shallower with each passing second.

"No longer will your greed bring ruin to the Warekin. No more innocent lives will be broken by your hand. Hear this judgment as you breathe your last. Your evil has ended…as it should have long ago."

Chapter 27

Rhane could sense his father's disappointment. He could feel York and Kali's horrified stares drilling into his back. What he had just done was pretty extreme. He knew that. He hadn't killed the eldest Prime because he was in some sort of blind rage or overwhelmed with emotion from losing Jethra and Rion in barely a week's time. No, if his plan was to have any chance of success, then Silas needed to die.

It would have been great to let York or Kali in on the decision to execute Silas prior to this moment, but he couldn't risk any of the warriors from Golden Mountain overhearing. Silas would have died by his hand anyway, but more blood would have been spilled in the process. Most were not privy to the evil deeds committed by their government, so were still loyal to the old regime. Misplaced allegiance would have made his people defend Silas and they would have been killed. Rhane couldn't allow that.

Steeling himself against the backlash, he addressed the Old Mother. "Silas lives with our ancestors now, and we must move forward. I cannot allow this world to be taken by the evil we have unleashed upon it. I will defend it, but I need your help. I need our warriors to fight."

"How dare you?" Seppina climbed to feet. Her face darkened furiously. Good thing her powers were tied to the mountain. "You leave me with nothing and then ask for my help?"

Rhane nodded toward the only remaining adult male in the Old Mother's bloodline. It was true. Seppina had lost a lot. Neither her oldest grandson nor her son's mate had survived the attack on Golden Mountain. And now her son was dead. But Cale's twin brother yet lived. "You still have Corbin. He may one day become Prime. Be careful, Old Mother. How you react now could cost him his life."

There were no tears in her eyes, only hatred. Panting heavily, her gaze flickered to Rhane's side. Silas' blood still drained from Bellefuron's blade. It probably helped drive the point home. Pulling herself upright, Seppina lifted her chin. "I could scream for the warriors."

"You will be dead before anyone reaches you. And I will slaughter them until surrender. Only those who submit will be spared."

"You're a monster."

"Right now, we need monsters."

Making one final effort to persist in defiance, Seppina turned to Jehsi. *"This,"* she practically spat. "This bastard is what you claimed. You should have left him to die."

Her words stung a bit, but Rhane was getting used to the reference. He couldn't see Jehsi, but the quiet anger in his voice spoke volumes as to how he felt about Rhane's new title. Everyone had always known or at least suspected. But now it was in the open. And their people were just as cruel and prejudiced as they had always been. At least Rhane was older now. Tougher. Jehsi didn't have to protect him, but the instinct to do so would never diminish.

Moving forward slowly, Jehsi looked the Old Mother square in the eye. She would never know it, but he felt Silas' death just as deeply. Side by side, they had ruled together for over two millennia. One could not do that without becoming as brothers. Jehsi couldn't know Rhane's thoughts but could easily see reason behind the extreme actions. Silas had still desired the death of the human world. Even after two-thirds of Golden Mountain was massacred, the Prime had still believed bringing Blight to life was the correct path. Silas clearly wasn't going to stop. He wanted to destroy the world, and Rhane wanted to save it.

Though Coren, the third Mother, and Cale, the third Prime, had died, the line of Greinwysh carried a majority of the ruling government. No doubt, Silas would have petitioned his son and Cale's twin brother, Corbin, to assume the third seat as Prime. Then he, Corbin, and the Old Mother would have sided against Jehsi and this whole nightmare would have continued.

No. Silas had to die. Jehsi was only glad Rhane had the strength to do it. He wished he knew Rhane's plan to destroy the creature. After witnessing Blight's power firsthand, Jehsi wasn't sure the feat could be done.

"Seppina, I have not forgotten how centuries ago your warning spared my grandson. Nor have I forgotten how you took part in the plot to murder me which culminated in me being parted from my son and him losing his entire family. One act does not pardon the other. Many of our people died for your actions, and you have yet to answer for it.

"However, you and I are all who remain of the Warekin regime. While you retain the title of Old Mother, you are in fact powerless here." Jehsi paused, allowing the unspoken threat to sink in. "Join us, Seppina. Help save our people."

Bottom lip quivering, the Old Mother took a long time to answer. Corbin's wrath over the demise of his father was sharply tempered by fear. The stink of it was all over him. Corbin recognized the precarious position he was in and thus far had behaved accordingly. He would accept whatever fate Seppina decided for them.

"You win, Jehsi. Now tell me. How do you plan to save us?"

Jehsi turned to Rhane. It was an excellent question.

*

"Rhane we need to talk."

"I know." Rhane winced. Kalista was just shy of mad, and there was news he had yet to deliver. No doubt that after hearing what he had to say, she would be even more angry—furious even. Rhane had promised to stop keeping secrets, but letting this skeleton marinate for a few more hours couldn't possibly make things worse.

He passed a fresh cloth along Bellefuron's blade, polishing the metal to shining satisfaction. Too bad it wasn't as easy to remove the stains from his hands. "Jehsi has asked to speak with me away from spying ears. I'll return as soon as I can."

"Rhane, it's the middle of the night," she said, propping both fists on her hips. "You need to sleep."

"I'll be back before morning," he promised.

"Okay," she relented unhappily, but made a swift change of subject. "If you really think Blight could already be on its way here, then my family is in danger and I need to go see them."

"You know you don't have to ask permission for these things."

She shrugged. "I know. I think I was just informing you that I will be away from the manor tomorrow. I didn't want to worry you."

284

After tonight, we'll both need the space. "It's a great idea. Warn them, Kalista. But understand that bringing them here would only endanger them further."

"Yeah. I guess we're kinda the bait now, huh?"

Rhane nodded. The dejected air about her made him set Bellefuron aside and pull her down to the space beside him. He kissed her forehead. "Somehow, we will make this right."

"Hearing you say so makes me feel better." She leaned back from him, looking slightly cheered. "Really."

"It's what I'm here for." After a quick debate on whether or not to jeopardize her improved spirits, Rhane decided to take the chance. "Would you mind if Orrin tagged along tomorrow? I know you can take care of yourself, but I feel better knowing someone is there to watch your back."

Kalista surprised him by barking a short laugh. "Look how far we've come."

Rhane grimaced. Tonight, he would definitely have to tell her.

She touched his arm. "Hey, don't look so serious. I simply meant I've finally outgrown babysitters and bodyguards in your eyes. It feels good."

"Yeah," Rhane said, telling himself to lighten up. "You've gone from sexy damsel in distress to sexy badass who takes no prisoners. My kind of gal." He grinned. "Well done." On seeing the faint blush dot her cheeks, he couldn't resist kissing her.

"Hmmm," she said. "Kisses and compliments. Too bad you have somewhere else to be."

When she tried to pull away, he responded by wrapping his arms more tightly about her. "Maybe I could reschedule," he said and pressed his mouth against her neck. He loved hearing her heartbeat kick into third gear as his teeth nicked her skin.

Whimpering, she angled her head to give him better access to her throat. Rhane obliged by licking and nipping until she panted with desire. With each kiss, the tension set deep in her muscles eased a little more, becoming putty beneath his mouth. Making her hot made him hot. Rhane moaned. He had been joking before, but now he seriously considered postponing the meeting with Jehsi.

Fortunately, Kalista possessed more self-control than he. With an agonized groan, she pushed him away and moved to put more than a foot of space between her body and his. "The last thing I want is your dad to smell sex on you and know what you and I were up to when you should have been having a really important discussion with him."

With a defeated sigh, Rhane stood up. "When did you become the grown up?"

"It's been a long road."

"That's an understatement," he teased. The remark earned him a punch in the shoulder.

She frowned, but Rhane could tell she wasn't really angry. "Just enjoy it while it lasts. Who knows when I'll be reset to zero again. Then you'll have to start from square one in winning my heart."

"Maybe I'll let you enjoy blissful ignorance instead. I can't handle too many more grey hairs. And you caused a lot."

"Whatever." Kalista folded her arms. "You don't even remember the sordid details."

Rhane had to laugh. "I remember enough."

"Do you remember what it feels like to sleep alone?"

"Ouch," he said, rubbing his chest.

"Uh huh. Get out of here while I still like you."

"Yes ma'am." Still grinning, he retrieved Bellefuron and sheathed the sword between his shoulder blades.

Kalista watched his movements skeptically. "I thought you were going to talk. Why are you taking your sword?"

"Jehsi also wants to tour the grounds. I'd rather be prepared." Kissing her goodbye, he strode quickly to the doorway. His father was probably already waiting.

Kalista called to him softly. "Try not to kill anyone."

He stopped and turned to study her expression but couldn't decipher whether or not she was joking. Sparing a curt nod, Rhane quietly slipped into the hallway. He took the stairs two at a time and paused long enough at the front door to thank Orrin for keeping watch in his absence. Seppina and Corbin had agreed to play ball, but Rhane was a long way off from trusting either of them.

He found Jehsi near the remains of Rion's funeral pyre. The old ruler stared down at the ashes with a solemn expression. If he had noticed Rhane's approach, he didn't show it. Rhane waited. Jehsi would speak when he was ready.

For a time the two stood quietly in each other's company. Rhane beat back the sadness of being so near the scene of Rion's recent memorial. Jehsi reflected on the decisions responsible for bringing their people to this point.

Finally lifting his head, Jehsi looked at his son. "You have my profound sympathies for your loss of the boy. You carry a grave weight about you Rhane. I miss the days when you didn't know such pain."

"I have always known pain, Sire. I think maybe I used to be better at controlling it."

Jehsi nodded. "Is this why you murdered Silas?"

"Emotion did not dictate his death. Necessity did."

"Explain."

Rhane streamlined his thoughts in order to present the most concise reasoning possible. "Silas would have never stopped fighting to end the human world. He was going to name his son, Corbin, into a position as third Prime. With Seppina, it would have made three royals united from the line of Greinwysh. Our people would have sided with them, and I would not command enough warriors to win this war."

Jehsi didn't bother hiding his relief. "I hoped your motives were as such but had to be sure. Forgive my doubt."

"There is no need for forgiveness, Sire."

"But there is." Jehsi's eyes filled with regret. "I knew all along of your mother's unfaithfulness. It is the oldest adage of all," he said with a sad shrug. "My mate was fated to fall into the loins of my best friend."

"But you forgave her."

"Not at first. When you were just an infant, it was my ire that drove her to try and end your life. It wasn't because of your eyes, Rhane, or some silly omen of the Glowing Stone. You carried none of the marks of a firstborn, and I knew you were not mine. The shame of it was evident in Roma's eyes. She could not deny it. I became angry. And I was cruel. You were a beautiful babe, but I could not love you. I couldn't bear the sight of you. Fearing how I might retaliate, Roma sought to remove the reminder of her shame. I caught her holding you beneath the water in small basin and begged her to spare your life. I told her I needed time to accept what was and sent her away with the warning that news of your death would mean she would never have my forgiveness. Your mother wasn't always the cold and calculating woman you knew. She used to be kind and loving. Loyal to the end, she supported me in every endeavor. She was a true partner." Jehsi closed his eyes at the memory. An anguished spasm rippled across his face

"She was already pregnant with River when I sent her to live in the village of the plains," he continued hoarsely. "I abandoned her. The disgrace made her bitter. By the time of my first visit, you had already suffered within her monstrous hands for many years. Roma was no longer the same, but it was you who I loved. I gave up my seat as Prime because I loved *you*, Rhane. You are *my son* in every way that matters. Don't let anything take that away from you. Please don't take it away from me."

Pressing the heels of his hands against his eyes, Rhane exhaled savagely. Then he grasped his father's forearm and rested his brow against Jehsi's. "I won't," he whispered. "I didn't love Roma. But my heart aches because yours suffers. I am sorry you lost her."

They stepped apart, each taking a moment to gather composure. There was yet another subject Jehsi hoped to approach. The violence he'd witnessed between his two sons after arriving here had been shocking and inexplicable. Were it not for his intervention, Jehsi truly believed Rhane would have taken River's life.

"River was always better with you," Jehsi said to test waters and immediately noticed renewed tension in Rhane's face at the mere mention of the name. "Shaded by your influence and love, he thrived. But something has changed, hasn't it? Last moon he returned to Golden Mountain as a haunted man. The shame upon him was heavy."

Firmly harnessing his temper, Rhane attempted to answer evenly. "The shame will remain upon him until he answers for past deeds."

"These deeds cannot be forgiven?"

"They cannot."

"And his only punishment is death?"

Rhane clenched his hand against the burning heat contained within his right palm. "I sent River away and told him to never return or else his life would be forfeit. He disobeyed my directive and has left me no choice but to carry out his judgment."

"This is your brother we're talking about. Do you hear yourself?"

Rhane lifted his chin. He hated to be the cause of Jehsi's grief. Under normal circumstances, he would surrender to Jehsi anything asked of him. But a promise was a promise. And considering the deplorable nature of River's offense, leniency was an invitation for disaster. He had failed to protect Kalista in the worst way. Rhane would die before allowing someone to hurt her again. "He is still my brother. And I still love him," Rhane admitted. "But what River has done cannot be pardoned."

"I have already lost too much," Jehsi said softly. "Do not take your brother away from me as well."

"He breathes for as long as you do."

Jehsi sighed. "I may have many years within me yet. Perhaps in time, River will convince you his life is worth sparing." He decided to move on when Rhane didn't answer. "I see you have armed yourself with Bellefuron. I can assume then you have agreed to take me to the kindred alpha?"

"I don't think he's very happy with me, but yes."

"How far is the den from here?"

"Nearly eighty miles. We can arrive in under an hour…if you can keep up."

Surprising them both, Jehsi actually laughed. "I assure you, my pace will not be the problem."

Chapter 28

Rhane wasn't exactly nervous, but he was wary of seeing Ian so soon after giving the alpha Cixi's body. She was the second of his soldiers to die under Rhane's watch. Unlike Ander, Cixi held position. She was a beta of significant importance. But this was war. And soldiers died in war. Rhane couldn't personally guarantee the safety of every kindred who served him at Ian's behest. Hell, he couldn't guarantee the safety of his own. And it was a hard pill to swallow. Hopefully, Ian would see things in a similar light. If not, then getting the alpha to agree to his plan for the eclipse was going to be an impossible sell.

At the edge of the preserve, Rhane announced their presence with a non-threatening howl and then moved forward into kindred territory. It didn't take long before two escorts arrived to guide him and Jehsi the rest of the way. Ian sat at the mouth of the main den, feet dangling beneath waters of a fall that dipped below the surface and flowed down into the kindred lair. Unblinking red eyes watched Rhane and Jehsi's approach, but the alpha did not rise to his feet. Dmiri was nearby. Though Rhane could not see the ancient kindred, his smell was unmistakable.

"Now this I never imagined to behold," Ian exclaimed softly, surprising Rhane with his cheerful mood. "Jehsi, Prime of Whytetree, draws near my humble dwelling. To what do I owe such pleasure?"

Neither escort had returned to human shape. Light from the blue moon eerily set aglow the spotted and gnarled skin of the ghoulish trolls as they towered above Ian, Rhane, and Jehsi. The alpha of course was stark naked and

293

more sullied than usual. Assorted debris clumped his hair while a thick layer of orange clay encased his skin from his head down to to ankles. Likely his feet too were once covered in mud, but the steady stream of water had washed away any traces.

It was plenty to take in, but Rhane was confident his father had witnessed far stranger things in his long lifetime. Showing no sign of discomfort, Jehsi's cool demeanor supported Rhane's theory. "Hello, Ian," he said. "Please forgive the late hour. It was I who insisted upon an introduction to new allies."

"Allies," Ian repeated in a somewhat darkened tone. The alpha nodded. "Yes. A union sealed by the spilled blood of fallen brothers. I am very glad to call Banewolf an ally as the eclipse approaches." He turned his red gaze toward Rhane. "Two nights remain until we are mortal."

"It's what we came to talk about."

"Oh?"

"I couldn't stop the rogues from awakening Blight. The creature has already consumed most of Asia, and I believe it will now come here."

Ian narrowed his eyes suspiciously. "And why would Banewolf think this?"

"The creature is drawn to its food source—power. Next to Asia, there is no other continent with a higher population of supernaturals than the one we're standing on."

"Your reasoning brings Blight to this land but not to our doorstep." Ian's gaze flitted from Rhane to Jehsi. "What are you not telling me?"

"The old one who watches us," Jehsi said before Rhane could answer. "Though I cannot see him, his scent is strong. He has lived through Blight's awakening more than once. He has witnessed firsthand how the creature ravages, destroying dens and razing hives. I also sense hatred from this old one."

Rhane was impressed. His father had figured out a lot from just a smell…and with no prior knowledge of Dmiri's existence.

"With every awakening," Jehsi continued, "Golden Mountain shined like a beacon to the creature because the powers within were irresistible. Until now, the strength of our Mothers repelled any attack against us, protecting our people from the scourge while outside, kindred and rogue kind were culled to near extinction. Tonight marks the first time Warekin have felt the full brunt of this curse. Tonight, we lost two-thirds of our people."

"And so you come to Banewolf for refuge."

"We have."

Ian looked at Rhane curiously. "It would seem your powers are in high demand. Though they are mighty, I question whether your wings can shelter us all."

Rhane smiled. "And that's where my plan comes into play." Hearing movement, he paused and searched the trees. Dmiri was nearby and listening, but obviously had no intention of showing himself. Rhane decided to ponder it later. "Blight is attracted to the energy of its food source. Contained within a hundred mile radius, we have the remnants of my people, your den, a powerful siren, and the immortal. Nyx marches toward us with an army consisting of two rogue hives. There is no way Blight won't come."

"I fail to see how this is a good thing, Banewolf."

"Ian, your people will be mortal. And since Blight only feeds upon the supernatural, kindred will be immune.

When Blight comes, we will fall back and let it consume the rogue armies. And then we will kill it."

"Your plan is quite clever, but how can you be certain of success? Blight has never succumbed to any power on this earth."

"Because I finally believe this is what Kalista and I were made to do."

Ian tilted his head to one side. "It would seem Dmiri believes in you as well. Very well, Banewolf. We will be your bait."

It was small, but it was a win. And after everything, Rhane sorely needed one. With no further matters to discuss, he and Jehsi moved to part ways with the alpha, but Ian called to them as they walked away. "Dmiri requests you to convey his regards to your siren. He mourns your loss."

"Thank you."

"He also believes you should know your trust has not been misplaced but gives warning. Great evil may yet visit in the night."

Knowing there was no chance of Dmiri explaining the meaning behind his cryptic message, Rhane inclined his head and left.

*

As promised, Rhane returned before daybreak…barely. Kali waited up for as long as she could. It wasn't difficult. She was wiped out but sleep did not come easy. Finally drifting off during an hour reserved for lonely ghosts and sneaking criminals, Kali became wide awake after the sheets stirred next to her.

A nearly full moon shone above the bedroom skylights, making it easy to see Rhane's long form stretched across the bed and his odd eyes watching her. Rolling onto her side, she climbed astride his torso, took his face in her hands and kissed him. His mouth was warm and eager, inviting her to deepen the kiss as his fingers massaged the curve of her bottom. Rhane made an appreciative noise in the back of his throat. "Someone is happy to see me," he mumbled.

Reaching behind her, Kali gently squeezed the growing bulge in his boxers. "You seem pretty happy too."

Smiling, she nipped his bottom lip and slid back to her side of the bed. Rhane reached for her with a clear intent of finishing what she had started, but Kali swatted his hand away. "You need to sleep."

"I'll be really quick then," he teased and grabbed her, tickling her sides.

Reduced to a fit of hysterical giggles, Kali struggled like a madwoman, but her series of bucks, kicks, and twists only succeeded in rolling them both off of the bed. She landed on top of Rhane in a tangle of bedcovers with his arms holding her tight. At least the tickling had ceased. Kali though, didn't stop laughing until his serious gaze subdued her. He buried a hand in her mass of curls. "You're so beautiful, beloved."

The comment stirred a lot of things in Kali. It warmed her heart, made her hot for him, and made her love him a little more. However, she wasn't going to show any of it. "You're just trying to get into my panties."

"You're not wearing panties." He dipped a finger into the moist slit between her thighs as if to prove it, and she was powerless to stop the moan from escaping her lips. His fingers tasted her again, melting her resolve. Those slow strokes would be her undoing. Shuddering, Kali grinded into his hand. It had been days since she'd last drank from his spark. Now it called to her and she answered, reaching toward those gold and blue tendrils of sustenance her siren yearned for. She drank deeply, humming with pleasure that only intensified when Rhane stripped off her shirt, rolled on top of her and slid between her quivering thighs. She moved when he moved, syncing perfectly with the rhythm she knew so well. He stared into her eyes, holding her gaze as the slow, deep thrusts of his hips explored her inner depths. Then a coil of heat took root, expanding and multiplying until it was as if her entire body burned from within. Suddenly, the pleasure between them was no longer enough. Kali needed more.

"Harder," she breathed.

Growling, Rhane obeyed and pounded into her with enough force to make her whimper as he pierced her womb even deeper. The fire within her intensified, reaching for her throat, making it impossible to breathe and threatening to rip her apart. Kali thought she would die unless it was sated. Reaching out, her nails dug into Rhane's biceps, shredding skin and drawing blood. His power flowed into her, halting the spread of the unbearable heat. She tore into his back until a slick of blood covered her hands. She knew she was hurting him but couldn't stop. Something else inside of her called for his blood, and Kali could not resist it.

Acting as if they belonged to someone else, her hands reached for the unmarked skin of Rhane's chest. Horrified, Kali pulled them away.

"No," Rhane said in a voice laced with pain. He touched her cheek, forcing her to look at him and stay in the moment. "Don't fight it."

For a moment, her eyes widened in confusion, but then the fire was back, roaring for control. Crying out, Kali succumbed to the heat. Primal desire took over and Rhane became her captive, an instrument to satisfy her cravings and fill the siren's thirst for blood as she mounted him. Using teeth and claw, she punished his flesh, leaving no part of him unmarked. Her hips drove downward, grinding and rocking against him as her body sought a different release. With the taste of his blood in her mouth, every muscle tightened, locked down to the point of pain…and then she was unleashed, bucking and writhing uncontrollably as her body came apart in a splendid storm of spasms. It was the most intense pleasure Kali had ever experienced. Sobbing, she collapsed onto his chest, unable to move as blissful aftershocks traveled through liquefied muscles.

Slowly, her other senses returned and she became aware of Rhane's heavy breathing and his hand stroking her hair and back. She noticed a pool of wetness against her cheek and the strong metallic scent in the air. The taste of his blood turned bitter on her tongue.

Kali bolted upright. Terror seized her veins like ice water. *Oh my god.* Tears filled her eyes as she looked at his wounds. Dim darkness hid the most of it, but she could see she had hurt him badly. There was so much blood. She hadn't lost control on this level in over a year. Starting to shake, Kali racked her brain for answers but came up empty. "Rhane," she whispered desperately, "What the hell was that?" Again, her gaze moved over the painful-looking scratches and bites covering his torso. "I—I hurt you," she stammered.

"It's okay," he said, still stroking her skin and apparently un-freaked by the whole scenario. "I'm already healing."

"But what happened?" Kali asked shrilly, fearing she was losing control again as she had in high school and after first reuniting with Rhane. She had joked about starting another reincarnation of herself and getting reset to zero, but being confronted with the reality of it happening again wasn't funny at all.

The look on Rhane's face gave Kali the impression he wanted to do anything other than answer her. Swallowing nervously, his eyes slid away from her questioning stare. "You're not changing back, Kalista. And you're not losing control."

"Okay," she said, and waited tensely for the rest. She knew better than to relax.

He finally looked at her. "You're pregnant."

Kali couldn't accept what she'd heard. "What did you say?"

To her horror, the sentence didn't change. "You're pregnant."

"I'm what?!" Fighting the sheets wrapped around her legs and torso, Kali scrambled to her feet. Her mind was a whirlwind. "I'm *not* pregnant. I just had my period. I take *pills* for this shit."

"Those are probably ineffective, considering your biology isn't truly human."

"And you tell me this now?" she shouted.

Rhane winced. "I should have said something sooner."

"Damn right." Kali started pacing. "How long have you known?"

"Uh…after the night we spent together on K2, I pretty much knew the next morning." Pulling himself up from the floor, Rhane took a step toward her, wobbled a little, and settled for a seat on the bed. Getting a full view of his battered body plucked several chords of sympathy in her heart, but Kali turned a deaf ear. If she had clawed the shit out of him due to some crazy storm of pregnancy hormones, then it was Rhane's own damn fault. His ensuing confession sealed the fact in concrete. "I should have stayed away, but your scent was irresistible. It was like you were everywhere, calling to me…taunting me." Rhane tiredly dragged one hand across his face. "I could barely think about anything else."

Suddenly, a few things clicked into place. Kali didn't know whether to be grossed out, humiliated, or continue being angry. "So, *that* is what Orrin meant when he said my smell was gone? And the pregnancy crack York made…I thought he was only being a jackass." Sinking slowly to the floor, Kali put her head in her hands. It felt like her life was over. Maybe Kalista the warrior from four centuries ago had handled childbearing without missing a stride, but Kalista of the twenty-first century wasn't ready to be pregnant. She had just graduated high school. As soon as they completed this business of saving the world, there were years of college to tackle before reaching her dream of becoming a marine archaeologist. Kali had already fit the idea of being a mother of two and a mate into her world view of the future. And now she had to come to terms with being pregnant as well.

Rhane touched her leg gently. Kali hadn't realized he'd moved from the bed. "Kalista, I realize you're technically only a teenager with several years of growing up ahead of

301

you. But just take a breath, give pause and remember the growth cycles of Warekin. This pregnancy won't change anything until eight years from now."

Fuck. Kali snatched away from him. "And for how many of those eight years will I be fat and tired and waddling because I'm swollen with child?"

Possibly missing the death stare and biting sarcasm or just blatantly ignoring it, Rhane actually answered the question. "Likely only the last ten months."

That was it. Kali had heard enough for one night. Furiously yanking on a pair of jeans and a tee shirt, she stuffed her arms into a sweater and jammed on a pair of Converse.

"Where are you going?" Rhane asked softly.

"I'm going to see my parents," she bit out.

He rubbed the back of his neck. "You agreed to take Orrin with you."

Rolling her eyes in exasperation, Kali threw open the bedroom door. "Well I guess he better wake the hell up."

Chapter 29

Staring at the painting of cheerful yellow daisies on her bedroom wall while listening to the morning song of finches perched outside her bedroom window, Kali began to resent everyone and everything seeming so damn happy. After leaving the manor, she had taken Rhane's truck and made the trip to her parents' house, managing to sneak inside without waking anyone. The last thing Kali wanted to do was explain to Greg and Lisa why she had come home at five a.m. harboring a mood fouler than a honey badger's.

The few hours of sleep she'd gotten post-fight with Rhane did well to cool the fires fueling her temper, and so Kali awoke with a slightly more positive outlook. It wasn't like she was a reckless teenage girl who had gone and gotten herself in trouble. Kali was older than any living human on the planet, a mother of two, and the mate of a pretty incredible guy who also held the title of being a one thousand year old warlord. Her life was far from ordinary. So, it wasn't rational to expect a normal progression of things in her life. Go to college. Land the perfect job. Marry the perfect guy. And then have the perfect kids. No. That sort of coveted path wasn't feasible. Sure, for her, Rhane was the perfect guy. Check. College and the perfect job were still very doable. Check. But as for the kids...well, she had two of those and they were two murders shy of being sociopaths. Kali touched her stomach. Maybe this one would be a chance for them to finally get things right. And it was a chance for Kali to experience and remember every second of every moment from start to finish of raising him or her.

"Are you feeling any better?" Orrin's voice startled her. She had forgotten he slept on the floor beside her bed. Next to the gentle kin of few words lay Bailen. Appearing from the darkness of the moors, he had jumped into the truck as well.

"A little," she admitted. "But I'm still mad at him. He should have given me a choice, Orrin. No one should go and knock a girl up just because her eggs smell delicious and he can't help himself. What was he thinking?"

"I do not believe Rhane was doing much thinking. The pheromones which poured off your skin were difficult to ignore. You were in estrus and your body begged to be fertilized."

"Okay. Please stop talking." Groaning, Kali buried her face in the pillow. She couldn't get over how everyone could smell the moment she had started to ovulate. What a freak show. "We're just not going to say anything else about this for awhile, okay?"

Though the pillow muffled her voice, Orrin seem to hear just fine. "If that is what you want," he said.

"It is," she insisted. A second later, she blew out a frustrated sigh and rolled over, pounding both hands against the mattress. "I mean, I haven't even told my parents about Bailen or Rhaven. Greg and Lisa are grandparents and don't even know it! How can I tell them a third kid is on the way? Greg will have a stroke."

"I thought you said you no longer wished to speak of the matter."

"I was talking to Bailen," Kali snapped.

Whining softly, Bailen bounded onto the bed and belly crawled toward her. Kali took his big head in her hands and planted a kiss on his nose. "Sorry, kiddo. Mom is having some issues with her hormones."

"No shit," Orrin agreed, surprising Kali. She promptly threw a pillow at his face.

A light knock sounded at the door and in walked Lisa. Seeing her mom again made Kali realize too long had passed since her last visit. She would have to be a better daughter in the future.

Even at such an early hour, Lisa looked flawlessly put together. Bouncy grey ringlets framed her glowing caramel complexion and round brown eyes bearing a minimal amount of makeup. Right away, Kali noticed her dress was far too casual for the law office where Lisa worked as the district attorney. The flowing teal skirt and white wrap-around sweater were more suited for an afternoon picnic.

"Hi, Mom," Kali said and shrugged sheepishly. "I would have called but…"

"Oh shoo. None of that. Kalista Metts, how many times do your father and I have to tell you this is still your home? There is no need to call, young lady."

"Okay, well, sorry for sneaking in."

Making a sympathetic noise, Lisa quickly moved to sit at the edge of Kali's bed. Bailen was kind enough to ease his big butt over and make room. "Did you and Rhane have a fight?"

"Why would you say that?"

"It's the oldest reason in the book for a woman to leave her husband and come home in the middle of the night."

"Oh." Kali laid her head against Lisa's shoulder. What she really wanted to do was climb into her lap. "It was bad."

"Do you want to talk about it?"

No way in hell was Kali ready to stomp around in that minefield. "Not yet. Why aren't you at work?"

"Your father and I saw you sleeping in your bed early this morning and both decided to call in."

"You didn't have to."

"Of course we did. No way were we going to waste an opportunity to have the whole family under one roof again."

A pang of regret hit Kali at the thought of her sister, Rosalyn. Their last time together had ended in a pretty big fight, and over Cal of all things. Kali had said some terrible things, and Rozzy was probably still angry. For some reason her sister was totally paranoid that Kali and Cal were destined to fall back into each other's arms. She was too insecure to accept Kali had truly let go and moved on. She and Cal were only friends now. "Summer will be over soon. Has Rozzy mentioned whether she's going back to classes or not? She's missed a ton of school."

Lisa shook her head sadly. "I don't know, baby. Rozzy hasn't been herself lately and…" Stopping abruptly, Lisa seemed unsure whether to go on.

"What is it?" Kali urged.

"Your sister and Callan seem to have grown really close. In fact, they've pretty much been inseparable since she came home from college. They're…dealing with something together."

"Like what?" Kali was genuinely interested but more so, she was worried. However, since her last effort to warn Rozzy away from Cal had ended disastrously, she thought it best to pass on offering any well-intentioned warnings. She didn't want Lisa mistaking concern for jealousy, which might have ended in her also thinking Kali still carried a torch for Cal.

Pursing her lips, Lisa patted Kali's leg. "I'll leave it for Rozzy to tell. You may be shocked, Kalista. But try to be supportive. Greg and I were hard enough on her already."

"O-kay," Kali said, dragging out the word. Lisa's vague explanation was near maddening.

Hastily rising from the bed, Lisa clapped her hands together. "Okay," she echoed. "Breakfast is almost ready. Get dressed and come downstairs."

"Alright. Alright." Kali yawned. She would worry about her sister's unending drama sometime after food was in her stomach. "Set a place for one more, if that's okay."

Confused, Lisa frowned. "Who else will be joining us?"

"Hello, Mrs. Metts," Orrin answered softly from the floor. He waved when Lisa turned to see who else was in the room. Her mouth formed a surprised *O*.

"Hi," she said, recovering quickly. "Orrin, isn't it?"

"That's correct ma'am." He stood up, towering over Lisa, and shook her hand. "It is nice to see you again."

Lisa looked him up and down. "Something tells me you don't eat turkey bacon."

Kali laughed. She didn't think Lisa would ever let Greg off the hook when it came to healthy eating. Anyone dining at their table also suffered. Trans-fats, cholesterol, and complex carbohydrates had been outlawed in the Metts' household since the early days of Kali's childhood. "Orrin will be fine with whatever you put in front of him, Mom. He didn't grow so big by being picky."

*

Downstairs, it didn't take long to uncover the mystery surrounding Rozzy and Cal's newfound entanglement. The curvier curves and protruding belly were a dead giveaway. Kali's mouth dropped open in shock. She had expected a lot of things, but never this.

Crap-ola.

Kali didn't realize she had actually stopped walking until Orrin nudged her forward. She stared wide-eyed at him over her shoulder and mouthed, "What the hell?"

"I told you that she smelled different," Orrin said in absurdly matter of fact tone, leaving Kali flabbergasted.

She spun around and shoved him sideways, away from the kitchen and out of Rozzy's view. "What are you talking about?" Kali whispered fiercely.

Orrin blinked. "You came here to visit at the beginning of summer when Rosalyn was home. After you two fought, you became upset and returned downstairs. I attempted to inform both you and Greg Metts of her situation."

Kali wanted to shake him. "I didn't know what you meant! You Warekin and your fucking noses. You can really smell pregnancy?!"

"Well, not really. Your estrus abruptly ceased after a night of copulation. It wasn't difficult to connect the dots. With your sister, her scent became noticeably less human and also she was far enough along to hear a second heartbeat."

Kali shook her head. Her mind was racing. Her stomach was in somersaults. The situation was ridiculous. Impossible. How could both she and her sister be knocked up? "Why does she look *so* pregnant?" she asked. Her mouth went dry. She was starting to panic. "I thought I had eight years before that would happen…before I would look like *that*."

"A true Warekin sired your child, whereas your sister was bred by a symbiote. Her condition will progress much faster."

Beyond shocked, Kali was speechless. She wanted to turn and run away without ever having to deal with her sister's situation and face the shitload of crazy Rozzy would have no shame in raining down at the breakfast table.

"Orrin, this isn't going to be pretty. Maybe we should go."

"I do not think doing so would make your parents very happy."

"It wouldn't." Kali sighed. She stood between a rock and a hard place made with jagged, spiteful edges. "This sucks."

"You will be fine." Orrin winked. "I've got your six."

Kali almost laughed. "I feel better now," she said with as little sarcasm as possible.

Resigning to deal with whatever came her way in the next few hours, Kali marched into the kitchen. The rest of the family was already seated and waiting with piles of delicious-smelling food in their midst. A mountain of turkey bacon was highlighted as the table centerpiece. Neatly situated around it was a platter of assorted breads—cinnamon toast, French toast, and baguettes—enough grits to feed a family twice their size and a vegetarian casserole with a copious amount of melted cheeses bubbling topside. But it was the sight of Greg's famous chocolate chip and pecan waffles making Kali's mouth water. Slinging her butt into a chair, she greedily picked up her fork. Every other worry was nearly forgotten. "This looks amazing."

Lisa smiled proudly. "Your father worked hard."

"Now that Her Majesty Kali has decided to join us, can we eat?"

Mining for patience, Kali greeted her sister as sweetly as possible. "Hi, Roz. How are you feeling?"

Rozzy gave her a withering stare. "How does it look like I'm feeling?"

"You look great."

"Right," Rozzy scoffed. "I saw judgment in your eyes the second you saw me."

"There was no judgment." *Trust me,* Kali added silently. "But I was surprised. Why didn't you tell me?"

Rozzy rolled her eyes. "Why would I?"

"Excuse your sister," Lisa interjected before Kali could answer. "The hormones seem to be wreaking some havoc on her emotions."

Throwing up her hands, Rozzy reared back in the chair with an expression of absolute disgust. "Why do you always take her side?"

"It is difficult for a human to carry the sort of offspring which grows inside you. The discomfort you experience now will not compare to the despair you will suffer during childbirth."

All eyes turned to Orrin. Rozzy's jaw practically sat on the table. Thankfully, she was too stunned to lash out at him. Kali hid a smile. If this was what Orrin meant by having her back, she'd gladly take it.

Clearing his throat, Greg raised a glass of orange juice. "Let's take a moment to celebrate being together again. To family," he said.

"To family," everyone echoed. Even Rozzy managed to mutter in agreement.

Fifteen minutes later, Kali was choking down her sixth waffle and third helping of casserole. She noticed Greg and Lisa's matching expressions of astonishment and made a slow retreat of the fork from her mouth. "Goodness, Kalista. You act like you're eating for two as well."

Kali badly wanted not to blush but couldn't stop the traitorous flush of color from reaching her cheeks. "Come on," she croaked weakly. "Orrin almost single-handedly devoured the entire pile of bacon. Give him a hard time."

"First of all, it was turkey bacon. It takes a lot more of that crap to put a dent in a man's stomach," Greg said. "And secondly, look at the size of him! No offense." He waved in Orrin's direction. "I understand Rozzy's appetite. But for you this is very different, young lady." Greg studied her suspiciously. "What aren't you telling us?"

Kali wanted to die. Or at least, she wanted to melt into the floor and slink away from her dad's interrogation. Luckily, Orrin was there to save her...again. "What Kali isn't telling you is that we only just returned from quite a dangerous mission. We climbed the world's second tallest mountain and traversed hundreds of miles through barren wilderness. Provisions were scarce, especially after several of our supply packs were lost. It will take days to replenish the fuel burned by our bodies. Kali seems to be determined to do it in half the time."

Greg and Lisa accepted his explanation, even chuckled a little at Orrin's attempt with humor. Kali could have high-fived him.

"Tell us more about this mission." Greg leaned forward in his chair. "Does it in any way involve what's been happening on the news? By the way, we saw when Rhane made headlines last week. Didn't know he could wrestle a semi-tractor trailer to a dead stop. Amazing." His awed gaze shifted to Orrin. "Are all of your kind so powerful?"

"No. Rhane is special," Orrin said, addressing Greg's second question first. "And yes, the mission within the Himalayan mountain range was to stop the spread of what you have seen in the news. But we failed."

"That's very unfortunate."

Her dad was trying to be understanding, but describing the outcome of Asia as unfortunate did not lend justice to the tragedy experienced there. "Because of what happened in Asia, things may become more dangerous for us here, Dad. The chaos in New York might come to our little town. I need all of you guys to stay away from anywhere large crowds will be. Don't go into the woods either."

Appearing more frightened than Kali had seen her in a long time, Lisa grabbed Greg's hand. "Callan has already given us the stay safe speech. He comes by every day to make sure things are all right."

So, Gabriel had kept his word. That was good.

Glancing quickly at her husband, Lisa blurted, "But he seems different. Callan acts older, calmer. Sometimes there is this strange, almost frightening air around him. Then at other times, he goes back to being the same young man we've known for so long."

Hesitating, Kali chewed her lip. She wasn't sure how much to tell. She looked from Orrin, to her parents, and then to Rozzy. Really, Greg and Lisa had been aware of the unusual path Kali's life was destined to take long before it actually happened. Greg had witnessed firsthand a fully transformed Gabriel after the fallen Prime attacked a police convoy. The existence of supernatural beings was no longer a thing of science fiction for them. That only left Rozzy. Angry, insecure, and mistrusting of anything her little sister had to say, Rozzy would never accept what Kali needed to reveal.

"Cal isn't just Cal anymore," she began. "He's changed. He now hosts within his body a second consciousness. A very powerful creature lives inside of him…a former Warekin ruler. But there is no reason to fear him," Kali added quickly. "He's still a friend. He wants to help."

Lisa shook her head, clearly struggling with the revelation. "Honey, are you sure? He still looks so much like Cal."

"He's very good at hiding the other side of himself."

Her dad almost looked angry. "And you say we can trust him."

Kali nodded.

"Then why hasn't Cal told us this himself? Why the ruse?"

"Well it isn't a ruse exactly. Cal's relationship with Gabriel—the being inside of him—is a symbiotic one. Unless danger is imminent, Cal retains dominance of both his body and personality. It's probably been mostly Cal who you've been dealing with. Gabriel doesn't concern himself with humans, but he promised to look after this household and a few other affairs while Rhane and I were away."

"Okay." Greg bowed his head thoughtfully and squeezed Lisa's hand. "Okay," he repeated. "Kalista, we love and trust you, but this is a lot to take in."

"I know," Kali said. "I'm only trying to be honest with you guys." *Just not totally honest,* she thought and tried not to squirm. There was a lot she was still holding back, but Kali swore to tell them everything in due time. Until then, a few secrets would have to remain on the shelf.

"Really though, Greg, considering all the footage we've seen in the news, from here and around the world…this isn't very high on the scale of unbelievable. Callan was very close to Kali at one point. It makes sense he would end up involved in all of this."

Her dad smiled at her mom with true love in his eyes, and Kali was reminded of how Rhane often looked at her. "I didn't marry you only because you were beautiful," he said.

Her mom returned the smile filled with love. "Well I only married you to get you to stop asking."

As Greg and Lisa burst into giggles, Rozzy stood from her chair, bringing her swollen belly into full view. Swallowing thickly, Kali had some difficulty tearing her gaze and mind away from her sister's pregnancy. It was like reality had slapped her in the face with the not too distant future.

"Are you kidding me? This is total bullshit."

Greg's dark complexion turned quite red. "Rosalyn, watch your language, young lady. I understand you're upset, but there are better ways to express yourself in this house."

Rozzy looked close to tears. "How can you guys believe this? Kali sounds like a total lunatic. Can't you see she's only saying these things to get attention?" Breaking down into a fit of hysterical sobs, Rozzy stopped to partly gather her wits. "Obviously, she's jealous of what Cal and I have." She turned a furious glare to Kali. "Now there's a baby, and you have no chance of ever getting him back."

"For the last time," Kali said in a volume close to a whisper. She held onto control by a thread. "I *do not* want Cal. And I sure as hell do not want his baby."

"Girls," Greg warned. "Language."

"Then what do you want?" Rozzy practically shouted.

"For you to be safe!" Kali yelled back.

"Okay. Stop." Greg stood up and pointed at Rozzy. "Rosalyn, sit down." He did nothing further until she obeyed. "We all need to take a step back." Rubbing his temple, he took a deep breath. "Rozzy, there are things about Kali your mom and I have known for a long time. You were too little to tell when your sister first came to us. And I don't know...I guess not long afterward, her past just didn't seem to matter anymore. You two were our little girls in every sense that mattered. You're also sisters, and I think it is past time for you both to start acting like it again."

Rozzy folded her arms. "Let me guess. You're about to tell me for one millionth time how special she is."

Greg sighed. "Lisa, will you help me clear the table?"

Even through her anger, Kali's heart was pounding. Rozzy already loathed her. What would knowing the truth of Kali's origins do to their already severely damaged relationship?

Once the dishes were cleared, Greg pulled back the tablecloth and revealed the scorch marks scarring the table's surface. "Do you remember the night you invited Cal to dinner and there was a fire?"

Still fuming, Rozzy conceded a little. "Of course I do."

"Well, your sister started that fire...*with her mind*."

Rozzy shook her head. "No way."

315

"I'll prove it," Kali said. She wanted to move past the animosity between herself and Rozzy more than anyone.

Greg quickly held up his hand. "Honey, you don't have to…"

"It's okay, Dad. I have a lot more control now." Turning to her sister, Kali opened her palm. *"Ont flamen,"* she whispered. A tiny ball of fire sparked instantly, the grey flames happily dancing within in her hand as they awaited the next command. *"Styganna lumas,"* she said, and the fire grew even larger.

Rozzy's eyes were about to pop out of her head. "Holy—"

Greg cleared his throat.

"Huckleberry," she finished. Her voice filled with wonder. "Kali, are you really doing this? Mom, Dad, look at her eyes! They're glowing."

"Orrece," Kali commanded, making the flames disappear. Then she mentally crossed her fingers and hoped the demonstration had been enough but not too much. Rozzy didn't appear to be on the verge of screaming and running away. She did, however, look more than a little wary. "What else can you do?"

"Uh…" Kali glanced at Orrin, but his attention was elsewhere. His body angled away from the table, and his head was slightly tilted toward the back of the house. "I can fight and handle knives pretty well."

If Rozzy was impressed, she didn't let on. "So, I guess the video of the giant white wolf wasn't faked then."

"No. It wasn't."

"Can you change into a wolf?"

"No."

"What about those things in the New York subway and the creatures overrunning Afghanistan? Can you change into one of them?"

"Ew. No."

Rozzy seemed relieved at Kali's last answer, but she wasn't done asking questions. "What about guns? Did Rhane teach you how to use them?"

"There will be no guns in this house," Greg said as Orrin abruptly left his seat and pulled the very weapon in question from a holster affixed to the back of his jeans.

From his station beneath the dining table, Kali heard a soft growl rumble in Bailen's throat. She tensed, instantly on alert. Rarely had she seen Orrin carry or use a gun. With the exception of Rhane, all the kin seemed to prefer to do battle with skins. "What's wrong?"

He didn't have to answer. Upstairs, a crash of breaking glass shattered the quiet. Heavy, lurching footsteps sounded against the hardwood floors. Strange, rasping breaths punctuated by eager snarls followed.

Lisa and Rozzy's whimpers became full blown screams when the hideously twisted form of a kindred appeared on the staircase. In full daylight, the creature should have been hidden behind a human appearance, but the newly changed lacked control. Operating solely on primal urges, changelings were wild and aggressive...exactly like this thing in their home.

Its mottled flesh seemed to absorb the morning light, keeping the creature in shadow. But dozens of knots were visible, covering its body. The largest of the growths were situated on the kindred's head, giving it the appearance of having horns. Malformed limbs moved awkwardly, advancing the creature toward Kali's family at an alarming rate. The incessant screaming originating from her mother and sister was completely understandable. This thing looked like something straight out of a horror movie.

Kali raised both hands, preparing to burn the kindred to ash, but Orrin shook his head. "Save your strength," he said, and fired five rounds into its chest.

The changeling tumbled to the bottom of the stairs but kept coming, crawling across the floor, driven to tear them apart even while breathing its dying breath. Holstering the gun, Orrin took the kindred's head into his hands and wrenched clockwise. The sound of snapping vertebrae echoed into the kitchen, and the creature's snarling at last fell silent. Rozzy's screams did not.

Lisa took her oldest daughter into her arms. Greg took Lisa into his.

Orrin took a long look at the three of them and turned to Kali. "I'll go upstairs and make sure there aren't any more."

"Bailen, go with him," Kali said. It wasn't like Orrin really needed the backup, but Kali felt better knowing he had it. And she very well couldn't leave her family in the state they were in. "Are you guys okay?" she asked gently and tried to recall her first encounter with a kindred but couldn't. Too many strange things had flooded her life in a relatively short amount of time.

Greg was in the middle of assuring Kali everyone was fine when four loud bangs hammered at the side door. Her parents froze. Even Rozzy's crying stopped.

"Stay here," Kali instructed and moved cautiously out of the kitchen and toward the noise. The knocking sounded again, more urgently. Then Cal's voice called out to her. "Kali, open the door. Do it in a hurry."

Running the rest of the way, Kali snatched open the door and Cal immediately staggered inside. His shirt was torn. A collection of scratches and cuts bloodied his arms and face. Wild blue eyes squeezed shut as he leaned against the wall to gather strength. Remarkably, Cal's blond hair was somehow still perfect. Panting, he straightened and fixed a troubled stare onto Kali. "We had a perimeter but couldn't hold them back. The changelings have broken through and are killing anything in their path. You need to get your family out of here."

"How many?" Kali asked. She had no intention of running away from this fight.

"Hundreds."

Rozzy chose this moment to wander in from the other room. On seeing Cal's condition, she let out a surprised shriek. "I thought I heard your voice. What happened?"

Moving Kali aside, Cal quickly went to Rozzy. Pressing one hand against her protruding belly, he kissed her cheek. "I'm okay," he said. "How's my girl?"

Her entire face lit up with a warm smile. "Great now that you're here."

"And how is my other girl?"

"Still making Mommy miserable," Rozzy answered with a pout.

Wow. Mom and Dad weren't kidding. Watching her sister and ex-boyfriend interact in such a way was bizarre, especially considering the growing bundle of joy currently situated between them. But Cal was happy, and really it was all Kali had ever wanted for him. She only hoped one day Rozzy would be able to let go of her insecurities, enjoy the happiness within reach, and be her sister again.

"Kalista!" Orrin's shout from upstairs wrenched Kali from thought. "You need to see this."

Taking the steps two at a time, Kali hurried in the direction of Orrin's voice. She found him in her parent's room but outside on the small balcony, leaning over the railing. From there, the only view overlooked the neighborhood street. This small oversight of floor planning had always been Lisa's chief complaint about the house.

Joining Orrin, she searched for what caused the quiet kin such alarm. The reason was instantly obvious. From their vantage point, dozens of changelings could be spotted moving throughout the subdivision. Kali was reminded of watching the nature channel and seeing African herds migrate across grassy plains in search of food and water ahead of the rainy season. Only…these creatures weren't migrating.

With a sickened twist in her stomach, Kali looked at Orrin. "They aren't here to attack. They're running from something. It's happening, isn't it?"

"I think so."

"We need to get back to the manor."

Orrin's expression was grim. "Agreed."

Hurrying downstairs, she found her parents and sister packing overnight bags. Cal paced nearby, intermittently offering remarks to encourage a speedier process. When Kali walked up to him, Cal looked at her in disbelief. "Are you nuts? We need to get out of here."

Kali didn't budge. "I need to speak with Gabriel."

"Why?"

"Because I believe you're letting emotion cloud your judgment. With Gabriel, I know that won't be a problem."

Cal scowled, but then his eyes flashed red and quickly returned to blue. "Hello, Darkesong."

There was no time for formalities. Kali jumped straight into the point. "Gabriel, you have to know that Callan is making the wrong move. My family needs to stay here and you need to make sure that happens. You promised to keep them safe."

"Did you not witness the changed ones? They have broken through our lines, and I can no longer assure your family's safety here."

"But the changelings aren't attacking. They are fleeing like zebras from a pack of lions. The aggression toward this home was a random, isolated incident. If my family stays here, they will be safe. I am certain of it."

Gabriel bowed his head. "Very well, siren. I will see to the boy and his rash emotions. Your family will remain here under my guard."

"Leave your Reapers, but I need you to come with me."

"Oh?" The fallen Prime grew very still.

"Blight is close, but not where we need it to be. Rhane has a plan to draw it to us, but in order to do so, we need to be a beacon of power to the creature—a buffet it couldn't possibly resist."

"So, we are to entice the creature and lure it here." Gabriel frowned. "And Rhane perceives this as the best course of action?"

"Yes." Kali put as much confidence in her voice as she could master. "Gabriel, it will work."

"We must hurry then." The fallen Prime's severe gaze at last slid away from Kali's face. "The destroyer draws near."

Chapter 30

With Gabriel's full cooperation, they made it back to the manor in record time. The fallen Prime hesitated on the porch, seemingly leery of actually crossing the threshold. Noticing Kali's questioning gaze, Gabriel lifted his chin. "This structure is filled with many ghosts. To them, I remain the demon."

Immediately understanding, she touched his arm. "They won't recognize you, Gabriel. Not in this form. Identify yourself only if you're ready."

Some of the tension left Gabriel's body. "Thank you, Darkesong."

Inside the manor, Warekin were everywhere, occupying every room and piece of furniture. But Rhane, Jehsi, and York were nowhere to be seen. She found War in the kitchen, conversing with a slender but capable-looking warrior who possessed kind eyes. "Where's Rhane?" she interrupted. Time was too short for polite introductions.

"He took York and his father and left."

"That much I figured out already, War. *Where* did they go?"

"I dunno. The eclipse begins soon, so they're probably out doing some final recon. You try calling him?"

"Of course I did, and I sent a text. No answer." She fidgeted. The plan depended on a lot of power being in the same general locale. If Rhane wasn't found soon, a lot of difficult decisions would fall on her shoulders.

Crossing his arms, War propped against the counter. "On a scale of one to ten, how important is this?"

"Are you kidding me right now? It's a freaking thirteen, War."

War held up both hands. "Yikes. Sorry. I thought it might've been a sex thing. Totally misread your body language."

"Absolute fumble," Orrin agreed.

Gritting her teeth, Kali said nothing. War got the point. Quickly digging into his pockets, he pulled out his cell. "Let me give it a try. Rion installed a program on York's phone capable of overriding its settings whether on silent or vibrate. I just have to block my number and call from my cell. Then York's phone will light up, vibrate, and play circus music. It pisses him off something awful, so you gotta pick the moments carefully."

Simultaneously wanting to laugh and cry, Kali shook her head. It was a stupid time to miss Rion so deeply. Thankfully, her cell buzzed and gave her an excuse to turn away, saving her the embarrassment of anyone seeing the misty look in her eyes.

Rhane's voice poured through the receiver, harried but still velvet in her ears. "I got your message. Where are you?"

"We made it to the manor. It's quiet here."

"We're headed back now, but there's not much time, Kalista. The rogues are almost to the reserve."

"Maybe a show of force will stave off their attack and allow Blight more time to come."

"Let's hope so."

"What do you need me to do?"

"Gather the warriors. I'll be there as soon as I can."

"Okay."

Rhane sighed into the phone. "Kalista, about last night...I understand why you're upset and why you had to leave. I heard you. And I'm sorry. I really am. If I could take it back, I would."

Squeezing her eyes shut, Kali swallowed thickly. *No, you dummy. I don't want you to take anything back. I want this baby.* But she wasn't ready to say words aloud yet. "We can talk about it later…when this is over."

"Of course," Rhane said quietly. "I'll be home soon."

Hanging up, Kali took a moment to steady her thoughts. It was a bad idea to approach the Old Mother with a head clouded by emotion. Considering the stern nature of Rhane's people, it would definitely be taken as a sign of weakness.

The unnamed man with the kindly gaze surprised Kali when he addressed her. "Be at ease, young siren. Seppina has already agreed to release the warriors, and we willingly serve your cause."

Regretting her earlier rudeness, a flood of warmth spread to her cheeks. "Thank you, uh…"

"I am Gareth."

"Just Gareth?" Kali was dubious. "No page-long description denoting title and bloodline?"

Gareth smiled, and she suddenly noticed how oddly attractive he was. "Just Gareth," he repeated.

"Okay, Gareth." Grinning back, Kali couldn't help imagining how handsome he must have been five hundred years ago. "Any idea where I might find Seppina?"

The old kin nodded, studying her carefully. "I would be honored to show you."

War chuckled. Gabriel rolled his eyes. Kali realized she had never seen him use such a human gesture. Ignoring them both, she accepted Gareth's waiting arm. He leaned in close as he guided her down the hall. "Don't let the Old

Mother intimidate you. Golden Mountain no longer stands, and without it she is powerless."

But Gareth's warning turned out to be unnecessary. Though Seppina was cranky, she presented no resistance to collecting the warriors. Male and female, they gathered. Nearly three dozen Warekin, all trained to be formidable in battle. Unfortunately, less than twenty of the warriors possessed war skins.

Before the massacre, Warekin armies had consisted mostly of people from the plains. It was the bloodlines of commoners which produced the most skins to populate Warekin forces. Royal blood started the wars. Royal blood controlled the armies. And common blood did most of the fighting. Kali could see a definite parallel to how things operated in the human world.

Two of the women, Zura and Idalis, stood out to Kali and not because of their extraordinary height—both were nearly as tall as York. Well, their stature wasn't the only reason. Instead of the characteristic white locks adorning nearly every royal head, Zura and Idalis sported locks streaked in black. Tattoos covered their arms and shoulders. Adhering to a clear theme of geometrical shapes and patterns, many of the markings were similar between the two. None of the other Warekin possessed tattoos to such an extent, not even Rhane.

"They are half-breeds," Gabriel said softly, and Kali strained to understand. "From my line of Bllacstag, Zura and Idalis are disgraced. They will never marry or continue the bloodline but still choose to remain within the mountain rather than seek a life outside of it. Fools," he finished in a harsh whisper.

"They seem strong."

"Oh yes." A hint of pride bled into Gabriel's voice. "They very much are."

Pondering the implications of Zura and Idalis being half-breeds, Kali made a mental note to dig a little deeper into their lineage. But she would have to do so discreetly. There was no better reminder than Rhane striding into the room and locking eyes with Gabriel. None of the newly arrived Warekin were aware of his true identity, and Kali didn't think it was the proper moment for the royals, especially Jehsi, to reach such a revelation.

Thankfully, a slight shake of her head vanquished the animosity from Rhane's face. And despite Gabriel's close proximity, Rhane came and stood at her side. When he didn't make a move to touch her, Kali slid her hand into his. Flinching, Rhane looked at her with open surprise. Then he relaxed into her grip and addressed the room.

"Before last night, many years passed since you last bled in battle. Before last night, you believed the mountain would shield you from the horrors of the outside world. Before last night, you thought our Mothers were invincible and you would never have to fight this war.

"Tonight, your blood and the blood of fallen loved ones freshly poisons your sense of security. Tonight, Golden Mountain is no more. Tonight, our Mothers are dead. Tonight, this war has finally come to our doorstep...and tonight, we must fight.

"On this soil, there are no royals. There are no bloodlines. There are only warriors."

Allowing that unifying thought to hang in the air, Rhane met the gaze of every individual in the room. Needless to say, a long stretch of silence passed before he gave one final command. "Let's conquer these bastards."

Chapter 31

When the kindred scout reported rogues had moved in position to attack ahead of the actual eclipse, some were hesitant to believe. Rogues rarely dared to bring war against a kindred pack at full strength. But Kali never doubted. Experiences over the past year taught her anything was possible, to expect the unexpected, and to hope for the best but prepare for the worst. It wasn't the worst, but it was bad, Kali thought as she stood next to Rhane with fully transformed kindred on either side them, facing off against the rapidly descending horde of masked rogues.

All Warekin who possessed skins now stood on all fours, spread throughout the ranks of kindred. They were beauties among beasts. Even in wolf form, Jehsi and River were similar in appearance, boasting nearly identical coats of silver fur. Jehsi's slightly larger wolf held a position on the front line, next to Ian. It was a shining demonstration of commitment and solidarity to creatures who were formerly enemies and who may again be so once the battle dust had settled.

Still hiding beneath the guise of Callan's appearance, Gabriel hovered near Idalis and Zura. Of those without the ability to transform, the half-breeds had taken up other arms. At least ten blades of assorted sizes adorned each of their Viking-worthy frames. Apparently, knives and swords were the weapon of choice amongst the Warekin. Some of the warriors were equipped with guns, but those were carried as secondary weapons.

Also among the unchanged, Rhane stood watching the enemy's approach with a sort of grim intensity. Kali understood his expression. This wasn't the plan, but there was no other choice but to see it through. "If Blight comes now, the kindred will not be immune," she said.

"I know." He looked at her, and there was fear in his eyes. "Stay alive, Kalista. Keep them safe."

Kali licked her lips nervously. "I will," she promised.

Squeezing her hand one last time, Rhane let go and moved to the front of the formation. "Do not allow your soldiers beyond this line," he said to Ian. And then he unleashed Banewolf.

The enormity of the immortal and its coat of pure white were a stark contrast to everything around it, especially the horribly twisted figures of the kindred. It towered above everyone and everything in sight. Only the forest trees stood taller. Confidence and power radiated from each step as the wolf strode forward, visibly hungering to meet the enemy. The sight was surreal, almost unbelievable, but awesome to behold. Even rogues were inspired to take notice of the immortal's presence. On seeing Banewolf, the horde abruptly slowed its charge, until an urgent command from the front lines pushed them onward. A ferocious growl ripped from his throat as Banewolf ran out to meet them. And he was unstoppable.

Barreling through the center of their mass, the wolf annihilated every rogue in its path. The utter collapse of their lines forced the horde to regroup around the immortal's devastating reach. Had there only been hundreds to rise against the kindred instead of thousands, it was possible Banewolf could have single-handedly won the war.

Several minutes passed before the fight reached Kali and the others. But when it did, Ian challenged the enemy with a screeching howl. His war cry was seconded by Jehsi's roar…and then the battle was on.

Gabriel finally picked his moment to shed his guise and become the nine-foot tall mixture of human and beast—an epitome of terror. Any Warekin witnessing the transformation was shocked by the end result, but it was unclear if Gabriel's true identity was recognized. There lacked opportunity for conversation about it. Rogues were upon them.

In the heat of combat, there was no time to think, only react. Kali stabbed with her long daggers and burned with fire, striking down every masked opponent who faced her. For every two she killed, three more appeared in their place. The rogue assault seemed to be endless. A brief but anguished yelp escaped Kali's lips when a large rogue broke through her defenses, clawing deep grooves into her forearm, which immediately welled over with bright red blood. She gritted her teeth and bore the pain of a second blow, this one from behind as another rogue took advantage of her faltered guard. Kali dropped to her knees, knowing the creatures would be drawn to perceived weakness like moths to a lamplight. When ten of them had surrounded her, she released an explosion of fire and incinerated them mid-breath.

On his way to assist her endangered state, Bailen was caught in the middle of the inferno but emerged unscathed. He was half siren, after all.

The blast cleared a good twenty foot radius all around her, giving Kali plenty of breathing room. She was still surprised when Bailen abandoned his canine form and his human form emerged still wearing faded denim jeans and the red "Jekyll Likes to Hide" shirt given to him by Rion. "Can you do that again?" he asked.

"Yeah," she said. "Why?"

Bailen smiled. "It is difficult for me to create fire, but I can control the element with ease."

"Okay." Kali had a pretty clear idea of what Bailen had in mind but… "Promise to make sure no on our side gets hurt."

"Trust me, *uskai.*"

Kali wanted to, badly, and so she did. As they moved through the battle, Bailen kept his word, eradicating only their foes and leaving kindred warriors untouched. She created the fiery blasts and Bailen directed them, intensifying her flames to consume rogues with incredible accuracy. In the case of many smaller skirmishes, she and Bailen secured the victory of kindred over rogue. Thousands had stood against them, but the tide of war was slowly being changed.

Moving through the field, Kali noticed fewer and fewer warriors advancing from the rear. It didn't make sense. A shift had happened. Rogues were being driven back. So, where were the fighters?

Turning around, Kali surveyed the dwindling battle. Many had fallen on both sides. Many more were wounded. Every kindred and Warekin in good enough condition to fight kept doing so, leaving only the wounded to assist the wounded. Dozens of them limped to the sidelines with the support of brother or ally. Feeling deep in her gut something was off but not immediately able to spot it, Kali kept watching. At last she saw.

A thin, elderly looking woman dressed in long, dark and tattered robes walked slowly about the battlefield. Her spine slumped with old age. Her eyes were sunken and hollow. She crept from body to body, lingering over those who still lived but were unable to rise. Stopping at the feet of an injured kindred, the old woman stooped as low as her ancient bones would allow and Kali saw a dim haze pass from the kindred's mouth and into hers. The kindred's chest expanded to a mass beyond normal limits. Then its body shuddered and finally stilled.

Kali's blood ran cold.

She looked around for help, but there was none. The war had moved on without them. Frantically, Kali considered the options. She could yell for help, but the sound would certainly alert Blight. She and Bailen could preserve the advantage of surprise, but it would mean facing the monster alone. Then Kali remembered. There was a third choice. Closing her eyes, she whispered, "Assemble," and then did a whole lot of hoping.

"Bailen, do you see it?" she asked, still careful to keep her voice as quiet as possible.

"I see it," he answered calmly.

The creature moved on from kindred to Warekin, draining the soul of its next victim until only a withered and lifeless husk remained of what was once a vigorous warrior. The ones fed upon never screamed or whimpered. Violent convulsions were the sole evidence of what happened to them. It was difficult to watch, but Kali held fast…until Blight's shadow crossed a form she recognized. Gareth.

Shit. "Bailen, we have to do something."

"Our advantage will be spoiled."

"Then let's hit it with everything we've got." Not waiting for his agreement, Kali reached down to the core of what she was and called forth the siren's powers, trusting Bailen to do what was necessary.

The fires built within her, multiplying until she could barely contain them. Clenching her fists, Kali demanded more. Grey scales flashed across her skin. Fingernails stretched into claws and dug painfully at the flesh of her palms. Hissing, she channeled the pain to increase her power. The inferno reached a climax where she could no longer control it, and so Kali let go.

Her fire thundered upon release, howling as if it possessed a life of its own. Bailen steered the flames, containing and then expanding them to extraordinary proportions. Engulfed by the blast, the creature disappeared from sight but the sound of its suffering was clearly heard. Horrible wails and moans lifted up beyond the smokeless fire, reaching past the trees and into the atmosphere. But when the blaze cleared, the old woman still stood.

Kali didn't waste time. Summoning another incendiary, she discharged a second blast with an intensity rivaling the first. The old woman shrieked but did not fall. Kali got the distinct impression of the grating cry being a product of rage rather than pain. Wrinkled features darkening ominously, the old woman advanced, lurching forward with halting steps. Gareth was spared, but now Blight's sole focus had turned to Kali.

Crapola.

"Anytime you guys," she muttered under her breath, sending a third and fourth blast that each hit the creature square on but barely staggered it. She and Bailen were only pissing it off.

Kali backed away as Blight advanced, knowing in her heart of hearts she did not want it to touch her under any circumstances. Bailen followed her lead, staying beside Kali and matching her retreat.

"Any ideas?"

"Let's not allow it any closer," Bailen suggested.

But Kali had no idea how to stop it.

Chapter 32

Kali and Bailen were in trouble. The first to heed her summons, Orrin and War left the primary battle without hesitation, forcing York to haul ass in order to catch up. He recruited Jehsi and River on the way. If Kali was asking for help, then York expected additional muscle might be needed. Their forces were close to beating the rogues, but it was too soon to claim victory. It was crucial that Rhane and Gabriel remain in the fight, anchoring the front lines in order to ensure the rogues' final efforts did not break through. But on being confronted with the scene happening just ahead, York was no longer sure his assessment had been the proper one.

A very creepy, extremely old hag with an awkward limp chased after Kali and Bailen. The scent coming from the woman wasn't human, but was also unlike anything York had ever encountered. Not good. The hag's face evidenced her ill intentions quite clearly. Bailen and Kali were about to be lunch. Also not good.

War, get between that thing and Kalista.

War didn't like that. *Why am I the bait?*

Just don't get eaten. The rest of us will flank it.

Without further protest the red wolf picked up speed, circled wide and blindsided the creature, launching itself right into its face. The old hag grabbed for the wolf, but War was too swift. He dodged out of the way in two quick bounds. *The flesh feels like granite,* he said and danced away as the hag lunged again, shrieking and frothing at the mouth, but a face full of fire distracted it.

York and Orrin took the opportunity to attack, simultaneously hitting the creature from behind. Orrin's

Kodiak-sized, brown wolf locked his jaws over the hag's head, while York wrested both legs from beneath it. War had made no exaggeration in describing the texture of this thing. To York, it felt like he may as well have bitten a slab of stone. It was a good thing Orrin seemed to be having better luck.

There was a distinctive crack of bone, followed by the old hag's body going slack. Orrin's wolf gave it a few shakes to be sure the creature was dead and then released it. The odd angle and bulge from the side of its neck should have been confirmation of the kill, but no one was really surprised when the hag started to move again.

Kalista, burn it.

She did so, and by hell, the girl gave it all she had. But the creature stood up from the midst of the flames, screeching as the clothes burned from its back and skin caught fire. Moving faster than what should have been possible, it latched onto the big, silver wolf that was Jehsi, still screaming as a strange light passed between them. Belting a furious roar, River slammed into the creature, knocking his father free, but then the creature began to feed from him. With every second, the burns on its flesh healed a little more.

Damn it.

York threw himself into the creature, ripping it away from River. Then it was his turn to feel the hag's burning touch. While Rhane was imprisoned at Golden Mountain, Kali had attempted to sustain herself by feeding on York's life force. It had only taken a couple of trials before both of them realized it wouldn't work. Kali's gentle, even if utterly draining, feeding paled in comparison to the agony of this thing's pull that reached past even the armor of the war skin. The very cells of his existence were being torn from his body via chest, stomach, mouth, and ears. York felt as if the flesh was being peeled from his bones while someone doused him in acid. Then Orrin and War were there, attacking the hag from both sides. Their efforts succeeded in making the creature release York. Collapsing to the ground, he forced the wolf to its feet by sheer grit. He wasn't ready to admit he was out of the fight.

"Orrin! War! Stand back," Kali yelled. Her eyes changed to grey, and scales of the same color appeared in patches across her face. A dark aura surrounded her figure. Curls spiraled in all directions from her head, blown by a powerful wind not present a few seconds ago. Even as she shouted the warning, two thick streams of fire blasted from her hands, barely giving the boys a heartbeat to avoid being scorched. She hit the creature again and again, driving it backward step by step.

Had York a human mouth, he would have smiled, even through the pain. This was when Kali was at her best—defending those she loved. Dropping to its knees, the creature screamed and Kali screamed back. A third howl answered…only this one came from the clouds. The pit of dread formed in York's belly before he looked up and saw the dark shape soaring through the evening skies.

The number of people he knew who could take the form of a dragon came to a grand total of one. And that psycho's double dealing had basically gotten Rion killed. A snarl bubbled in York's throat as he tried to keep an eye on Kali and the potential threat from above. But his judgment came prematurely. Circling overhead, Rhaven belched a torrent of flames onto the hag, mixing his orange fire with Kali's grey. Now the creature truly burned. Hair and flesh melting, the hag began to crawl toward Kali, leaving bits of skin behind as it made slow progress in her direction. This thing wasn't going to die.

To York's surprise, Bailen stepped forward. Raising both hands, he pointed one in Kali's direction and the other toward Rhaven...and then he closed his eyes. Something York had never witnessed before happened next. He shook his head to clear it...to make sure he wasn't hallucinating.

Where there were once two flames—Kali's grey and Rhaven's orange—joined into one, and the fire turned black. Swirling and churning, it compressed, surrounding the creature, intensifying until even York could feel the singe against his skin. The hag stopped moving, but the fire still burned, turning the creature to a lump of melted pulp, reducing flesh to charred bone, and then to ash.

Finally, it was over.

Chapter 33

Kali watched Rhane move throughout the remnants of the battlefield, exhausted but refusing to quit as he tended to wounded kindred and Warekin. In the end, Ian sustained the heaviest losses. Nearly a third of his pack either fell to the rogues or was consumed by Blight. Of the Warekin, five souls were claimed. Rhane healed the critical while Seppina trailed behind, tending to lesser injuries. Kali and Jehsi helped where they could. They wrapped bandages, applied salves, and offered herbal potions purposed to speed up healing or reduce pain. Kali drew on every memory within reach to aid them. Jehsi turned out to be a fine teacher, filling in the blanks when she could not and gently guiding her hands.

Reunited at last, Bailen and Rhaven kept to the sidelines. The two could be seen conversing in short intervals but mostly just stared in silence as Kali traveled among the warriors. They moved whenever she moved, always keeping her sight. Looking up on one occasion, she met their gazes and waved. Bailen seemed startled but bowed his head, letting a faint smile light his features. Rhaven had no reaction at all.

"My grandsons make a strange pair," Jehsi said in a quiet voice. His eyes never left the damaged thigh muscle he attempted to piece back together.

She couldn't deny it. In fact, Jehsi was probably being too kind. "They've been through a lot."

Nodding, Jeshi squinted as he examined his work. "Rhane once wore the same haunted expression. After years of abuse and never knowing love or a kind touch, only hatred and mistrust shaped his heart. He was lost."

"But you saved him."

"Yes." At last satisfied with the mending, Jehsi looked at Kali with eyes filled with warmth. "As your love will save them."

Hours after nightfall, the work was finally done. Funeral pyres were built to send the fallen Warekin to the ancestors at next sunset. The living returned to the manor. Kali wondered where all the refugees would go now that the war was over. They could safely return to Golden Mountain or choose to assimilate anywhere in the human world. York had offered to personally refuel the jet as many times as needed to shuttle the royals across the Atlantic. Kali wasn't sure the offer had been made simply from the kindness of his heart. She couldn't blame him though. Everyone was ready for things to be normal again.

Ian and his kindred were tucked safely away in their den with all of their dead given proper burials. During the battle and after, Kali pondered Dmiri's absence but was assured by Ian that the odd kindred was okay. By way of explanation, Ian said old wounds were sometimes the most difficult to heal. She took his words to mean Dmiri had no desire to suffer the company of anyone from Golden Mountain because of what happened to his family during Blight's last awakening.

Upstairs and alone at last with Rhane, all Kali could think about was feeding. The siren was starved, but Rhane was in no condition to give what she needed. Sleep was the next best thing. So, Kali stripped off her grimy clothing and turned on the shower. When she came back, Rhane had already sprawled across the foot of the bed. Both shoes were off but only one sock. It was as far as he'd gotten before collapsing. The sight tugged at the strings of her heart. He'd made a such valiant effort during the battle and healing so many afterward had definitely taken its toll.

The sound of his voice surprised her. "Don't stand there," he mumbled. "Get over here."

"I thought you were sleeping."

Climbing onto the bed, Kali sat next to him and combed her fingers through his hair. Rhane closed his eyes and sighed. "I'm too tired to sleep."

"How long has it been?" she asked, referring to when he'd last slept.

"Four...maybe five days."

"That's no good." Leaning over, she kissed the rim of dark shadows beneath his lackluster eyes. "Your brain is too worked up with all that's happened. Maybe a hot shower will help you relax."

Rhane groaned. Obviously, he held little enthusiasm for a suggestion requiring movement. "How about a sponge bath?"

Kali barked a short a laugh. "How about I help you finish undressing and get you into the shower?"

"Okay." Rhane sat up with painstaking slowness. "But if you leave me alone in there, I'll probably drown."

Smiling, she shook her head and pulled his arms free of his shirt. "People don't drown in showers."

"Sure they do," he insisted.

Noticing how pale and cold his skin was, Kali bit her lip and frowned. "Are you sure you're okay?"

"Yeah." Reaching for her hand, he brought her palm to his mouth and kissed it. "I'm great."

"Liar."

He grinned. "Eris called. He thinks there are many more changelings who can be tamed and returned to their human lives. He wants my help."

"And what did you tell him?"

"I said I would be there tomorrow."

Pursing her lips into a thin line, Kali swallowed her first response and bypassed the second. "You're not going anywhere unless you get a full night's sleep," she finally said.

"Yes ma'am."

"Rhane, I'm serious."

"I know. But I have to do this, Kalista. What's happening out there is a mess I'm responsible for creating. Commander Zed was right. We can't just ignore what's happening. I have to help clean things up."

"But you don't have to do it alone."

"I'm not."

As the hot water poured over Rhane's body, he started to shiver. Kali quickly stripped again and stepped into the shower, closing the door behind her. She pressed her skin against his and lent him her warmth as he had done so many times before. Slowly, his trembling began to subside.

"Rhaven wants to help too. I think he truly regrets his role in all of this. That's good isn't it?"

"Yeah." Kali remembered Jehsi's words. "There's hope for them, Rhane. We will just have to love them."

He kissed the top of her hair. "I can't help thinking maybe Rhaven was right to let the rogues awaken Blight. With it dead, whoever remains of the Faction has no reason to pursue us. We're finally free."

"But did our freedom have to come at so high a cost?"

When Rhane didn't reply, Kali looked up. His face was drawn, and fresh tears were in his eyes. She was referring to the battle on their doorstep and the countless number of humans whose lives had forever been altered by the power of the ark, but of course Rhane's mind would have gone straight to Rion. Kali wondered how long it would take before he forgave himself.

"York and the boys aren't too thrilled with having Rhaven in the house, so it will be good to take him with me on this."

"What about Bailen?" Kali thought of the eerie way they watched her earlier. "Those two are pretty inseparable."

"I might need your help in convincing him to stay. It will be easier, I think, to get an idea of where Rhaven's head is without him there."

"Okay."

Towel-dried and settled beneath the sheets with Rhane's arms wrapped securely around her, for the first in a long time, Kali felt things were really going to be okay. Just before he dozed, she pressed his hand against her belly. It was still flat and slightly defined, but according to everyone, there was a kid slowly brewing inside.

"Nothing or no one will ever take this one away from us. We're getting another chance."

Rhane's reply was so groggy, Kali couldn't make it out. But when he kissed her shoulder and pulled her closer, she knew he felt the same.

Chapter 34

Rhane slept so soundly, at first he didn't dream. Then terrible nightmares took over, tumbling him into an abyss of darkness and hopeless despair. He awoke drenched in cold sweat with the sound of a violent rainstorm pounding against the bedroom skylights. Wiping a hand across his face, he sat up and felt oddly disoriented. From the time on the clock he calculated he'd been asleep for less than two hours. No wonder.

Seeing Kalista no longer lay beside him, he turned his ears and searched for the sound of her heartbeat. He heard her, smelled her…and found the presence of something else that seized his heart with terror.

The snarl ripped from his throat as he pivoted, already changing, and leapt from the bed. Through shifting vision he witnessed sadness in her eyes and a gut-wrenching resignation to her fate. Her tears…Rhane knew those tears were for him. Kalista was well aware of what leaving him would do, but was powerless to stop it…she was gone before he had crossed the room.

She fell as if in slow motion. When her body impacted the hardwood floor, the echoes projected a million times over in his head. He screamed. But the sound came out guttural and twisted in a throat more beast than human. As Banewolf, he slammed into the thing responsible. Blight.

Even shadows couldn't hide the gaunt figure and paper thin flesh stretched too tautly across bony joints. A malformed skull was garnished by white horns protruding on either side. Blight rolled and the wolf rolled with it, destroying an armchair as they crashed through the room. Gathering his feet, Banewolf reared with snapping jaws, aiming for the kill. Blight grappled the wolf's forelegs, halting the immortal's momentum in an amazing display of strength. Its grip tightened, crushing the bones of one leg as it bared wide and flat teeth with primal intensity. Enraged by pain, the wolf buried its fangs into a face resembling stone rather than flesh and blood. Still, Blight's skull caved beneath Banewolf's crushing bite. Blinded and roaring with agony, Blight released the wolf and stumbled backward.

The bedroom door crashed in as a skylight exploded, raining splinters and glass onto the bed. A whirlwind of fire engulfed the atmosphere, blanketing everything in a blaze of orange. Blight retreated from the heat, hissing as the flames touched its granite skin. Seeing its intent to escape through the window, the wolf seized the creature, impaling it with tooth and claw as it held Blight within the core of the inferno's heat. There, they both burned, but the wolf would not let go and shared in the agony of Blight's slow death.

Astonishingly, the creature's flesh began to heal, renewing even as outer layers of skin melted away. Bucking against Banewolf's hold, Blight loosened the wolf's grip. It roared and the wolf roared back. But with one mangled leg, Banewolf's stance had weakened. And Blight wasn't dying quickly enough.

A third crash sounded and a second skylight ruptured. Only this time, a huge chunk of ceiling fell with it. Black and red scales glimmered in the moonlight as Rhaven glided into the room. Landing in front of the wolf and the creature it held captive, Rhaven's throat glowed orange as his wings expanded. Lowering his reptilian head, he breathed a stream of fire directly into Blight's throat, setting it afire from within.

Blight howled, but the sound was only gaping silence as its innards burned and melted away. With one, final raging roar, Banewolf tore the creature in two halves, bringing a gruesome end to its throes of death.

The immortal limped away from the kill, shrinking in size to become human once more. But Rhane never made it to his feet. On hands and knees, he crawled to Kalista's fallen form but stopped short of touching her. Bailen cradled her body in his arms, just as she had done with Rion only days ago. She didn't breathe. Didn't move. Her heart was silent. She was gone.

*

From the doorway, York had watched helplessly as the scene unfolded. Hearing the commotion, he and the others rushed upstairs. But in thirty seconds, the fight was over. Between Rhaven and Banewolf, Blight was dead...again.

Peering closer, York realized this creature differed from the first. Yeah, both possessed the same scrawny build better suited for nursing home living instead of terrorizing the supernatural world, but this creature had clearly been male and way more powerful. *Were they mates,* he wondered. All this time, they had operated under the impression of Blight being a singular entity and not a pair of soul-thirsty lovers. Way to go Builders for once again omitting necessary details.

Wiping the tears from his face, York refused to look at Kali's body again. He couldn't bear it. Her death was the biggest failure he had ever faced. His oath to protect any and everything his warlord held dear was nothing compared to the oath he had taken to protect Kali as a person because he loved her. From naïve, bordering on stupid teenager to her maturity into an amazing woman with the strength of at least three Amazons, York had always loved her. Of course, not in the same way as Rhane. Never that. But her loss weighed heavy on his heart and it was far, far too much to carry.

York wanted to comfort Rhane, but the red color of his eyes and the glowing symbol in his right hand were a clear warning to stay away. He didn't approach his friend until the fury dissipated. And then York gathered Rhane in his arms and cried with him.

*

Things were mostly okay until the evening of the burial ceremony. Until then, Rhane hardly moved or left his bedroom. When he did, it was to drift around the manor aimlessly, barely speaking to anyone, not even Jehsi. He always eventually returned to the same location—standing silently over the exact spot where Kali had died, but staring blankly ahead at nothing.

Admittedly, York could see him trying to be there for Bailen and Rhaven. Questionable morals and mental illness aside, those kids had loved their mother. Her death probably set them back a year or two of socialization. Maybe somehow, Rhane kept sight of this past even his own grief.

It was during the funeral when things got weird.

Rhane went through the motions. He did and said all the right things without shedding a single tear as Kali's ashes were sent away with the sun. Call it brave or call him stoic. There was one moment when York glanced over and saw Rhane smiling. The expression lasted for only a second, but it was there. And then it was gone.

The following day, Rhane's behavior didn't change much. Sure, his body resided in manor with the rest of them, but his mind was gone. He had no interest in food, conversation, or sleep. All he could do was stare at that damn death spot.

York went upstairs with the firm intent of giving Rhane the snap out of it speech. *Your kids need you. I need you and yada yada yada*...but when he entered the master bedroom, he found Rhane in the usual position, wearing the same blank expression. The symbols on Rhane's right hand were glowing again, but now the marks extended past his forearm, all the way up his bicep.

York realized calling out to him was probably a terrible idea, but it wasn't as bad a plan as setting one step further into that bedroom. It took two tries, but Rhane eventually turned to face him. Just as York feared, his eyes were scarlet red...and the strange smile was there again. When Rhane took a step forward, York automatically took a step back. Then Rhane shook his head and the homicidal expression cleared. Making up some bullshit about fixing tea and taking a walk, York suddenly thought remaining alone with him could turn out to be a fatal mistake. In the end, he succeeded in convincing Rhane to go outside. Bailen and Rhaven joined them. Together, Rhane and York came up with about a dozen stories to tell the boys about their mother. A time or two, Rhane genuinely smiled. For a little while the emptiness was gone. It was a good day.

Shortly thereafter, the murders began.

It started with big game found throughout the manor grounds and then spread even into Ian's territory. Deer, a couple of bears, several mountain lions—all were torn to shreds and partially devoured.

Kindred were the next to fall. A singular guard from patrol was discovered in morning light. The poor thing had been dismembered and had savagely broken bones and missing insides—heart, liver, and kidneys mostly. Ian strengthened the patrols, sending his men out in pairs or tripling the detail. And then those were killed too. The line was drawn when an entire squad consisting of ten kindred warriors was slain and fed upon by the invisible killer. Ian demanded Rhane's help as an ally to find out who was behind the attacks on his people. York didn't think anything the alpha said succeeded in penetrating the thick fog of apathy where Rhane's mind resided. But surprisingly, Rhane agreed to help. So, he and York spent days in the wood of kindred territory, babysitting patrols, making sure nothing awful happened to Ian's men. Rhane's eyes and hand glowed once. But there was no further incident. And nothing came to attack the kindred. Rhane, however, insisted on posting Warekin escorts with the kindred patrols to provide extra backup and make sure things stayed quiet.

For a while they did.

Or so York thought.

Turning on the news, he saw a story detailing a record number of missing person's reports filed in the past month. The number was well into the dozens. And for such a small city, this kind of statistic was a cause for concern, garnering even federal attention.

After that, entire families disappeared. But then the disappearances abruptly stopped. The murders, however, didn't. The killer just quit bothering to hide the bodies.

Suburban homes became bloodbaths, the attacks again attributed to a wild animal. Humans didn't have the necessary teeth or claws do the kind of damage inflicted upon the victims. And a human certainly couldn't eat them. Even The Kentucky Cannibal didn't consume over one hundred pounds of flesh from multiple bodies in single night. A brown bear could've made a good candidate, but authorities suspected someone would've noticed a seven hundred pound fur ball of terror strolling down the streets.

Of course, the cops had no leads. The only DNA evidence they had to go on was from an unknown species. Dental impressions matched no carnivore on record. No one survived to tell the tale. No one escaped.

York had a theory. And it was a terrifying one.

Then in one fateful night, the whole macabre situation came to a gruesome head.

More kindred were killed and the Warekin protectors alongside them.

Zura and Idalis, volunteers to watch over Ian's pack, were among the slain. Seppina was found dragged from her bed, throat slashed, and intestines strewn about the yard. Rhane did not smile at their funerals. For the first time, York noticed how pale he'd become and the significant amount of weight shed from his frame. Rhane was fighting a losing battle.

Risking a moment alone, he held Rhane back from the others. "Is there something you want to tell me? I'm not the only connecting the dots, buddy. I know you're hurting but this…this has gotten seriously out of hand."

Rhane closed his eyes. His face retreated behind a mask of pain. "The immortal…I think it's more than just a wolf. I can't control it anymore. I don't want to."

Folding his arms, York shook his head. "Bullshit. You've always had a handle on this. You made Banewolf disappear for four centuries."

"You don't understand," Rhane said quietly.

"That's where you're wrong. I do get it. We all lost her. And Kali...she wouldn't want this."

Bad choice of words. Rhane opened his eyes, revealing two very red irises. His features shifted ever so slightly, enough to alter them so he didn't look like Rhane anymore. This was a face of evil. Something hungering for death. A thing that would bathe in the blood of puppies without hesitation. This thing didn't recognize York. Familiarity was absent from those cold-blooded eyes. His best friend was gone.

Shit. I guess the pep talk was a bad idea.

York searched for the best exit. There was none. It was a wide open field with no place to hide. The manor was hundred yards away, but that was no good. Sure, he could run and harness a skin. But there was no doubt this thing in possession of Rhane's body would overtake him in seconds.

Facing the murderous red gaze, York readied himself for grisly fate, but help came from an unlikely source. Appearing from nowhere, Bailen put his furry little body between the bloodthirsty monster and York. He barked sharply once. And then again. The sound must have reached Rhane because his eyes cleared and the psychotic expression disappeared.

Rearing backward, he withdrew his outstretched arm as if a snake had bitten it. "I'm sorry." Looking down at trembling hands, he balled them into fists. "I just can't."

Kneeling to the ground, he put his face directly into Bailen's. "You must not follow me. It's no longer safe."

Bailen whimpered, huffing softly. But Rhane turned away and was gone. Shaking all over, Bailen started to whine.

"He'll come back," York said, not believing for one second his words were true. Rhane had barely survived losing the Kali the first time. And that was only because he'd known she still lived and would somehow find a way back to him. But now…now Rhane had lost her again *and* a third child. For him, there was no coming back.

Chapter 35

For the first time in his life, Rhane gave himself completely to the wolf. And that meant oblivion. No thought. No emotion. No pain. He was cocooned against it all. How long he remained in this state was unknown. Time held no meaning.

Until…something changed.

Rhane found himself returning to the land of the conscious but by no will of his own. His mind was cleared of rage. Hands, fingers, legs, and toes…all responded to his command. His back rested against a hard surface. Vertical bars intersected ten feet away in all directions. It was a cage.

Rhane lay still. He didn't know where he was. Nor could he begin to understand how he had gotten there. But Rhane didn't care. He could only think of Kalista…the baby…and Rion. Once again he had failed to protect those he had sworn an oath to. Closing his eyes, he started to distance his mind from the pain.

A male voice filled the room, pulling him back with strength resonating against unseen walls. "If you have lost your will, then you are of no use to us."

Though the voice sounded strangely familiar, Rhane lacked even the desire to recall its owner. Unmoved, he simply agreed. "I am of no use to you."

Anger flashed into the speaker's tone. "We cannot allow your rampage to continue. The balance of life has been upset."

The balance of life? Rhane stirred. The implications of the statement worried him. *How much time had passed?*

What had Banewolf done? Sighing, he let go just as quickly. "I don't control the immortal anymore."

"Have you no concern at all for the damage you have caused?"

"Not really," he lied.

"And those you have left behind?"

Covering his face, Rhane turned away from the voice. The words only brought agony.

"You must regain control, Rhane, Son of Bllacstag."

A chill ran through his body as the memory came into focus. Suddenly, he knew who the powerful voice belonged to. Inside the caves of K2, a strange being was encountered while crossing an equally bizarre lake. The creature called himself Alister. Rhane finally looked at his captor. Alister with the lavender eyes and diamond skin had given them the keystone. Why was he here now? What was his role in all of this?

While deciding whether or not the questions were even worth speaking aloud, Rhane felt a foreign presence nudge at the corners of his mind. The probe became more aggressive, digging through his brain and leaving a trail of white lightning. Gritting his teeth, Rhane bit back the sound to betray his suffering.

Alister's voice rang out in warning. "Einar, that is not the way."

After several more seconds that felt more like hours of pure torture, the probing ceased. "He remembers you," a second voice said, slightly feminine and likely responsible for the psychic lobotomy. "And you are correct, Alister. Force will not work with this one."

"You could have just taken my word."

Einar relented, sounding somewhat amused. "Perhaps next time."

Rhane's skull felt as if it had been split apart. Even blinking hurt. "Who are you?"

"To some civilizations we are gods. To others we are only legend. We are who Builders aspire to be."

"You created them."

Alister nodded. "We did…and many more."

"The immortal," Rhane said as the pieces fell into the place. "You created it too."

Alister's expression saddened. "No. The immortal was not created. He always was, just as we always have been."

"I don't understand. And I'm sick of riddles."

"Then allow me to explain. Frey—the one you call Immortal—he was the best of us but also the worst of us. The wolf is a manifestation of his life force, but if you allow this carnage to continue, Frey's powers will grow and he will return to what he was. We cannot allow that."

"So, the immortal is one of you?"

"He was."

"Why did you change him?"

Alister answered simply. "Because he tried to change us."

"So you cursed my bloodline."

"We honored your ancestors. And we honored our brother by tying his life force to the fiercest lineage made in our human likeness. But no other son of Bllacstag has ever controlled him as forcefully as you. And no other has given him such absolute control. Your bond is unique."

"If controlling him is what you want, then you have no choice but to separate us. Find another vessel for your brother. Your Builders made a good go of it."

Alister actually rolled his eyes as he tutted. "The Builders and their incessant meddling. They failed because Frey will have no other."

"I don't care what he wants. Your war is won. I'm done with this world. Your brother can have it."

"We do not care about the war. Everything you endured stemmed from the schemes of Builders. We simply observe."

Rhane gestured to the cage. "This doesn't feel like observing."

"Accept the honor bestowed upon you and reclaim control. Only then can we ever release you."

"No deal." Rhane shrugged. "You forget. I no longer care what happens. Keep me here forever if it suits you." He laughed bitterly. "Better yet, keep your precious Frey in this prison." Ever conscious of the other life force within, Rhane began surrendering his mind to it. The immortal immediately sensed his withdrawal and lunged for complete control.

"Rhane, wait!" Alister reached toward him, pleading for Rhane to stop. "What if we undo what was done? What if we bring her back to you?"

Battling back for ownership of his body, Rhane suppressed the wolf's influence and slowly reversed the changes. Three others had joined Alister, and now four figures occupied the infinite space outside of the cage. The newcomers were all female in appearance. Teal-colored hair, coupled with jet black skin and glowing, white irises made the trio quite a sight to behold.

Briefly distracted by the women's appearance, Rhane turned his attention back to Alister. "What you say is impossible," he argued. He refused to hope...refused to believe.

"Not often do we find just reason to interfere in the worlds we visit, Son of Bllacstag. However, few things are impossible for us. We are Masters. Our powers are near limitless."

Rhane didn't know what to say. Alister was offering something Rhane never could have hoped for.

"In exchange for the siren, will you again accept your mantle as the immortal vessel?"

It took a long moment to find his voice. "I will accept."

Alister snapped his fingers, sending rays of blinding light rippling across the room. "Then so may it be."

Chapter 36

Dark spots clouded Rhane's vision after the brightness cleared. Squinting through the haze, he saw the beings were gone and he was in a place he never expected to be. The pickup's engine idled, vents blasting in outside air where the smell of freshly buttered popcorn collided with the stench of day old garbage. Switching off the ignition, Rhane pocketed the keys and slid from the warm leather seat, putting his boots on the pavement. Nothing felt familiar about these surroundings. Searching his memory, he found no recollection of being here. His mind was still damaged, fragmented. For all Rhane knew, this theater could have been a location he often frequented...though Rhane didn't particularly enjoy sitting for two hours in a dark room with only one exit, surrounded by strangers.

When a gentle night breeze blew coolly against his skin, a thousand scents came with it. One of those scents was special. It was the only smell in the world capable of sending his heart charging forward faster than one hundred thoroughbreds. With fire burning in his belly, Rhane tracked the scent, jogging across the parking lot and up the concrete walkway. His mouth went dry, and the world moved as if in slow motion as he pushed through the double doors and stepped onto a plush red carpet. The smell was getting stronger.

He badly wanted to quicken his pace, but to move any faster would draw undo attention. Rhane wasn't ready to throw caution to the wind. He followed the trail down a dim corridor where the scent turned right and then moved behind another set of doors. Rhane licked his lips nervously. He needed to be on the other side.

But as Rhane stepped forward, a teenage theater worker placed a firm hand against his chest. "May I see your ticket stub, sir?"

Shit.

There was no way Rhane could risk going back and waiting in a long box office line. There was no way he could leave this spot without knowing...

Wrenching his mind away from infinite what ifs, he held it to the moment and thought to search his pockets, hoping he at least had a wallet. The kid waited. It was clear he was bored but also willing to give Rhane a hard time if necessary. Resurrecting his most charming smile, Rhane held up a fifty-dollar bill. "Those lines out there are crazy long. Would it be okay if I have a look first? I'm supposed to be meeting a friend."

Shoving a pair of thick-rimmed glasses back onto his face, the kid looked down the corridor both ways. Then he snatched the money from Rhane's fingertips and stepped aside. "Enjoy your movie, sir."

"Thank you," Rhane said, and hurriedly pushed through the doors.

Silver light from the screen provided more than enough illumination to search the room. He found her almost instantly, and all the air expelled from his lungs in one breath. As his legs threatened to buckle beneath him, he leaned against the wall and struggled to pull himself together.

She was really here. Kalista had come back to him.

He climbed the stairs slowly, never taking his gaze from her face. Her long locks were pulled back, showcasing every perfect angle and curve of her face. Everything else could have ceased to exist and Rhane would not have noticed. She was the center of his universe. The only piece that mattered.

When he was still three rows away, she turned and her grey eyes widened ever so slightly. But then she quickly looked away. He heard her pulse quicken, saw tension creep into the posturing of her neck. Undeterred, Rhane continued until he stood next to her chair. He smiled at the way she held her breath but stared straight ahead, pretending not to notice him.

Without waiting for an invitation, Rhane sat down. He knew this girl didn't know him but couldn't resist touching her skin. A small gasp escaped her lips. He had given her no choice but to see him.

Though her gaze was frightened, Rhane smelled very little fear escaping her pores. *Okay. Don't freak her out.* He extended a hand. "Come with me please."

She leaned away from him. "E-excuse me?"

"Please," he repeated softly. "Come with me." Rhane's heart was pounding so loudly in his own ears, he wondered if she could hear it.

Kalista bit her lip.

He waited, trying not to betray the intense emotion he was feeling.

When at last her hand slipped into his, relief poured through every fiber of his being. He led her out into the corridor and was grateful to find it empty.

She pulled away. He let her. "Do I know you?" she said.

Nodding, Rhane moved closer. He couldn't help himself. There was so much to say…so much to tell her. Too bad he had no idea where to begin. Burning tears stung the back of his eyes. He just wanted to wrap his arms around her and never let go.

"Okay." When her back bumped against the wall and she could retreat no further, Kalista folded her arms. "How so?"

He decided to start with the most important thing he could think to say but, in fact, it was the only thing he could think of. "I am yours forever, Kalista."

His throat was raw, so the words came out ragged and hoarse. "And you are mine. Please—" Rhane's voice cracked with emotion. He tried again. "Please remember me."

Confusion and fear crossed her features. He could see she was ready to run. But then surprise flickered into her eyes…Rhane allowed himself to hope. With a trembling hand, she reached out and timidly touched his face. Her shaking stopped as her fingers settled against his skin, but her expression was still a puzzled frown. Looking down at his hand, she silently traced her fingers along the markings in his palm and finger.

Rhane didn't move. Was too afraid to breathe. He desperately needed her to understand…to remember.

Shaking her head, Kalista stared up at him with wide, uncertain eyes. And then finally…finally, she whispered his name.

The End

Note from the Author

At least for now, Rhane and Kalista's journey has come to an end. I truly wanted a Happily Ever After for them, but in order to remain true to the tragic course of their history, I eventually realized that riding off into the sunset wasn't going to be possible for Rhane and Kali. But what they could have was a second chance.

Thank you, dear reader, for seeing Rhane and Kali through their journey this far. Who knows what future stories these two and their friends may enter?

On that note, *Thinner than Blood* is a novelette written and published a couple of years ago for a free download. *Thinner than Blood* continues Rhane and Kali's story…but far off into the future and through the eyes of a character yet to appear in previous books, but one who is intimately connected to them. Unfortunately, the novelette is no longer available for active download because I decided it needed to go back onto the shelf for a bit of a rewrite. But, if you happen to have a copy in your Kindle library, by all means check it out and leave feedback. Maybe it can be expanded into a full length novel at some point in the future.

Coming July 2016, I'll have a whole new story and entire new cast of characters for you to enjoy! *Love, Alchemy* is a new adult romance with a touch of fantasy…and I think you'll love it.

Available Now

Love, Alchemy
(New Adult Paranormal Romance)

Daveigh Little is no stranger to bad choices, but when one of them lands her in hot water, she finds herself on the run from a ruthless criminal who places a price on her head…and then there is Ethan.

From the moment she first laid eyes on Ethan Remington, Daveigh knew there was something very different about him…she just didn't know how different.

With the habit of showing up exactly when she needs him the most, Ethan displays an uncanny intuition towards Daveigh's whereabouts. But then the tables are turned and soon Daveigh realizes that it is Ethan who actually needs saving.

www.ingramcontent.com/pod-product-compliance
Lightning Source LLC
Chambersburg PA
CBHW020238200626
46816CB00001BA/32